Readers love
KELLY JENSEN

Best in Show

"…a quick, light read with funny characters in an odd situation…
Thanks, Kelly!"

—Rainbow Book Reviews

"…a pretty cute book, but definitely different!"

—Alpha Book Club

"…I found this one entertaining, and if you are in the mood for a fun,
easy shifter story you may want to give this one a try."

—Joyfully Jay

Counting Fence Posts

"Bottom line, this was an enjoyable shortie with a Christmas feel to it.
I'm looking forward to reading more from the author."

—Gay Book Reviews

"This is the first book I've read by this author, but I like her style and
will definitely look for more!"

—The Novel Approach

When Was the Last Time

"It's low angst, but with lots of emotion. *When Was the Last Time* is a
reminder that all relationships take work to flourish."

—All About Romance

By KELLY JENSEN

Best in Show
Block and Strike
Counting Fence Posts
Out in the Blue
When Was the Last Time

Published by DREAMSPINNER PRESS
www.dreamspinnerpress.com

BLOCK
AND STRIKE

KELLY JENSEN

Published by

DREAMSPINNER PRESS

5032 Capital Circle SW, Suite 2, PMB# 279, Tallahassee, FL 32305-7886 USA
www.dreamspinnerpress.com

ISBN: 978-1-63533-228-5
Digital ISBN: 978-1-63533-229-2
Library of Congress Control Number: 2016915176
Published January 2017
v. 1.0

Printed in the United States of America

This paper meets the requirements of
ANSI/NISO Z39.48-1992 (Permanence of Paper).

For anyone who has ever made a mistake, struggled with their identity, or had to learn how to make noise.

ACKNOWLEDGMENTS

A LOT of people helped me write this one. First, I want to thank Sensei Weaver for teaching me how to make noise. Without that skill, I might never have written a single book, let alone tried to get it published. Never-ending thanks to my first readers and eternal cheerleaders, Eileen and Jenn. You both helped me refine Max's character and make him more relatable. Thanks to Deb Nemeth for helping me refine Jake's character, so that he could better realize his goals.

I had to do a lot of medical research for this one. My favorite nurses, Jenny Grey and Lyndall Strong, answered all my emergency room questions—and then reminded me that if I got this book published, I'd need to mention them in the acknowledgments. Done and done! My more technical questions about brain trauma and recovery were fielded by members of the Crime Scene Writer Yahoo group. I'm grateful for all the questions I got in return, and for the willingness of some members to complicate Max's injuries so that he would need extra therapy (with friends like these…).

Thank you to my family for taking this journey with me.

Finally, thank you to the team at Dreamspinner Press for helping me put the best possible version of this story into the hands of readers.

CHAPTER ONE

A FEELING of menace rolled out of the dark alley. Jake's door was halfway down, the bulb over it dead for a week or more. Had it been lit, he'd still have been jumping from one puddle of light to another. Something else twitched his senses. Was it a memory or a figment of his imagination? Probably both. Since his release, dark spaces set his skin to itching and crawling.

Partway down the alley, he noticed the slumped shape. Closer, the stench of piss caught him and the shape resolved into a man curled up in the shadow of his darkened doorway. Wrinkling his nose, Jake readied his boot for a nudge. He had some sympathy—life was rough—but his front door wasn't a homeless shelter.

At his nudge, the guy twitched, groaned, and retched.

Wonderful.

Obviously too drunk to wake up and puke properly, the asshole gurgled and began to choke. *Seriously?* Only thing worse than a bum on his doorstep was a dead bum on his doorstep.

"Oh, no you don't, bud."

Swinging his gym bag from his shoulder, Jake tossed it onto the steps in front of the door and reached down to hook his hands under the guy's shoulders. He really didn't want him to choke outside his apartment. Or in this alley. Being caught dragging a body out onto Beech Street would be difficult to explain to his parole officer, though. He settled for rolling him into recovery position. The choking stopped immediately and a spooky groan drifted up with the stink of urine and puke. Jake resolved to scrub the skin from his hands when he got inside.

"Finished trying to die?"

He didn't expect an answer, and he didn't get one. Jake hopped up the steps and fished around inside the pocket of his sweats for his keys. He really needed to replace the burned-out bulb over the door. Mr. Wu of Wu's World, the Chinese restaurant on the street side of the building, would get to it in about a month if he asked. Easier to just do it himself and hope lighting his portion of the alley would discourage derelicts from dying on his doorstep.

Jake pushed open the front door and stepped into the narrow, dimly lit corridor. The odor of egg rolls, oil, and wilted broccoli permeated the air. He used to like Chinese food. He reached back for his gym bag and froze. A smear of red ran across his hand, from the soaked cuff of his long-sleeve T-shirt all the way down the side of his thumb. It had already seeped into the lines of his skin and around the flattened crescent of his thumbnail. Jake's stomach flipped and folded.

Then he recalled the labored breathing and all too familiar snuffle and rattle of spit. The lingering scent of copper under the puke and piss, the mottled appearance of the bum's face and the way he groaned and listed to the side. The absolute lack of alcohol fumes.

The guy on his doorstep wasn't a drunk. He was… "Oh, shit."

Jumping over his bag and down the three steps, Jake landed in the alley with a slap of sneaker soles. He dropped to one knee beside the crumpled figure of a man who, in the faint light now trickling through the open door, looked like he'd been beaten within an inch of his life.

"Fuck, fuck, fuck."

Panic kicked up his pulse until his heart hammered against his breastbone. Instinct begged him to run. No, he hadn't smashed this guy's nose or smacked his head into the wall. He hadn't pulped his face or laid into his ribs. Guilt had a way of elbowing into every situation, though. Even three months released, Jake still flushed at dark thoughts, or the urge to cross a street against the light.

He couldn't go back. Not ever.

He couldn't ignore the broken man crumpled against his stoop either.

Stitched letters over the breast pocket of the man's polo shirt caught his eye. *Wawa.* He must work at the convenience store three blocks over. Or maybe the one down on Lincoln. Couldn't walk a mile in Philly without tripping over a Wawa. Jake peered into the purpling, swollen face and quickly decided that one, he didn't recognize "Wawa" and two, he had to get him to the hospital. Except dropping Wawa off at the hospital would be about as damning as dragging him out of the alley. There would be questions and requests for identification. A possible call to his parole officer.

"Fuck!"

His frustrated yell echoed dully from the brick wall. Guilt slithered into the quiet pause, poking and gnawing. Jake wanted to do the right thing. He had to, for himself and for Wawa. But, Jesus H. Christ. He pulled his cell phone from the other pocket of his sweats and dialed his sister. Willa would know what to do.

"YOU FOUND him where?"

"In a heap by the front steps. Like someone had just tipped him there." Which, in Jake's defense, described the posture of most homeless folks.

Willa shook her head, her blonde bob twitching back and forth, and blew out a short breath. Gray eyes, same as his, pinned him with a look. "I wish you hadn't moved him."

"Well I couldn't leave him out there." Stinking up the alley. No, much better to carry him upstairs and have him stink up the couch. "I thought it might help to clean him up a bit." Jake gestured with the blood-soaked rag in his hand. "His face is a mess."

"His nose is probably broken." His sister crouched in front of the couch and ran practiced hands over Wawa's neck and shoulders. He didn't move. He didn't even groan. In fact, he'd done nothing but breathe in an awful, choky manner since Jake had carried him inside.

"He's breathing okay," she said.

Right. "Can you, ah, fix him up?"

"God no. He needs proper medical care." She indicated his scuffed and stained polo shirt. "Someone has really worked him over. He's out cold, and a concussion is probably the least of his problems. He needs…." She rattled off a series of tests or something, all of which sounded dire. "We should take him to Nazareth."

Willa worked shifts in the ER at Nazareth Hospital, about a mile away.

Jake grimaced. "Willa." Frustration and lingering panic left him with a tight sigh. *Do the right thing, Jake. Help this man.* "I…."

Wawa groaned and opened his eyes. Blood ringed one and the other only made a nasty slit in the swollen skin of his beat-up face. Willa put a gently restraining hand on his shoulder. "Shh."

The good eye revolved in the red-rimmed socket and then the retching started again. Jake ran to the kitchen and pulled the trash can out from under the sink. He didn't make it back in time. Vomit dribbled from Wawa's lips and pooled on the pale floorboards between Willa's feet.

He was going to have to burn the couch.

"We need to take him to the hospital now," Willa snapped. She pointed a finger at Jake. "Go get your truck."

"No," Wawa slurred.

Willa turned her attention to him. "Shh, don't try to speak. We're going to help you."

He produced a wet noise before repeating himself. "No."

Willa smoothed his dark hair away from the blood clotting at his temple. "It's okay. We won't hurt you."

"No money."

Had he been mugged? Was that what he meant?

"Can you tell us your name?" Willa asked.

His eyelids fluttered. Well, the left one did. The right was trapped in swelling flesh. "No hospital." He fell back, the white of his one eye, streaked with blood, flashing before he lost his battle for consciousness.

Willa turned back to Jake. "Go get the truck."

"But—"

Her gaze flicked to his knuckles. A flash of irritation burned through Jake. She looked up to meet his eyes, and he saw the relief there at the lack of bruising across his hands, at the proof he hadn't had a fit in the alley outside his goddamned apartment and beaten up a guy he didn't even know for no reason whatsoever. But he resented her for thinking it, for even a second.

The whole night was fucked-up.

Jake turned so hard the soles of his shoes squeaked against the floor, and went to get his truck.

He was home an hour later.

The ER had been a bright nightmare. They admitted Wawa right away, but after that, the rush had all been inside Jake's bloodstream until his adrenaline ran short. He spent thirty minutes pacing back and forth, waiting for news he wasn't entitled to. He wasn't a relative—he didn't even know Wawa's name. Willa promised to call him later.

Back at his apartment, the silence rang more loudly than the cacophony of the ER. Jake stood in the dark for a breath or two, appreciative of the relative peace, before dumping his keys on the table by the door and snapping on a lamp. Warm light spread through the room, giving his place a homey feel he usually enjoyed. Since his release, Jake had craved comfort. Cozy spaces lit only by single lamps. The aroma of fresh-baked pies, the sweet and savory kind. Clean linen that smelled of fabric softener rather than industrial-strength bleach. Anything soft.

He went to inspect his couch.

Willa had cleaned the floor while he brought his truck around from the garage at the end of the lane. The odor of vomit lingered, though, cutting through the antiseptic tang of pine. Jake cast a wary eye over his couch and thanked all the hells he'd bought leather instead of fabric or that weird microfiber shit. Leather could be cleaned and, wound up as he was, it would be a while before he slept.

He'd changed the bucket of water twice, for the couch and the floor, when his cell phone buzzed. Jake snapped off a glove and pulled his phone out of his pocket, answering with a quiet "'Lo."

It was Willa. "Why are you still up?"

"You said you'd call with news."

"Are you cleaning your couch?"

Closest in age of his three older sisters, Willa might as well have been his twin. She knew how he thought and how he felt, most of the time. When she didn't, she always seemed utterly baffled.

Jake dropped the sponge into the bucket and peeled off his other glove. "Yeah. What's up?"

"We got an ID on your guy. I thought you might like to know." In that respect, she knew him well.

Wawa hadn't had a wallet, only the shirt with the breast pocket logo, which the police had taken after the emergency room staff cut it off him. The police had taken Jake's statement, too, without looking at his knuckles.

"His name is Gareth Maxwell Wilson. Goes by Max according to his manager at the Wawa on Lincoln. He also works at the market behind the strip mall four blocks down from you."

"Hendrick's?" The family-owned supermarket had somehow managed to compete with the Pathmark across the road for longer than Jake had been in Philly.

"Yep. His insurance coverage probably sucks."

"Maybe that's why he didn't want to go to the hospital," Jake said.

"Or he could just be a wuss, like you."

"Hey, we don't all live for the scream of sirens and people in pain." How anyone could enjoy being a nurse was beyond him, but Jake was grateful, this once, for his sister's profession.

"Oh, and guess where he lives?"

"Um...."

"Under you."

"Huh?"

"Same building. The basement apartment."

Jake pulled his cell away from his ear and blinked at it. Lamplight glinted off the screen, blanking out the portrait of his sister. He put the phone back to his ear. "Seriously?"

"Yeah. I guess that explains why he was outside your door. It's his door, too."

Now Jake really felt like an ass for not replacing the light bulb or hassling Mr. Wu to do it. The basement apartment was a hole in the ground, literally—a cellar Mr. Wu optimistically advertised as a "studio apartment." The only light in the small, coffin-shaped room seeped down from two high windows covered by rusty old grilles. The bathroom was a moldy cupboard. The kitchen, as he remembered, consisted of a microwave on top of a bar fridge. Jake had painted the apartment for Mr. Wu after the last tenant moved out, just a month before. Not even the brightest rental white had improved the space.

Had he ever seen the new tenant? "Hey!"

"Hmm?" his sister answered.

"I've seen him. Skinny guy. Doesn't own an umbrella, or likes walking in the rain." A slice of memory, a bedraggled figure slipping through the door as Jake stepped out. Thin, wet, dripping. A flash of dark hair, vivid blue eyes, and pale skin. Though he still didn't know Gareth Maxwell Wilson, Jake felt his concern was now somehow warranted. They lived in the same building. They were neighbors—could have been friends. "How's he doing?"

"He woke up not long after you left. He's actually pretty lucid this time. We had his name before then, which was great. Can you imagine waking up and no one knowing your name?"

Maybe. Being in prison had been like that at times. Not the waking up part, the moving among strangers part. The sense of being out of place, of being someone else, or just unknown.

"Would be rough, yeah. So when is he being released? Does he need a ride home?"

"I don't know, and probably. Why, are you offering?"

"Ah, I guess? I mean, he lives in my building."

"We're trying to contact his family."

"Okay. Let me know, then."

"I will, and Jake?"

"Yeah?"

Willa hesitated. "I'm sorry."

He didn't ask what for. "See you at home on Sunday?"

The Kendricks clan went home to Doylestown every Sunday they could. Jake had resented the obligation when he was younger, but after missing those weekly gatherings for a whole year, he now craved the bosom of his family with something close to obsession.

Willa's tired sigh sounded like static against his ear. "Yeah. See you then."

Jake slid his phone back into his pocket and picked up the bucket and gloves. Breathing deeply, he inspected his couch. The dark brown leather looked clean and smelled clean. Maybe now he could sleep.

CHAPTER TWO

"Do NOT call my father." How many times did he have to say it? "I'm twenty-one. An adult. You do not have permission to call my father." Every word pulsed along his jaw and up into his skull, setting off a hundred clanging bells. Closing his eyes, Max made an attempt to swallow a groan. The sound vibrated low in his throat and that hurt too, dang it.

He opened his eyes again—just the one, really, as his left was swollen shut—and rolled his head toward the tall nurse at his bedside. Agitation and worry pinched her features and clouded her gray eyes.

"You really should have someone with you," she said. "You have a grade three concussion. I really can't advise leaving if you don't have someone to stay with you. There's also the matter of tests—"

"I can call my girlfriend." He didn't want to talk about the tests he couldn't afford. His head hurt. His whole body hurt. But he didn't need a CT scan or an MRI. If his head was going to explode, it would have happened already. He wasn't going to call Melanie, either. He'd never see a way clear if he invited her to hover.

God, why did he have a girlfriend? Of all the stupid, stupid—

"Okay, what's her number?"

"Ah…." He didn't know it. What sort of freak didn't know his girlfriend's number?

The sort of freak who shouldn't even have a girlfriend.

Let's not go there right now, eh?

"Mr. Wilson?"

"Huh?"

"You okay there?"

"Her number was in my cell." Which had conveniently disappeared along with his wallet. At least this time he'd been beaten up for a reason he could explain… and share.

"Maybe we can look her up?"

Ugh. Max put his hands to his head and instantly regretted it. His head was a massive bruise and every movement sent pain radiating toward his broken nose. He shut his eyes and willed away the flashes of feet and fists, the sound of knuckles smacking his jaw, his skull hitting the wall. The grunts, the groans, the stink of their breath. The harshly whispered threats. The world tilted. Groaning, Max dropped his hands to the bed in an effort to steady himself, despite the fact he was already lying down. Slitting his one eye open, he sought a focal point.

The nurse swam into view, her eyes wide with alarm. "Here, let me help you."

Her hands were warm on his shoulders. The back of his eyes burned. Max sucked in a breath, then another, the sharp edge of air hurting his chest. Pain surged through his temples and down his nose. Maybe he should reconsider the tests. No, he'd been hurt this badly before and survived. He allowed the nurse to push him back against the pillows and lay there, eyes closed, hoping she'd go away. He didn't want her to be nice to him—she'd make him cry. The sound of the hospital pulsed through him for a while before fading. Max followed it down the rabbit hole, only sort of hoping he'd wake up again.

He did wake sometime later, aware he was alone. Someone—the nurse, probably—had dimmed the light and pulled the door closed. Gingerly, Max rolled his head to the side. A curtain separated his bed from the next. He could see lumps under the blanket at the end of the other bed. A neighbor in hell. Had his roommate had the stuffing kicked out of him as well? Were they in the beaten-to-a-pulp ward, otherwise known as Stupid City?

Even sighing hurt. When could he go home? Alone?

Max hated his apartment. It was a hole. But he also loved the cramped space, because it was his and his alone. He didn't have to listen to the guy next door doing his girlfriend three or four times a night, bedsprings groaning rhythmically until the headboard knocked against the wall.

Mutinously, his memory served up the night he'd taken Melanie up to his room for a bit of privacy. He'd been sharing a house with three other guys and two of them often entertained downstairs. He and Melanie had sat side by side on his bed, hands joined like naïve teenagers, and watched each other's eyes widen as the rhythm of the springs next door raced toward a crescendo. It might have been all right if they could have laughed about it. But they hadn't. They'd stared at one another in morbid fascination. They'd blushed at the same time.

What Melanie saw in him, Max couldn't guess. She professed to like the fact he wasn't *handsy*. Little did she know.

Max pushed up out of the nest of thin, bleachy pillows and edged his legs toward the side of the bed. He wanted to go home—go hide in his cave until he had to work. He had a shift tonight and a thorough beating wouldn't keep him from doing his job. If he was ever going to make something of himself, prove he was a man—tall and proud—he needed to do his job.

The floor refused to stay flat beneath his feet and someone had taken to whacking him on the side of the head with a cast-iron skillet. One, two, three. The room pulsed in time to the clanging in his skull. Slowly, he picked his way across the floor. His pants were in an open closet opposite the bed. They didn't smell too good. His shirt had disappeared. Could he put the stupid hospital gown back on, right side around, with the closure at the front instead of the back? They'd probably all been looking at his ass in the ER.

The world dipped and swayed as he pulled his pants over trembling legs. Max caught himself against a wall and waited for his head to stop ringing and the vision out of his one eye to clear. The door to the room cracked open and a shaft of light thrust across the floor.

"Need help?" asked a deep voice.

Max turned to the nurse, a guy this time, easily seven feet tall and built like a linebacker. "Ah, no, just…."

"Here, let's get you back to bed." The nurse manhandled him with surprising gentleness, and his chuckle came from someplace deep when he discovered Max's pants. "Thinking of escaping?"

"No, I was cold."

"Right, sure." The nurse let him keep his pants on. Just pulled the sheet up over them. "Thirsty?"

Max shook his head and immediately regretted it. After waiting for the world to settle, he asked, "When can I go home?"

The nurse bent to check the chart at the end of the bed. "Says here you got a grade three concussion and you refused tests. You shouldn't go anywhere without someone to watch you for a day or two."

"But I've got to work tonight." Assuming Friday had bled into Saturday without skipping a week or some days in between. "What day is it?"

"Saturday, about four in the a.m., and you're not working tonight, my man."

We'll see about that.

"C'mon, let's ice those contusions."

Having the hospital gown on backward actually proved handy. Quick access to his ribs. The nurse pressed another crunchy plastic pack to his swollen eye. It hurt. Max had already investigated the stiches over his brow and had no inclination to do so again. The ice numbed the pain.

He waited until the nurse left before leaving his bed again. He paused by the door, head swimming, then cracked it open. The nurse's broad and cheerful face waited just on the other side. He waggled a finger. "Try that again and I'll have to confiscate your pants."

A blush crawled across Max's cheeks, prickling abused flesh. Quickly, he ducked his head, afraid the nurse would misinterpret his expression. He had a girlfriend, dang it. He was not the sort of guy who flirted with men. Not anymore. The nurse probably didn't mean anything by it anyway. He was just being kind to a patient.

The man's hands were large and warm. Max tried not to imagine them slipping across his bare skin as he was helped back to bed.

THEY WOKE him every hour. Waiting for his thoughts to coalesce every time, Max entertained fantasies of mauling each person who had touched him. Of giving back as good as he'd gotten, regardless of whether they'd been the ones who had put him in hell. The hospital *was* hell, and he'd be paying for his visit for eternity. His insurance wouldn't cover any of this. Maybe the stupid gown bunching up under his armpits or the gauze strips across his nose. His stitches? One ice pack for his bruised ribs? All he could probably afford was the cup of Jell-O the linebacker had brought him at *six in the a.m.* The big nurse had a name, but Max had forgotten it and didn't want to stare at the guy's chest. Where his nametag was.

Instead, he asked to go home. Every hour.

"Let's talk about that tomorrow, unless someone agrees to babysit you."

Stay here until Sunday? Absolutely not.

"I'm not a fff—" The curse died before it passed his lips. His mother hadn't liked him to swear and Max tried really, really hard not to do it. "I'm not a freaking child."

"No, but you got one wicked concussion. Threw up six times, I heard. And your nose is broke."

Irritated sighs hurt more than the regular kind. So did letting his head flop back into the thin pillows. "I can't afford to stay here. Can't you kick me out because I can't pay?"

"There's some forms attached to your chart. You can apply for assistance with the bills."

An hour crept by without a nurse and Max decided to make a break for it. Surely the linebacker had finished his shift by now—midday had come and gone. He crawled from the bed, waited for his stomach to settle and the world to stop spinning, then crept toward the door.

The blonde nurse was back and her pretty face did not cheer him up. "Do you need help?"

"Why does everyone keep asking me that?"

She tilted her head, her blonde bob acquiring an angular look. "You're out of bed."

"I want to go home." She moved toward his chart. Max held out a hand. "You can't keep me here. This isn't a prison."

Looking up from the page of bird-scratch he'd tried to read after his six o'clock wake up call, the nurse—Willa Kendricks, according to her name tag—said, "You could go, Mr. Wilson, ah, Max, right?" He nodded, perplexed. He didn't remember telling anyone he preferred his second name to his first. In fact, he didn't remember telling them his name at all. "But it's not recommended. A concussion can be pretty serious. Have you had one before?"

"Yes, and I lived."

Her gray eyes squinted a moment. Her lips pressed together. Max didn't even try to guess at her thoughts. "My brother can come get you," she said.

"Huh?"

"He's the one who brought you in here and he offered to drive you home if we couldn't contact your family."

"Huh?"

He'd taken a knock to the head. Eloquence was not required.

"He lives upstairs."

Max looked up at the ceiling and immediately regretted it. Pain swirled around the back of his skull and down his spine. His nose throbbed. Straightening, he swallowed a groan. Willa's mouth had curved into a sympathetic smile. "You really don't like hospitals, do you?"

"No."

"Not many folks do, I suppose. So, want me to call him?"

"Who?"

"Jake."

"Who's Jake?"

"My brother."

Oh. So weird. Why would some stranger offer to drive him home? "Wait, you said he lives upstairs?" Did she mean the guy who lived in the apartment over Wu's World? The blond-haired, gray-eyed demigod who'd held the door open for him the day it'd bucketed down rain? "Ah, um, I could call my girlfriend." The words were ground-up gravel in his throat.

"Oh, did you remember her number?"

"No."

Willa pulled a pen from the pocket of her scrubs. "What's her name?"

"Melanie."

"Last name?"

He really didn't want to see Melanie and he couldn't remember what lies he'd told last night. "Can't I just go? Please?" Annoyingly, his voice broke on the plea.

Pen poised over the small notepad, Willa gave him a long, hard look. Then she dipped her head into a gentle nod. "I'll fill your prescription for you and organize the paperwork. And find you a shirt. Okay? Just let me do that and I'll let you go."

It was as good a deal as he was likely to get, so Max returned her nod, his as gentle, and parked his butt on the side of the bed.

Half an hour later, sheaf of paper in hand, loose, borrowed T-shirt flapping around his hips, Max limped slowly toward the double glass doors of the hospital. A single word sang through his blood: freedom. And it hurt. Everything hurt, but he was used to it. Wasn't like he hadn't had the stuffing kicked out of him before.

The doors whooshed open, revealing bright sunlight, and pain stabbed him directly through the eyes. Or the eye. The thing about having one closed eye was that he couldn't see the shocked looks from anyone on his left side. He could see the man standing in the open doors, though, a corona of sunlight flaring around his blond head, and the shock on his face seemed worse, somehow.

It was the guy from upstairs. Willa's brother.

"Hey," the golden man said. He reached for Max's arm. "How are you doing? All right to walk? I'd have come upstairs, you know."

Max jerked his arm free of the man's grasp. What was his name? Willa had mentioned it. "I think you've got the wrong person," he said.

"Nope, I'm here for you. Max, right?"

Sighing hurt. He had to remember sighing hurt.

The golden man thrust out a hand. "Jake."

Max looked at the hand before giving it a brief shake. His mother hadn't raised him to be rude. Or maybe he was just too tired and sore to continue being an ass. "My girlfriend is coming to pick me up."

Jake's tentative smile folded up and left his face. "Oh."

"Yeah." Max started to swipe his hair out of his eyes, then remembered that would hurt. "Um, sorry?"

"Yeah, no, that's cool. Want me to wait with you?"

"Why?"

Jake's mouth flattened, and Max studied the line it made across his handsome face. Everything about Jake was square but not rigid. He just had angles. Big gray eyes, same as his sister's, defined cheekbones and a strong jaw. He kept his hair short, and it looked both bristly and soft.

Eyes narrowing, Jake offered an upward nod. "Your girlfriend isn't coming, is she?"

Max thought about lying. Blurring the truth had always been a good way to make himself less distinct, less defined. But he'd taken a breath and Jake still held his gaze and Max just knew he'd see the lie tripping off his tongue.

"'S okay, I get it," Jake said. "If I were you, I wouldn't want my girlfriend to see me like this either. Listen, I know you don't know me, but I'm only trying to help. I'm the one who found you. Brought you in. I called my sister and we carried you in here. Last night."

Max's throat quivered as if it might close. He swallowed. He didn't want to accept this man's help, no matter how beautiful and golden he was, and he didn't want to... crap. He dipped his chin too quickly and made the mistake of sniffing. Fire shot up his nose and into his head and the world took another spin. Jake caught his shoulder and eased him away from the door where Max might have been making a scene.

"I'm sorry."

"No worries, man. You're messed up. Let's get you home."

The short ride back to Beech Street became a blur of motion and time. Max could barely account for any of it when Jake's truck rolled over the rough pavement of the alley and turned into a garage. He was grateful to have someone to follow from there to the apartment door, but paused when he found himself halfway up the stairs.

"I live downstairs."

"Willa wants me to keep you upstairs with me. Just for a night."

"I have to work tonight."

"Max, there is no way you're working tonight."

"I'll lose my job."

"Call in sick. It's the Wawa on Lincoln, right? Your manager knows you were in the ER last night. The police had to call him to ID you."

Not good. He'd probably already been replaced. One month did not equal any sort of seniority. Max turned on the stairs. "I should call in."

"You can do that from my place." Jake shuffled in place and produced a cell phone. "You can call from here if you want." From the stairwell, because if Jake let him go downstairs, he'd lose the battle?

Talk about stubborn.

"Why can't I go down to my place?"

"First off, your place is like the *Lair of the White Worm*. It's fucking creepy down there."

Max did his best to look offended. His apartment was…. Okay, it was a lair.

"Second off, Willa really thinks you need someone to keep an eye on you. Knocks to the head can be nasty business. You were out cold for a while. We don't know how long." Jake tilted his head. "Do you remember anything?"

The police had asked him that and he'd told them a bunch of useless facts. For Jake, Max shrugged and sighed and neither hurt because he was just so tired.

"Ready to go upstairs?" Jake asked.

"Yeah."

"You can take a shower and I can burn those pants. Maybe the shirt, too."

He did stink—of the hospital and piss. Whoever thought of hospitals as clean and sterile places was seriously deluded. "I don't have any other clothes." He figured mentioning he had some downstairs would incite another lecture on why he couldn't go to his own apartment.

"Not a problem. You can borrow something of mine until we get a key from Mr. Wu."

Because he'd lost his keys last night, as well.

Suddenly it was all too much. He craved a shower, time alone in a small space with lots of hot water and billowing steam. A place to hide. And a couch sounded good. If it had to be Jake's couch, well, life could be worse. It could be Melanie's couch.

CHAPTER THREE

JAKE HAD never met anyone as stubborn as the waif from the basement apartment. Max looked like a good wind would knock him over. Actually, he looked like a good wind *had* knocked him over, and rolled him along until he hit every lamppost and collected every piece of trash in Northeast Philadelphia. Smelled like it too. Still, he stood there on the stairs, bruised and purple face set into a scowl, one blue eye flashing angrily and….

Damn, he was cute. Really, really cute.

His dark hair had flopped across his forehead and Jake's fingers itched to smooth it away. He'd seen Max attempt it a couple of times and he'd seen the wince that followed. He was in serious pain. No way he was collapsing on the couch without a shower and clean clothes, though. He reeked.

Max shifted from foot to foot and offered one of his truncated nods. "Okay." He said something else, uttered in a low rumble that was surprising, given his lean frame. The deep voice suited him. Went with the whole gruff persona thing.

"Hmm?"

"Thanks." Slim shoulders hitched up and down in a quick shrug. Pain pinched Max's brow. "For, you know…." He gestured vaguely.

Picking him up off the ground, carrying him up a flight of stairs—and down again—and taking him to the hospital. Jake didn't imagine Max actually wanted to thank him for all that. He seemed to have hated being in the hospital. But someone had taught him some manners and he was grudgingly exercising them.

"It's all good."

Max offered a grunt in reply and looked pointedly up the stairs.

Jake leaped up the last couple, pulled out his keys, and opened the door. "Remember being up here last night?"

A single blue eye looked up from inspecting the apartment and pinned Jake with a considered glare. Another shrug then deflated Max somewhat, returning him to his waif-like state. He looked back through the door. "Yeah, maybe. Willa was here, right?" The glare renewed itself. "I asked you not to take me to the hospital."

"Right."

Jake moved through the door and dumped his keys. He beckoned Max inside. Max stopped by the door and wrapped his arms around his torso. Jake watched him look around and turned to view his space through another man's eyes. Sunshine splashed through full-length windows lining the front and rear walls, bathing his living area with natural light. Those windows had sealed the deal. The place was small, but it had two bedrooms. The second, which he'd set aside for his daughter, if Kate ever let her visit, was little more than a closet. But the bright and airy space of the main room more than made up for it. The front half of the apartment served as his living room. Couch, chair, TV, and a long, low coffee table he'd just finished staining. He'd picked it up off the side of the road one Sunday night on the way home from his parents' place.

He had a den sort of space along the bare wall between the living room half and the kitchen half. A bookshelf and narrow table repurposed as a desk.

The kitchen had the same airy feel as the front of the apartment, even though the windows looked out over the alley. He had another half-finished project there, the round table he'd sanded, but not stained. A collection of chairs that worked in pairs, two by two. One set refinished, the other not.

The walls were brick, the floors wide, golden planks. He'd sanded, sealed, and buffed the floor before moving in. The interior doors, too. The kitchen cabinets could use a strip and sand. Or maybe he'd replace them with something from a job site.

"Nice place," Max said.

Jake smiled, proud his home could be considered nice. "I like it."

"Makes my place look like a hole in the ground."

"*Lair of the White Worm*," Jake reminded him.

Max's bruised features moved toward a smile. "Nah, it's too small for that. More like *The Crypt* or something. Just one. A small one."

So, he had a sense of humor under all that piss and vinegar.

"C'mon, I'll show you the bathroom." Jake opened the door. "Towels are in the closet, behind here, and I'll get you something to wear. Just leave your gear on the floor. Washer and dryer are in there, too." He peeled off toward his bedroom. Over his shoulder, he asked, "Want something to eat? Soup, probably. Chewing will hurt for a while, I reckon."

"Yeah." Max touched the side of his nose. "For a few days, at least."

"Had a broken nose before?"

"Once." His one eye narrowed slightly as he pushed open the bathroom door and disappeared inside. He left the door ajar, which seemed odd until Jake remembered he was supposed to be delivering clothes—not standing there wondering if Max needed help undressing.

Max had a girlfriend.

Casting a sideways glance at the bookshelf beside his desk, Jake looked for the picture of him and Kate together. They'd been seventeen at the time, and supposedly in love. Old hurt circled his heart for the space of a breath until he looked away.

He chose an old pair of sweats for Max, the soft and comfortable kind, debated including underwear, and settled on a pair of shorts. Shorts didn't hug a guy's junk, so it wouldn't be as weird, right? He snagged an old Phillies T-shirt from the top of the pile and, as an afterthought, a pair of socks. The shower started before he left his room and Jake paused outside the bathroom door a moment, thoughts running wildly and inappropriately. He needed to get laid. It had been, what, a year in prison, months before that and three months since? *Too long, man.* If he was fantasizing about the beat-up kid from the basement apartment, the guy with a girlfriend, it had been too damned long. He'd give Eric a call, but his oldest friend and regular booty-call was not currently *in between.*

Suppressing a sigh, Jake nudged open the door, slid the clothes onto the corner of the vanity, and pulled the door closed behind him. In the kitchen, he inspected the contents of his fridge and pantry, wondering what sort of soup Max might like. Maybe he should just get some egg drop from downstairs. Wu did make good soup. How hard it could be to actually make egg drop soup? Wasn't it just chicken broth with some tofu, green onion, and an egg? He'd give it a try, minus the tofu because he wasn't some hippie-dippie vegetarian. He'd use some leftover roasted chicken instead.

The soup was about done when Max emerged from the bathroom, pulling the drawstring on the sweatpants tight around his lean hips. Jake caught a flash of material at the waist there, the shorts—good call—then the T-shirt flopped down, looking something like a sack slung over a clothes hanger. Max had fairly wide shoulders and his arms were long.

Legs, too, under the sweats. Despite his slim appearance, Jake knew Max had a little heft to him. He'd carried him up and down the stairs last night, after all. Max might look like a waif, with his large eyes (one) and pale skin—but he wasn't. He had presence. It was just a shorter presence than Jake was used to with everyone in his family being tall.

"Feel better?"

Pushing wet hair back from his face, Max nodded. "Yeah." He moved slowly, obviously in pain, and the shower had done little to improve his appearance. He had a pair of stitches closing a cut over his swollen eye and a couple of moist scabs near his hairline on the opposite side.

"You need to cover those?" Jake couldn't help wincing slightly as he pointed out the cuts.

"Nah, they'll heal quicker if I let 'em dry out." The voice of experience? "Soup smells good."

"We'll reserve judgment until we taste it. I probably should have just gone to Wu's."

"You eat there much?"

"Not really. The hall always smells like Chinese food. Sort of puts me off."

"I know what you mean."

Jake waved at the table. "Have a seat. Can I get you a drink?"

"Just water." Max pulled out a chair and sat carefully. "How long have you lived here?"

"Just over three months."

"Dang. So if I'd ditched my old place a couple of months earlier, I could have had this one." Max's crooked smile looked like it hurt. "Not that I could afford it, mind."

"Where were you before?"

Max waved in an easterly direction. "Closer to the park. I was sharing with some other guys, but it ended up just being too noisy. I guess I'm a country boy at heart."

"So, you're from the country, then?"

"Mechanicsburg, it's—"

"Out past Harrisburg, yeah, I know it."

Max nodded. "You from Philly?"

"Doylestown. I moved down here a few years ago to be near...." His gaze flicked to the picture of him and Kate, then back to the soup pot. "Friends, and work, I guess. And my sister."

"What's your work?"

"Construction. Residential, which is mostly renovation at the moment."

Max smoothed his hand across the table. "So these tables are your projects, then?"

Tables, plural. He'd noticed the others? "Yeah."

"Nice."

Jake nodded in acknowledgment. "What about you?" Admitting he already knew Max also worked at the supermarket could sound stalkerish.

He hadn't noticed how open Max's expression had become, despite that one swollen eye and all the bruises, until his face closed again. Max looked down at the table and traced a finger along the grain. "I work at Hendrick's on weekdays and some shifts at the Wawa in the evenings."

That was a lot of hours. "Why do you work two jobs?"

"What else would I do?"

Jake blinked at the blank question reflected all over Max's face. "I dunno. Go out. See your family, friends."

Max's shoulders crept toward his ears. "I s'pose."

"Your girlfriend."

A long, low sigh deflated Max's shoulders. He stretched both arms across the table. Okay, time to change the subject.

"Is all your family in Mechanicsburg?"

Max shook his head halfway and offered another of his habitual shrugs. Silence fell between them with an audible thump and Jake turned back to the stove, disconcerted and confused. Max was like a cactus or something. One with those rare flowers that only opened up for an hour a day.

Not able to think of another topic, he served up the soup. It worked out okay. Didn't really taste like egg drop, but it had the chicken thing going.

"It's good," Max said before tackling one of the soft pieces of meat. He winced and snuffled as he chewed.

"Are you in pain? Where did you put your prescription?"

"In the bathroom. I took a pill after my shower. I figured I'd take it before I got really sore. Not that I'll not be sore somewhere for the next week or two."

"Sounds like you're speaking from experience."

"Sure. Who hasn't been in a fight?"

"Willa said…." Jake trailed off, sure Max didn't want be reminded of the beating.

Max looked up, his one startlingly blue eye pinning Jake with a look. "Said what?"

Fuck, here goes. "It looked like you didn't fight back."

"I didn't."

"Why?"

"They finish up quicker when you let them get on with it."

CHAPTER FOUR

THE SOUP was really, really good. It was about the best thing Max had eaten since forever. He slurped up that last piece of chicken and set to chewing it slowly, which didn't really hurt his face any less, but he wanted to savor the flavor of something that had been cooked rather than microwaved.

His enjoyment of the soup was interrupted by the sound of Jake's spoon clattering to the table. "Just how many times have you been beat up?" he asked.

Didn't Jake know sighing hurt? Max had figured out how to shrug with minimal pulling. He did that.

"Is it the same guys?"

"Huh?"

"Picking on you."

"What? No. I don't know who these guys were. I guess I ran into their deal or something. They were all huddled outside the door."

"Here? Outside this door?"

"Yeah."

"Damn it!" Jake pushed up, away from the table, and paced over to the windows. He looked down into the alley. "I should have replaced the light. I'm sorry."

"Not your fault."

Jake turned around. "So you didn't know them, then?"

"Nope."

"What about the others?"

"What others?"

"These people beating you up!"

Geez, take a pill. "That was in high school. And once in college. And, whatever. What does it matter?" Why was Jake interested?

"What do you do that…." Jake rubbed at his forehead, then pushed his hand up over his short blond hair.

"I'm just the kid people pick on, okay? I'm a runt." And a freak. "Can we talk about something else?" Max looked around the apartment for a better topic of conversation. He saw the series of photo frames on the bookcase between the kitchen and the living room. He'd seen them before, when he'd made his initial inspection of the apartment, and had decided they suited the homey feel of the place. They were family photos. Jake, obviously younger, with a pretty woman. Jake with a little girl. "Is that your family?"

Jake took a turn at looking uncomfortable. His gray gaze flicked toward the shelves, over the collection of frames, and seemed to linger on one. He stepped away from the windows and dropped back into his chair with a sigh. "Yeah."

"Who's the kid? Your niece or something?"

Jake fiddled with his spoon—and his thoughts, by all appearances—and leaned back, folding his thick arms. "That's Caroline. My daughter."

All of Max's fantasies evaporated with a near audible pop. He glanced around the apartment, but saw no Barbie dolls or pink things. He reevaluated the furnishings and they still said "homey, but not feminine."

"Oh. So, you're divorced, then?" Tactful. Really tactful.

"Never married." Jake scrubbed his face again. "I got Kate pregnant, just after high school, and…." He shrugged. "She wanted to do it herself."

Huh. "You still see her, though? Caroline?"

"Sometimes."

Max supposed he should revel in how completely he'd managed to turn the tables on his host, but he didn't. Jake seemed sad rather than angry, and his sorrow made his eyes grayer. He kept glancing over at the pictures, himself and a blonde woman, Caroline's mother by her looks, and then at the picture of himself with the little girl draped over his shoulders.

"She's cute."

Jake cracked a smile. "Yeah, she is. She really, really is."

"How old is she?"

"Nearly nine."

Whoa, so Jake must be close to thirty? He didn't look that old, but then again, he didn't look young, either. He just looked sad.

Max drained his water and set the glass down. Before he could ask any more awkward questions, fatigue caught up with him, wrapping a warm and heavy blanket around his shoulders. His stomach felt pleasantly full and the flavor of the soup lingered on this tongue.

He glanced toward the couch. "Did I wreck your couch last night?" Broken noses bled like nothing on Earth and he'd apparently thrown up several times. His pants had also had that faint odor of piss. He must have wet himself while being beaten. Or afterward. Lovely.

"No, it's fine. Leather cleans up easy."

"I don't suppose you're going to let me go downstairs now?"

"Nope."

Max sighed. His eyelids were heavy, and his eyes—both of them—felt gritty. "You don't have to do this, you know. I can look after myself."

"I'm sure you can. But… I found you, all right? I thought you were a bum. I nearly left you in the alley. If I hadn't got your blood all over my hands, I probably would have, and I should have replaced the light. I'm sorry."

"Not your fault."

"Let me look after you. Just for the weekend." He smoothed his hand over the unfinished table between them. "You can be one of my projects."

"I don't want to be sanded and stained. I'm already in enough pain."

Jake's eyes widened, then narrowed. "That almost sounded kinky, man."

Kinky? Max met Jake's gaze for a second and they measured one another, just for that second. They looked away at the same time. As he sucked in a tight breath, Max heard Jake breathing as well. He had no idea what that meant.

Jake stood. "I'll, ah, get you a pillow and shit."

Imagining his mother's reaction to Jake's casual cursing, Max smiled. "Thanks."

The leather couch proved surprisingly comfortable. The pair of pillows held his head up at a good angle and the "shit" turned out to be one of those down blankets, all light and soft and warm. It smelled of fresh air and sunshine. Pillows smelled good, too. For a moment, eyes drifting closed, Max could almost imagine he'd returned home. Or had never left. That the past few years hadn't happened. His mother was well, and alive, and she had never heard his secrets.

Hearing a soft shuffle of socked feet, Max opened his eyes. Jake stood over him, his expression unreadable. Or maybe too weird to read.

"You okay?"

"Yeah." He was so tired he no longer hurt.

"I'm going to head downstairs and see about getting you a new key."

Max nodded.

"My cell number is on the fridge."

"Okay."

"You'll call if you need anything?"

"Sure." The need to sleep pulled at every inch of his body. Jake shuffled in place and scrubbed at his hair. "Right. Okay. See you."

"See you."

WHEN MAX woke, he noted the dimness first, as if someone had switched off the sun. It took a while for the realization to form that he'd missed the day—the afternoon portion, anyway. Mild panic gripped him, the sense he'd left stuff undone. He usually cleaned and did his laundry on Saturdays.

The couch beneath him squawked softly as he slid against the leather, but it didn't loosen its warm embrace. Max thought about dropping his head back into the stack of pillows, but his bladder had had time to wake, as had the various aches and pains now rippling through his body. He hurt. All over, he hurt. Lying there with his eyes open— both of them, he thought—he compared the pain to the last time he'd been caught in an alley and taught the error of his ways. He quickly found he couldn't remember how bad he'd been hurt that time. Maybe the pain from his ribs, the gentle poke every time he breathed too deep, was making everything hazy. More likely, the concussion had robbed him of perfect recall.

He remembered the annoyance of having a broken nose, though. His face would hurt for days, longer than it took for the swelling around his eye to subside or the bruises to fade. Running, climbing stairs, hitting his shoulder on a door frame because he hadn't judged the space properly. All of these things would send waves of pain rolling through the center of his face and into his brain.

His sigh highlighted the fact he really needed to take a leak.

Only after he'd lifted himself from the couch—his slow and awkward movements designed to not jostle anything, and failing, completely—did Max realize that he might be alone. The apartment felt empty. Had Jake not returned from his outing? Where had he gone again?

He looked around for a clock and saw the green display on the cable box under the TV. 4:45. Craning forward, he blinked a couple of times to clear his vision and looked again. 4:46. A glance through the uncovered windows placed the time at early morning rather than late afternoon. He'd slept through the night. He'd slept for over twelve hours.

There were a couple of vague shadows on the coffee table resembling familiar objects. Max picked up the wallet-shaped one and discovered it *was* a wallet. His wallet. He could tell by the faint whiff of old leather and the worn binding on the lower fold. He opened it up and hefted it, measuring the weight of the contents. He peeked inside the billfold and saw notes. Money.

"What the…." How had his wallet, presumably stolen, ended up on Jake's table? Were those his keys? That his phone?

Yep.

Jake had plugged the phone into a charger. The cord snaked across the table and disappeared into the shadows on the floor. Max picked it up and woke the screen. The fact he had no messages came as no surprise. He had about five contacts. Really, he only had a phone because…. He didn't know why he had a phone. Probably because normal people had phones.

He scrolled through his contacts, expecting a pang of guilt when he got to Melanie's name, and noted a new entry: Jake Kendricks. Jake had put his number into Max's phone. Max peered at the name and the digits. He scrolled up and down looking for information, found none, and looked at Jake's name again. He couldn't decide if it was weird that Jake had put his number into his phone, or if it was nice. Friends did that, didn't they?

Were he and Jake friends now?

Staring at the screen tempted his head to ache. Max pushed off the couch and tiptoed to the bathroom. His clothes were missing from the floor and the bathroom smelled faintly of laundry detergent. He peeked in the dryer and found his clothes resting in the bottom, all tumbled, wrinkled, and clean. At that point, he decided Jake was a little weird. Who did all this stuff for a stranger? For some guy found in an alleyway—neighbor or not. Jake had carried him around, all broken and bleeding. Upstairs, downstairs, and into his truck. He'd taken him to the hospital and had picked him up. He'd made him soup and a bed on his couch. He'd performed the certain miracle of finding Max's wallet and keys and phone, and then he'd plugged in the phone to charge, because good guys thought of that sort of thing.

Back on the couch, Max considered his escape. Jake's care felt oppressive. Surely he'd want something in exchange? What would someone as normal as Jake want?

Did normal guys wash another man's clothes?

Next to his wallet stood the bottle of pain relievers from the hospital. Max stared at it a moment, then decided his various aches didn't necessitate being knocked out for another twelve hours. He didn't want to lose another day ensconced in Jake's couch. He didn't want to get used to his care. He crept back to the bathroom and dressed in his rumpled pants and the T-shirt they'd given him at the hospital. It had a V-neck and looked like an old man's undershirt. He put on his socks and shoes. He folded the gear Jake had lent him and put it on the corner of the vanity, just where he'd found it. He folded the blanket and set it in the center of the couch and put the pillows on top. Then he gathered up his stuff and crept toward the door. The pills rattled gently in his pocket. His shoes sounded all clompy on the floor. The door clicked loudly when he pulled it closed behind him. The stairs creaked.

Jake apparently slept like a dead man. Or maybe he'd gone out again. Either way, Max didn't look back.

CHAPTER FIVE

EVERY COUPLE of years, April served up a handful of bright, sunny days that properly belonged in May. It was a tease and a promise, that lick of warmth on the skin. Seated in a chair on the back patio of his parents' house in Doylestown, Jake soaked it up. He had his eyes closed, head resting on the high metal back of the chair. He could hear two of his sisters talking quietly. The sound of the TV drifted out of an open window, a golf game judging by the hushed tones interspersed with polite applause. In a corner of the yard, his nephews argued over a ball or something. It was the sound of family and he absorbed it all with the spring sunshine.

"Hold this for me, will you?"

Something solid landed in his lap. Squinting against the sun, Jake glanced from his sister's exasperated expression down into the snot-crusted face of *this*, otherwise known as Antony—which was entirely too much name for a two-year-old. Jake called his youngest nephew T.

"Hey, T." Jake bounced his knee. T gurgled and sneezed, fine droplets and one unattractive clump of something spraying toward Jake's forearm. The lump landed with a splat and slide, and Jake stared at it a moment, wondering if this was his week to wear other people's bodily fluids. "Has he got a cold?"

"He's teething," Abby said, dropping into the chair next to him. She had a glass of wine clutched in one long-fingered and bony-looking hand.

"You look tired."

"I've been tired for years, Jake. Now I just look dead. A walking cadaver."

"Speaking of cadavers." Willa looked up from her tête-à-tête with Dawn, the oldest of the Kendricks siblings. "We had an interesting case roll into the ER this week. Death by fork."

Dawn shuddered. "Fork? I don't want to know."

"When was this?" Abby asked, reaching over to curl her finger through T's hair. Jake bounced his knee again and T rewarded him with a giggle. He grabbed a napkin to wipe the goo off of his arm.

"Thursday. Most exciting thing to happen all week until Jake's guy."

Three pairs of eyes turned toward him, the color varying from gray-blue to gray—and there *was* a difference, though sometimes it was just mood.

"Jake's guy?" Abby smiled, which did wonders for her drawn features. Put life back into her tired eyes. "You have a boyfriend? Since when?"

Dawn, seated on the other side of Willa, leaned forward to make sure she was heard. "ER doesn't make a great date night, Jake."

"He's not my boyfriend." But as he denied the claim, his gut clenched and his pulse kicked up—just slightly. "He's straight, anyway. He has a girlfriend."

"A girlfriend he refused to call from the hospital. Two or three times," Willa said.

Jake recalled the look he and Max had shared across the kitchen table after the kinky comment. That second of curiosity as they measured one another's gaze, the way guys did when trying to figure out—without asking the obvious question—if the other was straight. With only one very blue eye open to scrutiny and his face all swollen and purple, Max hadn't conveyed much of an impression, or invitation. He hadn't called his girlfriend, either.

Of course, he hadn't had his phone handy. Mr. Wu had had the phone, which had been really, really strange. Mr. Wu had found the wallet, keys, and phone by the Dumpsters the restaurant shared with the other stores on the block, begging the question: why had Max been jumped? If he hadn't been mugged, he'd had the shit kicked out of him for some other reason, one Jake couldn't fathom.

Waving a hand to dismiss his thoughts, Jake said, "Look, I just met the guy, and he snuck out before six this morning and didn't answer his door later." Why did every comment out of his mouth make it sound like he and Max had gone on a date? T grabbed his waving hand and moved it toward his mouth. Jake let his nephew gnaw on a finger as he continued. "He's my neighbor. He got beat up on Friday night. I took him to the hospital, that's all. I never met him before that."

"Someone really worked him over," Willa put in, shaking her head. "How did he do Saturday night? He actually stayed with you?"

"I nearly had to tie him down." Brows arched. "Jesus, you guys. That's not my thing, okay? He's just a stubborn shit, is all. Didn't seem to like having someone look after him."

"Point me at him," Dawn said. "I'll swap him for Bernat, who likes being looked after all too well." Bernat, Dawn's husband, was the man-she-should-not-have-married. Jake had always thought him nice enough. Bernat obviously loved Dawn, and their two sons were good kids. Neither of them had tried to bite his finger off.

"Ow." Jake pulled his finger out of T's gaping maw. "I think he grew that tooth."

"He grew those at six months, Jake. He's working on the back ones now."

"Is he always so drooly?"

"Mmm-hmm." Abby drained her wine, then gestured with the empty glass. "So I know North Philly has a reputation,"—for looking postapocalyptic—"but I thought you lived in the nicer part."

"I do. But people get beat up in Doylestown, too. Shit happens."

"You should stop swearing in front of the baby," Abby said.

T gurgled.

"Did you ask him about Friday night?" Willa tilted her head. "I know the police took a statement, but I got the idea he didn't give them much, even though he seemed pretty lucid."

"You know what he told me? I asked him about not fighting back and he said they finish up faster if he doesn't."

His sisters all gaped at him, their mouths open at various degrees. Dawn recovered first. "You need to move to a new neighborhood, hon."

"Jake can take care of himself."

"He's not meant to be fighting." Willa lifted her chin toward him. "You show up for a meeting with your parole officer covered in bruises and it's trouble, right?"

"Yeah, but that's beside the point. Max seems like he's had a rough time. He's a small guy. I think he got picked on in high school and college. I guess he's just resigned to it." Which was wrong.

Abby echoed his thoughts. "That's wrong."

"It is." Willa sucked on her lip. "And he's not that small."

Dawn waved for their attention and T stretched up to grab a new hand, his chubby arm flailing clumsily. "Jake, you should take him to your dojo. You still study, right?"

Jake hummed. "Yeah. You know, that's a great idea."

Sensei Alyssa Fabrizio was shorter than all her adult students. But she could take them down, every single one of them, and delighted in doing so. She'd share his opinion of Max, too, about being cute. Instead of imagining him naked, she'd wrap him up in a motherly embrace, from down there at five-feet-and-a-bit. Then she'd introduce him to the floor and teach him how to get back up.

Abby dug an elbow into his ribs. "Helping him out would be good karma, too."

Jake answered her with a sideways look. He already had a PO, and Officer Spet didn't feel the need to punctuate his advice with sharp elbow digs.

He should be grateful his family still seemed willing to touch him.

"Helping who?" Annabel Kendricks asked as she stepped onto the patio carrying a wine bottle and another pair of glasses.

While Willa related the tale—hospital style—Jake watched his mother refill glasses. She offered him one and he shook his head. He didn't want even a whiff of alcohol on his breath when he drove back to the city, not with his record. Sighing quietly, he looked down into T's ruddy face. He remembered Caroline at that age. He didn't recall her being as snotty. She'd been his little princess. He should call Kate again. He'd let another month go by, hoping she'd simmered down a bit.

Would she ever forgive him?

MAX LOOKED terrible. Worse than terrible. Standing in the doorway to the basement apartment, expression mutinous, he looked as though someone had worked him over again.

"Are you all right?" Jake asked. He could see Max thinking about his answer and even that looked painful. Jake held up the bag of food, the lunch leftovers his mother had packed up for the *poor dear*. "I have ribs and beans and apple pie."

The kid's eyes actually brightened at the mention of pie. He dithered in his doorway for another long second, then stepped back, the movement inviting Jake in. "I'm probably not much company, but, yeah, I could use some pie." He looked down as he spoke, as if holding his head up caused pain.

"Have you taken your meds today?"

"No, Mom." That one blue eye flashed. Max huffed out a sigh. "But I probably should. I feel like I got hit by a bus."

"You look it." Oh, he hadn't…. "You didn't try to work today, did you?"

"No. I called in, but they let me go."

"From the Wawa?"

"Are you coming in or what?"

"Oh, yeah."

Jake stepped inside and looked around. For a dingy hole, the place was remarkably clean, probably cleaner than when he'd painted. The walls were still white and bare. They seemed forlorn without any decoration. Under the two high windows, Max had a small TV and a bookcase. Any books on the shelves were hidden by a motley collection of potted plants. One of the shelves held model cars. In fact, there were cars everywhere—except the windowsills. More forlorn plants hugged the glass, some with pale tendrils drifting partway down the wall. Little Matchbox models and the larger kit-models covered every other available surface. The TV showed a motor race.

"Plants and cars. Interesting combination."

"I like cars." Max delivered the simple statement in a defensive tone. He said nothing about the plants.

"I know next to nothing about cars. I can commentate a hockey game, though."

That sly smile tugged at Max's mouth as he aimed a pointed look at the bag in Jake's hands.

"Want some ribs or beans before the pie?" Jake asked.

"Just pie."

Max moved toward the kitchen—or the slice of wall that served as a kitchen with its half fridge and microwave stacked next to a single counter with a sink at one end. Cabinets overhead and a table with two chairs completed the nook. The table looked newish and as Jake crossed the living room, he noted the pine surface hadn't been finished.

"Planning to stain or paint this?"

"Maybe."

"I could recommend some techniques if you want."

"Sure."

Jake forgave him his single word answers. Max looked like human wreckage, after all. He opened the bag, set out the Tupperware, and pulled the pie forward. Two hefty slices. He smiled as he levered one out onto a plate he retrieved from the draining board. He liked that Max was the sort of guy who did his dishes promptly. In fact, he liked that Max was the sort of guy who kept his apartment clean, even if such a sparsely furnished place would have a hard time messing itself up.

He put the plate on the table, and Max dropped into the chair and picked up the fork. Jake opened the fridge to store the rest and froze. Max had a jug of milk, a tub of butter, and a jar of strawberry jam. No ketchup or mustard. No weird pickles bought on a whim. No moldy containers of Chinese food or limp stalks of celery. Just those three things.

"If you need some help shopping, I can give you a ride to the store sometime this week."

"I shopped today," Max said around a mouthful of pie.

When, where, how? "Where's all the food?"

"In the freezer."

Jake opened the smaller freezer compartment set inside the top portion of the fridge. Wedged into the tiny space were three Hungry Man frozen dinners and a box of lime-flavored ice pops.

"This is what you eat?"

"We're not all Betty Crocker."

Jake frowned at the kid shoveling apple pie into his mouth as if he'd never had anything so delicious. "It's not hard to make a few simple things. That soup I made was pretty basic."

Shruggy McShruggerson shrugged. "Pie's good. You make it?"

"No, my mom made it. Dad did the ribs and the beans might be from a can, but she dresses them up with stuff. You like beans?"

"Maybe."

"You ever had beans?"

"Sure, it's been a while, though."

Maybe Hungry Man didn't have a dinner with ribs and beans. Jake looked back at the dinners and saw two of them were Boneless Fried Chicken and one was Bourbon Steak Strips. What the hell were Bourbon Steak Strips?

"I usually get the regular fried chicken but wasn't up to eating my way around a bone this week."

"You live on Hungry Man fried chicken?"

"The steak strips are new. They look soft."

"This is really sad, man. You're like a bad cliché."

"You're letting all the cold air out of the freezer."

Jake closed the freezer and set the other leftovers in the fridge. "Want some milk with your pie?"

"Sure."

He poured Max a glass of milk and sat opposite without waiting to be invited. Max didn't look hostile, exactly. But he didn't have his friendly face on. Not that Jake knew that one yet. "Sorry to hear about your job at the Wawa. Did you, ah, will that make things tight for you?" *Do not offer him money. He already thinks you're weird.*

"Nah. I'm good."

"How come you work so many hours, then?"

"I like to stay busy."

Why? Jake swallowed that question and asked a more appropriate one. "Where are your meds? Best to take 'em on a full stomach."

"In the bathroom." Max half rose.

Jake waved him down. "Finish your pie, I'll get them."

He ducked into the bathroom and noticed again how clean everything was. The faint odor of bleach in the air hinted the cleaning had been performed recently. Jesus, did Max not know how to convalesce? The inside of the medicine cabinet had exactly five items: deodorant, dental floss, shaving foam, a razor, and the little orange container of pills. A cup on the sink held Max's toothbrush and toothpaste. The shower stall had a 2-in-1 bodywash/shampoo bottle. Max sure valued the minimalist lifestyle.

Back in the kitchen, Jake sat and pushed the pills across the table. "You don't have a car, right?"

Max shook his head.

"So you walked to the store and then came home and cleaned your apartment. What else did you do today while you were supposed to be resting?"

The glare brightened his one eye. God, his face looked awful.

"I took my laundry to Arnolds." The Laundromat around the corner.

"You—" Jake clamped his lips shut. He had been going to offer Max the use of his washer and dryer, but decided Max would probably kick him out if he tried to help him any more than he already had. Instead, he drew in a quick breath and tried to exhale slowly. "You're not good at relaxing, are you?"

"I usually relax on Sundays. I go for a run and watch TV. But seeing as I spent most of Saturday sacked out on your couch, I had to get stuff done today."

He hadn't mentioned his girlfriend. When, exactly, did Max see this girlfriend of his? Jake swallowed yet another question. It was none of his business. "So, what do you do for fun?"

"I go to Pennypack, run along the creek. Do a portion of the trail."

"It will be pretty down there in May."

"Yeah."

Finally, something they agreed on.

"Listen, I wondered if you were interested in martial arts," Jake said.

"What do you mean?"

"I study at a place two blocks from here and I thought maybe you might want to check it out. Learn some self-defense."

"Why would I do that?"

It should've been obvious. Jake flipped his hand toward Max's beat-up face and the kid snorted softly and reached for his pills. He wrestled open the canister and swallowed two. He looked more thoughtful when he set the container back down.

"First lesson is free," Jake said, "and I can get you a deal on tuition if you like what you see."

"I'll think about it."

The small thrill in Jake's chest felt like victory. He smiled at Max and nodded at the empty plate. "Want the other slice now?"

"Sure, and thanks."

Jake's smile widened. Max could be gruff and kinda rude, but he always seemed to remember his manners at the end of it all, which just made him all the more interesting. And cute.

"Hey, where did you find my wallet and stuff?" Max asked.

"Oh, Mr. Wu had it all. He found it by the Dumpsters."

"Weird."

"Yeah, but lucky."

After the second slice of pie had been demolished, Jake wrestled the plate out of Max's hand and directed him toward the futon arrangement that obviously served as Max's couch and bed. "Go rest. I'll clean up."

Max hesitated only a second before complying, his fatigue obvious. He eased down onto the futon with a weary sigh and picked up the remote.

Jake washed the plate, fork, and glass, and then he stopped in front of the couch, prepared to take his leave.

Max surprised him with an invitation. "You can hang out if you want. They raced Bahrain this weekend. Formula One."

Jake sat on the couch and tuned in to the race. A comfortable quiet blossomed between them, punctuated only by the whine of race cars and the speculative tone of the commentators. Now and again, the broadcast would break for an ad—always motor-sport themed. Max watched those as avidly as he did the race. Jake found it interesting that Max didn't talk. Whenever he watched golf with his dad, Tony Kendricks dissected every swing, putt, and choice of club. The golfers' shoes sometimes came under scrutiny, and the behavior of the crowd. If nothing interesting was happening—and very little about golf held Jake's attention for long—then his father would talk about the weather over there, wherever there was, and share information about the location as if he'd been there, which he hadn't.

In comparison, Jake found Max's quiet companionship restful. A man who didn't feel the need to talk was rare. Or maybe Max was just used to spending time alone.

During an ad break, Jake glanced over and noticed Max's head had listed to one side. One of the snuffling breaths drifted over, then a soft snore. Max had fallen asleep. Probably the pills. They'd knocked him out completely the afternoon before. Jake had actually feared Max had died. Sort of. When he finally tired of checking on him, he'd gone to bed himself—and had woken to an empty apartment and tidy piles of clothes and blankets.

He indulged in a minute or so of unabashed and close inspection of Max's profile. With a face full of bruises and a swollen eye, Max could only claim cute—and even then, only when that one eye of his flashed with anger, defiance, or more rarely, humor. He had delicate but defined features. Eyes of a deep, velvety blue and dark hair that only seemed to highlight the paleness of his skin. He had the slightest shadow of stubble over his top lip and around his chin. Rubbing a hand along his own bristled jaw, Jake supposed Max might be one of those guys who couldn't grow a full beard. Probably just as well given the state of his face.

A flash of memory, there and gone, left a pinch between Jake's shoulder blades. Shaving in prison had been a fast exercise done with cheap soap and paranoia. If he'd had smooth skin like Max's....

Deep breath. Let it go.

Next to him, Max snored softly again. Asleep, he looked too young to be living alone, though fewer than six years separated them—Jake had peeked at his driver's license. Max would be twenty-two at the end of summer. Jake had just turned twenty-seven. Sometimes he felt much older.

When he got to wondering if the skin across Max's torso was as smooth and pale as his face, Jake decided he should go home. First, he arranged Sleeping Beauty, stuffing pillows under Max's head and pulling his legs up onto the futon. It didn't look that comfortable, not like a real bed. He wondered if Max usually folded the back down at night. Jake decided not to fiddle with that now. Max needed his sleep. He snored through the entire process, even when Jake tucked a comforter around him. Jake resisted the urge to sweep a lock of dark hair away from Max's forehead for about a minute—hovering, feeling both irrationally tender and stupid. Then he went ahead and smoothed the hair away, the very tips of his fingers lingering a second longer than advisable against warm skin.

He needed to leave.

Jake left the TV on, the sound turned down a little. The apartment seemed too quiet and lonely otherwise.

CHAPTER SIX

THE TABLE didn't quite turn out as he'd imagined. The green tint in the sealant Max used streaked along the grain in uneven ribbons. Off center, a green whorl stared at him like a single, baleful eye. It was seriously ugly, but contemplating it, Max couldn't help a grin. He and his table could be freaks together.

After a week, the swelling around his left eye had subsided, leaving behind a deep purple bruise. A blue and green bruise curled under his right eye, courtesy of his broken nose, giving him the appearance of a demented raccoon. More bruising extended from around his left brow and into his hairline, this mottled patch a sickly shade of green. Small scabs decorated the mural. Thumb-sized bruises, each a greenish gray, trailed along his jaw. His nose was a mess. Not squashed across his face—he'd managed to keep the sharp line that defined his features. But the bridge had a second bump, larger than the first. His ribs were still tender, the left side of his torso as colorful as his face. He also had a dark mark across his left hip and bruises on his thigh. A couple more on his forearms from when he'd tucked his head in, not exactly defending himself, more acknowledging that one more kick to the temple might scramble his brains permanently.

His phone vibrated in his pocket and Max dug it out. It was another series of texts from Melanie: *Where are you? Are you at home? Can I come over? Call me.* She'd been calling twice a day, texting more often, since Monday. She'd missed him at work, obviously. He'd thought about going to Hendrick's, but one look at his face in the mirror on Monday morning had been enough to discourage him. Plus, he'd seriously overestimated his capabilities on Sunday—his awakening on Monday morning had been about three levels south of rude. For the first time in the year he'd been employed at the supermarket, he'd called in sick. After he explained the nature of his injuries—the bruises would be obvious for a couple of weeks, at least—he was told to take the week if he needed it.

Unused to having so much time to himself, he'd spent the week climbing the walls of his lair. His sorry collection of plants only needed so much tending, and he hurt too much to run the Pennypack Trail. Hence the table project.

Mild panic knotted his gut as Max stared at the messages. He didn't know how to answer any of her questions. How could he explain what had happened? What would her reaction be? She knew he wasn't some kind of action hero, but being beaten to a pulp was the other end of the spectrum entirely.

Max scrolled through the small list of contacts on his phone and paused by Jake Kendricks. What would he say if he called? *The pie was good. Sorry I fell asleep. Thanks for tucking me in.* "No, you could have just asked about the table stuff, stupid." Jake had offered his advice, hadn't he?

Sighing, Max nudged the display with his thumb and paused again as he noted the name just above Jake's: Elaine Honeycutt.

Elaine had been his only friend growing up. His neighbor and confidante. She hadn't been able to stop Bryce and his pack from dragging Max out behind the gym, but she'd always been there afterward with lime popsicles and a tube of Neosporin. Neither assuaged the shame nor did anything for his bruises, but Elaine's company had always been the balm he needed. Simple and accepting, no matter what—until she'd gone to college in California. She'd met a guy over there and never come back.

Tapping her name, Max brought up their last exchange of texts. Two months ago. Wow. He typed a message, knowing it might be weird after two months of radio silence. But Elaine would get it. Elaine had always understood him. He kept it short and sweet: *Hey.*

She didn't reply right away. She had a life, obviously. Max tucked the phone back into his pocket and bent to collect the newspaper he'd spread across the floor under the table. His back was stiff and his nose and head ached, but cleaning the paintbrush proved a meditative exercise— warm water flowing across his fingers, alternately pale green and clear, depending on whether he squeezed the bristles or not. Finally, the water ran completely clear and somewhat cool. He'd emptied the tank again. Still, he showered, not minding the nearly cold water.

After he dressed, he picked up his phone, weighing it in his palm. He might not have a lot of friends, but he spent much of his time surrounded by people. Being alone in his apartment was lonely.

The phone vibrated in his hand. Max woke the display.

Hey? Two months and all I get is a "hey"? Call me!

He dialed Elaine's number and she answered immediately with, "Hey!"

Max laughed at the cheerful greeting, the same one she'd chastised him for. The laugh scraped a throat dry from disuse and emerged as a strained cackle.

"Jesus, Max, are you all right? You didn't call me to die on the phone did you?"

"No," he croaked.

"Are you sick?"

"Not really."

"What does that mean?"

"I, um, had an accident. So I've been home for a few days."

"Home where?"

"Still in Philly."

"Tell me about the accident. Is that why you called?"

He could tell by the tone of her voice she suspected that was pretty much exactly why he had called. Why he had sent a feeble text. Something had happened to him and he'd reached out to the only person who had ever shown a lick of care or compassion. Well, except for his neighbor, who'd been conspicuously absent for five days now. He'd half expected Jake to knock on his door every evening. He'd been disappointed when he hadn't.

"Max?"

"I got mugged." Being mugged was different to being beat up.

"Oh God! What happened?"

He shrugged, aware that Elaine couldn't see the gesture, but taking a certain pleasure in being able to do so without triggering a hundred sharp pains from head to toe. "I was just trying to get into my place."

"You need to get out of the city."

"I'm not really in the city and it's quieter where I am now."

"Sure sounds like it. Are you going to move again?"

"No."

"Well, is it safe? God, Max." He heard Elaine sigh and he could imagine her pinching the bridge of her nose. "How bad is it?"

"Just a broken nose. Some bruises."

"Have you got anyone to look after you?"

"Kind of?"

The beat of silence felt speculative. "A friend?"

Max nearly scoffed. Elaine knew she was his only friend. Instead, he thought about Jake, whom he'd like to have as a friend. "My neighbor took me to the hospital and gave me a ride home. He watched me the first night. I, um, stayed at his place."

"Go you! Is he cute?" Jake wasn't cute. He was gorgeously handsome. "I'm going to take your silence as a 'yes.'"

"He's just the guy upstairs."

"Have you been out with anyone since you moved?"

Max blew out a breath. "I have a girlfriend."

"A what!"

"I've been trying to just fit in down here."

"I thought the whole point of moving to Philly was so that you could be yourself."

"Maybe this is me."

"Don't make me fly out there."

I wish you would. Max let go another sigh. "I'll be okay. You know me."

"Yeah, I do. All too well. Why don't you ever check your voice mail, Gary? I've left messages."

Max gritted his teeth. "Don't call me that." He'd chosen long ago not to share a name with his father, a decision Elaine had heartily supported. "You could just text me."

"I want to *talk* to you. We need to talk more often."

"I'd like that." His cheeks warmed, the skin beneath his bruises prickling. "So, ah, tell me what's up with you?"

"I'd love to, but I've got work in half an hour. I'm going to call you on Sunday, okay? We'll have a good, long chat and set a schedule for you to call me back. Regularly. I want to hear all about this neighbor."

That she did not mention his girlfriend didn't surprise him. Elaine obviously had the same attitude toward Melanie as he did. She was a prop—there to hold something up, but not important enough to be noticed. He really should answer one of her texts, though.

The day ebbed into late afternoon without him doing much to stop it until a knock sounded at his front door. Max nearly tripped over his feet getting up off the futon and had to pause to catch his breath before answering. Jake might be waiting on the other side.

Melanie stood in the dim hallway.

"Mel."

"What happened to your face!"

"I got mugged."

"Oh my God!" Fright diminished her and Max felt the urge to pull her into his arms. He liked holding her. He liked the idea of being there for someone more frail and delicate than he was, someone less prepared for the real world. "Why didn't you call me? I've been leaving so many messages. At work they said you were sick, but this. Max…." His name left her lips in a breathy rush. "Does it hurt? Are you in pain?"

Yeah, but admitting as much would only give her an excuse to linger. *This is your* girlfriend, *man.* Max opened the door wider. "Want to come in?"

After giving him an odd look, Melanie slipped through the door and paused just inside. He watched as she absorbed the small space of his new apartment. When she looked back at him, he saw her trying to think of something nice to say. A smile tugging at his mouth, he waved a hand toward the single, sparsely furnished room. "It's a cave, I know. But it's cheap."

Melanie nodded once and turned to him. "I'm angry with you. I know I shouldn't be, seeing your face and all, but we've been together for nearly two months." Already? "You should have called me. I need to know when you're hurt."

"I'm sorry."

Her dark brown eyes narrowed. "No, you're not. Why didn't you call me?"

"I didn't want to worry you."

"But, Max…." She closed her eyes and rubbed her forehead. "Isn't that sort of the point of being together? Having someone to worry about you?"

He shrugged.

Melanie stepped closer, lifting a hand to his cheek. Her fingers were cool against his skin. Should he kiss her? Melanie had a nice mouth, with very kissable lips, and she made sweet sounds when he kissed her—little moans that shot right through his chest, warming him. He liked the idea a woman might be hot for him, even if she'd initially rejected any advance of his hands so that he now kept them to himself. Probably better that way. What would he do with a breast, anyway? Squeeze it? Hope the weight of her bosom or the poke of her nipple against his palm would magically turn him straight?

A different mouth edged into his thoughts. One wider and bolder. A masculine mouth and a strong jaw. Blond stubble. He recalled the way Jake smiled, as if it were no effort at all, and the amused glint that sometimes lit his gray eyes, making them appear almost blue. He thought about the man's broad shoulders and how muscular his chest might be. Must be.

Max stepped away from Melanie's hand and waved toward the couch. "You want to sit?"

Brows crooked together, Melanie perused the single room of his apartment again. "Don't you have a bedroom?"

"Why?" Surely she hadn't come over here to lift the no-hands rule and entice him into bed. Dear God, no.

"That's your bed, isn't it? All folded up."

"Yeah. It's both. Want something to drink?"

Instead of sitting, Melanie followed him into the kitchen. "We need to talk."

Well, shi—shoot. Life had definitely become more curse-worthy in the past week or so. Max pulled out a chair for Melanie and sat on the other side of his ugly table. "Okay. Um, is this about me not calling you?"

"God, this is hard. Your face. Why didn't you call me?" She held up a hand. "Wait, no, that's why I'm here. I didn't want to do this over the phone." Do what? "I don't think this is working."

"You're breaking up with me?"

Melanie had a pretty face, her features as sweet and delicate as she was. When she'd first asked him out, he'd been surprised and flattered. He'd planned to be brave. Tell her he wasn't exactly straight, ask if they could be friends. Her attention felt good, though, the relationship they had fallen into too simple to resist.

"I feel like a bitch doing this now."

Max reached across the table and took her hand in his. "You're not a bitch. You're a really sweet woman."

"Now it's like you're breaking up with me."

Was he? He was genuinely fond of Melanie. But he was also afraid of her in a way he couldn't describe. Probably because most of what they had was a lie.

"You're not upset, are you?" Melanie said. "Which means I was right."

"About what?"

"Sometimes it feels like we're just friends, Max. That you have no interest in taking things further." Melanie turned her hand beneath his and rubbed her thumb across his knuckles. "You're a really nice guy. I like being with you. But…." She licked her lips. "This past week is a good example. You were hurt, really badly, and you didn't call."

"I'm sorry."

"Why didn't you call?"

"I didn't want you to worry or fuss or something."

"That's what girlfriends do, Max." Her slim shoulders dropped. "You're so distant. Always. I mean, this is the first time I've even been in your new apartment. It's like I don't really know you."

Was this the usual two-month conversation? What should he say? "Maybe you don't."

"What's that supposed to mean?"

"I dunno. It's just I know I'm different. I'm…." He really should just tell her.

"You're not invested in our relationship, are you?"

His head had started to ache. Max rubbed his temple—the right. The left still hurt just to think about.

"Maybe this isn't a good time," Melanie said.

"No, it's not." Her brows arched in surprise. "I think you're right. I'm not… I don't…." Man, this was hard. "I do like you. A lot. I like being with you. But I don't think I'm in a good place for a serious relationship right now."

Melanie looked hurt, as if she'd expected him to fight for them, refute the fact he was distant and unemotional, promise to eat lunch with her every day, take her out more than once every couple of weeks and maybe put his hand inside her shirt next time they kissed.

Instead, Max fought rising bile, which made no sense at all until he recognized the burn as shame. He'd been lying to this nice woman for months, and he was lying to her now.

"Can we stay friends?" he asked.

She tugged her hand from beneath his. "I don't know." She ducked her head. She wasn't going to cry, was she? Pushing her chair back, she said, "I think I should go."

"I'm sorry."

She shook her head. "Don't."

Max followed her to the door and when she passed through without a word, he followed her up the stairs and out the front door, into the alleyway. "Mel."

She turned, finally, and flung herself against him, wrapping her arms around his waist, tucking her head into his shoulder. Max pulled her close. He dipped his chin and the scent of her shampoo slid inside him like a memory, one already tinged with melancholy. He inhaled again and kissed the top of her head.

Melanie pulled away and swiped at her cheeks. "Good-bye, Max."

He fought the irrational urge to pull her close again. It would only make this harder. Then there was the fact that he suspected the hurt he felt—the burn of shame—wasn't so much because he'd been dumped, but that even then, he hadn't had the courage to tell the truth.

CHAPTER SEVEN

JAKE WATCHED the slip of a girl walk away, then looked back at his downstairs neighbor. In the late afternoon light, Max looked rough. Shoulders rounded, back hunched, face still multicolored. Max kept rubbing the right side of his head, as if it pained him. He didn't look away from the retreating figure of the young woman. Feeling guilty for interrupting the scene, Jake scraped his boots against the pavement as he walked closer. Max turned at the sound. Jesus, his expression. He looked as though he'd lost something he hadn't understood the value of until it was gone.

"You okay?" Jake asked.

Max nodded, the motion obviously automatic. Then he shook his head once. Then he shrugged and looked down at his hands.

"Was that your girlfriend?"

Another nod, another shake. "We broke up."

Hence the forlorn look. Jake searched for something to say. "She left you when your face looked like that? That's harsh."

Two blue eyes snapped up and Jake sucked in a startled breath. The swelling had subsided around Max's left eye and he wasn't prepared for the intensity of color times two, or the weight of his gaze. Glare. "What makes you think she left me?"

Well shit. "Ah, I meant now. Not...." He gestured helplessly.

"Heh, doesn't matter anyway. She left me because of my face."

"Oh."

"And because I'm distant."

"Ah...."

"I didn't call her or answer her messages. She didn't know I'd been mugged until half an hour ago."

"Oh, man, that's.... Yeah. Okay. I can see why she'd be pissed."

Max treated him to another glare, and it *was* a treat. He could pin Jake with those magical blues whenever.

Swallowing, Jake offered a conciliatory smile. "Sorry. Hey, want to come to the dojo? There's a class tonight. You could look on, see if it's something you're interested in. Might be a good distraction?"

"I dunno."

"Not like you got anything else to do."

One of Max's dark brows arched. Rather than glare, however, he snorted, and the vaguest hint of humor twitched across his face. "Sure." He looked down at his jeans. "Should I change?"

"Nope. Just observe. In another week, when your nose is more set, you can try some stuff out." Jake tilted his head and considered Max's face. "Probably no sparring for a month or so."

"Sparring?"

"Oh, yeah. You'll love it. Really gets the blood going."

"If you say so."

"Just gonna go in and get my gear. Want to come up for a sec?" Jake had the idea if he let Max out of his sight, he would disappear.

Max patted his pockets. "I should get my keys and stuff. I could follow you up, or…."

"I'll leave the door open for you."

Max took his little cloud of despair and disappeared down the stairs to the basement apartment. Jake went upstairs and jumped right into the shower. He'd get sweaty again during class, but after a day swinging a six-pound sledgehammer, he already stank, and he had time to get clean before round two.

When he emerged from his bedroom, bag in hand, he saw Max over near the kitchen, one hand skimming across the surface of the table.

"I'm going to sand it again before I finish it. Give the wood a satiny texture."

Max offered a doleful nod.

"You okay?"

Less swollen, Max's face showed more expression, despite the bruising. He glanced over, the blue of his eyes less intense, as if he guarded the color on occasion, then looked back down at the table. He smoothed his hand over the wood, pausing when he reached a swirl in the grain. "I've had a crap week, I suppose. Lost a job, my girlfriend. Had too much time to think." Briefly, his eyes cut sideways. "Then there was pissing myself in an alleyway and bleeding all over your couch."

"To be fair, you had the shit kicked out of you first."

"Yeah."

Jake put his bag on the table. "Wait here." He ducked into his room and grabbed a pair of jeans. Back in the kitchen, he stuffed them into his bag. "After class we'll go get a drink and you can tell me all about it."

Max offered a skeptical look.

"It'll do you good. You've been stuck in your lair all week, haven't you?"

"I went out a couple of times. I needed more fried chicken." There it was, the hint of a smile.

"We're going to get some dinner while we're out, too. Something other than chicken." Shouldering his bag, Jake nodded toward the door. "C'mon. We do not want to be late. Sensei will have us drop and push out fifty on the sidewalk."

JAKE PAUSED in the doorway of the dojo to bow, and Max smacked into the back of him. One of the kid's slender arms wrapped around his ribs, holding him close for the second he needed to regain his balance.

"Sorry," he said, his voice muffled by the back of Jake's shirt.

Regretfully, Jake pulled out of the accidental embrace. "'S okay. I should have warned you I was stopping."

"Did you just bow?"

"Yes. I'm paying respect to the dojo."

"Oh. Do I have to do that?"

"It's not about what you have to do, it's about…." Jake tried to think of a way to explain the less well-known aspects of martial arts. "Showing your appreciation for the space, I guess."

"Okay." Max dipped his chin a little, obviously shy about making more of a gesture his first time there.

Jake moved inside and toed off his shoes. After a moment's hesitation, Max did the same. Jake hid his smile in his bag, ostensibly looking for the top portion of his gi. Beside him, Max studied the assembled students with open curiosity. Jake pulled his T-shirt over his head and basked in satisfaction when he diverted Max's attention. Did something other than casual interest spark that sapphire gaze?

"What do you call the pajamas?" Max said.

Jake laughed. "My uniform?"

"Yeah." Max nodded toward the black pants and wrap-style shirt Jake wore.

"You can call it a uniform or a gi."

Max tested the unfamiliar word. "Gi." Jake pulled his belt out of his bag. Max's brows shot up. "Wow, could you kill me with your bare hands?"

"Don't need a black belt to do that. In fact...." Jake's shoulders drew up and in. The subject brushed uncomfortably close to his recent past. "That's not what karate is about."

"Yeah, I know." Max smiled his sly little smile.

Jake tied on his belt and fiddled with the knot until the tension between his shoulder blades eased and motioned toward the other students. "Ready to meet everyone?"

Max's small smile faded instantly. "Ah...." He looked around nervously before squaring his shoulders. "Um. Okay. If that's okay."

"It's why I brought you here."

A blush stole over the skin unblemished by bruises. Jake wished for a pocket to shove his fingers into so it'd be easier to resist the temptation to caress Max's cheek. Instead, he tightened his belt again and reminded himself, silently, why they were there.

A small woman approached them first. Her black belt had two red stripes across one end, indicating she'd progressed beyond the first degree of black. Alyssa Fabrizio extended a hand toward Jake and he clasped it and bowed slightly over the firm shake. "Sensei."

"Sempai," she said. The sparkle in her eyes softened her formal greeting. Turning to Max, she smiled and held her hand out again. "You must be Max. I'm Sensei Fabrizio. Welcome to our class."

Looking surprised, Max took her hand. "Thank you." He let go and wrapped his arms around himself.

"I might have mentioned you on Monday night," Jake put in to clear up any assumption that a red-striped black belt imbued the wearer with mystical powers.

Alyssa tilted her head, obviously inspecting Max's bruises. "It's not easy to stand up after you've been knocked down. I'm really glad you're here." The kid's throat bobbed a little as he swallowed and offered a short nod. "I hope you'll consider joining us."

Max made an effort to loosen his posture at that. Arms by his sides, fingers digging for his pockets. "Okay."

The rest of the students came forward. Arthur, a talk black man with salt and pepper stubble for hair, clasped Max's hand between both of his. "Peace," he said.

Jake grinned.

Taking note of Max's bruises and defensive posture, Barry offered a perfunctory shake.

Jill pumped the kid's hand up and down enthusiastically. "Great to meet you!"

Elsa, a deceptively delicate septuagenarian, mimed swiping at his head, then shook his hand. Grant made a more solemn greeting. Then Alyssa called for class to begin. Jake pointed Max toward the bench at the back of the dojo and went to take his place at the front.

Because they had a guest, the class remained quiet and focused during the meditation and warm-up. Their voices blended as they counted out their fifty jumping jacks and fifty push-ups, Elsa and Barry both pausing at thirty, rising to their knees until the rest of the class punched through the rest of the count. Then there were calisthenics and kicks, stretches aimed at preparing their bodies for the rigors of training. Jake always enjoyed the warm-up. As he bent this way and that, muscles stretching and pulling along his side, down the backs of his legs, through his shoulders and arms, he let go of the stress of his day. By the time they were dismissed for a small break, Jake felt loose in body and thought. It was his favorite state of being—almost postcoital. Not that he'd share that comparison with Sensei Fabrizio.

Alyssa stepped up to him as the rest of the students grabbed a drink of water. Quietly, she said, "Your friend looks like he might take flight at any moment."

Jake glanced toward the back of the room where Max sat perched on the very edge of the bench. "He's kind of shy, I guess."

"Let's see if we can keep him, hmm?"

As he'd suspected, Alyssa had fallen for Max. He could see it in her eyes. She wanted to pick the kid up and set him properly on his feet—much as she'd done for another young man some years before.

Bobbing his chin, Jake replied, "Yes, ma'am."

Alyssa raised her voice. "Everyone get a partner, please. We're going to show our guest a few tricks."

Elsa trotted toward Jake, a wide smile wrinkling her sweet face. Jake wasn't fooled by her grandma look. Nope. She meant to take him down, and hard. He shook her hand and waited for further instruction.

Without looking at Max, Alyssa explained the exercise. "Tonight we're going to work on defense off a punch. Vary your strikes, people.

I do not want to see the same punch twice. If you do not want to hit the mat, let your partner know."

She clapped her hands and walked toward the back of the room where she stood near Max. He looked up at her, all five-and-a-bit feet of her, with something like awe, then turned his focus back to the class, Jake in particular. Jake winked and promptly rocked to the side as Elsa's fist glanced off his jaw.

Max's quick grin served as a pretty good balm for the sting to both his skin and his pride.

He recovered quickly enough to deflect Elsa's next strike, one aimed at his ribs. From there, they worked through several strikes and blocks, each resulting in a takedown. A captured arm could be pinned, momentum then used to turn the attacker around, pulling them off balance. Jake did this twice. He heard a gasp the first time he set the "little old lady" on the ground and pulled her arm into a chicken wing, causing her to tap out. Next strike, he captured her hand and twisted her wrist. She went down to her knees in front of him. They danced a little longer, Elsa trying to catch him unawares, Jake trying to exercise finesse, then they switched positions. He threw the punches and Elsa went for the takedowns. She got him, off the very first punch. As Elsa attempted to fold his arm into something resembling a pretzel, Jake risked a quick look at Max. His eyes were wide and his lips were curved in a proper smile, maybe the first Jake had ever seen.

"Oh, stop looking at your boyfriend and pretend I'm actually hurting you," Elsa muttered as she continued to twist his arm.

Jake could have rolled out of the hold, but as senior student, it was his job to teach. "That way, twist my wrist more," he instructed, directing her torture. "And he's not my boyfriend." He'd blame the heat prickling his cheeks on exertion. Yeah.

While Elsa worked toward optimum torque without dislocating his wrist, he wondered if he should reject her assumption he might date a man. Jake hadn't shared his sexuality with the class, mostly because it wasn't anyone's business but his own. He also had the idea the other guys—Barry in particular—might have an issue rolling around the floor with someone who slept with men as well as women.

He tapped out of the hold and got to his feet without saying anything else, but found it difficult to look over at Max for the rest of the evening. Every time he glimpsed that dark brown head, his heart did a stupid pitter-patter and, with Elsa aiming to humiliate him, he couldn't afford to be distracted.

CHAPTER EIGHT

MAX WAITED outside for Jake to change out of his uniform. He peeked through the window once and saw Jake had stopped to talk with the instructor. Sensei Fabrizio was not what Max had been expecting. She was tiny, and without the uniform, not particularly remarkable. Max could more easily picture her swinging a golf club than taking down a man of Jake's size. The mixture of students had been a definite surprise as well—especially the ages. Elsa looked like a grandmother, except she'd managed to floor Jake twice, obviously enjoying herself. Arthur had the kindly old man thing going as well.

Everyone else looked as though they had ten years on him, at least. In a way, that was comforting. Max didn't think he'd consider a class full of kids. Being taken down by Elsa would be humiliating enough. Being pressed to the mat by a twelve-year-old? A dark alley and a piss-soaked pair of pants seemed more appealing. Max hadn't decided if he wanted to join the class yet, though. The idea of being so physical with other people made him nervous. What if he grabbed a guy's ass and they accused him of being gay?

What if he grabbed Jake's ass?

Heat rippled through him, causing his breath to hitch and his heart to pound. Okay, there was one good reason he should take the class. He'd get to touch Jake.

You are so deluded.

The door opened and Max glanced up expectantly. Barry stepped out and offered a smirky sort of smile before he swung his bag over his shoulder and strode off in the opposite direction. Then the lights went out in the studio and both Jake and Sensei Fabrizio stepped outside.

The small woman offered her hand again. "Thank you for coming tonight, Max. I hope we'll see you again."

Max did the firm shake thing. "Thanks." He wanted to say more, enthuse about the idea of studying karate, but his tongue decided to knot right then and a familiar wave of uncertainty rolled through him. He dropped the instructor's small hand and stepped back.

If she was offended, she gave no sign. Instead, she hugged Jake and stood on tiptoe to kiss the cheek he bent toward her. "Stay out of trouble." She stepped off the curb, pulling keys from her bag. Lights flashed as she disabled her car alarm.

"So, what did you think?" Jake said.

"She's so little."

Jake chuckled and the deep, warm sound pulled Max's attention away from the little woman climbing into the big SUV.

"What does semp-something mean?" Max asked. He'd figured out *sensei*. He'd watched enough movies for that one.

"It's semp-eye. S-E-M-P-A-I. It means senior student."

Ah, right. Jake had been the only black belt in the class, aside from Sensei Fabrizio. "What if there are two senior students?"

"One will always be senior." Meaning Jake must have worked with Sensei Fabrizio for quite some time.

"Okay."

"Ready to eat?"

Max's stomach groaned and they both looked down. "Ah, yeah."

"Let's go to Shay's. We can eat and drink at the same place."

Shay's was an Irish pub one block over from Beech Street. Easy walking distance to their apartments and they didn't serve Chinese food. "Sounds good."

Falling into step beside Jake, Max asked more about the class. Jake seemed pleased by his questions and answered each carefully, giving more information than really necessary, but also confirming the fact he really enjoyed the sport. It was a sport, right? Definitely more than a hobby. Max learned the system name and that it was really a combination of styles, one of which he'd actually heard of. "I've seen aikido on TV, I think. A tournament." Occasionally he watched something other than motor racing. Very occasionally.

"It's a really great style," Jake said. "I'm glad it's part of our system. Aikido is especially useful for people like Elsa. It teaches you to use your opponent's force and momentum against them."

Max grinned. "That was kinda funny, watching her take you down to the mat."

"You could do that. Think that's something you'd like to learn?"

Hell yes. But not for the reasons Jake might imagine. Regardless, Max's mind wandered, taking him to a place where he lay on top of a warm and sweaty Jake. The fact he could smell the other man next to him only enhanced the brief fantasy.

An arm shot out in front of him, catching Max across the middle of his chest. "Hold up."

Max looked up to see Jake had just stopped him from crossing against a light and plunging into traffic. "Ah, thanks."

The warmth of Jake's arm disappeared. "No problem." He grinned down at Max. "You kinda need a bodyguard, don't you?"

Max ducked his chin. "Heh, yeah." He felt his shoulders draw up as his usual defensiveness took hold. Taking a deep breath, he forced himself to relax. "I get caught up sometimes. Thinking about stuff."

"I think we all do that from time to time."

The light changed and they crossed the street. Jake opened the door to Shay's and waved him through. Max had been to Shay's only once before. He'd grabbed a meal there his second night in the apartment, after discovering that living and breathing Chinese fumes somewhat dampened his appetite for beef with broccoli. The pub had a warm and convivial atmosphere. It was the sort of place where friends met up and locals could command a bar stool on a busy night. Lacking in friends, Max had felt a little out of place, even though he'd enjoyed his meal. He'd imagined himself visiting more often, and even bringing Melanie in. His imagination was often more exciting than his real life.

Jake walked up to the bar with the attitude of a local. He didn't secure a pair of stools. Instead, he enquired after a table. After shaking his hand, the bartender—a wiry woman with steel-gray hair and don't-mess-with-me eyes—pointed him toward a booth.

"What do you want to drink?" Jake asked over his shoulder.

"A Coke."

Jake turned back to the bar. "Two Cokes."

Max arched a brow at the order, but stayed quiet. Jake pushed a menu toward him. "Have you eaten here before?"

"Yeah, I have. I had the Guinness pot pie and it was about the best thing I've ever eaten." Max handed the menu back. "I'll just have that again."

"Good choice." Jake ordered two of those as well and picked up his bag. "Can you grab the drinks?"

"Sure."

They eased into opposite sides of the booth. Max breathed out a small and satisfied sigh as he leaned back, already lulled by the atmosphere and the fact he had company. It was a nice end to a pretty crappy day.

He nodded toward Jake's glass. "You didn't have to drink soda with me."

"I got out of the habit of drinking anything stronger a year or so ago." A shadow flicked through Jake's eyes, a memory, perhaps. Or just the shuffling of patrons in front of the bar. "What about you?"

"I don't drink," Max said.

"Ever?"

"A couple times at college, but I don't like the idea of being drunk." Or the resultant loss of control. What inhibitions might he lose after a single beer or a shot of something? No, it was better to stay sober and keep his secrets.

"What did you study?"

"Business."

"Yeah? Did you like it?"

Max shifted in his seat. "It's a practical degree." Not that that had convinced his father. If not for his partial scholarship, he'd not have gotten away at all.

"Doesn't sound like you were into it."

"I had to drop out anyway, so it doesn't matter."

"Oh?"

Max studied his glass intently, watching bubbles rise through the dark caramel liquid. "My mom got sick and I had to look after her."

"Oh."

His mother's illness had left him and his father in debt they might never clear, no matter how many jobs Max worked. There would be no more college, regardless of how *practical* his degree. "She was sick on and off throughout high school. The summer before I graduated, her cancer finally went into remission. I thought it would be all right to go away, you know?"

Jake nodded.

"But it came back. So I went home."

"Is she...."

Max shook his head. "She's gone. Nearly two years now."

"I'm sorry." Jake observed a respectful beat of silence. "Why didn't you go back to school?"

"Couldn't afford it."

"Is that why you work two jobs?"

"I'm not going back." And it was time to change the subject before Jake asked any more questions. "Anything in particular break your habit of drinking?"

Rather than look perturbed by the direct question, Jake grinned. He pointed across the table at Max. "Now that is a perfect block and strike."

"A what?"

"You didn't want to talk about college or your mom, so you chose a question that would make me squirm instead. A block without a strike only prolongs the fight. Sometimes that's all you can do. Better to stay in, if you can. But a block and strike together is how you take control, gain the upper hand."

"Are you going to answer my question or continue with the defense lesson?"

Jake laughed. "You're cute when you're angry."

Max blinked and sucked in a breath as heat rushed to his cheeks. Jake thought he was cute? Why did a straight guy think he was cute? Wait, he wasn't cute! Not by any stretch of the broadest imagination. "Still waiting for my answer."

Jake lifted his chin. "Nice, Max. Good." He put his hands flat on the table. His expression sobered and the shadow returned, darkening the gray of his eyes. "I made a mistake a couple of years ago. One that will mark me for the rest of my life. I wasn't drinking at the time, but afterwards, I had a lot of time to think. Time to work on my issues."

Jake had issues? He seemed about the most balanced individual Max had ever met. "So you decided not to drink?"

"I don't like the idea of being drunk, either."

"So, we're sitting in a bar and neither of us drinks."

Jake's grin returned, easing his face back into familiarly handsome lines. "How 'bout that."

"The food is good, though."

"That it is."

Max shifted on his seat. "And the seats are comfortable."

"More so than that thing you call a couch."

"Hey." Max's indignation faded quickly. He snorted and allowed a small grin. "It is pretty crappy, isn't it? It'll do for now, while I'm in the crypt."

"Your lair."

"Whatever. When I get a proper place, I'll get a proper bed, I suppose." He had no idea when that would be. Currently his life, his state of being, felt very, very temporary, as though he skimmed across the surface of the Earth, sampling, but missing most of the good stuff.

His smile fell away with practiced ease. In an attempt to stifle the sigh welling up in his chest, Max picked up his Coke and drank half of it down.

Jake did the same before addressing Max's southward mood. "Thinking about your shitty week again?"

"Yeah."

"I've had worse, if that makes you feel any better."

"You've had the stuffing kicked out of you?"

"I've been in some scrapes."

Whatever had happened a couple years ago, the incident that had caused Jake to reevaluate his habits, must have been more than a scrape. He hadn't seemed eager to talk about it, though, and as much as Max wanted to probe for more detail, he respected the fact they both had stuff in their closets.

"Sounds trite, but there will be other girls and other jobs," Jake said.

"Yeah, I know. What about you and… Kate, was it?"

Jake's mouth slanted into a sad smile. "We were over a long, long time ago. Before Caroline was even born. We were best friends in high school and probably shouldn't have ever tried for more." Jake seemed pretty cool about the whole thing, but when he started to talk about his daughter, his tone deepened and softened. "If I have a regret, it's that I'm not more a part of my daughter's life. Again, a lot of that was my choice."

"You didn't want to see her?"

"No, I did. I do." His mouth twisted as he gripped the back of his neck. "Things just aren't good with Kate right now."

"Oh?"

"She has shitty taste in men."

Max frowned, wondering how Jake could, in any way, represent a poor choice.

"Her boyfriends, I mean. After me. I am absolutely perfect, of course."

Of course. "Except for that one mistake, heh?"

Jake leaned back into his seat, but did not lose his smile. Not entirely. "Yeah," he said. "Except for that."

The conversation remained light for the rest of the meal, and Jake didn't fuss when Max insisted on paying his half of the check. Outside, the April night had cooled considerably. Max hugged his torso as he walked beside Jake, who seemed to have no issues with personal space. He walked so close to Max their arms brushed on occasion. The warmth of him was nice.

Jake could also do the companionable silence thing. He hadn't tried to talk over the racing commentary last Sunday, or pepper him with questions. Instead, he just watched the race—a pleasant change from trying to watch anything with Melanie. It was restful to sit with someone and not feel the need to entertain them.

At the mouth of the alley leading behind the block, Jake stopped and raised a hand. Alarm tickled across Max's skin, but he shut his mouth and remained silent. When Jake grabbed his arm and pulled him backward, out into the street, Max followed. Jake turned after two steps, his hand only shifting on Max's arm. Without letting go, he tugged Max along Beech Street, back toward the main avenue fronting their apartments.

Max waited until they hit the corner before speaking. "What did you see?"

"There was someone in the alley, near our door."

Max stumbled. He reached for the wall to steady himself, fingers grazing the brick.

Jake's grip tightened. "It's okay."

No, it wasn't okay. Max felt as if an elephant had just squatted on his chest.

"Breathe, Max."

"I'm sorry." Max allowed Jake to pull him along Cottman Avenue. He breathed carefully, trying not to gasp or wheeze. Or whimper. Instinct begged him to cling to the nearest wall. To drop down low, make himself small. Maybe they wouldn't see him.

The scent of Chinese food cut through his panic. Max looked up to find the lucky cat inside Wu's front window waving at him, the plastic arm flicking back and forth. Jake tugged him into the shop, the bells over the door tinkling happily, the bright atmosphere of the restaurant so different from the foreboding that had shadowed them from the alley.

He pulled out a chair, dropped into it before his shaking legs betrayed him, and turned to look out the window. A cluster of people walked by on the other side of the avenue, and then two men lurched into view, just outside the shop. Both were dressed in dark clothing, but neither looked like a typical mugger. Neither had hats or bandanas pulled down to mask their features. No gold chains sparkled from their chests. Hands were not shoved into the deep pockets of too-loose pants.

The men who had attacked him in the alleyway hadn't been dressed like typical muggers, either. Being beaten up by someone who didn't look as though they might hurt him only made the world a more confusing place.

Bells tinkled as the door opened again and Jake stepped into the street. He walked right up to the men and spoke to them. Max couldn't hear them through the window, he could only see mouths moving and faces showing snarls. Were these the men who'd been lurking in the alleyway? Were they two of the three who had attacked him just a week ago? A sharp needle of pain shot through his head when one of the men met his gaze. God, those eyes. Those dark, dark eyes.

Disparate urges clawed at him. He should go out there. His shaky legs laughed at the very idea he might stand. The stronger urge suggested he crawl beneath the table and cower. He looked out the window again, at Jake—so strong and confident in his defense—and willed himself to stay seated. To at least do that.

Jake stabbed a finger through the air at the dark-eyed man. His body canted forward, silent threat held in check. The sound of voices rose on the other side of the glass, words still muted, tones not quiet. When they broke apart without violence, the moment of separation was oddly anticlimactic. Jake remained in place, shoulders rigid, as the other two backed off. He watched them as they walked away. Max looked after the men once, then back at Jake, knowing he was seeing another side of his neighbor—knowing this was the Jake who had gotten into a few scrapes. The anger in Jake's eyes was a banked fire, a low flame held with visible control.

The tinkling of the bells over the shop door broke an eerie, oily silence. As Jake approached the table, Max fought the urge to cower again. "Who were they?"

Jake shook his head.

Max dipped his chin, knowing the blush was coming. It burned across the back of his neck and stung his cheeks. His stomach cramped and he swallowed convulsively.

The very last thing he wanted to do was throw up in front of Jake.

Max pushed up out of his seat, brushed past the hand Jake extended and slammed through the door. The bells jangled overhead, the sound angry, discordant, and perfect. He broke into a run, every thud of his shoes against the pavement sending a jolt of pain through his bruised body. He thought the back of his head might burst open, that he might just explode in a flash of agony.

"Max!"

Jake caught his arm and jerked him to a halt. Max tried to shake his hand off, but Jake held firm. "Stop, Max. It's not safe."

Max whipped around. "I know!" Breath heaved out of him. "I know it's not safe. What does it matter, Jake? They'll find me anyway, and I'll just do what I always do."

"What's that?"

"I'm such a goddamned coward."

"No, you're not."

"Yes, I am! I hid in Wu's while you told those guys to back off. They'd come back for me, hadn't they? Because they know I'm an easy target."

"That's not how it has to be."

"Easy for you to say, with your black belt and all."

"Belts don't matter. Not really. It's what's up here that counts." Jake tapped his head. Then he let go of Max's arm, gently, as if he suspected Max might still make a run for it. "Can you imagine Elsa taking shit from those guys?"

Max's stomach twisted again—then eased as he remembered how easily she'd taken Jake to the ground, and the self-assured manner with which she had approached the rest of the class and the lesson. He looked away, shame burning more hotly than anger, making his temples pound.

"Hey." Jake's tone had softened. "I didn't mean… I just meant…." He sighed. "Did any of the guys look familiar?"

"Yes." Even as he said it, Max wasn't sure, though. "Maybe."

"Well they won't be coming around again. No one hurts my friends, you understand?" The banked anger returned, simmering in Jake's gray eyes. "No one touches my friends."

My friends. Jake had just called him *friend,* or implied it, which pretty much meant the same thing. Max didn't flinch when Jake grabbed his arm once more, his hand wrapping easily around Max's biceps.

"C'mon," Jake said. "You look like you're about to fall over."

Now that his own anger had faded, Max felt like he might at that. It was time to retreat to his lair. He followed Jake back to Wu's to get Jake's gym bag.

Mr. Wu slid out of the kitchen, his wide face creased with agitation. "Everything all right?" he asked, looking between them.

"Yeah. Those guys,"—Jake jerked his chin toward the front window—"might have been the ones who jumped Max last week."

"Not good!" Mr. Wu shook his head. His eyes narrowed on Jake. "You bring trouble to me, Mr. Jake?"

"No." A muscle jumped in Jake's cheek.

Mr. Wu studied his tenant a moment longer before nodding. "This not good at all. Come." He beckoned them. "You use the back door."

The kitchen door opened out into a small alcove at the rear of the building. Jake thanked Mr. Wu as the metal door banged closed, leaving them in cool-wrapped quiet once more.

"Want to come up for a bit and chill?" Jake asked.

A deep fatigue pulled at Max, making his limbs and eyelids heavy. Passing out on Jake's cozy couch was an attractive option, but he'd rather go downstairs, curl up on his hard futon, and cherish the fact he had a *friend*. One he quite liked, even before his thoughts bounded off into unhealthy fantasies.

"I'm kinda tired," he said. "Um,"—he chewed on his lower lip—"thanks for taking me to your class tonight."

"I'm glad you came." Jake smiled. They were on safe topics now, despite the near violence of the evening being a close memory. "Think you might want to try it out?"

The idea of spending time with Jake appealed, yeah, and he could even see the value in learning self-defense. Tonight had served up a pretty good incentive. Could he overcome his fears enough to put people down onto the ground, though? Could he throw a punch in return?

His shrug was instinctive. "I dunno. I'm not sure I'm the right sort of person for a class like that."

"No such thing as the right sort of person, Max. For any situation." Jake spoke with a smile, but something darker lurked behind they gray of his eyes. He wanted to believe what he was saying as much as Max did.

CHAPTER NINE

JAKE EASED back against the park bench and stretched his legs out. The late morning sun lacked the warmth to ease his sore muscles, but it felt nice on his face. He'd been stiff and achy all morning, a sure sign he hadn't slept well. He didn't often suffer from nightmares, but when he did, his whole body got into the act and he woke disoriented, startled by the relative quiet of his apartment.

Prison had never been quiet.

Pulling out his phone, he thumbed down the list of contacts and wondered if he should call Max. If anyone rated a rough night's sleep, it was Max. The fear on his face last night—Jake had never seen anything like it. Then there was the shame regarding his fear. Someone had fucked him over, and royally.

The display dimmed and switched off. Jake tucked his phone away. If he were Max, he'd want time to rebuild some sort of fence. Jake wouldn't mind being on the inside of that barrier, but given Max's prickly attitude, he reckoned too many people had forced themselves in there. He'd wait to be invited. He wouldn't wait indefinitely, but he'd give him the space he needed. Then he'd be the friend Max needed.

Could he do that without testing a different sort of boundary? Last night, when he hadn't been sleeping, dreaming darkly, Jake had imagined holding Max's slender body to his—in a protective way, back to front. He'd wanted to hear Max's breathing as he wound down and drifted off. He wanted to keep him safe through the small hours. More than anything, he wanted to see Max smile. The kid was cute, but when he smiled…. Man, he was just gorgeous. All big blue eyes and wonder, as if he'd just discovered happiness.

Jake looked up as a tall, brown-haired man approached the bench. A genuine smile pulling at the corners of his mouth, he pushed to his feet and stepped into Eric's embrace. "Thanks for coming."

Eric hugged him hard, and it felt good to have someone's arms around him. Max wasn't the only one who needed a friend right then.

"So." Eric pulled out of the hug and draped his lanky frame casually across the bench. He reached down to tug a crease from the artfully distressed denim of his jeans. "Why are we meeting in Pennypack Park? Are we planning a visit to the bushes? Please say we are."

Chuckling, Jake flopped down next to him. "No. You're not available, anyway."

"I'm always available to you, Jacob."

Eric was the only person who used his full name regularly. Jake never minded it. He smiled. "Not like I need you to be." They both snickered. "How are things with Rob?"

"Surprisingly, I'm not bored yet." Eric did look surprised, and his brown eyes were all warm and gooey looking.

"You know, when you started calling him Rob instead of Robert, I assumed it was a different guy."

Eric whacked him. "So not fair, but—" He broke off with a chuckle.

Eric wasn't exactly a tramp, but he didn't usually settle for long. Having someone now served not only to highlight the fact Jake had no one, but that he'd been drifting from hookup to hookup for years, counting on Eric to be there *in between*—which wasn't fair, not to either of them. Of course, then Jake had been locked away for a year and Eric had met Rob. Had Jake's extended absence finally given Eric the freedom to find something real?

"It's been six months, right? You gonna put a ring on it?" he asked.

"Much too early to be choosing wedding china. I haven't even moved him into my place yet."

"But you're thinking about it."

Eric smiled. "Maybe." He turned slightly, arranging himself so that he faced Jake, more or less. "So why are we here? It's a gorgeous morning, but I could use a coffee."

"We can get one later if you want." Jake nodded toward the small playground just over a hundred yards away. A couple of kids hung from the monkey bars and a toddler clung to the top of the smallest slide. Squeals from behind the primary-colored structures indicated more kids played on the other side. Jake could just hear the creak of swings. The taller figures scattered around the outside of the equipment leaned against posts and trees in casual poses. The parents.

Jake had been there, once. Before he'd fucked up. He'd been that guy by the tree. No, he'd been the dad in the sandbox, covered head to toe in a funk that wasn't just rotting sand. Damned feral cats. He'd been the dad who followed his daughter down the slide, after wedging his shoulders through that tiny opening at the top. Or the one who pushed the swing endlessly. Caroline never had to say "More, please."

That had all been before Dominick. Before Kate had gotten herself mixed up with a fucking psychopath.

"Caroline's babysitter texted me," he said. "She's bringing her to this park this morning."

Eric stiffened. "Are we far enough away?"

"I think so. Actually, I don't know." He'd never actually read the restraining order. The purpose seemed pretty clear. "I just want to see her. Not going to leave this bench. I just want to see my daughter."

"I kept an eye out while you were away, Jake. As much as I could."

"I know you did."

"Kate—"

Jake shook his head. "I don't want to talk about Kate. I just want to see Caroline."

Eric grabbed his hand.

Jake laced his fingers through Eric's and squeezed gratefully. "Thanks."

"Don't thank me. I'm going to hold you here so you don't do anything stupid."

Snorting, Jake said, "Then thanks for that, too."

"Anytime." Eric turned a narrow-eyed look on him. "So what else is bothering you?"

"Who says something's bothering me?"

"Me."

Jake borrowed one of Max's shrugs and eased his hand away from Eric's. He leaned back into the bench and stretched his legs out. "I'm nearly four months out of prison, meeting weekly with a parole officer who looks sideways at me every time I sniff, and work is kicking my ass. Oh." He waved toward the playground. "And I haven't been able to talk to my daughter in nearly two years."

One of Eric's brows lifted into a lazy arch. "And…."

"And what?"

"You didn't invite me here to bitch and watch Caroline play. Though, I'd have come for that. Her. You know I love your little girl. What's eating you?"

"Dominick."

Eric's brows drew low. "How? Did he contact you? Isn't that, like, against some rule?"

"That's one of my restraining orders, yeah." Jake shook his head, momentarily stunned, again, by the realization he had become a person he didn't understand. That something fundamental had changed. His life would never be the same. "He sent his friends to do the talking, only they met my neighbor first."

"Yeah?"

"They put him in the hospital."

"Holy fuck."

"He's a nice kid, Eric. Really inoffensive. Works two jobs and minds his own business. I just don't get how anyone could pick on a guy like that. Beat him so badly and then just leave him in the alleyway like some piece of trash." His hands curled into fists. "Who does that sort of shit?"

Eric eyed him warily a moment, then curled a hand around one of his fists. "Not you, Jake. That's what I know. That's not you."

"But he got beat up because of what I did. He didn't deserve it, and on top of that, Max is messed up. He's…. Remember the dog my dad found on the side of the road? We called her Maggie. Sweetest animal ever. But if you moved too quick, she'd shrink in on herself and pant. Eyes rolling. You could never raise your voice around her. That dog had been hit too often. Someone has done that to Max. He came to the city to get away from a bad situation and Dominick's friends tried to spread him across the pavement."

Unable to sit still with his anger, Jake pushed up off the bench.

Eric caught his wrist. "Jacob. You need to calm down. Take a breath."

Jake opened his mouth to tell Eric to fuck off. He had had enough anger management counseling in prison. Then he listened to the thrum of his blood, the way it sang through his veins, and realized he needed to do as his friend said. He needed to find that place of control. Anger was dangerous, especially for him.

He breathed. He sat.

"So, we've got two issues here," Eric said. "One, Dominick is being a prick."

"Nothing new there."

"And, two, you're afraid for your friend."

"I barely know him."

"Bullshit. You know enough, and you care." Eric put his arm around Jake's shoulders. "That's a good thing. You're a great friend, Jake. Max is lucky to have you in his court."

"I took him to the dojo last night. I thought he could use some self-defense training."

"No kidding."

Jake shook his head. "Not just so he can defend himself against Dominick's creeps, but because he needs some self-respect, you know?"

"Absolutely."

"After, we went to get a bite to eat."

Eric's brows rose.

Jake elbowed him in the side. "Shush. It was purely platonic."

"I'm sure it was."

"He has a girlfriend. Or had. She dumped him yesterday. He's really had a rough week."

Ignoring the invitation to move on, Eric said, "You've had girlfriends, Jake."

Two. He'd had two girlfriends—Kate, and a woman he'd dated about five years ago. Ellen. They hadn't gone out for long, but it had been fun while it lasted. Kate had been another matter entirely. She'd broken his heart.

"Your point?" Jake asked.

Whatever Eric said in response, Jake didn't hear it. Caroline had arrived at the playground. Even after eighteen months, and from a hundred yards away, he knew his daughter. Her posture, the golden blonde curls, the laugh floating in on the breeze. The way she skipped and turned at the same time. Were her legs longer? His throat tightened. He leaned forward and Eric caught his hand. A small sound edged from his lips, something not quite human. Eric's fingers slipped between his, not restraining, but in support.

His heart ached. To be so close, but so far. To be stuck on this bench, instead of behind the swing. Did nearly nine-year-olds still love the swings? She'd want to go higher now, wouldn't she? Could she do all the monkey bars still, pull herself down the long line of rungs, her body apparently weightless? Did she still rescue ants from the sandbox?

Tears clouded his vision. Jake blinked them away. He would not lose a moment of this, would not lose sight of his daughter for one second. He wanted to savor every last sun-drenched minute. Every painful breath.

CHAPTER TEN

A SUDDEN gust of wind pushed in under the awning, blowing the spray from the hose back into Max's face. In the summer months, he'd welcome the cool blast. In April? Not so much. Angling the hose away from the wind, he continued watering the racks of early tulips and daffodils. The pot at the end had only one anemic bloom. None of the other sheaves of green hid a bud, so this would be the only flower in the pot. Max shut off the water and considered the singular and lonely tulip. No one would buy this one. People wanted bright clusters of color, not single sparks of sweetness.

Touching the side of the pot, he murmured, "I'll take you home." His apartment didn't really have the light for flowers, but he hated seeing neglected plants.

Maybe Jake would like it?

"Talking to the plants again?"

Quickly withdrawing his hand, Max turned to find Melanie standing a short distance away. Her arms were crossed over her green supermarket apron and her head was tilted to an imprecise angle, attitude undecided.

Max couldn't decide his, either. "Um."

"Your face looks better."

Not by much. His nose didn't ache all the time. Instead, it delivered a precise stab of pain into the middle of his brain every now and then. His jaw remained stiff, as did his left hip. His ribs didn't bother him unless he breathed hard. All in all, the headaches were the worst. A follow-up visit to the outpatient clinic netted him some more pills, but Max hadn't used them more than once. They made him too sleepy.

"Yeah. I, ah...." Working with an ex-girlfriend was definitely more awkward than working with a current girlfriend. "How are you doing?"

"Okay, I guess. I came to ask if you were interested in taking some of Lorenzo's shifts. His wife is due soon and he wants to switch to days."

"You mean switch? Or extra hours?"

His back pocket buzzed. Melanie watched as he pulled out his phone and woke the display. The message was from Jake.

Coming to class tonight?

A blush crawled across his cheeks, all prickly and warm.

Melanie huffed softly. "Frank will take the shifts if you don't."

With a scrape of heels, she turned and stalked away. Max didn't look up from his phone. How could a simple text make him so happy and so anxious at the same time? He'd begged off on Monday night, citing fatigue. Given he'd come back to work then, his excuse had been solid. He'd limped past the studio late Tuesday afternoon. The window had been dark, door locked, but a sign in the window announced the hours. Adult classes were Monday, Wednesday, and Friday nights. It seemed a lot until he considered the amount of practice needed to get a black belt.

Jake hadn't invited him on Wednesday, which had been both a relief and a concern.

Now Friday was here and, staring at his phone, Max wondered if answering Melanie might have been easier. Did he want to go to class tonight? It was either that or go home and continue fiddling with his next project: a '68 Mustang GT model kit. Not terribly ambitious, but it kept his fingers busy. He could only clean his apartment so many times and if he tended his sorry collection of houseplants any more, he'd kill them.

He texted back: *What time?*

6:30. I'll come get u.

MAX REMEMBERED to stop at the door and he managed not to look at Jake's ass as he bowed. Didn't seem respectful. Besides, he'd get plenty of opportunities to look when Jake did the warm-up exercises. He then took a turn at bowing, dipping a little lower than last time. It seemed weird to show respect to a room, but he supposed he understood the theory of it. Respecting a space set aside for training made the place more special, more purposeful.

Elsa greeted him the moment he stepped inside.

"You're back!" The little old lady swiped at his shoulder, causing him to twitch sideways. Then she caught his hand and pumped it up and down. "Good to see you."

A small smile insisted on pulling at his mouth. She just looked so pleased to see him. Genuinely pleased.

So weird.

Jill shook his hand next, then Arthur, who again wished him "peace." The other two guys offered more solemn handshakes. Max couldn't remember their names, but he supposed if he attended more regularly he'd sort them out. For now, he dubbed one Surly and the other Smiley. Then the instructor, the tiny little woman who could probably kill him with her pinky finger, had his hand in hers.

"Good evening, Max."

Surprisingly, Sensei Fabrizio left her greeting there. No: *I'm so glad you're here*, or: *When are you going to join us?* Or: *You're still standing!*

Max wondered for a moment if perhaps he wasn't welcome. Then he figured he'd moved beyond welcome and into some sort of sly expectation. She'd known he'd still be on his feet, she'd known he'd be back, and she knew he'd join the class, even if he hadn't fully decided that himself.

Was it weird she knew all that?

Maybe.

Dressed in his black uniform and black belt, Jake looked pretty danged sexy—and sort of dangerous, which only added to the whole hotness vibe. Max swallowed as Jake stepped close.

"Think you might work out with us tonight? Or just observe?"

Max sucked on his lower lip. If he observed, he'd get to watch Jake in action, which was just about better than TV. Heck, it *was* better than TV. But Sensei Fabrizio had passed on that sense of expectation and Jake hadn't just brought him here to watch. Max knew he hadn't come just to watch, either.

"I'll give it a go." He looked down at his sweats and T-shirt. "Am I dressed okay?"

Jake smiled. "If we don't break you tonight, we'll get you a uniform."

Break him?

"Relax, Max." Jake's wide grin did not look feral. Nope. "Do what you can of the warm-up. If something hurts, rest until we move on. Ask questions at any time, okay?"

Max nodded and tried to relax. It wasn't going to happen. He'd relax when he died. Until then, he'd try to get through this one class without embarrassing himself too much.

"Okay."

As the lowest of the low, Max found himself at the back of the line, which suited him just fine. No one to watch him flail uselessly.

No one checking out his ass. Everyone in front of him dropped to their knees, butts resting on their heels, and Max discovered his first limit. His bruised hip and thigh made folding his legs difficult. Sensei Fabrizio waited for him to settle without giving away any hint of either impatience or irritation. There was a bit more bowing, some murmuring, and then everyone clasped their hands in front of them and held very still. Sensei Fabrizio's eyes closed. Max sat there, skin prickling, wondering if he should close his eyes. Wondering if the instructor would open her eyes and admonish him for not closing his.

Her eyes opened and she caught him staring. Max's breath hitched. She smiled.

Then they were up and jumping.

Max didn't do the jumping jacks. Only an idiot jumped up and down fifty times with a recently broken nose. He attempted the side and back bends, wincing as he tested the limits of his sore body, and gratefully sat down again for some more intensive leg stretches. He managed a few of the crunches before his ribs poked at his lungs; he counted out ten push-ups before his lungs pushed back at his ribs. But the exercise felt *good*. Aside from the oddness of spending every evening home, not being able to run had eaten at him. Max had been running since he could walk. Running was one of his escapes—his aloneness never felt quite so lonely when he ran, when his body moved without the effort or benefit of thought, when his mind roamed free, the air plucking at the very corners of him as miles disappeared beneath the steady drum of his feet.

After a quick break, the class lined back up to work through a series of moves together. They started with easy strikes and kicks, counting off ten of each before moving to the next. No one told him what to do, but Sensei Fabrizio waited for him to finish his ten before moving to the next. Max watched and learned. He knew his careful imitations lacked grace, but he also guessed he wasn't expected to pick everything up in one night. By the time they took their next break, Max's shirt clung to his skin and he suspected his hair might be sticking up. Yep. He smoothed the damp spikes down.

Elsa bounced up to him. She might have been baking cookies instead of throwing punches and kicks while yelling at the top of her lungs. "How's it so far?" she asked.

Wiping a hand on his sweatpants—in case she wanted to shake it again—Max offered what he hoped passed as an enthusiastic nod. "It's fun." The corners of his mouth lifted as he fell into the simple truth of his statement. He *was* having fun. For the past half hour, something other than his current funk had occupied his thoughts. He'd moved and breathed.

"Good, good." Elsa picked up a towel and swiped at her perfectly dry forehead. "How old are you?"

"Um, twenty-one."

Her eyes twinkled like Christmas lights. "Are you single?" The Christmas lights flicked toward Jake and then back at him.

"Ah…."

"I have a granddaughter, you see. Four of them, actually. But Carrie—"

Sensei Fabrizio's voice cut through the quiet murmur of students clustered at the back of the dojo. "All right, everyone get a partner, please."

Oh thank God. Max didn't care if he got thrown to the ground and tied in knots. Anything to escape a blind date. Likely as not he'd end up with another girlfriend.

"Arthur, would you work with Max, please?"

Max glanced at Jake, which he'd been trying not to do after Elsa looked his way, because, well, he didn't really know why. Just seemed he shouldn't draw attention to the fact he liked looking at Jake, or that he wanted to go out with Jake, or that—

"You seem a little out of breath." Arthur's tone was quiet and solicitous. "Need to sit down a minute?"

Max pinned his hands to his sides where they wouldn't flap about. "No, sir. I'm fine."

"Sir?" Arthur smiled, exposing very white teeth. "Call me Arthur."

"I'm Max." Really? *He already knows that, you dork.*

Arthur had the same smile as Sensei Fabrizio. Not patient, not too kind. Just… serene? Then he leaned forward in a confidential manner. "It's okay to be nervous. I don't think I spoke my first few lessons. There's a lot to take in. And, a course, I was scared I might break someone."

Max really looked at Arthur and noted that despite his height, Arthur did not have a lot of bulk. He did look strong, though, and the brown belt wrapped around his hips hinted that he could probably break Max easily enough.

"Ready?"

"Um, sure."

"We're going to run through some simple aikido. Wristlocks and such. This is all white belt stuff, so exactly your level. But what we're going to practice will form the fundamentals of every other self-defense technique you will learn in this class."

Max fell quickly into the rhythm of Arthur's voice, drawn in by the quiet but absolute confidence of his tone, and the idea that, wow, he might actually be learning something. Arthur instructed him to grab his wrist. Max complied. "Tighter," Arthur said. "Really grab a hold of me and don't let go until you feel like you have no choice. If I hurt you, tap out by slapping the side of your thigh, or simply telling me 'enough.' Got it?"

"Okay." Max tightened his grip.

Suddenly, he was on his knees, his wrist a hot point of pain. Max gasped and Arthur let go long enough to grasp his arm and haul him back to his feet. "Don't forget to tap out if it's too much."

Eyeing the other man warily, Max rubbed his wrist. "Okay."

Arthur smiled. "I'll go slowly this time so you can see what I did."

Max grabbed Arthur's right wrist again, tightening his grip when Arthur turned his wrist back and forth to show how easily he might break free. Then he watched as Arthur clapped his left hand down over Max's, trapping it, and maneuvered his right hand up and over Max's wrist, effectively forming a lock. Pain twanged along his forearm, but he didn't tap out until Arthur stepped in. Against his will, Max's knees began to buckle again.

"That's your body telling you to drop down so your wrist don't break." Arthur let go. "Ready to try that on me?"

Max nodded. Arthur wrapped long fingers around Max's scrawny-looking wrist and instructed him. "Place your right hand over mine to capture it. Then make a blade out of your left hand, that's right. Now try to angle your fingers up over my wrist. No, the other way. Yeah, like that."

It was magic. Max felt it the moment he did it correctly. He felt the tension in Arthur's wrist and caught the other man's wince as he increased the pressure. Then, just like that, Arthur dropped down.

Holy crap!

"Did I really do that?" Max asked, amazed he had just forced a man six inches taller and several inches broader to his knees.

"You did. Now, I could've got out of it. But not everyone you meet is going to have training, and some will just be idiots. We'll teach you how to deal with them, too."

Max didn't have a reply to that. His mouth was busy spreading itself into a wide smile, which felt strange, but also really, really good. When he risked a glance at Jake, his neighbor winked at him. Max thanked the stars his face already carried a healthy flush.

By the time they left the dojo he was tired, but a weird sort of elation warmed him from the inside.

"How did you like the class?" Jake asked as they walked side by side back along Beech Street.

Max showed Jake a smile. "It wasn't what I expected."

"Did you think you'd be breaking a board your first night?"

"Hah, no. I kinda figured I'd end up on the floor more, though."

"We'll save that for after we've given you a promotion and you look like you're gonna stick around for a while."

"Promotion?"

"Yeah. After you've had a white belt for a while, we make you sit on a wall to prove you're tough enough."

"Sit on a wall."

"You sit with your back against a wall, no chair. Just your legs bent. It's an endurance test."

"Oh, yeah! We used to do that in cross-country training."

A blond brow arched. "You ran cross-country?"

"In high school."

Jake offered a sober nod. "Yeah, I can see it. You've got a runner's build."

Max hoped the low light hid his sixth blush of the evening—not that he was counting. Jake had checked out his build? Of course, he'd checked out Jake's. Guy was perfect. In fact, Max had been kind of annoyed when Elsa blocked his view of Jake changing into his gi. On Monday night he'd angle himself better.

"You said you run the trail at Pennypack, right?"

Huh? "Oh, yeah. I'm hoping to get back out there soon." Real soon. He was so done with all this thinking time.

"Maybe I'll come with you."

Disregarding the heat in his cheeks, Max smiled. "I'd like that."

Jake paused on the corner of Beech and the avenue. "So, we going to duck through Wu's or brave the alleyway?"

Max sucked his lower lip between his teeth and pretended to consider both options. He leaned toward the alley, then rocked back on his heels and dipped his chin. "I, ah…. Wu's."

Jake gripped his arm. "Ever hear that one about the better part of valor being discretion?"

Max looked up. "Um, yeah. That's...."

"Good advice is what that is. Living to fight another day is smart, right?"

"I suppose." Max looked at the brightly lit windows of Wu's. The plastic cat waved at him. Then he glanced along Beech Street, toward the dark shadows gathered at the head of the alley. Foreboding and fear tickled his insides. "I feel...." Mouth clamping shut, he searched Jake's gray eyes for a clue, for the correct answer. "You must think I'm so stupid."

Jake's eyes didn't convey that. Nothing in his posture did. Still, Max couldn't help but compare himself to the strong and confident man standing next to him and come up short.

"You're not stupid, Max." Jake jostled him with an elbow. "C'mon. Let's go sneak into our apartments."

"If they're outside the door, it won't matter which direction we come from."

"Then you'll just have to catch one in a wristlock while I kick their asses."

Max fought a smile. He didn't think, even for a minute, he'd succeed in catching anyone in a wristlock, but he'd enjoyed learning that one simple move. It opened his eyes to the possibilities, and to the suggestion that maybe he *was* the sort of person who could study self-defense, and make a more than half-assed attempt at it.

CHAPTER ELEVEN

"WHAT DID you do to this table?" Jake asked.

Two weeks ago, it had been a rough canvas. Now… "Is that mold?" It couldn't be mold. Max's apartment reeked of bleach. Jake traced his fingertip over the streaked green surface and encountered a hardened bubble. Instantly, the puzzle fell into place. "You used that colored sealant, didn't you?"

Next to him, Max shifted. Jake looked up. Max had his jaw all stuck out. He was going to defend his ugly-ass table, wasn't he? And damn if angry Max wasn't a cute Max. With a faint smile, Jake recalled the sweet look of confusion that had wrinkled Max's brow when he'd passed a "cute" comment at Shay's that night. He just hadn't known how to process it.

"I like green," Max said.

"Green is cool. Streaks of green that look like mold, not so much. You have to eat off this, man." Jake lifted the bag he held in his other hand. The aroma of pie—still warm from the drive down from Doylestown—drifted out. "This table could contaminate the whole pie experience."

"You brought pie?"

"Mmm-hmm." Jake waved the bag. "You wouldn't come out for a meal, so I brought you dessert."

He hadn't really expected Max to accept the invitation to his folks' and, after spending the afternoon fielding questions about his love life (or lack thereof)—the attack incited by an evilly gleeful Willa—he was kinda glad Max had turned him down. Still, he'd brought home some pie. Max seemed to really like pie.

Max had two plates out. "Did you bring enough for you, too?"

"It's all yours."

"I don't want to eat in front of you."

"You mean you don't want to have to sit at this table and pretend it's normal."

The corners of Max's mouth turned way down and Jake's heart took a nosedive through his chest, ending with a splat somewhere near his intestines. Shit. When had he turned into such an insensitive clod?

"Hey, listen, I'm sorry. I'm not normally such an ass. I just spent the afternoon with my family and it was my turn under the microscope and…." Jake trailed off with a vague shrug.

Max returned the shoulder hitch and sat down. "'S okay."

No, it wasn't.

Jake sat opposite and pushed the bag across the table. "Here." Then he tapped the bubbled and stained wood. "What I should have said is, ah, fuck it. This is what I do, Max. I mean, sure, I work construction, but restoring furniture is kinda like my thing. It's what I'm passionate about. So I tend to go overboard." He pointed out the model cars lined up in front of Max's books. "If you saw a badly constructed model, you'd need to pick it apart and put it back together again, right?"

"I guess."

Jake watched as Max's lower lip disappeared beneath his teeth. He found that habit about as engaging as the sly smiles, or the way Max's eyes blazed when he got worked up about something. Dragging his gaze away from Max's mouth, he looked down at the table again and smoothed his hand over the slightly tacky surface.

"I can help you fix this." He flipped his fingers up, wordlessly asking for a minute to explain. "The all-in-one sealant isn't the best product. It's difficult to use and it won't protect the table well. What you need is a stain, any color, then a clear coat over the top. Or, you know what would work really well here? A polish. Sort of like wax. It would deepen any color you chose and highlight the grain of the wood as well."

Max's belligerent look faded into something more akin to interest. "Yeah?" He eyed the table. "I thought about just painting it, you know? But I like the way the wood looks."

Jake smiled. "Me, too. All the wandering lines." He traced one, then nudged the bag toward Max. "Eat your pie. I promise not to insult your table anymore."

One side of Max's mouth twitched. "Okay." He fished one slice out of the bag and dug in with his fork, cherry filling spilling out around the plate. Jake's mouth watered. Glancing up, Max arched a brow—elevating Jake's pulse by an unhealthy degree—and shoved the bag over. "Eat it."

Damn him.

Jake served himself the other slice of pie and forked up a mouthful of sweet pastry and tart cherry. God, it was good.

"Your mom makes good pie."

"Yep."

They ate in a quiet punctuated only by the smacking of lips and scraping of forks until both plates were empty. Glancing over at the flattened bag, Jake wished he'd grabbed more than two slices.

"So when can we fix the table?"

Jake looked up to meet a sweetly intense gaze. *Dear God.* "Next weekend work for you?"

MAX MIGHT'VE been slender, but he had a wiry strength to him. Watching the lean musculature of his arms bunch and flex, Jake wondered why Max had cowered under threat. He had backbone. He got angry and had verbally defended himself countless times when Jake overstepped. But he caved if physically intimidated.

There had been no shadows lurking in the alleyway for the past couple of weeks. Jake didn't know if his threat of a police report—texted to Dominick the day after meeting his *friends* outside Wu's—had put an end to the trouble, or if Dominick had found someone else to play with. So long as everyone left Max alone, Jake didn't care. What mattered was that Max seemed to be gaining confidence, and in the right environment. His steps were slow, but Jake could see how hard he tried.

Max definitely had a backbone.

"Step in." Jake watched the battle play out across the delicate lines of Max's face. Even with fading bruises coloring his skin, he was like some sort of art—beautiful in repose, breath-stealing when nudged toward an emotional response.

"It doesn't feel natural to step in," Max said.

"I know. It's hard. Most people would step away. Think of it as an element of surprise. Your opponent usually won't expect you to move in. But if you do, you'll have all the advantages. You'll shorten his reach and distract him. You'll be in his space and you know what that's like."

Hell, even Jake knew what it was like to be crowded. No such thing as space in prison. He'd hated anyone touching him while he'd been there. If someone got close enough to touch you…. Shaking off an involuntary shudder, Jake focused on Max. On the frisson of excitement that curled around his belly every time his downstairs neighbor got close.

Max stepped in and the angle of the hold changed. Pain flared in Jake's wrist. "Good." He backed up to relieve the tension. "Now I'll show you another one. Grab my lapels."

Max did so, his thumbs grazing the hair on Jake's chest. Another shiver pinched Jake's shoulders together, this one much more welcome. Looking up, he met Max's sapphire gaze for more than a brief glance.

He sucked in a breath.

Max looked away.

What was that? Was Max…?

Jake's thoughts whirled for a moment, and down in his groin, things stirred. *Down, boy.* Before his mind could settle, he pondered the very distinct possibility Max might be gay. It might explain the bullying. All sorts of kids got picked on for all sorts of reasons, but Max hadn't been ripped to shreds by the breakup with his girlfriend, and it seemed as if he'd had a very perfunctory sort of relationship. Had she been a cover?

Max was looking at him again, less intensely. Obviously waiting for instruction. Fervently, Jake wished Arthur were in class. Working with Max was dangerous. He spent half his time afraid he'd break him and the other half restraining the urge to touch him more intimately.

Drawing on the focus a black belt should have, Jake slid his fingers beneath Max's and turned his hand until he found that point of tension. "Okay, this is called the ikkyo pin." With Max's wrist turned, his elbow popped up. Jake took advantage of that to keep him off balance, grasping the elbow and pushing gently until Max figured out he was going down. Once he had Max on the floor, he bent the captured arm into an angle, explaining every step, then backed off before he could act on the fantasy of covering Max's body with his own.

Alyssa stepped into the gap he'd put between them and offered her newest student a hand up. "How are you doing?"

Max showed her one of his shy smiles. "Good." He straightened his gi, looking stupidly adorable as he did so, and glanced up at Jake. "I'm learning a lot."

Alyssa patted him on the shoulder. "I'm glad." Turning to the class, she raised her voice. "Let's take a break. Grab a drink, everyone." Before Jake could move toward his gym bag, Alyssa cocked her head toward the front of the room. "A word?"

Jake followed her forward. She waited until they had relative privacy before speaking again. "Are you all right to work with Max?"

"What do you mean?" Jake wondered if she could hear his heart pounding.

"Now is not the time to send him mixed messages, Jake. He needs solid reassurance."

What do you mean? He didn't say it again, he only thought it, and the answer came quickly, which did not surprise him. He knew what was happening. What did surprise him was the fact Alyssa had picked up on it.

Jake scrubbed the back of his neck. "I...." He met his instructor's steady brown gaze. "Um...." Fuck, he didn't know what to say. What if she had an issue with him being bi, or with him being attracted to another student, or with him being.... Shit, shit, shit. Maybe this wasn't a sexuality thing. Maybe this was an overprotective friend thing.

Alyssa reached for his arm and Jake shrank back. Was this an ex-con issue? Had he been too aggressive with Max? Did she regret letting him back into her class?

"Jake."

He looked up at her gentle tone and saw the softness in her gaze that had won him over eight years ago. This little woman could break him, but she had no intention of doing so. Ever. More, she wanted to build up her students. She wanted them to be confident, regardless of their perceived handicaps—height, weight, temperament.

"Lord knows, he needs someone like you. Just try to keep it professional in class, okay? If he gets distracted, he won't learn, and he really needs to learn. He needs to feel good about himself inside and out."

"He's... ah...." Damn it, he sounded like Max. When was the last time he'd been this tongue-tied?

"Very impressed with you."

Jake sucked in a quick breath and took a risk. "Not sure I'm his type."

Alyssa smiled. "That's something you can figure out outside my dojo, hmm?"

Message received. Oddly relieved, Jake breathed out a long sigh.

"Now go show him why I awarded you a black belt."

"Yes, Sensei."

Jesus, his knees felt weak. Having to tell Alyssa he was going to prison, and why, had been hard. Really hard. She hadn't judged. She'd simply listened, and when he'd approached her after his parole, she'd invited him to study with her again. That had been huge. Jake credited a large part of his sanity to that very thing. Between his family and this class, he had what a lot of men didn't, ex-con or not, and he wanted to share it with Max.

Having Alyssa figure out what else he wanted to share with Max almost terrified him more. Jake wasn't ashamed of his sexuality, but he didn't wear it like a badge. Was no one's business but his. He glanced over at Max, who had been caught by Elsa. She was probably trying to fix him up with one of her granddaughters.

Maybe he should tell Max how he felt, or at least clue him in.

Elsa looked over, caught him staring, and arched a brow. Max followed her gaze and smiled when he saw Jake. Heart pounding, Jake smiled back, then fought every urge to blush, duck his head, or do something really stupid like wave. He wasn't five.

His friendship with Max felt so damned tentative. He didn't want to ruin it, not yet. He didn't want to find out whether Max had a bias against bisexuality, or that his feelings weren't welcome. Max needed a friend right now. That was all.

Taking a deep breath, Jake shoved all his unresolved issues into a little box and locked them away. Anger management—not. Fuck it, he'd deal with it all later, after he'd taught Max how to pin him to the floor.

CHAPTER TWELVE

SPRING HAD been teasing Philadelphia for weeks. Max didn't mind. He loved the chill mornings and cool evenings. They made for perfect running weather, and now that his nose no longer sent random spikes of pain into his brain, he fell easily into his old schedule. He ran five mornings a week, the early exercise doing much to restore his equilibrium. He'd managed a mile on Monday. On Friday, four weeks after he'd been beaten down, he'd done two miles. Not a lofty goal, but Max knew all about small steps. He was the master of little victories. They were the kind a man could hug to himself and hide away somewhere safe.

Sundays he ran Pennypack Trail. Last Sunday he'd walked out there, stupidly breathless after covering the mile from his apartment to the park. This Sunday he took the mile at an easy lope, opening up once he hit the trail. The newly green trees, weeks from forming a canopy, let enough sunshine through to dapple the ground. The scent of mulched leaves and dirt competed with the river. Max could even smell his own sweat, which he counted as a good thing. It had been too long since he had the drive to really push it, to stretch his legs and just run. The path wound beneath his feet and the trees seemed to jog alongside. He inhaled and exhaled in a steady rhythm and, when he hit his stride, the place where pace and breath matched perfectly, the world fell away. He entered Max-Space.

Max didn't think when he ran, he daydreamed. His mind flew far from his small existence and expanded over a place where he could be anything. Anyone. In Max-Space, he had the courage to be who he wanted to be. People liked him and he was happy. He often carried a slice of that joy home with him, at least for a little while.

He reached the mile post he'd designated as his turning point. One day, he wanted to catch a bus to the top end of the trail and run the whole ten miles, down to the Delaware River. That was his intermediate goal. Sometime after that, he'd run both ways, do the whole twenty. Complete a personal marathon where the only audience was his dream-self, the

Max who lived somewhere wonderful. The joy of such a large victory would keep him warm for a week or more.

Running back toward Lincoln, Max stayed in the real world a moment, checking his rhythm, his breathing, listening to his body. His ribs grabbed at his lungs a little and his left hip ached. So did his jaw and nose. He didn't feel that bad, though. He was fitter than he'd been in a long time. Stronger. Two weeks at the dojo helped there. He hadn't done that many push-ups since a deluded week in high school when he thought he might actually face down Bryce and crew with a single flex of his puny biceps. Heh.

A figure reclined on a bench caught his attention. Max nearly tripped as he recognized Jake. Jake hadn't seen him—his attention seemed to be focused on a playground about a hundred yards away. Max fidgeted in place a minute, sweat rolling down his back in a tickle he'd not have felt in Max-Space. Should he say hello? That's what friends did. Something about Jake's faraway look and posture had him holding back. Also, it was Sunday. Jake usually went home to his folks' on Sundays. He'd invited Max three times now and had taken to dropping by on Sunday evenings with leftovers and pie.

Why wasn't Jake in Doylestown?

Swiping his forearm up over his brows, Max attempted to mop up some of the sweat creeping out of his hair. He smoothed the inevitable spikes, wiped his hands on his sweats, and stepped off the trail.

"Jake?"

Jake startled and turned, gray eyes momentarily wide. "Max! Hey." He leaped off the bench and shoved his hands in his pockets, extracted one to maybe offer a handshake, then shoved it back into his pocket again.

Max glanced around, wondering if he'd walked in on a secret tryst or something. Maybe Jake planned to meet a girlfriend and he'd bumbled in. "Um, I was just running by and saw you."

"Cool." Jake's gaze traveled up and down Max's body, leaving a heated flush in its wake. Then he smiled. Man, it felt good when Jake smiled at him like that. As if he was really pleased to see him. As if they actually were friends. "How are you doing?"

"Good! I missed running, so it's great to get out here."

"I hear you. Want to sit for a bit or will that mess up your run? I can walk alongside if you need to keep moving. Or, um…." He trailed off, looking helpless.

Max stared at him a moment, confused. Jake was usually more cool. Unflappable, easily amused. Stoic when he needed to be. "Is everything all right?"

Jake opened his mouth and shut it again. His shoulders hitched up and down, and then he tugged his hand from his pocket and gripped the back of his neck. "Yeah, kind of."

"Kind of?"

Jake hooked him with a searching gaze. After a moment, he seemed to arrive at a decision. He waved toward the playground. "I thought my daughter would be here today, but they never showed."

"Oh." An inadequate response, little more than a noisy exhale. "You don't get to see her much?"

"Nope. I'm not allowed."

"Why?"

"Because I'm a fucking idiot, that's why."

Max had no idea what had gone down between Jake and the mother of his child, but he knew the whole situation was Jake's *big mistake*. Sometimes he wondered what Jake had done, what haunted him, and he tried to figure out how it was related to Kate and Caroline. He could ask, but he knew all about the weirdness of unwanted questions. Seeing Jake stripped bare, looking so miserable, though, Max wanted to know it all. Maybe he could help. That's what friends did, right?

"What happened?"

"You don't want to know, Max. Trust me on that one. Listen, I should go. I'll catch you later, okay?" He started to walk away.

"Wait."

Jake turned back, surprise etched across his face.

"We're...." *Don't be shy now.* "We're friends, right?"

Jake returned a guarded nod.

"It's cool if you don't want to tell me, but you look rough. Let me walk with you. We can talk about something else." Having made his offer, Max concentrated on not dancing from foot to foot.

Jake looked about to refuse, then the tension along his jaw eased. One corner of his mouth twitched and he nodded again. "Okay, sure."

Fighting a grin of his own, Max fell in beside his friend. "So what pie are we missing out on tonight? Seeing as you've skipped out on your folks and all."

Jake shot him a surprised look and laughed. "I have no idea. We might be forced to pick up something from Shay's." He sobered a little. "That's if I'm welcome without a bag of Kendricks's finest leftovers."

"I'd consider it. For good pie."

"How 'bout if you come upstairs instead? I got a new game for the Xbox."

"Yeah?"

"Ever played *Saints Row*?"

"Nope."

"It's fun." Jake nodded at nothing and no one, as if trying to convince a ghost of his point. "I could use some fun."

Max opened his mouth and stopped. He'd been going to ask about Caroline again, about what had Jake so down. Then he realized that maybe he could ask—not only to assuage his own curiosity, but in a way that might lift Jake up again.

"Tell me about Caroline. The good stuff. The stupidly proud parent stuff."

Jake's expression shifted a couple of times, and Max wondered, briefly, if he'd messed up. Then Jake nodded again, at him this time.

"The day she was born, it was raining. It had been thundering and carrying on for hours. Perfect weather for the whole ordeal if you ask me. Childbirth is fucking scary business. I don't know how women do it. Anyway, Caroline came out of all that noise, quiet as a lamb. Just as serene as you please. Wide blue eyes and a single golden curl." He paused and Max wondered if that was it. But, no, after a breath, Jake continued. "You know how after a storm, the sky looks kind of unreal? The blue is too blue and the air has this sort of glassy feel to it?"

Max knew exactly what he meant.

"It was like…." Jake sucked in a breath and hummed softly.

Max took the opportunity to study his companion, the line of his jaw and the way the sun glinted off his perpetual stubble. The shape of his mouth, his full lips. His nose, the angle of his eyes, the way his face was all straight angles, but not at all severe. Just handsome. Perfectly content with his view, Max waited for Jake to finish his thought.

"I got it, you know? Right then. Why people had kids, why Kate wanted to keep the baby. I'd been shit-scared and I was angry about a lot of things, but then I saw my little girl's face, all golden and sweet, and I just fell in love and it was the most profound thing that has ever happened to me. Ever."

Max hadn't ever considered kids, but listening to Jake, seeing that light in his eyes, he could almost imagine wanting them some day. Or imagine, at the very least, what all the fuss was about. Jake continued on, detailing Caroline's first few years. All the gross and mundane things that parents marked as milestones and treasures. Max interrupted once or twice, to ask a question, or just to show he was still interested. He was, but really, Jake could've been talking about dirt. Just to hear him talk, to watch him gesture and smile. To have Jake's presence at his side, all companionable. It was like being in Max-Space, only better.

AFTER PIE, Jake taught him how to play *Saints Row*. Stealing a car and driving it along the sidewalk while pedestrians fell away like bowling pins shouldn't have been so much fun. Every time a body bounced from the car, the Xbox controller vibrated against Max's hands. He yelped the first time it happened, causing Jake to laugh. Trying to avoid carnage also had Jake laughing.

"That's not the point of the game," he said.

"I'm not sure there is a point to this game." Max valiantly tried steering through another knot of stupid people and ended up with his vehicle wrapped around the side of a building. The controller jerked and whined in his hands. On screen, someone pulled open the car door, yanked his character out, and began beating on him. Max rocked back, momentarily disturbed by the violence, then he mashed the keypad in combination, trying for a block. "These guys do not play by the rules."

"Nope. But they're predictable. Hit enough of them and a mob will come after you." Jake grabbed the controller. A few moves later—one of which involved the main character jumping high up into the air before plummeting back to Earth in a nuclear strike—he'd incited a riot. "Duck and cover, man!" he yelled with entirely too much glee and handed the controller back.

Elbows rising, Max began leapfrogging his way over obstacles in an effort to leave the scene. An alien ship descended and he got caught in the crossfire. He mashed a few more buttons. "How do I jump up again?"

"A! Hit A! But hold it if you can."

"They're dog-piling me!"

Jake took over again, the poor sod onscreen wading into the knot of bodies, virtual fists flying. "You need to put more points into the—Shit! Time to pull out your baseball bat."

That shouldn't have been fun, either, but it was. Max preferred the tentacle bat to the baseball bat, though. Felt a bit less real. They cleared the scene and began leaping across the landscape toward another minigame.

"Time for some Tank Mayhem," Jake announced.

An hour later, Max called for a break. "My thumbs are sore."

"Wuss."

Chuckling, Max handed over the controller and watched as Jake cleared the mission. Jake's jaw flexed and shifted, a muscle in his cheek jumping. One shoulder hitched up and down as he moved with the controller. His feet tapped across the floor. He leaned to the side and a flash of pink darted between his lips, the point of his tongue held by his teeth as he executed a precise combination. Then his arms shot up in victory.

"Woo! I am the man." He turned to Max, one palm up to invite a high five. Max slapped his palm to Jake's and his fingers were captured and his arm pulled up into the victory yell. "We rock!"

Max laughed. "No, you rock. I'm just the distraction."

"Hey, everyone has their strengths." Jake's blond brows rocked up and down. "Next time I'll play decoy and you can do the jumping puzzles."

Max wiggled his sore thumbs. "Sure, after I grow some new thumbs."

"You just need some calluses."

"On my thumbs?"

"Yep, and some gaming muscles."

Max laughed again and the sound of his mirth felt curiously unfettered. He grinned at Jake, who returned the smile. Then Jake was reaching for him, pulling him into a half hug.

"You're all right, Max. You know that?"

Heat slid across Max's skin, touching off points of fire at his extremities before gathering in his groin. His skin prickled and his palms itched. Beneath his sweatpants, his cock stirred. Panic gripped him by the back of the neck. Breath hitching, Max jerked away.

Jake tensed in response and lifted his arm. "You okay? Did I catch a bruise?"

The loss of heat across the back of his shoulders was nearly worse. Max wanted to grab hold of Jake's arm and pull it back around himself. Long forgotten words tickled the tip of his tongue, the urge to flirt, to say something to invite Jake to wrap him up again. Max swallowed them all. If he hadn't flinched, or....

Say something! "No. Ah... no. I'm fine. You just surprised me."

Brow furrowing, Jake shifted on the couch. Max fought the urge to glance at his crotch. How deluded was it to think Jake might also be turned on by their half hug? More likely he thought Max was just plain weird and wanted to put distance between them.

Then something sad crawled into Jake's eyes. Something suspiciously like regret. "I wish I'd been there. When you were growing up. You needed a friend like me."

Well, dang. "I…." Max clamped his mouth shut, unsure of what he should say. A breath huffed out of him. "I had a friend. Elaine. She lived next door. She's gone now, but we still talk sometimes." Max squared his shoulders. "She's really happy where she is. So it's all good." He forced a smile. "I'm good."

"Yeah, you are." Jake reached out again, his movement gentle. He appeared to wait for Max's go-ahead before clasping his shoulder, his strong hand so warm, his grip so reassuring. "This time next year, you are going to own that dojo. You'll have us all on the floor."

Just the idea he and Jake would still be friends this time next year was enough to make Max's heart soar. A lingering sadness crept beneath his joy, and he tamped it down. This time next year, he would be friends with Jake and that would be enough. He'd have gotten over this stupid infatuation by then. He'd have stopped needing to be touched, even when those touches had him leaping away. He'd be able to lean into a hug without getting a hard-on. He'd have stopped searching those gray eyes for a reciprocal spark.

Reaching up in a sudden movement, he grabbed Jake's hand—the one on his shoulder—and slipped his fingers beneath, just as he'd been taught. He twisted. Jake responded by folding his arm up and back, turning the lock back on him. Max yelped, thought about tapping out, then remembered that if he had a free hand to tap out, he had a hand to attack. He drove a strike toward Jake's ribs. Not hard, just enough to score a point.

Eyes widening, Jake breathed out sharply and loosened his hold. "Nice!" he said, rubbing at his ribs. "Six months, man. I predict you'll be mopping the floor with me in six months."

"Ha!" Max shook his head. "Let's give it five years." Five years. Yeah, he could handle that. He sucked in a breath and forced himself to stick out his hand. "Shake on it?"

Jake's large hand engulfed his. "Absolutely."

CHAPTER THIRTEEN

JAKE PICKED up a pot holder and plucked the lid off the saucepan. The aroma of tomatoes, onions, and garlic wafted up with a billow of steam. He inhaled deeply and breathed out pure satisfaction. He might not have an Italian bone in his body, but he made a good sauce. After replacing the lid, he ducked down to check on the chickens. Behind the oven window, the birds sizzled. He resisted the urge to open the door and poke at them. When the skin on the legs crisped up, they'd be ready. Then he'd put on the pasta and give the salad a toss.

Jake leaned against the counter and crossed his arms. Damn, it felt good to be *here*. To be doing something so simple, so utterly fulfilling. There had been too many blank hours in prison, and the work had all been stuff he hated. He hadn't been there long enough to get a position he wanted—and he'd never regret that. But even then, none of it would have been for him. Work in prison had been meant to keep him busy and that was all. Now, he saw projects take shape under his hands. Bits of furniture, pieces of his home. The jobs with his uncle.

They'd just finished a job over in Havertown. It had been an ambitious renovation and, to meet the client's deadlines, the crew had worked more nights and Saturdays than usual. Not that Jake was averse to working hard, he just didn't like the idea of leaving Max alone. He'd sounded pissed when Jake arranged for Alyssa to drive him home from the dojo last Friday night, but Jake took it in stride. As long as Max was safe.

The excuse of keeping Max safe had started to wear pretty thin. Sure, Max needed a friend, and over the past six weeks, they'd formed a pretty easy relationship—except when Jake forgot himself and tried to put his hands on him. Max had started to return the shoulder-bumps, and he didn't pull out of the occasional half hug anymore. It killed Jake to keep things there, but Max *had* actually become a friend. Effortlessly. More and more, they simply hung out together. They'd run the trail at Pennypack, they'd caught a bite at Shay's, and they found Max a coffee table to sand and stain. Last Sunday they had finished *Saints Row IV* and had started talking about getting *Call of Duty*. Something they could play together.

But tonight Jake had a different plan. Rather than take the chance of damaging his friendship with Max—a friendship Jake could admit they both needed—he'd see how Max reacted to the company of an obviously gay man and take his cues from there. Beyond any suspicions regarding Max's own sexuality, Jake would like to think he was open-minded. Max read a lot, mostly science fiction stuff. But even the most confused and/or forward-thinking dude could be biased. Jake didn't want to consider what that outcome might mean for their friendship, but if pressed—and he had been, by Eric—he'd admit that if Max had an issue with him being bi, then their friendship might hit the skids anyway. If so, Jake would still look out for him. Eric could just take a flying leap off that one.

But if Max seemed cool with it, maybe Jake could broach the next step. Carefully, as always.

A knock at the door pulled him out of his reverie. He tossed down the pot holder and strode across his apartment. It was Eric and Rob.

"Speak of the devil," Jake murmured.

"That's me." Eric pushed inside and gathered Jake into a hug.

Over his shoulder, Jake could feel Eric's head turning. "He's not here yet," Jake said.

Rob came in next. Though shorter and wider than Eric, Rob's brown hair and brown eyes were almost a match for his boyfriend's. If Rob and Eric could've made babies together, they'd be adorable. With his square shoulders, Rob looked like a laborer, but he had soft, white-collar hands. He and Eric both worked for the same investment firm.

Jake had met Rob twice before and liked him. "Rob." He extended a hand. "Good to see you." He turned back to Eric and appraised his friend's outfit. Eric had dressed down, thank Christ, in a lavender cowboy shirt and boot cut jeans. His belt buckle was the size of Texas, but Eric had to sparkle somehow, and his boots... "Where the fuck did you get those boots? Are those rhinestones?"

Eric sniffed. "They were a gift from Rob."

Jake glanced at Rob, checked his outfit for sparkly cowboy touches, and found none. Rob wore a long-sleeved polo, a pair of Dockers, and loafers. Very business casual. He held a bagged bottle of wine in one hand

and a cake box in the other. Glancing up, Jake caught the amusement lurking in Rob's deep brown eyes.

"He likes to sparkle," Rob confirmed.

Chuckling, Jake lifted his chin. "Shine on, you crazy diamond."

Eric smiled a pleased smile. "I intend to. Now, when is Cute Stuff arriving?"

Jake's smile faded. "In about fifteen minutes and please don't call him Cute Stuff."

"Boring!"

"Jesus. You do remember the plan, right?"

"To expose Max to the wonders of man love, yes?"

This had been a mistake. Gritting his teeth, Jake pulled out his phone. Eric snatched it from his hand and waved it over his head. Damn him for actually being taller.

"Give me my phone," Jake growled.

"You are not cancelling your date."

"It's not a date."

Eric tucked the phone behind him. Rob dropped the cake box onto the side table and took the phone out of Eric's hand.

"Behave." Rob smacked his lover on the backside and handed the phone back to Jake.

Eric pouted. But before Jake could unlock the screen, he said, "I'll be good. I promise."

God, he could use a drink.

Obviously in tune—and when hadn't he been?—Eric put his hands on Jake's shoulders and steadied him. "Take a deep breath. Now hold it, hold it." Jake held it. "Let it go slowly."

Jake breathed out and breathed in again. Beneath the firm and familiar grip of Eric's hands, his shoulders inched down. He didn't exactly relax, but his pulse calmed. His heart stopped slamming against his breastbone and the evening teetered back from the edge of disaster.

"He's not even here yet," Jake mumbled.

"I know, and you're already a mess." Eric kissed the side of Jake's head. "I hope he's worth it, babe."

Jake had dreams, but no expectations. "Don't scare him, okay?"

"I'll try not to."

A quick glance at Rob showed he seemed completely comfortable with the display of affection between old friends. Jake then understood that Rob knew the whole story, how long he and Eric had flirted around the idea of a relationship and why they hadn't ever really gone there. He felt their really close friendship, and was cool with it. He probably even knew why Jake had been in prison. Resentment flickered briefly and died. Instead, Jake found himself glad Eric had someone like Rob, someone to listen, someone to understand. Someone so damned confident, he could stand there holding wine and cake while his boyfriend cuddled another man.

Smiling, he beckoned Rob forward. "I hear you know a bit about wine. What did you bring?" Not that Jake would be drinking any, but he could be polite.

Rob explained his choice while opening the bottle to *breathe*. He then begged a taste of sauce and rolled his eyes in a close approximation of ecstasy. "So good."

"Thanks."

Eric set the table and the cozy domesticity of the scene tugged hard. Jake drifted back toward happiness. Another knock sounded at the door. Jake strode toward it, cutting Eric off with a scowl. Eric grinned widely—evilly—and positioned himself by the desk, arms folded above his ridiculous belt buckle. Rob hung back in the kitchen. Jake paused for a deep, fortifying breath and opened the door.

"Hey."

Max's face lit up as it always seemed to when he saw Jake. "Hey." He held up a long loaf-shaped bag. "Bread." He'd asked if he could bring something. "It's got garlic and butter inside."

"Awesome." Jake opened the door wider and Max stepped in. They passed that awkward moment where they sometimes did the half-hug thing by shuffling in place instead. Then Max's gaze lit upon his other guests. As Max processed Eric and all his sparkly, lavender glory, Jake indulged in a lingering look of his own. Max cleaned up well. He was the smallest, slightest guy in the room. The skin along his jaw glowed the way skin did just after a close shave, and his hair had a slightly damp sheen to it. He'd dressed in a blue checked shirt that brought out the intense color of his eyes and had it tucked into a dark blue pair of jeans. No sparkly belt buckle, no fancy boots. In fact, he had work shoes on his feet. Black lace-ups.

Okay, stop staring and introduce your friends.

"Max, this is Eric"—he pointed out the Rhinestone Cowboy—
"and Rob." Rob ducked out of the kitchen, looking blessedly normal and
pleased to meet Max.

Eric got to him first. Thankfully, he didn't try to hug the kid, nor
did he camp it up to eleven. He shot out a hand, which Max immediately
took. "A pleasure to meet you, Max. Jake's told us a lot about you."

Max blushed adorably, the tips of his ears turning dark pink. "Ah,
hi. Jake's mentioned you, too."

In passing.

Rob shook Max's hand next, and then Eric made one of his
signature moves. He put his arm around Rob's shoulders, bumped his
hips sideways, rocking Rob's stout frame a little, and turned him toward
the kitchen. "Let me take the bread, Max. Lover and I have to go see if
the wine has managed to choke yet."

"*Breathe*, Eric. Breathe."

"Yes, that." Eric winked at Max and turned Lover toward the
kitchen end of the apartment.

Jake did a little breathing of his own into the minivacuum his best
friend left in his wake. Then he looked at Max. "You get a run in today?"

Max rearranged his features from stunned to serious. "Yeah. Six miles."

"Wow, that's awesome."

Max nodded his agreement. "How 'bout you? Did you get to see
Caroline?"

Jake showed a grin. "Yeah, I did."

"Good days all around, then."

"Yep."

Max side-eyed the kitchen. "So, ah, your friends. Are they—"

"Gay?"

"I was going to say, um, together."

"Oh, right. Yeah, they are."

Max's brows pinched briefly, and then he nodded before turning a
shy smile on Jake. "Thanks for inviting me."

Resisting the urge to pull Max to his side, Jake simply returned the
smile. "C'mon, let's make sure Eric puts that bread in the oven."

DINNER CONVERSATION roamed the topic of hobbies, from furniture
restoration to model car building, to gardening—something Max and

Eric discovered a shared and keen interest in—and, finally, golf. Rob apparently spent every Sunday on the green, weather permitting, and had a membership at an indoor driving range for when it rained.

"I sometimes play caddy," Eric said. "I wear the spiffy outfits. Rob refuses to wear pink or even checks."

"Pink is like a golf mainstay," Max supplied.

Jake grinned. He still couldn't quite believe how relaxed Max was with Eric. He blushed at every innuendo, but laughed when Eric turned on the camp.

"It doesn't suit my skin tone," Rob said. "I like blue, and that one shirt I have is sort of checked. Like that." He pointed out Max's shirt.

Max looked down at his shirt. When he looked up, his eyes had an intense cast to them.

"Max looks gorgeous in blue," Eric said. "Makes his eyes pop." He rolled his gooey brown gaze toward Jake. "Don't you think so?"

Offering a noncommittal grunt, Jake gestured at Max's glass. "Another soda?"

"Sure."

Max held his gaze a moment, as if waiting for something, and Jake wondered if he should tell him his eyes were beautiful. Or popping. Or…. Jesus Christ. He pushed back his chair and stood. "Anyone else need anything while I'm up?"

Eric stood. "I want more chicken. It's delicious. You'll have to give us the recipe for your sauce, Jake. I'd forgotten what a good cook you are."

"Help yourself." Smiling, Jake leaned into the kitchen and stuck his head in the fridge.

Eric's head appeared beside him. "Oh, my God," he whispered. "Cute Stuff is utterly adorable. If you don't want him, I'll dump Rob. Or talk him into a harem."

"Whoa, cowboy," Jake hissed. "Can we do this tomorrow?" *And, no, you may not have him.*

"Take me to lunch at your parents' and we'll all gang up on you."

"Wonderful."

Jake grabbed the bottle of Coke and returned to the table.

"I'm surprised you made chicken," Max said. "You're always after me to eat something other than chicken."

"Hah." Jake snorted. "You'll notice I did not fry the chicken, or wedge it into a microwave tray with gloopy mashed potatoes and hard little kernels of corn."

Max produced one of his shy smiles. "You do know how to make fried chicken, though?"

Jake turned to explain the conversation to his friends. "Max here lives on Hungry Man dinners. Fried chicken, specifically."

Eric looked the kid up and down. "Another five years and that diet of yours will soften your angles, Max."

"Soften?"

"You'll end up like me," Rob put in, leaning back to pat his stomach.

Rob did have a bit of a gut, but his wide frame almost required it. Besides, he looked—

"You, my dear, are perfect. Properly cuddly."

Cuddly, yeah.

Jake glanced at Max and wondered if Max was a cuddler. Further, he wondered if all his angles, elbows and knees, folded neatly when he slid into a lover's arms. He might pass himself off as awkward, but Max actually had quite a lot of grace to him. He moved carefully and methodically, even in class. Watching him work through his assigned strikes, blocks, and kicks had become a definite pleasure.

"You're ogling, Jacob."

Fuck. Hoping the warmth in his cheeks was good food and good company, Jake looked from Max to Eric and smirked. "Just wondering where he'd put a gut."

"Mmm-hmm." Eric sounded unconvinced.

Another brief glance at Max showed him plucking at his blue shirt, his downturned face flushed with color. Jake looked quickly away.

"Jake does know how to fry chicken, just so you know." Eric twirled his wine glass. "He's an amazing cook, just like his mother."

"Oh, yeah?" Max smiled.

"He's tried to teach me a few times, but I am a disaster in the kitchen."

"Yes, you are," Rob put in.

"Hush, you. You liked my cookies well enough."

Rob shrugged. "Cookies are cookies, man, and I don't mind crispy."

"They were a little burnt."

Max chuckled and the sound of his amusement had Jake's shoulders winding down a little. Food was a good topic. A safe topic. So long as they didn't go back to how each of them wore their appetites, he'd be fine.

"So how long have you all known each other?" Max asked, gesturing between the three of them.

Jake leaped in with an answer, unsure if Rob knew how to talk around the fact he'd been absent for a year. "Rob and Eric have been together for six months." He aimed a quick smile at Rob. "But they work together at Franklin Investments."

"In Center City?" Max asked.

"Yes, the black and blue building that looks like an elongated hexagon," Eric said.

"I think I know it. I used to walk around the city a lot when I first moved down here. There are so many parks and gardens."

Rob interjected here. "My cousin is involved with the horticultural society. If you're interested, I can give her your details."

"They have a great summer program," Eric added.

"Yeah? I think…. Yeah, that would be cool," Max said.

Jake smiled. This had been a great idea. By the end of the night, Max might have two more friends and a line on something he was really interested in, given all the sad little plants gathered around his apartment. Jake glanced at the cluster of pots by his front window and the lone tulip on his coffee table. Yeah, Max could use access to a proper garden or two, before he filled both their apartments with the supermarket's castoffs.

Eric nudged his arm. "Earth to Jake."

"Huh?"

"Rob asked if you were interested in the community garden program. They need guys to help build the beds and frames." Eric arched a brow. "And you like getting your hands dirty."

Jake snorted. "Sure."

Typical of Eric to try to include him. He felt a warm rush of gratitude toward his friend. Jake glanced over at Max and met a curious gaze. God, he could just drown in those velveteen eyes.

"What about you two?" Max asked. "How do you know Eric?"

Jake pondered the subtext of Max's question long enough to miss the jump on the answer. A warm body pressed to his side and a hand crept around his shoulder. Eric, claiming him. Jake didn't know whether he should look at Eric, or watch Max's expression for warnings. What he did know was that Eric would not be stopped now. He just hoped he would exercise some tact.

"Jacob stole me from his sister when we were fifteen."

Fuck.

"Stole?" Max asked, his dark brows drawing together.

"She found us lip-locked in the basement." Eric's lips brushed Jake's cheek. "We've been besties ever since."

"Lip-locked." Max's gaze flipped back and forth between Eric and Jake. "Like, kissing?"

Jake's stomach twisted and rolled. He didn't try to shrug out of Eric's embrace. To do so would be just pissy, and wrong. He'd be feeding Eric's nuts through a food processor later, but not because the dick had outed him. Because Eric had stepped outside the program.

"Yes, kissing. Jake has gorgeous lips, don't you think?" Eric pulled away then, and leaned back toward Rob. "But we're just friends. Always have been, which is just as well, or I'd not have Rob, here."

Max's gaze hadn't shifted from Jake. The color of his eyes had darkened. Then his skin paled, visibly, except for two spots of color right over his cheekbones.

"You're gay?" If not for the complete quiet, no one would have heard him. His mouth had barely moved.

"Bisexual."

Max swallowed, his throat jerking with the movement. Then color rushed back into his face, making his eyes bright. He leaned back from the table and gripped the edge. Looked down. He pushed back from the table a moment later, mumbling "Excuse me," and broke for the bathroom. As soon as the door shut, Jake turned on Eric.

"You asshole."

"What?"

"You know fucking well what."

"Look, if he's not cool with your gay side, then he's not worth your time, even as a friend."

"That's not…." Jake kicked at the leg of the table. "Fuck it, Eric. I was going to tell him, and he'd probably have been cool with it without you draped all over my shoulder and telling him what a gorgeous fucking mouth I have."

"Guys, I'm pretty sure he can hear you from the bathroom."

Jake's stomach lurched. Jesus H. Christ. What had that look been? Hurt? Why had Max looked hurt? At least he hadn't looked disgusted, as if he might puke. Unless he'd gone to the bathroom to do just that.

Fuck, fuck, fuck.

Kicking the table again, Jake huffed out a breath and reached for a space of calm. His thoughts swirled along with his gut, greasy as chicken, and neither would settle. He stood and paced toward the kitchen. Eric moved up behind him.

"Go away," Jake growled. "Take your sparkly fucking self and get out of my apartment."

"You don't mean that."

He did and he didn't. He was scared he might hit his best friend, or rip the legs off a table, or smash something. Anger swamped him, thick and heavy. His nails cut into his palms. His anger refused to settle on a direction, however. Eric had pissed him off, but he might also be the only man who could talk him down. Max…. Jake swallowed against the desire to push into the bathroom and demand answers. Or to explain. Yeah, explain.

The bathroom door opened with a quiet creak, and Max stalked into the middle of the apartment. He had one hand pressed to the side of his head. Jake approached with a caution that burned, flinching as Max rocked back, away from him.

All the ease between them was gone.

"I…." Max didn't seem to know where to rest his gaze. In between all the flicking about, he stuttered, "Head hurts. Sorry I should go. Gonna go."

"Don't," Jake said.

Max looked at him then. Really looked at him. Etched across his face was the hurt Jake had glimpsed before, and something else, something deeper. Sadness or… betrayal. "Sorry," he mumbled, edging toward the door. He slipped through, apologizing again, and the door closed behind him.

The continued apologies made no sense, but they did dull the spark of his rage. Jake was simply angry when he strode toward the door, intending to follow Max downstairs, but a hand caught him around the arm. Jake turned with his fist up and curled, ready to hit whoever tried to stop him. Rob stood there, blocky and square, his expression weirdly calm.

"Let him go."

"I need to explain—"

Rob shook his head. "No, you don't."

"But he thinks…." What did Max think? What had pulled him up from the table and out the door, and why had he looked so hurt?

"He likes you, man. A lot. He's just surprised, is all, and a dude like that needs time to think. He'll come 'round."

"Cute or not, he's an idiot."

Jake turned on Eric. "No, he's not, he's just…. Fuck it. I told you how sensitive he was."

"Like a wounded dog, I know. Still, he just dissed you. I'm not liking him so much right now."

"You don't know him."

"I'm not sure you do, either."

"Fuck you."

"Fuck you," Eric spat back. "Is that the best you have, Jake? Is that what they taught you in prison?"

Growling, Jake turned on Eric only to find himself again restrained by Rob. He swallowed another *fuck you* and wrenched out of Rob's grip, turning away from both of them. "Go. Both of you."

"You know, if he'd fallen into your lap, you'd be thanking me right now."

Jake looked at Eric, stunned by the suggestion. Then he shook his head and pointed toward the door. "Just go, before I show you what else I learned in prison."

CHAPTER FOURTEEN

BEING LESS than six feet tall should've meant you could curl into a ball. Max had never managed it. Despite being on the short side, the slender side, he'd always found one of his legs stuck out when he tried to curl up, which could be why he ended up with so many bruises from every beating. He didn't have a proper shell. He couldn't even roll well.

Half curled on his hard futon, he let his thoughts roam across a field of pathetic—all his flaws, the reasons why a handsome gay man—a bisexual man—might keep him as a friend, as a little buddy, but never make a move on him. Max understood his biggest fault—lack of confidence. If he sparkled like Eric, he might find himself *lip-locked* with Jake. Of course, Jake had no idea he wanted anything like that, or even that he'd spent nights—and some mornings, afternoons, too—dreaming about it. Because Jake didn't know he liked guys.

The big, deep closet Max had stepped back inside since moving to Philly was supposed to be a safe place. But it never had been. It had never protected him from the thoughts of others, because he always came across as awkward, gay or not. He made stupid decisions, one after the other. He didn't know who he was, and so he never gave up much of himself. He'd figured Jake might know him—they certainly spent enough time together. Now, Max figured he'd been a project. Jake had felt sorry for him. And for as much as they'd shared, Jake hadn't thought well enough of him to be himself, either. He'd hidden a huge part of his life.

Because Max didn't matter.

Because Jake would never consider dating someone like him—deep, dark closet aside.

Max heard the front door of the building open and close. A minute later, someone pounded on his apartment door. He knew it was Jake. He remained tightly curled, except for the leg defying his requirements. His left hip ached and his head thudded alongside. Briefly, he considered taking one of the pills he'd gotten from the clinic. Even more briefly, he considered taking all of them. Surely no one would miss him.

God, it had been a while since he'd felt the searing burn of humiliation quite so keenly. Being kicked into a wall felt better. Physical pain always trumped mental anguish.

Max remembered a party, one for a kid at school. He'd been surprised by the invitation, and when he'd rolled up to the house, he'd half expected to find he'd been invited on the wrong day as a joke. The party had been in full swing. Max sat in a corner for most of it, picking at a Rice Krispies treat, wondering if his mother would ever make something so frivolous. He played a couple of games, but his awkwardness made the other kids nervous. He'd known that, even then.

Then he'd heard it, the reason he'd been invited. The school had a rule. Either invite the whole class or no one at all. He hadn't accepted any invitations after that, and soon enough, the other kids had grouped together and exchanged phone numbers. Had planned their get-togethers outside of school hours. By then he'd befriended Elaine, so the Monday morning recounting of all the awesomeness of the other guys' weekends hadn't really bothered him. Except, it sort of had.

Jake knocked again and Max continued to ignore the booming invitation. Jake didn't want a friend, he just felt sorry for the kid downstairs.

"HEY!" ELSA swiped at his jaw and Max blocked gently. "Not used to seeing you on a Wednesday," she said.

Max had skipped Monday, ignoring the texts, voice mails, and the knocks at his door that had started on Sunday. He suspected Elaine might have left a message in among Jake's, but couldn't bring himself to admit his folly to the only friend he might have left. Best to pretend his phone was broken. Tuesday night, he went to see a movie—leaving his phone at home. Afterward, he walked the alley to the front door, braving the dark on his own, the small victory squashed flat by the fact he had no one to share it with.

His phone had stopped buzzing sometime this afternoon—the battery had died—but the idea of sitting home, alone, with it not ringing…. "I had a free night."

"Right! Well Jake's not here on Wednesdays."

"I know." Max turned away to pull off his shirt—not that he expected Elsa might check him out. He just wasn't comfortable being rude to her face. If undressing in front of someone was rude. Avoiding conversation might be. As he fastened the white belt around his gi, he breathed out and acknowledged that coming to class could be the best idea he'd had all week. He enjoyed the lessons, and he needed an outlet. He'd never be an aggressive guy, but sometimes he craved something more than running.

Maybe he just needed to hit someone.

Sensei Fabrizio made her rounds, greeting every student. She lingered in front of Max, brown eyes searching his face as she held his hand in hers. "Is everything all right, Max?"

"Yes."

"How are the headaches?"

How did she know he got headaches?

"I have a prescription for them." He'd been using it, too. Those pills had a way of swallowing what remained of his evening, rolling extra hours into long and dreamless nights.

"We missed you on Monday."

"Sorry. I…." A lie danced at the tip of his tongue, then curled into truth. "I didn't feel up to class."

She squeezed his hand. "Take care of yourself, okay?"

Max moved to his customary position at the back of the lineup and quickly fell into the routine of greeting and warm-up. The jumping jacks still jarred a little, a month and a half after the attack. He figured the last three nights of dead sleep had left him stiff and sore. He managed forty push-ups, his pleased glow fading somewhat when he remembered he had no one to share that victory with, either. Then came the line work, the series of blocks, strikes, and kicks, from his level on up. By the time they took a break, his blood hummed and his thoughts were all but blank.

"Pair up for defense off a punch," Sensei Fabrizio instructed.

Max paired with Barry—formerly known as Surly. Barry had about an inch on Max and was built like Eric's boyfriend. The permanent sneer negated any cuddliness. Being the lower rank, by one belt, Max assumed the role of attacker. He adopted a fighting stance and aimed a punch at Barry's face. Barry performed a simple block and strike, obviously thinking his way through the process. Max tried a second punch. Barry caught his arm, locked it, and turned him around, using Max's own momentum. Max barely caught his feet before Barry snapped him back, pitching him toward the floor. He landed gracelessly, head bouncing off the mat.

He scrambled up and readied another punch. Barry went for the lock again and Max tried to follow his movements as his opponent folded his arm into a pretzel and flung him back toward the ground. Max stiffened his neck the second time, avoiding the head bounce. The third time, air gushed out of his lungs and an ache took up residence in his hip.

"Let's see something else, Barry," their sensei said as she passed by.

Something else turned out to be a flip in the opposite direction, over Barry's hard hip. Max groaned as he rolled onto his side and pushed back to his feet.

"Too much for you?" Barry asked quietly, eyes glinting mirthlessly.

Max shook his head and lined up again. Again, he found himself on the floor. This time, Barry had simply tripped him. After another hard fall, Max asked for a turn and received a fist to the jaw. His head rang and a second ache throbbed into being.

"A little slower, please."

"Jake been taking it easy on you, has he?"

Ignoring the taunt, Max waited for the next punch, guessing Barry would give him all he had. He did. Max went for a simple block. Barry must've had concrete for bones. The connection between their wrists as Max swept the punch aside sent a jarring shudder down his arm. He'd have a bruise later, no doubt.

"Block *and* strike, Max," Sensei Fabrizio called out. "Always follow up."

He tried again and managed to perform both together, the block and the strike, while stepping out of the way, lessening the impact of bone on bone.

Again, and he got in a good, solid strike.

"That all you got?" Barry asked, brows tilted to a sardonic angle.

"Pretty much." Max had run through some of the more complicated moves with Jake, but six weeks in, he was still a newbie. He didn't trust himself to try a takedown with anyone but Jake. Or maybe Arthur.

Barry muttered under his breath, the end sounding like "pussy."

"What did you say?"

His opponent flicked his fingers up. "C'mon, get your guard up. Wouldn't want to mess up your pretty face."

Blushing, Max missed the block and rocked back as Barry's knuckles grazed his jaw for a second time.

Sensei Fabrizio appeared at his side. "We're not brawling here, Barry. Pull your punches, please."

Max resisted the urge to rub his jaw and thrust it out instead. He didn't need a five-foot woman looking out for him. He didn't need anyone looking out for him.

Barry threw another fast punch and Max batted his arm away while stepping in, his own arm extended to catch his opponent across the throat. He kicked back with one foot, catching Barry's ankle, and stepped down, just as he'd practiced with Jake. Stopped short and put off balance, Barry dropped to the ground. His head bounced.

A glow of satisfaction went partway toward soothing the aches in Max's head and hip. Hiding a smile, he extended a hand toward Barry in an offer to help him up.

Yeah, coming to the dojo tonight had been a good idea.

After class, he refused a ride home from Alyssa Fabrizio. "It's not far."

"It's on my way Max, I don't mind."

It was hard not to scowl at the woman he wanted to respect. Did respect. "I appreciate the offer, but…." *I can take care of myself.* "The walk helps me cool down after class."

She considered him a moment before nodding and letting him go, and Max affected a casual stride as he walked away from the dojo. He kept his cool as he continued on toward home. The pretense fell away as he spotted the shadow lurking outside the front door of his building.

Pulse tickling wildly at his throat, Max called up the moves he'd made in class that night. His confidence quickly waned with each beat of his heart. His jaw hurt and his head ached. His hip, which hadn't bothered him in a while, felt like an overstretched rubber band. Fatigue pulled heavily at him. He wanted a shower, a pill, and eight dreamless hours on his futon.

Instead, he set out to prove he could take of himself. Squaring his shoulders, Max approached the door. Relief did not trickle through him when Jake stepped into the light.

"Hey."

"Hey." Max hunched and searched his bag for his key.

"You're ignoring my texts."

"I know."

"What gives? I thought we were friends."

Keeping his gaze pointed down—because it hurt more than all his aches together to look at Jake—Max shrugged. He felt rather than saw Jake reach for him and stepped back. Jake dropped his hand and sighed.

"Look, I'm sorry. I don't know what I'm apologizing for, but I'm sorry. Just tell me what's going through your head, okay?"

Max looked up. "Where do you go on Wednesday nights?"

"Huh?"

"You don't go to class on Wednesdays."

Shadows crept across Jake's face, darkened by the abstruse angle of the light. "I have another thing I have to do on Wednesdays." A thing he didn't want to share, obviously. "Listen, Max—"

"I'm tired and I don't feel like talking."

"Then how about tomorrow? After work. Or I can come by the market and meet you for lunch."

"No." Defeat swirled in his belly. He didn't want to do this. He didn't want Jake to try so hard. "Just let it go. I get it, all right? You found me on your doorstep and felt sorry for me. Well, I'm all right now, see? I'm good. You can go. I don't need you."

Jake looked like he'd been caught, flipped and tossed to the floor of the dojo. He even breathed out on impact. "That's—fuck." He scrubbed at his hair and gripped the back of his neck. "You think I've been…." He shook his head. "Damn it, Max. We're friends, aren't we? You've helped me out, too."

He had? Max tried to conjure up a situation where he might have helped Jake, but his head ached too fiercely. Wincing, he rubbed at his temple. Jake advanced on him, reaching out again. Max ducked his chin toward his shoulder, eyes closed, instinct overriding all sense.

"Max!" Jake grabbed his shoulders. "Don't do that. Jesus, I'm not going to…." He growled under his breath and let go. Shoe soles scraped the pavement, Jake turning a circle. "Shit. Don't shut down like that. Open your eyes. Please."

Max opened his eyes and stared down at his shoes. Another growl of frustration drifted toward him.

"You're not going to listen to me, are you?"

No. Because he didn't want to hear what Jake had to say. He'd apologized and that was all well and good. But they couldn't be friends. Nursing an unrequited crush for the past six weeks had been difficult enough. Knowing Jake was available but not interested? Way worse.

"Just tell me one thing. Just answer one question." Jake sounded about as tired as Max felt. "Tell me this isn't because I'm bisexual. Is that an issue for you?"

Max glanced up. Jake looked wrecked. Someone had ripped him open and pulled out his stuffing. Not him. It couldn't have been him, could it? Max didn't want to lie to Jake's face, handsome even in distress. Nor did he want to be a hypocrite, treat Jake the way he'd been treated his whole life. But the answer to the question had to be yes— because Max did have an issue with Jake's sexuality. With the fact he also liked guys.

Guys that weren't him.

Maybe he should admit to his crush. Watch the shock and amusement wrestle for dominance on those angular features. Let Jake reject him. Let that be the end of this… this thing. This hurt, this confusion, these questions. Maybe….

The pounding in his head intensified, sparking off reciprocal aches down his arms and legs, and the moment stretched too thin.

Breath hitching in his throat, Max shook his head, the vague movement unconvincing, even to himself. It was cowardly and it hurt, but it was all he had right now. Turning, he pushed past and put his key to the lock and opened the door.

He half expected Jake to call him back.

He half wished Jake would.

CHAPTER FIFTEEN

RESTLESSLY, JAKE paced the back corner of his parents' yard. He had his nephew cradled in his arms. T gurgled contentedly, happy to be carried and bounced. Jake tried to drift with the happy sounds, to become one with the toddler. For the first time, T's burbling failed to inveigle him. Jake couldn't stop thinking about Max.

He'd had worse weeks, certainly. Being arrested had sucked. His arraignment and sentencing had been about the most stressful events of his life. Kate's absence from the courtroom had driven a spike through his heart. Then there had been his year in prison. He still woke sometimes, breath caught painfully in his throat—as he had so often *inside*, waiting for the ever-present miasma of violence to coalesce into something more than a threat. It had been a long, slow year.

Being on parole sucked. He hated missing Wednesday nights at the dojo, especially now he'd taken an interest in Max, which brought him to the latest arrangement of suckiness. Jake still didn't understand what had happened, why Max had freaked out after Eric's neat little bombshell. All he knew was he missed Max with an intensity that left him breathless. He hurt, physically and mentally, and he wanted to know why.

A finger poked into his ear, drawing Jake to a halt. He turned, and the finger moved with his ear.

"Is your finger stuck in my ear, T?"

T mumbled something and poked harder. The sound of a finger plunging into his ear canal distracted Jake from his woes. He pulled his nephew's hand away and the action started a game. Every time Jake pulled T's finger down, it somehow ended up back in his ear.

"Quit it."

T giggled in response and said something that might be "quit it." Jake pondered swearing, just to see if he could get T to imitate him. Then he could surprise Abby with her son's first word. Something truly scandalous like *fuck* or *shit*. *Crap* would be appropriate, given the kid knew all about the process, and that word wasn't the worst he could pass on.

"Crap." Jake said.

T stuck his finger in Jake's ear.

"Crap."

The finger wiggled, creating the odd pressure again.

"That's just too weird." Jake pulled the finger out again and bounced his nephew. "C'mon. Let's go find something else to play with."

Abby met him at the edge of the patio and pulled her son out of Jake's arms. As soon as he let go of the warm little body, Jake missed it. He followed Abby over to their chairs and flopped down next to her. He tapped T's knee and said, "Can you say the word Uncle Jake taught you?"

"Oh no you didn't."

Jake arched a brow at his sister. "Didn't what? It was a clean word. Sorta."

"Honestly, Jake. This is why I never ask you to babysit."

"You never ask me because I live near the city."

"Exactly. I'd have to check my baby for tattoos and track marks every time I picked him up."

"Wow." Jake shook his head. He pushed out of his seat. "I'll take my tattooed self over to the other side of the patio, okay?"

He had one tattoo. One. And he'd gotten it when he turned twenty. Not after he got arrested and joined the ranks of those with a criminal record.

"I didn't mean you, Jake. Where did you leave your sense of humor?"

"In the gutter with all my sharps."

Willa pulled her sunglasses down and looked between them. "Are you two going to start drinking soon?"

Scowling so hard he could see his eyebrow hairs, Jake pushed off the end of the patio and looked for his path along the back fence. He'd completed his second lap when Willa fell into step beside him.

"What's up?"

Jake answered with a grunt.

Willa put a gentle hand on his arm. "Talk to me."

Jake turned to her, but didn't stop his pacing. If she wanted to have a conversation, she'd have to keep up. "I don't drink anymore, remember?"

"You were in a mood way before I suggested you have a drink."

"Not every day is a sunny day."

"Did something happen? Is it Kate? Has that asshole Dominick sent his friends around again?" When he frowned harder, she tried a new tack. "Is it Max?" Jake shook off her hand and strode away. Willa quickly caught up. "What happened? Is he all right?"

"How the fuck should I know? It's not like we're friends or anything."

"Since when? You guys have been practically living in each other's pockets for weeks."

"Well we're not anymore."

"Why not?"

"I don't *know*."

And that was the worst fucking part. Had Max lied about the bi thing? Or had Jake missed something else? Something subtle, but crucial? Wouldn't be the first time he'd misread a gesture or misinterpreted a signal. There was a reason he'd been single since forever.

"Slow down. It's Sunday. We're supposed to be lying on the patio waiting for Mom to stuff us with food." Jake slowed, but did not stop. Willa caught up. "Now tell me what's going on."

Jake looked over at his sister, at the face that so closely resembled his. Gray eyes and blonde hair. A wide forehead and angled jaw, though Willa had the more delicate versions. He'd always been close to Willa. Now he regretted sharing so much of himself with her, particularly over the past few weeks. Given that she'd helped treat Max, it seemed natural she should take an interest in him. Heaving out a sigh, he decided to test her theories on what the hell had happened.

"He found out I was bi and freaked out. Left in the middle of dinner and has been avoiding me ever since. He won't answer my texts or calls and when I confronted him on Wednesday, he brushed me off."

Jaw slackened, Willa stopped and stared. "Seriously?"

Pausing in his mission to wear a track in his parents' lawn, Jake offered a nod.

"That makes no sense." She shook her head, setting her blonde bob swinging. "No, I don't believe it. Not Max. He's too sweet to be so bigoted."

"Different strokes, Wills." At another time, in another universe, he'd be laughing at that comment.

"Are you sure it's not something else?"

"That's what I've been trying to figure out, but it seems pretty clear."

Willa stepped in, slim arms extended, and Jake allowed her to pull him into an embrace. "Oh, Jake, I'm so sorry."

He didn't want to hear how sorry she was. He wanted to hear how wrong he was. Still, Jake returned the hug. He even patted her back, as if she were the one requiring comfort. When she pulled away, he summoned a wry smile.

"For what it's worth, I think he's an idiot," she said.

"You and Eric both."

Her gray eyes narrowed. "Still. It's so weird. I mean, I had an idea Max might be gay, and halfway besotted with you."

Jake's skin prickled. "What makes you say that?"

"The way he talked about you when he came into the clinic."

"When did he visit the clinic?"

"A couple of weeks ago. I happened to be subbing down there that day. He said he'd been getting headaches. You know, I meant to check up on him, but the days have a way of rolling together when I'm working shifts in there and the ER."

"Headaches?" Jake thought about the way Max often rubbed his head and worry instantly pinched his gut, despite the fact he was mad at Max. Furious with him.

"I'm sure he's fine. It's not unusual to suffer headaches for a while after a concussion."

Jake nodded while worry continued to gnaw at his insides.

"Listen, while he was there, he told me about the classes you'd taken him to and dinner out. Some game you've been playing? I could barely get a word in. I'd not have picked him for a talker. He only talked about you, though, and he had this look on his face, like you'd invented the wheel or something. So when you kept talking about him, too, I just figured you two were...." She gestured vaguely. "You want me to call in on him? I could make up an excuse. Say it was an outpatient sort of thing, or just tell him the truth, that I'm worried about my brother."

"No." Jake searched her face for answers and saw only sisterly concern. For a second, he was tempted to change his answer to *yes*. Let her classify the bug Max had up his ass. But ultimately, if he wanted to know, he needed to be the one to do the asking. "Maybe I'll try talking to him again."

JAKE SAT in his truck with a paper sack of leftovers in his lap. Barbecue pork, coleslaw, and strawberry rhubarb pie. Listening to the cooling engine tick, he planned out his attack. The food in the bag was for Max. Jake resolved to make one more attempt to get through to him and he wasn't ashamed to try an ages-old method. Pie hadn't worked last Sunday. The bag he'd left by Max's door had still been there on Monday night. Jake forgave him the slight. He'd have done the same thing—and didn't he think Max's stubbornness was cute?

But a week without Annabel Kendricks's pie could wear on the hardiest soul.

A surprise awaited him in the apartment hallway. Max sat on the stairs, cell phone in hand. Eyes widening, he stood and tucked his phone into his pocket. His hands followed, fingers crawling deep.

"I...." Max blushed deeply and for once, Jake didn't enjoy the sight. The tips of Max's ears didn't pink adorably, he just looked plain awkward. "I need to talk to you," Max said before dropping his gaze.

Arching a brow, Jake waited for the slow roll of anger to move through him. His temper was his greatest fault, he knew that. Losing hold of it now would not help his case, or his cause. And hadn't he planned to do just this? Talk?

"Okay." He affected a nonchalant shrug. "Want to come up?"

Max's gaze touched on the paper bag, lifted to Jake's face, and skittered away. He returned the shrug. "Sure." He flattened himself against the wall so Jake could pass, then followed him upstairs.

Dropping his keys onto the small table inside the door, Jake lifted the bag in his hand. "Are you hungry?"

Max shook his head. "I just want to talk."

"Okay, so talk." Jake winced at his own tone, but managed to swallow bitter recrimination. He wasn't the one at fault here.

Max fidgeted, biting his lips and pulling his hands in and out of his pockets. Then he got right to the point. "I wish you would have just told me you were bi. At the beginning."

"Why?"

"Because I felt like a fool last Sunday. I'm sorry I left, I know it was rude, but it was like you all had this secret and I was the odd man out."

Jake processed that for a moment. Took it, walked across the room with it, toyed with it as he dropped his sack of food onto the table. "Okay, I guess I can see that. Thing is, Max, my sexuality isn't really anyone's business but my own. I don't identify as bisexual first, human second. It just is what it is. I'm not ashamed of it. I just don't wear it as loudly as, say, Eric. I've had girlfriends and I've had boyfriends. He's had girlfriends, too. Just so you know." Eric's sexuality wasn't in question, but the fact he came across as more obviously gay while still having had a period of figuring himself out sort of made Jake's point, didn't it? He waved toward the fridge. "Want a Coke or something?" Max shook his head. He still stood halfway across the room. Jake beckoned him over. "Come sit?"

Max crept forward and put his hands on the back of a chair.

"Can I ask you something?"

Max nodded.

"Why is it such a big deal?" Jake squashed the urge follow up with a qualifier, give Max reasons to duck, or a range of acceptable answers. Instead, he simply waited for one of those spikes to be driven through his heart, and wondered why this kid—this man—held such power over him. Why he mattered so much.

"Because I was with a guy in college."

Well, damn. He should have seen that coming. Hadn't he wondered about Max's sexuality? If only it was considered polite to ask which way the wind blew or whatever. Straight up ask if someone was gay.

"Okay, then." Jake wrapped a hand around his nape and squeezed. So, Max was gay. Not bi, not questioning. Gay. Had to be, because the picture in Jake's head sure looked like the result of a lot of little pieces slotting neatly together.

And the blush darkening Max's skin looked downright painful.

Jake pulled a chair out from the table and flopped into it. "Okay, I need to sit." He waved at the chair Max was gripping. "Sit, before you fall down. Let's talk this out."

Max looked confused for a second—more confused—then he jerked the chair out and dropped down.

"What happened with the guy from college?"

"Henry." Max's voice was so quiet. Sucking on his lower lip, he skimmed a fingertip along the edge of the table. "Mom got sick again and I had to go home and they, well, they didn't like it. Him. Henry. They knew, I think, that he was more than a friend. Dad did, anyway." He paused for a long, quiet moment, then looked up. "Mom was so sick. They hadn't told me how bad she'd gotten. So I had to stay and that meant I had to let Henry go. I had to be there for my folks." His voice rose at the end, as if in question.

Reliable as the tide, Jake's anger rolled back in. The picture in his head expanded. Max had spent his childhood being picked on, and his parents hadn't supported him, obviously. His mom had been too sick and his dad sounded like a right prick. So Max had gone into hiding. But a kid never really lost the need to impress, did he? A guy always craved the approval of his folks. So when they rejected who Max wanted to be, Max retreated into what he thought he needed to be.

How fucking exhausting.

The tide of his anger rolled back out, leaving Jake contemplating a move around the table. Surely Max could use a hug. When was the last time someone had passed on a quiet word of reassurance? Told him he was a good guy, blessed and beautiful and perfect in his own way? Max's tense posture warned him off. One touch and Max might fly up and away, likely never to return.

Okay, maybe not all of his anger had drained away. It would take more than a few minutes to forget the whole fucking off halfway through dinner business, and the week of silence after.

Breathe, Jake.

"So how come you had a girlfriend down here?" Jake asked. Might as well deal with all of it now that they were talking.

Max pushed his arms onto the table. His shirtsleeves caught the edge and slid back, revealing the slim but leanly muscled forearms Jake had admired so often. Running at Pennypack had brought out some freckles. A glance up confirmed freckles also converged around Max's nose. Because he wasn't already cute enough. Swallowing a sigh, Jake waited—and tried not to stare. Tried to remember all the times he'd caught Max looking at him. Had Max ever looked at him like this, with desire spiking through his veins? Could that be why things were so awkward now?

"She asked me out and she seemed nice and I didn't have any friends down here yet."

What was Max talking about? Oh, his girlfriend. Right. "So you ended up with a girlfriend." Jake smiled at that. "That's kind of how I ended up with Kate, you know. We were friends and I just liked her." Had loved her.

"Yeah, I wondered about that. So, you slept with her?"

"Uh, yeah? I got her pregnant, didn't I?'

"How does that work?"

"Well, when a man likes a woman very, very much...."

The twitch of Max's lips held no mirth. "Okay. I guess it was kind of rude of me to ask."

"It's not like you've never been rude before."

"I know. I can be an ass. Elaine calls me on it all the time." Max pushed out a sigh. "So, have you had a lot of girlfriends?"

Jake spread his hands across the table surface. "Listen, Max. I'm happy to talk about my past relationships, but another time, hey? Right now I'd rather talk about you."

"Not much to tell."

"Why didn't you tell me you were gay?"

With another soft blush, Max acknowledged the strike. "Because." His dark brows pinched together in the middle of his forehead and his shoulders hunched together. Then he pushed back from the table. "I... I'm... I...." He stood.

Jake stood as well and rounded the table. He put a hand on Max's arm. "Hey. It's just me, remember? I won't hurt you, Max. Is that what this is all about? Did someone hurt you because of this?"

"Yes."

"Shit, it wasn't your dad, was it?"

"No." Max gave his head a quick shake, brow furrowing more deeply. "He didn't like me being a sissy, but he never laid a hand on me."

"Telling you that was bad enough. What about your mom?" Jake's father had been slower to accept his son's sexuality than his mother, which Jake sort of got. Tony Kendricks had wanted another *man* to take his place. But after he'd figured out that alternating between boyfriends and girlfriends hadn't made Jake any less of a guy, he'd come 'round. Mostly.

Max shook his head again. He opened his mouth and a strangled sound came out. He tried again. "I told her. My mom. I told her the truth before she died. I shouldn't have done it. I shouldn't have let her go like that. But she had this day, a week before. She got up and dressed, she hadn't done that in months." His words were stumbling over themselves, picking up speed. "She made breakfast. She actually cooked. She hadn't cooked in years. Then she sat and tried to eat with me, but she couldn't, because it was in her stomach. The cancer. It was everywhere by then. She couldn't do anything a normal person could do, but she tried and I guess I knew that was it, you know? The last time she'd try."

Jake squeezed Max's arm gently.

Sucking in a quick breath, Max continued in a low, almost confidential tone, "So I told her. I figured... I wanted her to know the truth before she died. So I told her. I told her I was gay and she said, 'I know.'" The blue of his irises deepened with sorrow. "Then, when she died, that last day, she was in such pain. She gripped my hand so hard I thought she might break something. I told her I was sorry. I was, for everything. I tried so hard to take good care of her. But she had to go. It was too bad for her to stay."

Jake knew what heartbreak felt like, and the sharp stab in his chest was suspiciously close. Who had Max had to tell all of this? Not his father, obviously. Probably not his girlfriend either. He'd had to keep this grief bottled up for two years.

"She told me," Max whispered. "She said 'I forgive you,' and I figure she meant for being gay. I don't know if she made peace with it, or if she just figured I was all wrong inside but she wanted to love me anyway."

Wrong inside? Jake pulled Max into a hug then, whether he wanted it or not. Max became a conglomeration of stiff angles, all wriggling elbows and knees. Throat tight, the edges of his vision *not* blurry—because this wasn't his pain, damn it—Jake held on until Max stopped struggling. "You're not wrong inside," he said. "Not at all. You're a beautiful person."

Coming out could be rough. He didn't know anyone who'd just stepped across that line without it hurting in some way. But had Max's parents had to make it so damned hard? No wonder he was so messed up. Max trembled against him and Jake shifted his arms so he could stroke the back of his dark head. He squashed his wonder—at how many times he'd dreamed of doing just this—and concentrated on comforting his friend. The young man who so badly needed him as a friend. His heart twisted and turned as he acknowledged that—he wanted to be so much more to Max, especially now, but pushing his own agenda would only invite disaster. He'd learned patience in prison; now was the time to exercise it.

After a moment, Max pulled away. He kept his head downturned. Jake wanted to lift Max's chin, show him he was there—with him, but understood Max needed to be somewhat alone in his skin. Fuck, being a friend was hard. But if he did this right, the reward would be worth more than his own satisfaction. To see Max truly shine, to be himself, that would be something.

"Okay, so there's something I still don't get," Jake said. "If you like guys and I like guys, why aren't we friends anymore? What happened last week? Why were you so freaked out?"

Max scrubbed at his cheek. "Because it was easy for me to be your friend when I thought you were straight. But knowing you're…." If he shook his head again, it was gonna roll right off his shoulders. "I know you don't like me like that. So I got embarrassed. I just figured I was in the wrong place, pretending to be someone I wasn't and—"

"Wait up. You mean you…." He'd interrupted Max so he could offer a half-formed question. Wonderful. Jake swallowed, but the hope spreading bright wings inside his chest didn't care for such little things as breathing, swallowing, thinking… speaking. Because now, with another of those sudden clicks, the hurt and betrayal on Max's face last Saturday finally made sense and, just like that, Jake could feel his *friendly* resolve crumbling.

He grabbed at some words and put them out there. "You want to be more than friends?"

CHAPTER SIXTEEN

JAKE LOOKED surprised… no, stunned, as if he'd never considered the option. He'd slotted Max permanently into *friend* territory, and why wouldn't he be? Regardless of whether Max wore sparkly outfits like Eric or carried the square confidence of Rob, he really wasn't Jake's type. He didn't have a black belt, and he sucked at *Call of Duty*. He didn't even really want to be gay (mostly) because he lived in fear God or the specter of his mother would strike him down from Heaven. But he'd blurted it out, like the stupid fool he was, and now Jake was stumbling around the polite way to brush him off.

He should have just stayed in his lair.

Jake grabbed his arm again. "Hey. Look at me. Let's get this all sorted."

This was a complete mess. Max had meant to apologize. To try to rekindle the friendship he'd destroyed. But, heck, now he'd spilled his guts and Jake wanted more.

"It's okay. I'm good with being friends," Max said, peeking up at Jake.

"No, you're not."

What?

"Want to know what I think?" Jake asked.

Focusing on the hand clamped around his biceps, Max vacillated between nodding and shaking his head.

"I think we've fucked this up from the start," Jake said. "There's no easy way to say some of this stuff, especially for guys like us. But if we'd been a little more open and honest, we wouldn't be in such a mess."

Lord, he like the sound of *we*.

"I really like you, Max, and I would have made that clearer, sooner. But you're so damned shy. I wanted to make sure you were good with my company before I made a move."

Wait, what? Max's chin jerked up. "You…." His throat locked.

"That's kind of what the dinner was all about. I figured if you were good with Eric and Rob, I'd tell you I liked guys too and if you were good with that, I was gonna ask you out on a date."

The air in Jake's apartment was suddenly very thin. "Me?"

"Yes, you." Jake huffed out a breath. "You really don't see yourself, do you?"

"Sure I do. I'm awkward, skinny, and my hair sticks straight up if I don't push it down. I'm strange and quiet. I'm the guy who gets invited to parties because it would be rude not to, but then I get left in a corner. Unless someone wants something." Bitterness flowed in over the fear that had been pinging through his veins. He didn't really believe Jake would play him. There were good guys out there. Henry had been one. Jake could be another. But fear was a much, much older friend.

Jake considered him for a moment, mouth set into a serious line. Max studied his mouth, as he had so many times before, and wondered what he'd have to do to taste those lips. Was that what Jake meant by asking him out? Was that what Jake wanted, too? Or was he just being kind?

"Know what I see when I look in the mirror?" Jake asked.

Max grunted at the unexpected question.

"I see eyes that aren't really a color. Hair so thick and curly, if I grow it out, I look like a girl. The fact I'm big only makes that whole image more ridiculous. Trust me, a guy my size should not have golden blond curls." His smirk did wonderful things to his mouth. "And I'm a fuckup. I've made so many mistakes in my life. I have a daughter, for Christ's sake, one I've never had a chance to be a proper father to. I'm not husband material. I work construction and I fiddle with furniture on the side. Never even considered going to college. They don't hand out scholarships to 'C' students. I'm not smart. Hell, I don't even follow politics 'cause I don't figure I could ever be a part of it. I just swing a hammer. That's what these big shoulders are good for."

"But you're perfect."

Jake let out a harsh laugh. "I'm so far from perfect, I'd have trouble spelling it."

"That's not true. You're good and kind. You picked me up out of the gutter and let me bleed all over your couch."

"I didn't tell you I considered dragging you out to Beech Street for someone else to find."

"But you didn't. You called you sister and took me to the hospital. And ever since then you've looked out for me."

"Because I like you, Max."

Max's breath hitched. The way Jake said it, with a spark in his *not* colorless eyes. The way his mouth curved into a warm smile, his whole face round and happy. At least Jake hadn't tried to deny being handsome.

"I like you, too." Max nearly choked on the words, but he got them out.

Jake's smile was wry. "If we were in a movie, this would be the part where we kissed."

Max contemplated passing out instead. The air in Jake's apartment was still too thin. His knees shook inside his jeans and his palms itched. Oh, man, he really, really wanted to kiss Jake. But should he? Could he? Why didn't Jake swoop down and get them started? Was he toying with him?

He lifted a shaking hand and put his palm against Jake's chest. Warmth seeped through the cotton of Jake's shirt. He studied the pattern of thread beneath his fingers so intensely, his vision blurred. Jake leaned into his palm.

"It's not enough to reach for what you want, Max. You have to grab it. Take it."

What did that mean?

Max glanced up at the face hovering so close, Jake's breath brushed his skin. He studied the variations of gray and blue in Jake's irises. How could he think his eyes were colorless? "Your eyes are like metal. Warm and cold and sometimes they shine."

Jake's eyes widened at that.

Then Max mustered every ounce of courage he did not have and lifted his chin the bare inch required to close the distance between Jake's mouth and his. He died a hundred times in the second it took to lean forward and take what he wanted—to give it, too. He kissed Jake. He pressed his lips to those more fabulous and sighed as they softened beneath his, as Jake welcomed him, kissed him back. Their lips moved against each other, then together as they caught a rhythm. A hum rising in his throat, Max leaned in for more. Jake's shirt bunched beneath his hand as his fingers curled. Jake snuck a hand around the back of his shoulders. Teeth clacked against teeth. Jake laughed softly, air puffing across Max's mouth. Then Jake leaned in closer and deepened the kiss.

Max closed his eyes and lost himself in Jake's lips, the way they danced with his. The taste—all man, with a hint of pie. The beat of Jake's heart beneath his hand, the scent of his body. Warm and musky. The rasp of stubble as their mouths aligned and realigned, chins bumping together, noses colliding. The graze of Jake's tongue.

Max fell. The kiss claimed him like no other. He was with a man and it felt good and right. As if he'd come home, at last, and found himself there waiting. The scratch of Jake's beard was perfect. The shape of Jake's mouth, the musculature bunching and shifting beneath his roaming hands. The tang of sweat with nothing sweet. The power of the arm banded across his back.

Too soon, the kiss robbed him of breath quicker than he could replenish it. Gripping Jake's shirt, Max pulled away, dizzied, sure the floor would claim him if he let go. He opened his eyes and the world swayed. He looked up and saw Jake looking at him, his gray eyes heavy-lidded and unfocused.

"Wow," Jake whispered.

Wow?

"We could have been doing that since we met," Jake said.

Swallowing a mad cackle, Max shook his head. Then he found his other hand. He'd looped it through Jake's belt. Producing the required blush, he extracted his fingers and rubbed the side of his nose. "I couldn't have kissed you like that for a couple of weeks after you found me."

"Thank Christ I didn't drag you out to Beech Street."

To that, Max could only smile.

Jake stepped back, withdrawing his arm. He pushed his fingers through his hair and just breathed. Max chewed on his deliciously tender lower lip.

"I need to sit down." Jake stumbled toward the table. He dropped back into his chair and put his arms across the satiny wood.

Max sat opposite, noticing as he did so that his jeans were tighter than they had been before. Crap, had Jake looked down? No, he didn't think he had. Oh, man. Was that why Jake had had to sit?

"This isn't what I planned," Max said.

"You didn't plan to make my knees weak?"

"I made your knees weak?"

"Hell yeah. Why do you think I'm sitting down? It was either that or throw you across the couch."

The situation in Max's jeans got harder.

"You're like a secret weapon," Jake continued. "Where did you learn to kiss like that?"

Max's ears rang. "Um...."

Jake waved weakly at him. "'S cool. Best not to divulge all your secrets at once."

Was he serious? Had Max really kissed him breathless? "I only stopped because I thought I might pass out, and not just because I needed air."

"Good to know, man. Good to know."

A grin overtook Max's face, pulled at his mouth so that he could see his cheeks bunching up. He ducked his head and pushed his hands across his thighs, easing the itch, the need to reach across the table and grab Jake's hands.

"Remember that time I told you that you were cute?" Jake asked.

"At Shay's."

"If you could see yourself now."

Now his ears were burning. Max cleared his throat.

Jake indicated the bag sitting in the middle of the table. "Okay, it's time to eat pie. Then we can talk about what we want to do on our date."

"Da-te?" Max swallowed and tried for another smile.

"Yeah." Jake grinned. "Hey, I heard you took Barry down on Wednesday night."

"I tried the tripping thing you taught me."

"Good, I'm glad. Did you go on Friday?"

Max shook his head.

"I texted you, said I'd stay away."

Eyes closing, Max shook his head again. "Jake, I'm so sorry. What I did...." He opened his eyes. "I acted like a child."

"Yeah, you did." Though the comment stung, Max respected the fact Jake hadn't pulled the punch. "You leaving like that kinda twisted everything I thought I knew about you."

Shoulders hitching up, Max considered dodging the issue. He'd given an explanation before, one Jake seemed to have accepted. But now that they had kissed, now that they were planning an actual date, he figured he could offer up the truth. "I...." His lip required a quick nibble before he could continue. "This is kinda stupid, but I felt like an idiot. Not so much because I was surprised, but because I've had this... crush,

I guess? On you. For weeks. Then I found out you liked guys and you'd never made a move, so I figured I was wasting my time. Which is dumb, right? I mean, we were friends. We are friends." Max pushed out a sigh. "I guess you're seeing why I don't have many friends."

"You don't have many friends because you don't let people in."

"Yeah, I know."

Jake stood and went to get plates and forks. He served out the pie, two slices, and pushed one plate across to Max. Digging his fork through the golden pastry, Max watched as red fruit oozed out the sides. Strawberries and odd little square things. "What's this?" He speared one of the pale red pieces and lifted it up.

"Rhubarb."

"Rhu-what? Is it fruit?"

"I dunno, man. It's a stalk thing. All cooked up it's kind of sweet and tart at the same time, like a green apple. It's great in pie."

Max poked the strange fruit into his mouth and bit down. Flavor exploded across his tongue and a low groan set up residence in his chest.

"You're not allowed to groan like that when you eat pie," Jake said.

"Why?"

Jake tipped his head toward the couch and smiled.

Another blush prickled Max's skin. "So, um, does your mom know why you bring home two pieces of pie every week?"

"Yep."

It would be easier to just peel off his skin, Max decided. Just let his blood pulse around freely, making him all pink and awkward looking.

"She wants me to bring you out there. They all want to meet you."

A piece of rhubarb lodged in Max's throat.

"And Willa was going to visit you if we didn't sort ourselves out."

Max managed a painful swallow. "Elaine was going to call you. Or fly over here and kick my ass." That had been a fun conversation.

"Women think they have it all sorted, but they're just as messy. Willa? She's had more boyfriends than I have."

"Is she older or younger than you?"

"Older. They all are. I'm the baby of the family."

Three older sisters. Max had an idea Jake had shared that tidbit before, but every word they exchanged now suddenly felt new and precious. He looked at Jake's mouth, at the lips he'd kissed pretty thoroughly, and felt a twinge in his groin. Jake caught him looking and grinned.

"You like making me blush, don't you?" Max said.

"You know it." Jake scraped up the last of his pie and sucked the tines of his fork. "So, where do you want to go for our date?"

"Um." Max blanked.

He and Melanie had done the movie thing a couple of times. Mostly, they'd just eaten lunch together, or he'd followed her around a shopping mall, pretending he knew the difference between purple and mauve. Mel would talk and talk, pulling on his hand in emphasis every now and then. He'd liked that—holding hands and being the center of someone's attention.

He and Henry had had one date: coffee on campus. They'd spent the next two months naked in one narrow bed or another—when their schedules allowed.

"Maybe we could just stay here?"

Jake had a nice apartment. A very roomy bed.

"Nope. If we stay here, I am going to throw you over the couch, or drag you into my bed and we're not going there until we've had a proper date."

Max frowned. "Why?" His dick could go there right now. In fact, the very mention of couches and beds had him hard again.

"Because I want to do this right, Max. You're not just someone I want to sleep with. I meant it when I said I like you. I'm not looking for a quick fuck."

"Okay." Wow, so... "You want to 'go out' go out, then. Not just one date. Like, be together." He gripped the edge of the table again. He'd slipped and hit his head on the stairs, hadn't he? The kiss, this pie, they were all a dream.

Jake reached across the table and tickled the tips of his fingers. "That's exactly what I want."

"With me."

"With you."

Max gulped at precious air before a helpless smile caught him. "You choose, then. Surprise me."

Jake returned his smile. "All right. Make sure you bring that big grin with you."

CHAPTER SEVENTEEN

TIME HAD passed oddly in prison, some weeks being interminable, others disappearing when he turned his head. Jake supposed time moved like that always, he'd just noticed it more when his days had been strictly regulated. Still, he didn't think he'd ever experienced a week filled with such expectation. Well, maybe waiting for Caroline to be born. But that week had most definitely not been filled with such temptation.

Keeping his hands off Max on Monday night nearly undid him. Thankfully, Alyssa had clued in to the issue right away and assigned them separate partners. While Jake wiped the floor with the sneering Barry, Max worked with Arthur. He snuck in a kiss at Max's door, one that jellied his knees all over again, and bit his tongue over an invitation to more. Max's eyes held a similar spark of urgency.

Why were they waiting until Saturday to go out?

Wednesday, Jake met with his parole officer. He planned to spend the rest of the evening practicing his anger management techniques. Wednesday always seemed a good day for that. Instead, he fell into a brood, as he sometimes did. At least he wasn't out there stirring up trouble, even if his brooding often included creative ideas for fixing the Dominick problem permanently.

Looking for distraction, he called Eric. After verbally ripping his friend a new one, he outlined the events of Sunday night. Eric proclaimed his life more interesting than *The Real Housewives of Atlanta*.

"What makes Atlanta so interesting?" Or more interesting than New Jersey.

"It's not, hon. That's kind of the point."

"You watch crap TV."

"Mmm-hmm, and I will continue to do so, waiting for the date report."

Jake huffed. "I'm not going to call you and tell you about the date."

"Yes you are."

"I'm still pissed at you, Eric."

"You're always pissed at me. That's why we're not together."

"That's not true."

Eric sighed into the phone. "I guess not. You never indulged me like you do Cute Stuff, though."

Jake thought about that for a moment. "Did you want me to?"

"No."

"Then I'm not sure I get your point."

"You're making a fool out of yourself for Max."

At least Eric hadn't called Max *Cute Stuff* while making that particular observation. Jake stared sightlessly at his TV. An immediate denial would only give Eric something to gnaw on.

"I care about him," he said at last. "He needs a good friend." Hell, Max needed a lot of things, but a good friend, even in the guise of a lover, would make a great start.

"Be careful, Jacob."

"What's that supposed to mean?"

"It means I love you, you idiot, and I don't want to see you get hurt."

Jake swallowed the tight lump that had formed in his throat. "Love you, too, Cowboy."

Friday afternoon delivered a text message from Max: *Can't make class tonight. Headache.*

The Date wasn't until tomorrow, but he'd looked forward to seeing Max at their Friday night karate class. Jake pocketed his phone and threaded his way through the remnants of the kitchen he'd been pulling apart, looking for his uncle. He found Brian Kendricks, his father's younger brother, wedged through a ragged hole in the bathroom floor.

"Tell me you didn't just fall through the floor."

Brian stopped pushing at the sides of the broken floorboards and reached up toward him. "Gimme a hand?"

"Did you change the name of your business to Kendricks Destruction while I was away?"

"Har har. It's called renovation, Jake, and if that's what this economy serves up, we're going to keep ripping out kitchens and bathrooms."

"And falling through floors." He pulled his boss out of the hole and spent ten minutes working with him to secure the floor before making his request. "I need to duck out early today."

"Everything okay?" Brian side-eyed him shrewdly.

"It's my neighbor. He's, um, sick I think."

"The kid who got beaten up?" Brian nodded. "Sure. I hope he's okay."

Expressing his concern out loud and getting a response served only to tighten the small knot of worry in Jake's gut. He tidied up his tools and packed up his truck. Then he debated driving to the supermarket to pick Max up from work. The clouds lining up to the west all day had finally started to roll out across the sky. A storm was coming. Max could be prickly about accepting something as simple as a ride, though. He'd turned Alyssa down twice now.

Best just to meet him at home.

The drive was hell. Halfway there, thin raindrops striped his windshield as the clouds finally gave way. The drum of rain against the roof of his truck provided a chaotic soundtrack to visions of Max slipping on the wet pavement, or simply shivering in the sudden downpour.

The rain intensified as he pulled onto Beech Street, the fall of water so thick, Jake could barely see through it, even with the wipers on full. He managed not to hit anyone as he turned into the alley and nosed into his garage. Pulling his shirt up over his head, Jake ducked out of the garage and down the alley. As he pushed the door open, he flashed back to the first time he'd seen Max. It had been a day just like this one and Max had come out of the storm, slim and wet, all pale skin and large blue eyes under a dripping cover of dark hair. Skin prickling, Jake checked the alleyway, but saw nothing but rain. He let the door close with a bang and made for the stairs leading down.

Max opened his door seconds after Jake's knock. His expression brightened immediately, and then a wince of pain creased his forehead. Smile dropping away, he opened the door wider. "Got caught in the storm?"

"Yeah. Did you?"

"Nope. I got in about a minute before it started raining."

"Oh, good." Jake hesitated on the threshold, starting up a puddle and filling it. "Okay, well, I just wanted to check on you. I was worried about you getting caught in the rain and I wanted to pick you up, but I wasn't sure if...." He shut his mouth in an attempt to stop rambling.

Max's brows drew together. "Are *you* all right?" He beckoned Jake inside his apartment. "Let me get you a towel."

"Thanks." He'd just stay a minute, make sure Max wasn't about to hemorrhage from his ears, then head upstairs for a hot shower.

"You want a shower or something?" Max called from the bathroom. He stuck his head through the narrow door. "You look half-drowned."

Warmth bloomed in Jake's chest. Concerned Max was about as cute as Stubborn Max, and for as much as he enjoyed looking out for the kid, having that care returned lit a spark inside. Then he imagined Max in the shower with him. He ached to slide his fingers across his smooth skin, explore his leanness, find the soft places and sensitive spots. A groan tickled his throat and he swallowed it. Right then, right there—wet, cold, and now obnoxiously horny—Jake found it difficult to remember, again, why he wanted to romance Max. Take him out before he took him to his bed. They were guys, right? They were physical beings.

"Jake?"

Jake met Max coming out of the bathroom door. Heedless of his wet clothes, he pulled Max's body against his and bent down the necessary inches to kiss him. As happened every time their lips touched—this would be the fifth time; he'd kept count—Philadelphia receded into a pinprick of nothingness, taking the rest of the world with it. All that mattered was the man in his arms, the mouth beneath his, a tentative flick of tongue, and the hint of peanut butter on Max's breath. He heard and felt a groan. It might have been Max. It might have been him. Didn't matter—all that mattered was Max leaning into him, returning his kiss, fingers pressed into Jake's back, no doubt forming divots in his shirt and flesh.

What was it about Max? Why did the universe begin and end right here, at their lips, the point of contact between them? What would happen when they did have sex? Jake had never felt so simultaneously thrilled and terrified. He'd never wanted anyone this much before.

He pulled out of the kiss and framed Max's face with his hands. Panting, he watched those lovely blue eyes blink open. God, Max was beautiful. With his dark hair and pale skin, he sometimes seemed sylph-like. Insubstantial, but not. The man before him was definitely *there*.

Max's hands were hooked together behind him and they'd squashed any space between them. Tension vibrated off Jake's skin, thrumming just below the frantic beat of his heart. Jake sucked in a ragged breath and commanded his hips not to rock forward. If he felt a similar heat in Max's groin, encountered just a hint of hardness, he'd lose control.

"How's your headache?" he asked.

The crease reappeared between Max's brows. "Is that why you're checking on me?"

"Yes."

"So the plan wasn't to drown me, then. Or kiss me senseless."

Snorting, Jake let go of Max's face and stepped back. Cool air slicked along the skin at his shirt collar and down beneath the sodden fabric. He shivered. "No. Um, towel?"

Max scooped a towel up off the floor and thrust it into Jake's hands. It was thin and nasty, the sort you found at a dollar store, and it smelled the same as everything else in Max's apartment: bleach.

"Do you actually use laundry detergent or do you just bleach everything?" Jake scrubbed his face with sandpaper masquerading as cotton.

"I use both. After my mom.... It's a habit, I guess. From when I was looking after her."

Oh. Right. Jake reached for Max and pulled him into a gentler embrace. Tension kept Max stiff for a breath before he relaxed.

"You're making me even wetter."

Jake dipped down to kiss him, pulling away before control escaped them both. "Do you have any idea what you do to me?"

"I don't think so." Max shared one of his sly smiles. "But I think I like it."

Grinning, Jake backed up again and pulled the thin towel across the front of his shirt. It was hard to tell which piece of fabric was wetter. He was cold, too. "Okay, I need a shower and some dry clothes." He planted another soft kiss on Max's upturned lips. "I'll be back in a few." Was he being presumptuous? "If that's all right."

"It's fine. I'd offer you dinner, but I've only got peanut butter and jelly sandwiches and milk."

"Sounds perfect."

The sudden light in Max's eyes was more perfect.

When he got back downstairs, he found the door to Max's apartment ajar. Jake closed it, joined Max on his uncomfortable couch, and accepted a plate with a sandwich in the middle and a tall glass of milk. Max had changed his shirt, too, and he looked downright cozy in sweats and a long-sleeve T-shirt, legs tucked beneath him, hands loosely folded in his lap. He also looked tired, with dark thumbprints beneath his eyes and a crease between his brows. In front of them, the TV buzzed quietly. Glancing at it, Jake saw a race in progress, probably recorded. He smiled at the thought that the only luxury in Max's hole of an apartment was the DVR situated under his small TV. He sure did like his motor racing. Hopefully he'd enjoy what Jake had planned for their date.

"You going to be up for tomorrow?"

"Yeah. That's kind of why I wanted to stay home tonight." Max frowned. "Is that bad? To skip karate so I'm all good to go out with you?"

"Yep. Shows a complete lack of discipline."

Max sucked in a quick breath. Jake nudged him gently with his elbow. "'S okay. I'm skipping, too. We can either say I'm setting a terrible example, or that I'm pretending to be a mentor or something."

"So if we talk about karate for a bit, we can say we did something."

"Sure." Jake grinned. "Okay, conversation done."

Max laughed and reached out to nudge him in return. "You *are* setting a bad example."

Jake shrugged and finished his sandwich. After draining his glass of milk, he set his dishes aside and turned back to Max. "So, these headaches. Is this a usual thing with you?"

"No. Maybe? I don't know. I guess." He flexed his hand as if that had started to pain him as well. "It's been worse the last couple of weeks. Probably stress," he admitted with downcast eyes. "I've been taking those pills I got from the hospital clinic, but I don't know if they're helping. They just knock me out." He cut a sideways glance. "Fair warning, I took some when I got home. So I'll probably pass out in the next ten minutes. I've already lost feeling in the lower half of my body."

"Huh, I guess I won't be pouncing you tonight, then."

Max grinned and blushed at the same time. "Guess not. I'm okay, though. You didn't have to check on me, or skip karate to sit with me." A note of defensiveness had crept into his voice.

The panic that had driven Jake home that afternoon had subsided. A bit. "I was worried about you."

Max looked ready to prickle, thrust out his thorny spines before retreating into the thick shell he so casually wore. Jake was actually surprised when his shoulders relaxed instead. "Okay."

Jake scooted over. "C'mere. Put your head in my lap. I'll rub it until those pills catch up with you."

Max studied him warily before complying and, even then, he didn't settle the full weight of his head onto Jake's thigh until a minute later. Then a deep sigh left him on a moan, and his head settled in beneath the press of Jake's fingers. "That's good."

"Isn't it? Having your head rubbed is up there with ice cream and sex as the best things in life."

"I don't like ice cream."

Jake's fingers stopped moving. "What did you say?"

Mumbling with fatigue, Max said, "I like popsicles. Lime flavor."

"You're weird."

"I know."

Max didn't say anything after that and a few minutes later, his breathing evened out. Bending forward, Jake studied his face and was relieved to see the lines of pain eased. The tension had disappeared, leaving his forehead smooth once more. Shadows still dwelled beneath his eyes, but it was Friday. Everyone was tired by Friday.

He should go, let Max sleep, but moving was suddenly difficult— the hard and uncomfortable futon had developed some sort of attraction field. So he just sat there, Max's head in his lap, and watched the race. He had no idea who was who, or which car was which. But the steady drone of the engines proved soothing enough that he fell into an easy trance, his heartbeat slow and steady, the warmth of Max creeping through his skin, the swirl of hair beneath his fingers.

He couldn't remember when he'd last felt so relaxed.

CHAPTER EIGHTEEN

"WHEN DID you last service your truck?" Max cocked his head as he spoke, listening again for the telltale syncopation of a loose timing chain. "There. Hear that?"

Jake frowned at him. "Hear what?"

"Your timing is off."

Frown deepening, Jake tipped his head toward the dash and appeared to listen. Then he reached for the radio and turned up the volume of the music. "Hey, I love this song." After humming along for the last line of a verse, Jake bellowed out the chorus.

Max wanted to smile at the joy in Jake's song. The lyrics were ridiculous, but Jake didn't seem to care. Still singing, Jake glanced at him, then reached over. Max ducked the threat of an incoming hair ruffle.

"Your grumpy look is cute," Jake said, "but we're heading out on a date. Smile."

Max fought the natural response to being told to smile. He wanted to scowl more profoundly, though he wasn't sure why. Perhaps because since he and Jake had started kissing, all of his smiles felt goofy.

"We won't be going anywhere if your truck breaks down," he pointed out instead.

The truck had been garaged regularly, that much was clear, but it was old with a capital O. The exhaust was loud, the spark plugs needed cleaning, and the timing was off. It'd rattle like an old man's teeth on the interstate. Max looked up at the windshield where a mechanic usually left the service sticker and squinted until the faded date became clear. That couldn't be right. Jake didn't strike him as the sort of guy to neglect routine maintenance.

"Is that an old sticker?" He pointed it out.

Jake looked up. "I dunno." He fell quiet for a moment. When he spoke again, his tone was guarded. "I guess it's been a while."

"Nearly two years?"

"What makes you so sure there's a problem, anyway?"

"I can hear it." At Jake's quizzical frown, Max continued. "My dad owns a garage. I worked there all through high school and after college."

Jake's brows rose. "Yeah? Awesome." His brows dipped once more. "Oh, so that whining sound—"

Whining? Oh, no. That was bad. "Got any tools?"

"Um, maybe? A few."

"I'll take a look tomorrow."

Jake nodded and a secretive smile crept across his full mouth. "Better make it early. My mom is expecting us for lunch."

"Lunch? I'm not sure if I'm ready to meet your folks."

"How 'bout next weekend, then? Sunday, for Memorial Day. It'll be great. We'll stuff ourselves on burgers and dogs." Jake's smile widened. "And pie. Then there's the parade on Monday."

"Monday is the next day."

"Yes, it is."

"We'd go up there two days in a row?"

"Nah, we'll stay over."

"Stay over?" Timing issues forgotten, Max looked for something to grab, grip, or shred. "I can't stay over at your folks' place. I don't know them."

Jake turned his attention away from the traffic clogging Roosevelt Boulevard to leer at him. "Scared they'll listen for the squeak of bedsprings in the night?"

"Squeak?" He might as well have been a mouse. "But, Jake, we haven't—"

Raucous laughter interrupted him. Jake leaned forward to fiddle with the radio knob again. A breath later, his laughter rolled into the chorus of yet another song, this one featuring a female vocalist. Jake did a reasonable job of matching her, word for word, before her voice soared above his range. He tried to follow, squeaking and squawking. Max clapped his hands over his ears. A glance confirmed Jake continued to laugh at him while singing. Max shrank into his seat and gave in to the flush burning across his skin.

Jake turned down the radio. "You okay over there?"

"I can't stay overnight at your parents'."

Jake smiled gently and reached over to squeeze his knee. "I know. I was kidding about the parade. But they'd all love to see you next Sunday."

"Okay." He'd been outmaneuvered and knew it, but couldn't help being just a little bit excited about having a second date planned before the first had ended.

The truck veered right as Jake left the middle of Roosevelt Boulevard, passing through a gap in the tree-lined median and into the access lane. Car dealerships flanked both sides of the highway, the uniformity of their lots and snapping pennants inducing a sort of calm.

Jake pulled to the curb and killed the ignition. "Here we are." He pushed open his door, checked for traffic, and hopped out of the truck. He had Max's door open before Max finished peering through the window, looking for someplace date-worthy.

"Where's here?" he asked.

Jake pointed to the dealership in front of them. Max absorbed the details without really processing them. The tall Ford sign looked almost black against the early afternoon sky. Sunlight glinted off the top of the oval. The ubiquitous flags and pennants flapped, and the large square of glass covering the front of the showroom seemed to sparkle. Cars and trucks filled the lot. All new, all shiny. As places went, it was a good one. Max loved cars. But why would Jake bring him to a car dealership on a date?

A man approached them, sliding between two small SUVs before stepping over a low barricade. Dressed in dark pants and a crisp white shirt, he possessed a wide, toothy smile and perfectly groomed hair. He was obviously a salesman.

"Jake!" he said, extending a hand.

"Dan the Man. Good to see you." Jake pulled the salesman into a half hug. Backslapping ensued. Jake had several inches on him, but Dan had the comfortable bulk of an older guy. Not fat, just the weight that came with a happy life. Max would bet most folks noticed his handsome face before the fact his shirt billowed a little over his belt buckle.

Dan turned toward Max and stuck out his hand again. "You must be Max."

"Hi." Max shook the offered hand, then stuck his hands in his jeans pockets. When Jake sidled up to him, he squinched in a little, as if making room for him to pass. He flinched when Jake touched his arm.

Jake quirked an odd smile at him. "C'mon. Dan's got a surprise for us."

"Oh?" Weirdest date ever.

"You guys are going to be the first to drive it," Dan said.

Drive it? Max's heart skipped a beat.

It was a Mustang Shelby GT350. Max stopped just outside the halo of its glory and tried to remember how breathing worked. Lord, she was beautiful. Magnetic gray, nineteen-inch wheels and digits on the front quarter panel that had Max's pulse racing. Stepping closer, he reached out to caress the paint, reveling in the feel of something other than model plastic or die-cast covered in lumpy acrylic. He leaned in to peer through the tinted driver's side window and noted the six-speed manual transmission.

"Can you drive a stick?" Dan asked.

Max looked up into the man's very white smile and nodded.

"So, it's a V—"

"Eight, five point two liter DOHC Ti-VCT Shelby." Max turned to Jake. "We're really gonna drive this?"

"You are."

"Why?"

"Because you have Mustangs all over your apartment. I figured you'd like to drive one. Ever driven one before?"

"No." A small tide of sadness rolled through him. The end of his career as a mechanic had arrived with a Mustang. A guy who'd smiled a certain smile, encouraged him to flirt, and caught the adverse attention of Max's father. Shoving away those thoughts, Max produced a grin for the man standing next to him. The big, blond, and beautiful man who had planned the most unusual and amazing date ever. "Thanks, Jake."

Jake smiled and the sun surely dimmed.

"I'll need to see your driver's license," Dan said. When Jake reached for his wallet, Dan waved him off. "Not yours, man. You can't drive it. Sorry."

Max darted a look between Dan and Jake. It was on the tip of his tongue to ask why, but the expression on Jake's face forestalled the question. Instead, he dug out his wallet and produced his license.

Dan took it and waved toward the showroom. "I'll just go get the key."

Dan strode toward the glass cube and Jake sidled up to Max and poked him in the side. "I know next to nothing about cars, but this looks like a pretty sweet ride."

Max laughed. "Yeah, it is. I mean, it's not that a Mustang is the pinnacle of engineering or the car that wins the most races. It's just...." Max searched for a way to explain what made his favorite car so special. "It's the original pony car. It inspired so many other manufacturers. The Mustang came before the Camaro and Challenger. Then there's the name. Did you know it's named for a P-51 Mustang fighter plane?"

Jake's expression hinted he didn't know.

"This is a close as some of us will get to flying."

"It doesn't have wings, does it?"

"I was being metaphorical. It's meant to be fun."

"Well it looks like fun."

Why wasn't Jake allowed to drive it? Max swallowed the question and bit his tongue as Jake's arm landed across his shoulders, drawing him into a casual embrace. He tried not to squirm. Jake had done this wonderful thing for him. Rejecting his hug would be rude. But people could see them standing there, together, looking like they were *together*.

Jake looked down at him. "What's up?"

"Um." Max sucked on his lip and glanced over at a family inspecting an Expedition. His shoulders hitched up and he stepped away, flushing so hard his head swam lightly.

Jake looked at the family and back at Max. The corners of his mouth turned down. Offering a short nod, he stepped back. "Okay."

Of course that made Max want to hug him, but fear kept him still. It was one thing to confess all to Jake in the cozy light of his kitchen, to snuggle against walls, kissing, to rest his head on Jake's lap while they were alone in his lair. But out in public?

Dang it. Jake looked so disappointed and it was weird. Large, tall, and strong men shouldn't look like that. Ever. Swallowing, Max stepped to his side. "Sorry," he mumbled.

Jake pressed a quick, soft kiss to his ear, sending another heated flush across his skin and arcing through his torso, directly to his groin. "It's okay, Max. Take your time. I'm not going anywhere."

A glance confirmed Jake's sincerity, but that extra tinge of gray had not left his eyes.

Dan returned with the keys.

Jake claimed the front passenger seat. Dan happily folded himself into the back. Max sat in the driver's seat and stared at the cockpit, jaw slack, the smell of new, clean upholstery addling his senses. He caressed several of the controls before tweaking everything, learning the layout. Then he started the engine and listened to the pitch rise and fall as he depressed the accelerator. The sound moved through him with the thrill of deep-rooted lust and when he glanced over at Jake's heavy-lidded expression, Max thought he might never manage a full breath again.

He adjusted his seat and mirrors and eased off the clutch. It had been a while since he'd driven, but the Mustang responded beautifully to his tentative step, surging forward with an eager purr. "Oh, my God." He hadn't even left first gear.

Moments later, each counted and catalogued, Max merged onto the left lane of the turnpike. With Saturday afternoon traffic, he couldn't really open her up. His foot itched with the need to press down, unleash the power of all eight cylinders. "I wish we were on the interstate right now."

Dan laughed. "I can let you have her for about fifty gees. Then you can take 80 all the way to San Francisco and back." He tapped Jake on the shoulder. "Hey, there's a plan for you, Jake. Rent your boyfriend a Mustang for a couple of weeks. Take a trip."

Boyfriend.

"Might have to check that out," Jake murmured.

Max dropped back a gear, swerved into the right lane, accelerated and popped forward, back into the fast lane. Jake let out a whoop. "Man, I wish we were on 80 as well. Or somewhere out in the middle of nowhere."

"You know, they've got a test track at Penn State," Max said.

"Yeah?"

"At the College of Engineering. I went to check it out one time. They were test-driving buses. Not that exciting." Driving a Shelby around that track would be much, much more thrilling.

He wove through traffic for another mile, used the next exit, roared across the flyover, and merged back onto 276, heading south. More familiar with the beast, he took more risks, delighting in each whoop from Jake and every hiss from Dan in the backseat. By the time they returned to the dealership, his cheeks hurt from grinning. When he stepped out of the car and reluctantly relinquished the key, he had to squash the urge to jump up and down. Adrenaline still pumped through his veins.

Turning to Jake, Max socked him on the arm. "I'm still buzzing."

Jake beamed. Even Dan's raised brows didn't detract from Max's joy, from seeing Jake so happy. The shadows had disappeared from his eyes. He looked calm, seemed calm, until Max asked, "You don't want to have a go?"

Expression sobering, Jake shook his head. "Hey, if I can't tell my truck is about to keel over, I don't belong behind the wheel of a Mustang."

"Maybe you've just been driving the wrong car all this time."

Jake snorted. "Find me fifty grand and we'll talk about which car might be right for me."

Dan flipped the key up and down. "So, you guys done for now?"

Max nodded and stuck out his hand. "Thanks, Dan."

"No problem. Come by again. If she's still here, we can take her for another spin."

"Sure. Thanks." Jake hugged Dan again and they headed back to Jake's truck. "You look like you're still flying," Jake observed over the roof as he fitted his key into the lock.

"I kind of am," Max said. "That really was awesome." A truly amazing thing to do for a friend, or for a date. Jake really was a great guy. "Thanks. This was the best date I've had."

"Oh, we're not done yet."

"We're not?"

Jake shook his head. "The best dates include a meal."

"They do?"

"Have you actually ever been on a date, Max?"

"I took Melanie out a couple of times."

"Dinner and a movie?"

"Mostly just the movie part. You know, when I think back, I was a pretty crap boyfriend." He pulled open his door and slumped into his seat. "It's a wonder she didn't dump me before I messed up my face."

"If it's any consolation, I don't think she dumped you over your messed-up face."

Max pondered that a moment. "Not a consolation." A smile pulled the corners of his mouth. "But I suppose I'm glad that things didn't work out with her."

Jake winked at him. "I am, too." The truck coughed and spluttered to life. "You like noodles?"

"Maybe. Like spaghetti?"

"No. Not like spaghetti. Vietnamese noodles. And crispy little bits of unidentified animal parts. And shit that will sear your tongue like nuclear waste."

"I'm not buying whatever you're selling, Jake."

"Adventure, Max! I'm selling adventure and you're going to love it."

"Can we stop by the auto parts store first?"

Jake chuckled. "Sure."

CHAPTER NINETEEN

THEY STOOD in the alley, just outside the garage, Max waiting while Jake lowered the door. The sky glowed a dusky purple and the street sounds were muted. But the night hadn't deepened enough for shadows to threaten, and the cooler air touched Jake's skin in a gentle caress.

"My lips are totally numb," Max said, touching his mouth.

Jake laughed. "I told you not to eat the red stuff."

Max shot him a confounded look. "But you *did* tell me to eat the green stuff and that was disgusting. Like eel guts or something."

Laughter rolled through Jake again, from his belly all the way up through his chest. The deep laugh felt good, really good. "Okay, the salad was definitely weird. But the soup was good, right?"

"The soup was awesome. Even with the lemon juice, which was weird. But it worked." Max's expression sidled into coy. "Could you make soup like that? With the noodles?"

"I bet I could try."

Max's mouth moved, framing words, and then he sucked on his lower lip. Jake reached over to touch his shoulder, just gently, aware of the virtual prickles Max had extruded earlier that afternoon. Public displays of affection apparently unnerved him. Jake hoped that particular fear would fade with time. But watching Max drive the Mustang had been like seeing the sun peek out from behind a rain cloud. He'd glowed, well and truly. He'd smiled wide enough it must have hurt. His confidence as he shifted through gears and steered the car with an amazingly deft touch had been incredible. Max drove well, really well, and he obviously knew how to treat a sports car.

He'd demonstrated a verbal mastery of shifting gears at dinner as well, cranking the subject away from his father whenever Jake managed to turn it there. After two attempts, Jake stopped trying. He didn't need to know all about Max, not yet. He knew watching Max try food he couldn't pronounce made him about as happy as watching him drive a car. He knew he needed to kiss those numb lips, encourage the blood to flow back there, incite a tingle.

"How about if I look up a recipe some time and we try to make it together," Jake said.

Max's smile exceeded the limit of shy. "I'd like that."

As Max hadn't stiffened at his touch, Jake wrapped his hand around his shoulder and pulled him a little closer. "You want to come up? Or do you have other plans?"

"Other plans?"

Jake nodded toward the garage. "Like getting frisky with Tanya."

"Tanya?"

"I didn't tell you my truck had a name?"

"You did not." Max stepped forward. "I think Tanya can wait until morning."

Hallelujah.

"I had a really fun day, Jake." The earnestness in Max's expression plucked at everything inside Jake's chest.

"Good." He bent down and spoke against Max's mouth. "This is not a good-night kiss, just so you know. This is a come-upstairs-with-me kiss."

He pressed his lips to Max's and found them ready to receive, softened and parted. Max's hands slipped around his waist in a gesture that had already become familiar. Jake skated his fingers along Max's jaw, cradling his beautiful face, and leaned in more, needing to possess his mouth, his tongue. Wanting to leave Max breathless and devoid of thought. When a soft moan rose out of Max's throat, Jake figured he was halfway to his goal. A moment later, Max pulled away, though his hands remained tangled in the back of Jake's shirt.

"How are those lips doing?" Jake asked.

"What lips?"

Jake grinned. "Not sure that's the response I was looking for."

Max's mouth twitched. Then he seemed to notice his fingers were still attached to the back of Jake's shirt and that they were standing pressed together, their words bouncing off each other's mouths. "Hard to think when we're this close."

Jake cupped the back of Max's head and sifted his fingers through soft brown hair. "Mmm-hmm."

"Can we go upstairs?"

"God, yes."

He'd had a plan for when they got upstairs. That plan had not included pushing Max up against the nearest wall and claiming his mouth again. Thankfully, this derailment went a lot more smoothly than his runaway dinner party. Max did not ease out of his grasp, did not back away, did not turn tail and run. The lingering heat of chili and spice on Max's lips drove Jake's desire higher, nudging further thought aside, and Max's response, the moans building in his throat and the eager thrust of his tongue, the fact his hands had slipped beneath Jake's shirt and started tracing a path up his back, tended to indicate he was okay with Plan B.

Lips thoroughly engaged, Jake fell into the myriad sensations of a close kiss: the scent of another man, the heat of his skin, the taste of a sweet mouth and tongue, the press of another body—hard and lean. Max dug his fingers into the flesh of Jake's back, sparking a thrill that traveled inward and down. He was like some weird drug. The more Jake had, the more he wanted. Ignoring the mental whisper to slow down, Jake rocked his hips forward. A loud groan tore from his throat as the hardness beneath his zipper bounced off similarly strained denim. What little blood he had left shot south, stiffening him further. Max made a sound and clutched at Jake's skin. A moment later, he rocked back, his head connecting with the wall. The muffled thump echoed through their short gasps.

"You okay?" Jake reached behind Max's head to feel for a lump. Their hips were still attached and he found it difficult to think with all his being centered at his groin.

Max stared at him, eyes darkened by pupils blown wide, lips parted in invitation. He pulled his hands out of Jake's shirt. "Need air."

With the moment suspended, Jake eased himself away. Jesus it was hard. *He* was hard.

So was Max.

"Are you good with this, Max?"

"Why wouldn't I be?"

Jake examined that response a minute, but his blood-starved brain served up little. "I was gonna suggest we play Xbox some after dinner, but I think we're way beyond that."

Max's mouth, kiss-reddened, quirked into a smile.

Jake suddenly felt like the twenty-one-year-old. Briefly, he worried the situation took advantage of Max's obvious naiveté. But logic couldn't argue with the fact they both panted irregularly, or that both of them seemed about ready to bust out of their jeans.

"I want to taste more of you," Jake said, leaning in to nuzzle the slender line of Max's neck.

Max stuttered. "Okay."

"But not up against a wall."

Max's teeth grazed his earlobe.

Growling, Jake pulled a grinning Max off the wall and led him across the apartment to his bedroom, where Plan B escalated quickly. In the half dark, Max's silhouette called to Jake. He slid his hands across Max's waist and up under his nice, neat polo shirt. As he whisked it over Max's dark head, he caught the familiar odor of bleach and detergent. He leaned down to nip Max's ear and a shiver caught them both. Max tugged Jake's button-down upward and huffed impatiently when it got caught on Jake's upraised arms. Jake flinched when warm lips touched his bare chest. With his arms over his head and his shirt covering his face, he could do little but stand and gasp as Max trailed kisses across his skin. A tongue flicked across his nipple and a string pulled taut beneath the sensitive point and his groin. His cock jumped. Jake groaned and wrestled with his shirt. He got it over his head, tossed it to the floor, and wrapped his arms around the spare figure before him. Max worked across his chest to the other side.

Jake stroked Max's jaw and tilted his face upward. He could only see the shadow of his features, the hint of a bump at his nose, dark pools where his eyes were. Still, Max seemed beyond lovely. Jake had never considered another man beautiful before. Handsome, sure. Attractive, sexy, doable. Max fell into a different category altogether.

He leaned forward so their foreheads touched and indulged in a reciprocal exploration of Max's lean chest. His callused fingers discovered firm lines of neat musculature and raised goose bumps.

"Cold?"

"No, just really, really turned-on."

Jake smiled. Max's eagerness didn't entirely surprise him. He didn't know if it was the whole "still waters ran deep" thing, or the fact Max simply continued to stand, stubbornly, despite the obstacles in his path. A core of iron existed inside this man, an indomitable will, and that spoke of passion—for life and right now, for him.

It was a potent thought.

Max's fingers spread across his chest, sifting through fine golden curls. Jake explored Max's form in a similar manner, noting the smoothness of his skin, the hint of hair beside tiny, tight nipples. Max pushed at his chest and Jake rocked back toward the bed, grinning stupidly. Max's expression showed determination, which further roused him.

"God, you're sexy."

Eyes widening briefly, Max cleared his throat. "So are you."

Lifting his chin, Jake preened for Max, squaring his shoulders, flexing in the most unassuming manner he could muster. Max grinned. Then they were on the bed together, lips attached once more, time and space suspended by heady exploration, fingers pinching and caressing all the way down to belt buckles. The brush of warm skin against his bare skin pulled a deep groan from Jake's chest. His hips acquired a rhythm, one Max met. Grinding up, Jake gasped and growled. The clink of belts and rasp of zippers interrupted a pattern of needful breath. Cool air tickled Jake's bare hips.

Jake rolled over Max so he could explore that smooth chest with his tongue, intending to work his way down to his loosened jeans. He licked the underside of Max's jaw and kissed his way across the hollow of his throat. From there, he advanced upon a tight nipple. The soft bite of his teeth pulled a moan from Max. Long fingers drove into Jake's hair, nails scratching at his scalp as he bit Max's other nipple. Dragging his tongue down the hollow between Max's ribs, Jake paused at the divot of his navel. There, he pressed a kiss. Max chuckled and his abs tensed as he raised his head.

"Did you just kiss my belly button?"

"I did."

He licked the skin below the tiny puddle of shadow, and finally encountered the sparse hair of Max's happy trail. Max's head flopped back and another groan drifted down. Jake grinned as denim brushed his chin, Max's hips following an involuntary current upward. He worked Max's jeans down to his knees, pausing only to lick at his thighs. Max had a runner's legs—long and lean with every muscle apparent. Fine, dark hair shaded every line, making him appear delicately sculpted. There was not a spare ounce on his entire body. Beneath his jeans, Max wore very conventional underwear: white briefs. Jake pulled the waistband out and down, grinning as a very erect penis bounced back up. Long, not quite slender. Beautiful; and the bead of moisture at the crown called to Jake's tongue.

With a hiss, Max curled his fingers into Jake's scalp. His hips bumped up again, thighs quivering with palpable tension. Jake pressed his tongue down, rode the buck, and wrapped his lips around Max's cock. The kick of Max's hips became more restrained, which Jake appreciated. The fingers curled against his hair spread as Max gasped and moaned. Jake hummed in response and those narrow hips jerked. He'd barely gotten his hand around Max's shaft, fingers riding up to meet his lips, when the pitch of Max's moans changed. A single nudge to his tight nuts sent him up and over.

"Jake! I'm gonna…." A soft shout followed the rest of the warning.

A hot rush of fluid hit the back of Jake's throat, nearly choking him. It had been a while, a stupidly long while, and he'd never been a fan of swallowing. The idea of leaving Max's experience half done had him persisting, however. He wanted to ride the high with his lover, taste him, and bring him down slowly.

When Max finished shuddering, Jake crawled back up the length of him and pressed a kiss to his slack mouth. Max's tongue flicked out, surprising him, and his deep blue eyes opened.

"That was embarrassing." His voice was dry and creaky.

"That was sexy," Jake countered. The pace of Max's desire and quick release stoked his ego.

"I… I want to do you, too."

God, yes. Still caught in his boxers, Jake's erection jerked. Pressing his hips forward so that he nudged Max's thigh, he said, "If you wanna." *Please.*

"I feel like a noodle."

Chuckling, Jake tucked his face into the crook of Max's neck. He licked at the sheen of sweat there, and kissed the underside of his jaw. Max's skin pimpled again and another shudder rippled through him.

Max had his hands draped loosely across Jake's shoulders. He slid them downward, fingers sculpting Jake's biceps. Kissed his cheek before touching his lips to Jake's ear. "Thank you."

"I've wanted to do that for a long, long time."

A flush stole across Max's skin, darkening his cheeks and the top of his chest. "Me, too. Both ways." Max slid a slender hand between them, fingers fanning out across Jake's chest. "I've wanted to touch you all over." His expression darkened momentarily before he smiled and pushed at Jake's chest. "Okay, my turn."

"You mean my turn."

"Works both ways, doesn't it?"

Yeah, it did.

Max took his time exploring Jake's chest and despite the near pain in his groin, Jake exercised his patience. He ran his hands over the back of Max's shoulders, admiring the smooth skin as Max dotted kisses down between his pecs, sucked on his nipples, and explored the bumps of his abdominals. Jake's caresses were somewhat absentminded, though— Max's touch had all his attention. Plus some. He'd fallen under the spell of his lover, of those sweet lips and the pattern they wove across his skin. Of the brush of Max's lean limbs against his own. The slight weight of him as he moved steadily downward.

His hips strained upward as Max pulled his jeans farther down. A second later, his boxers joined the fold of material at his knees and a warm hand had grasped his cock.

"Yes," Jake hissed.

He looked down at Max and met his steady gaze. Eyes locked on his, Max bent to swipe his tongue over his tip. Jake thought he'd come right then. The look in Max's eyes, the way he held his attention. Then Max released him, but only visually. Lashes lowered, he took Jake into his mouth and began to work. And… Jesus H. Christ he'd done this before. Jake had been prepared for inexperience, he'd almost looked forward to the role of tutor, but the firm press of Max's tongue, the tight ring of his lips, and the perfectly synchronized motion of his hand pushed all such thoughts from his mind.

Dropping one hand to the bed so he could clutch at the quilt rather than Max's hair, Jake worked at not snapping his hips upward. Experienced or not, he did not want to choke the man so lovingly tending his cock. It was hard to hold back. He wanted to grind up and in, he wanted to rut. He wanted to fuck Max's mouth. Lose himself in Max, be forever connected to him. Ride him, be ridden. Slip inside and claim him.

Max's hand plowed beneath his hip, fingertips digging into the meat of his ass, encouraging him to move. Jake gave in to the urge and rocked gently against Max's mouth. The suction increased. Before he could establish a proper rhythm, his body betrayed him. For nearly two years, his only partner had been his hand. A warm and willing mouth was always going to undo him in minutes.

Tension snapped all his tendons tight and a wave rolled down his spine, into his groin. His nuts drew up and he shot through the eye of the needle—all of him, every last inch of self. He echoed his own yell, chasing his voice across the room. Max's mouth was still there, milking him. Jake tried to pull him away, the push of his hands little more than a nudge, but Max seemed wonderfully content sucking his pulsing length. The sight of that nearly had him coming again.

Time stretched and contracted. Then a familiar scent tickled his nose. Lips touched his, a reciprocal kiss, and Jake flicked his tongue out, mimicking Max's earlier tease. He tasted himself and Max. He tasted their evening and whatever had bloomed between them. Opening his eyes, he met the expected gaze, deep and velvety blue, and reached up to wrap his arms around the man smiling down at him.

"That was 'mazing," he slurred.

Max's smile widened and a deep flush crept across his cheeks. "Good."

Dipping down, Max kissed him again before sliding off to the side and flopping onto his back. Jake let him go. He felt slack—like a noodle—and the warmth of Max at his side was just right. He rolled his head sideways and studied Max's profile. Max's lower lip disappeared and his brow furrowed. The lip popped out, wet and shiny.

Uh-oh. Max's thinking face. Jake waited for the penny to drop— not really wanting to hear it.

"We still have our shoes on," Max said.

Laughter rolled through Jake, cramping his belly before flowing up and out. This was the second round of deep laughter Max had pulled from him. The second proper, all-consuming laugh he'd given in to in more than a year. He reached to his side and found Max's hand. Jake threaded their fingers together, noting the stickiness of their skin. His spunk and maybe Max's as well. He reveled in the knowledge they wore one another's pleasure. That the tang of it lingered on their tongues.

Max's fingers squeezed his and that gorgeous face tipped toward him, lips upturned in one of his sly little smiles.

CHAPTER TWENTY

"WANNA TAKE a shower?" Jake asked.

Max scratched at the flaky patch of semen on his cheek. He suspected his other hand was stuck to Jake's. Sure enough, when he tugged, he pulled both of their hands up off the bed. "You might have to chisel us apart first."

"Not if we shower together."

"Oh. Okay."

Jake grinned. "You thought playtime was over, didn't you?"

"I hoped it wasn't."

"See, this is why I like you."

Jake made a show of pulling their hands apart, peeling Max's fingers away one by one. It was silly, funny, and somehow sweet. Freed from the clasp, Max sat up to finish undressing. By the time he'd kicked off his shoes, jeans, and underwear, Jake stood by a similar pile of castoffs.

He pulled Max to his feet. "C'mon, slowpoke."

Max allowed himself to be led toward the bathroom in much the same manner he'd allowed himself to be led toward the bedroom. Jake was a huge, sexy magnet, and he was compelled to follow.

Mixed memories assaulted him in the bathroom. He remembered being there the day he'd been released from the hospital, fuzzy and disoriented. He hadn't really known Jake then, or what to make of him. A month and a half later, he'd rushed in here after learning about Jake and Eric's lip-lock. Of all the idiotic things to do. If he'd stayed for the rest of dinner—if he'd remembered he was nearly twenty-two, not twelve—he and Jake might have been showering together two weeks ago.

Or last week.

Or....

Jake turned on the shower and nudged Max gently against the only wall not cluttered by cabinets and appliances, a slender slice of space between the closet and shower. He put his hands to either side of Max's shoulders and leaned in, lips brushing over Max's temple. "What's up?" he murmured.

Max looked up into eyes that twinkled with gentle humor and concern. What could he say that didn't sound weird? "I was just thinking—"

Jake cut him off with a kiss. After robbing Max of breath and thought, he moved away just far enough to touch their noses together. "All gone?"

"What?"

"Perfect." Jake opened the shower door and pulled Max inside.

Steam wrapped cautious fingers around his skin. Jake pulled him in closer. Their bodies slid together, half-wet and tacky, skin sticking as much as slipping. The hair on Jake's chest and thighs tickled. The press of his hard body excited. Max gasped as arousal shunted through him, hot and cold. Spray bounced off the walls, stinging his eyes, so he closed them, and that just made it all the easier to lean into Jake's embrace. With one hand, Jake cradled the back of his head. Max loved it when he did that, when Jake held his head, pushed his fingers through his hair. No one had touched him this way before, with such unaffected fondness, as if he were something precious.

Tucking his arms around Jake's waist, Max pressed his cheek to Jake's shoulder. A sigh stuttered out of him. Only slightly embarrassed, he sucked in a much shallower breath.

The sharp scent of soap cut through the sweaty steam. Jake rubbed at his back, washing and massaging at the same time. So blissful. After a full day and a suborbital orgasm, a soapy back rub was just what he needed.

Jake moved his hand down. Breath rushed from Max's lungs as Jake groped and squeezed his ass, fingers brushing past the cleft between his cheeks. Max shivered at the tease of it, the difference between gentle washing and obvious exploration. Involuntarily, his hips jerked forward. Jake's half-hard cock twitched against his hip. He imagined Jake behind him, hand replaced by something harder, thicker. He hadn't gone there in his fantasies. Hadn't allowed himself to imagine the feel of Jake inside him. He didn't dare. But now, with Jake's fingers sliding below one buttcheek, he couldn't think of anything else.

Jake growled softly. "You drive me wild, Max. The way you move, the sounds you make." He'd been making sounds? "You make me so hard." Jake nuzzled his ear. "Have you any idea how many times I had to adjust my pants, just today?"

Pulling his face away from Jake's shoulder, Max looked up. Their cheeks slid together, Jake's rough with stubble, and before he could say anything, their lips connected. The magnet thing again. Kissing Jake could be Max's favorite pastime—probably even better than watching motor racing, totally on par with driving a Mustang. Maybe even better than that, considering what kissing had led them to a half hour ago, what it might lead to now. Jake's lips were incredible. Full, like Jake. But not hard. Jake's tongue touched his and Max sighed into the kiss. The fingers cupping his ass dug into his flesh and his groan seemed to echo in the small space. Max ground forward, then remembered he had hands. He stuck one between them, grabbing Jake's erection, and smiled into the kiss as Jake's groan chased his.

Jake broke the kiss and leaned back to grab the soap. He sudsed up and dropped a pile of pink foam onto Max's hand. Max worked the slippery bubbles down the length of Jake's cock and reached under to squeeze his balls. He grinned as Jake's legs vibrated against his. A shudder. He'd made Jake shudder.

Jake widened his stance and tucked a hand between them to tend Max's erection, tugging and sliding with soapy fingers. Then Jake pulled their dicks together. The velvet slide of hot flesh to hot, sensitive flesh was incredible. Wrapping his hand around them just above Jake's, Max rocked his hips up and in.

"Max," Jake panted.

Realizing he'd said nothing for a while, Max attempted to speak and produced only a strangled grunt. Fingers slid up between his buttocks, almost but not quite touching the place he most wanted to be touched. He burned with the need to be touched there, to have Jake stroke his hole, breach the tight ring of muscle. He was grateful for the more restrained gesture, too. He felt safe. Jake would respect his wishes even while pandering to his desires.

With two hands wrapped around their erections, Max was close. The tease of Jake's fingers at his backside only pushed him higher, closer. Jake's hitched breaths and growly groans indicated he couldn't be far off—that and the jerk of his cock, the buck of his knees and hips as they rocked together, rutting under the warm spray of the shower, bodies slick with soap and water. Max bent forward to flick his tongue over one of Jake's nipples. He'd gotten a good reaction to that before, and this time, Jake did not disappoint. He hissed and shuddered. Max caught the firm nub between his teeth and sucked, the soft blond covering of hair over Jake's chest tickling his lips. Jake shook again and the larger hand between them, the one truly holding their cocks together, gripped just a bit tighter.

Max felt that rocket ship launching again, engines burning, roaring. Or maybe that was him.

"Oh, God." Yep, definitely him, and he couldn't manage more than that.

The press of a finger right where he wanted it, *needed* it, two more sure strokes between them, the weight of Jake's body against his, harsh breaths gusting across his ear, and Max took off, shooting so hard his body screamed. Stars exploded across his vision and the light in the bathroom grayed and dimmed. Jake roared across his ear and liquid heat covered his hand and stomach. Their rhythm faltered, aligned and jerked out of sync again. Jake gripped his ass, pulling him close, and the world tilted as they rocked into a wall. Throughout, the hiss of the shower continued unabated, an odd accompaniment to their off-key symphony.

When he could see again, Max blinked into the spray of water. His cheek was smooshed up against Jake's chest. He could hear Jake's heart thudding. His breath was unsteady. The last orgasm, coaxed out of him by Jake's fabulous mouth, had been amazing. This one? Max wasn't sure if he still lived, if the breath whispering across his lips had any life-sustaining power.

"Holy hell."

"Pretty sure hell isn't holy," Max muttered.

Jake laughed quietly, his body rocking against Max's, knocking him gently back into the wall.

"You're probably right." Jake wrapped a hand around his shoulder. "Tell me you're as whacked as I am."

"If you move away from the wall, I'm going to fall down."

"Good enough."

Jake dipped down to kiss him, and Max had no choice but to lift his chin. He'd never wanted a kiss more. Rather than steal his breath, Jake tasted his lips delicately, the kiss sweet and light. Again, Max felt cared for in a way he couldn't quantify, so he simply fell into Jake's embrace.

It was easier than thinking. Thinking was overrated. For now, he just wanted to exist. To be happy.

Moving them back from the wall, Jake reached for the soap again and they washed each other, slowly and carefully, both at the same time. Max grinned as Jake tickled his hip. Jake sighed as Max dug soapy fingers into his lower back. Each caress edged toward sensuality, but never quite crossed the line. Lust thrummed just below the surface. Sated, they managed restraint. Instead, Max spent the time admiring the body of the man before him. Tracing every line of muscle, every unexpected curve. Discovering small scars and, when he moved behind, an impressive tattoo etched across the back of Jake's left shoulder.

Max smoothed his hands across the patterned skin, over the circle of two fish, each chasing the tail of the other. One was outlined in sinuous strokes of black ink, the other almost all black, unmarked skin forming the outline and suggestion of movement. Max had seen the design before, but not with fish. One dark, one light.

"Is this a yin and yang symbol?" Max traced the outline of the darker fish, his finger running over a strip of smooth, unmarked skin.

Jake glanced over his shoulder, as if he'd forgotten he even had a tattoo. His cheek rounded as he smiled. "Yeah."

"Do the fish mean anything?"

"I liked the idea of one driving the other, or chasing. It could be either, right? That's what balance is about. Movement. Life isn't a spectator sport." Leaning forward, Jake braced against the wall, hands flattened against the tile. "It's also me, in a way. I spent a lot of time wondering who I was when I was younger. I guess we all do. Being attracted to both guys and girls had me spinning in place a little longer than most, I suppose. When I got the tattoo, it was my way of making peace with the duality of being, of not being what I sometimes appear to be."

Max's postcoital state lent both more and less meaning to Jake's explanation. On the one hand, he understood it perfectly, and the confession—if it had been that—warmed him. He wasn't the only guy to struggle with his identity. On the other hand, he didn't get it at all. Jake was the strongest guy he knew. The most settled and even. He saw no yin to his yang, or vice versa. But he did appreciate the fact Jake had a new depth to him, a thoughtful, almost philosophical nature that made absolute sense. This was why Jake was kind and good. Why he took the time to do things right. Why he breathed easily and contentedly. Why he laughed and sang. Why he seemed to be such a complete person.

Jake turned around and slid his hands around Max's shoulders. He didn't pull Max into a hug, just rested with him in a loose and easy embrace. "We're all struggling, Max. Each and every one of us. Every day. Some of us just hide it better. Or cope better." He moved one hand up over Max's shoulder to caress his neck, the underside of his jaw. "You're going to get there before I do."

Max shook his head.

An easy smile pulled at Jake's full mouth. "Oh, yeah, you are, and I'm gonna be the one clinging to your coattails. I'm going to ride up with you."

"Why?"

The hand at his jaw tipped his chin up so Jake could lean in to meet his lips. "Because that's what I want to do."

Not a philosophical answer, but honest.

The water cascading over Max's shoulders had lost most of its heat. Jake leaned around him to shut off the shower and they stepped out together, arms wrapped around their elbows. Jake pushed a fluffy towel at him and Max scrubbed his face and hair before swiping his back and shoulders, then bending to dry his hips and legs. He patted gently at his groin, smiling at his flaccid length.

"Did I wear you out yet?"

Max looked up, grin intact. "Pretty much." He could be coaxed back to life. The tingle beneath his skin suggested it wouldn't be hard. But much as he'd like to explore more with Jake, Max would rather bask in the contentment he had gained. The sense of peace. The closeness they had forged.

"Will you stay?"

Max froze, contentment sliding from a happy buzz to a panicked chirp.

Jake gripped his shoulder again. His thumb poked up, nudging Max's chin. "I promise I won't molest you in the night." Sparks lit his gray eyes, a sure sign Jake was amused. "Maybe." His thumb swiped along Max's jaw. "I just want to fall asleep holding you."

Breath caught in Max's throat. He looked up properly, searching Jake's gaze for the joke, the hint he had something more to say, a punchline. Instead, he saw affection and kindness. The warmth he'd experienced from Jake since the day they'd met. And something else: a quiet yearning.

The image of Jake's tattoo flashed through his mind, of two fish chasing one another in an endless swirl. He'd found that interpretation frustrating, and he'd wondered how it applied to Jake, who seemed so sure of himself. Always. Staring at the man who just wanted to cuddle him—after milking him dry, twice—Max thought that maybe he didn't really know Jake very well at all. But he wanted to. The need in Jake's eyes echoed something Max had carried inside for a long, long time.

He put his hand over Jake's, caressing the thumb at his jaw, and turned to kiss Jake's palm. The skin there was soft, but he found a callus at the base of Jake's thumb. He kissed that, too, before looking up and mustering a smile that might have wavered. "I'll stay."

CHAPTER TWENTY-ONE

"READY?" JAKE asked. They were standing outside the front door of his parents' home in Doylestown. The rambling split-level ranch had a lot of windows facing the street, but no one had spotted them yet. Likely, everyone was sitting outside on the patio. Normally Jake would walk around the side, barrel through the gate, and claim a spot. For Max's first visit he'd decided on a more formal approach.

"Yes." Max's tense little smile said otherwise. Thumbprints shadowed his eyes again with the startling effect of deepening the blue of his irises. Or maybe it was his shirt, the same blue check from dinner three weeks before, tucked into the same jeans. Both had been laundered recently; Jake could smell the strong detergent Max used. Idly, he wondered how Max's clothes didn't end up stripped of all color. He reached out to smooth the hair flopped casually across Max's forehead and stopped, turning his hand toward his lover's cheek instead. Max leaned into the caress, but his smile didn't strengthen. If anything, he became more nervous.

"I know it's kind of soon, but if we were just friends, I'd have brought you out here anyway."

"Yeah." Max's smile quirked up on one side. "You've only asked me every week since the first." He had, at that. "Do we have to tell them we're... you know?"

Resignation clutching his gut, Jake shook his head. "No. We're still friends, right?" Despite the fact they'd gotten each other off five times over the past week. Trying not to touch Max inappropriately during their shared karate lessons had been hell.

Stuffing his hands into his pockets lest he pull Max into his arms, or simply caress him, embarrass him, Jake continued, "I meant what I said on our date. Take your time. I'm not going anywhere. I just want to spend time with you. When you're comfortable with me smooching you in public, let me know, and I'll try not to embarrass you with my affection."

Max ducked his head, but his smile had widened.

Jake rocked forward onto the balls of his feet and pressed a kiss to Max's forehead. "Last kiss," he murmured. He could be patient. He'd breathe through the spikes of need, apply the techniques he'd learned in class, in prison. He'd be what Max needed him to be.

The front door opened.

"Busted."

Jake rocked back, away from Max, and looked up to meet Willa's triumphant gaze. "Shit."

Beside him, Max stiffened. He had his back to the door and looked for all the world as if he planned to bolt. Jake put a restraining hand on his arm and greeted his sister. "Willa, you remember Max." He didn't urge Max to turn, but hoped his usual polite manner would halt his flight, compel him to turn around and at least acknowledge Willa.

Willa spoke first. "It's great to see you, Max." She looked at Jake. "Why are you lurking outside the front door instead of barging through the side gate?"

"Max and I were sorting some stuff."

Her gray eyes narrowed as she looked between the two of them. Max half turned. One of Willa's manicured brows arched slightly and she offered a wicked smile. "He looks tired, Jake. Did you keep him up all night?"

Groaning, Jake let go of Max's arm. He was surprised when Max didn't immediately take off then. Instead, he stood his ground, shoulders drawn in, chin pointed down.

"Willa…." How to phrase his request without offending everyone?

"It's okay," Max said quietly. He looked up, eyes wide and dark. His throat moved convulsively. He glanced at Willa, then back at Jake. "Your family knows, right? About you."

"Yes."

"And they're good with it?"

"Yes."

"Then it's okay," Max repeated, a little breathlessly.

Jake wrapped his fingers gently around Max's elbow and leaned in. "I'm still going to play it cool."

Jake looked at Willa again and lifted his chin. She caught his gaze, eyes narrowed shrewdly, then stepped off the porch and leaned in to press a quick kiss to Max's cheek. He didn't flinch, but his eyelids fluttered.

"We're an affectionate family, Max. Always kissing each other. Foreheads, cheeks. We hug it up all the time." Hug it up? She laced her fingers through Max's. "C'mon. I'll introduce you to Mom and Dad."

Wide-eyed, Jake watched as Max allowed himself to be led away by a different Kendricks. Then he acknowledged Max had been stolen by the perfect Kendricks, the one who could ease his introduction to the family without tripping over her words, accidentally landing lips first on a guy who had issues with public displays of affection.

Thank you, Willa.

As if she'd heard him, she looked over her shoulder and winked.

THE FOOTBALL seared his fingers and slammed into his chest, nearly knocking the wind out of him. "Jesus, Brian. I was right behind you. You didn't need to attempt a twenty-yard pass into my rib-cage." Jake heaved in a breath and winced as a dull ache gripped his lungs.

"Just making sure you caught it," his uncle huffed as he ran past, turning his shoulder into Dawn's husband.

"I caught it." Now he had to pass it because Bernat had avoided Brian's meaty shoulder and was coming right for him. Shit. Jake looked down the yard for opportunities.

"Here!" Willa flung her arms in the air. "Here, Jake!"

He measured the pass, got a good hand on the ball, and threw. Bernat knocked him down a second later, growling in Spanish the whole time. One of Jake's nephews leaped into the pile, cursing his father in the same language. Jake resigned himself to being grass-streaked and battered. The Kendricks family holiday football games were rough and ready.

He heard Willa yelling. "Run, Max, run!"

Sticking his head out from under the pile, Jake looked down the yard. Max had the ball tucked tight against his chest and he was running toward the back fence. Like a fucking sprite, he dodged nephews, nieces, and cousins until he crossed the wavy chalk line delineating the end zone. There, he pounded the ball into the turf and jumped up, both arms raised over his head. Willa slammed into him a second later, wrapping her arms around his middle, and the pair danced a circle. Jake thought he might die happy in that moment, squashed by his family, in sight of the one of the most wonderful things he'd ever witnessed. Max smiling and cheering, happily hugging someone, and obviously having a good time.

Jake decided then and there he was going to buy Willa the best Christmas present ever, and present it to her in July. He'd kidnap that actor she adored—or maybe not. His parole officer wouldn't go for that. Such a thought couldn't pluck him down from the clouds today, but he did want to pick himself up out of the dirt.

"I think you broke all of my ribs," he complained to Bernat.

Dawn's husband clapped him on the shoulder. "You're welcome."

Sometimes Jake wondered at Bernat's command of English.

Heads bent together, Max and Willa plotted as they crossed the yard. Jake met them in the middle and clapped his hands together. "Okay, what's our next play?"

Willa eyed him critically. "Putting you in a body bag."

Jake looked down at his stained jeans and rumpled shirt. "I'm still standing."

Max's lips twitched and humor lit his eyes. "Barely. Bernat is like a steam train."

"That he is," Jake admitted ruefully.

"Better you than me." There was the sly smile.

Jake nudged his shoulder into Max's. "Can't have our best runner groveling in the dirt."

Max's shoulder moved back into his. "If Bernat jumped on me, you'd be digging me out of a grave."

Willa laughed and circled Max's shoulders with her arm again. She'd warned Max they were an affectionate family, but she was the only one wrapped around him. Max didn't seem to mind. She'd dutifully stayed at Max's side all afternoon, engaging him in lively conversation and deflecting pointed queries from others. Anyone might assume he'd arrived with her, that she'd been the one rolling around naked with him the night before. Jake had a handle on his jealousy, though. Mostly. He'd be the one taking Max home tonight, right? And Max was leaning against him now, panting softly, lips still curved in a relaxed smile.

Tony staggered into the huddle, one hand braced against his hip. "I'm too old to be rolling around in the dirt with you kids." He nodded toward Max. "Nice play." Max's smile widened carefully. Tony tipped his head toward Jake. "You can bring him again."

It was a small thing, and Jake could see the heat rising across Max's skin. But to have even a casual stamp of approval from his father—who knew exactly *who* Max was with, despite Willa's play-acting—made it a big thing. Jake's heart lurched and flopped again. But he kept his cool, for Max and for his dad. "Yeah," he said. "I think I will." His cool evaporated as he shot Max a wink.

"Who's ready for pie!" came a welcome call from the patio.

Instantly, the game dissolved. Jake had no idea who had won or lost, but he didn't really care. None of them did. The holiday scrimmages were more about rolling around in the dirt than anything else.

Max ended up in a tug of war between brother and sister and seated happily between them. Jake leaned around him to challenge Willa. "You're not taking him home."

Willa produced a pout. "Aww!"

Max blushed.

Plates circled past them, each with a generous portion of pie. "Ice cream is self-serve," Annabel announced. She angled her way around the table, two plates in her hands, and sat on the other side of Jake. She put her plates on the table and pulled one close. Pointing her fork toward the other, she said, "That is for Max. Either of you touch it and I will jab you with my fork."

"She'd do it, too," Jake said. He chuckled as Max's brows arched upward.

"Mark my words." His mother hummed happily as she ate her pie, leaving them in relative peace until she'd finished half her portion. "I hear you were quite a fan of the strawberry rhubarb, Max," she said, forking up another mouthful.

Max nodded with genuine enthusiasm. "Best pie I ever had, ma'am. But all your cooking is good." He cast a shy look toward Jake. "Jake's, too."

Grinning at the compliment, Jake tipped his head toward his mother. "I learned from the best."

Annabel smiled. "Please call me Annabel." She punctuated her third such request by pointing her fork at Max. "Unless you want me to call you *sir*."

"That would be weird," Max said.

"Yes. Yes, it would," Annabel agreed. She turned her attention to Jake. "I spoke to Kate last week. She said you haven't called."

Jake frowned at his mother. What the fuck was she doing, poking a hole in his cozy bubble? "I'm not supposed to call her, Mom. That's part of the agreement."

Annabel sighed. "I don't understand why you still can't talk to her. Is there an expiry date to all this nonsense? I want to see my granddaughter."

Aware of Max's curious attention, Jake shrugged and rubbed at the back of his neck. He paused to let the short hairs there tickle his fingers, concentrating on the sensation rather than the anger swirling up from his gut. "Her babysitter texts me when she's taking Caroline to the park. I go watch her sometimes."

"It's not the same."

If he shrugged again, he'd turn into Max. Still, his shoulders twitched up.

Annabel looked between the three of them—Willa, Max, and Jake—and said, "It seems to me you're getting sorted, is all. You look happy, Jake. I like it. I want to see the rest of your life falling into place for you."

It might, if she'd stop poking.

Jake huffed out a sigh. "I'm getting there, Mom." He glanced at Max and back at his mother. He'd been careful to give Max space the whole afternoon, letting Willa monopolize his time. But he supposed it was damned obvious he cared for Max. He'd brought him out to Doylestown after all, and hell, he couldn't look at Max without smiling while his heart knocked and twirled in his chest. Eric had called it—he was a damned fool, and he'd never been good at hiding how he felt. And they knew—his whole family knew what Max was to him, so they figured Max should be included in *everything*, even if Jake hadn't quite gotten around to mentioning *everything* yet.

Thankfully, his mother seemed to sense his agitation. Funny how before *everything*, they'd never really mentioned Jake's temper, except to note he was a slow burn. Now, they seemed hyperaware of every twitch.

Annabel finished her pie without saying another word and pushed Max's second slice toward him. "Eat up, *sir*. You're much too thin."

"Chimo's got the ball!" yelled someone from the backyard.

"Let him have it," Tony returned. "We're on a pie-out." The family version of a time-out could extend well into dusk.

Stretching his legs out, Jake leaned back in his chair, closed his eyes, and tuned out of the conversation, letting it settle into the rising buzz of cicadas. It'd taken him years to get over Kate. He was only six months distant from his latest mess. Why was his mother in such a rush to get him sorted?

Couldn't he take a little time to enjoy Max first?

CHAPTER TWENTY-TWO

"NOT SO fast, you don't want to completely break the eggs."

Hadn't they already broken the eggs before putting them in the pan?

Max shivered as Jake's stubbled cheek rasped gently past his. Jake stood behind him, leaning close, his chin hooked over Max's shoulder.

"Over there, get that bit." Jake's chin bobbed down.

Max sent the wooden spoon after the clump of egg at the side of the pan and saw he'd left it alone too long. The underside had browned a little. Scrambled eggs weren't supposed to be brown. They should be thickly clumped and slightly wet. His looked like someone had stepped on them and then taken a flamethrower to the mess.

He lifted the pan off the burner and turned to share the tragedy with Jake. To his credit, Jake didn't laugh right away. He looked down with all proper solemnity until his lips twitched. Then he looked up, eyes sparkling with mirth.

"It looks edible, which is good for a first try."

"Yeah, okay." Edible was good enough. Max sniffed as the faint odor of burning something tickled his nostrils. "Oh no."

Jake whirled toward the toaster. "Aw, shit." He smacked the side of the shiny appliance and two slices of blackened toast shot up into the air. They fell back to the countertop, landing with a dry rustle, one on top of the other.

Jake picked one up and slathered it with butter. "There, now we can't see the black bits."

Except they could, swirled all through the creamy yellow.

Max dumped his pathetic eggs on top of the mess and served up his first attempt at a cooked breakfast. "You don't have to eat it," he said.

"Trust me, I've had worse." Jake sat down and dug in. He inhaled the awful food in a few bites and washed it down with a generous gulp of coffee.

Max ate more slowly, doing the meal no favors, and daydreamed about the food he'd eaten yesterday. Ribs and beans, corn on the cob, potato salad and coleslaw. And pie. Fruit of the forest pie, which could, quite possibly, be his new favorite. There seemed to be no end to the wonders that came from Kendricks's kitchens.

"I had a really good time yesterday." He showed Jake a smile. "Your family is great."

Jake leaned back so that he sat with his coffee cup nestled into his ribs. "Yeah, they are, when they're not being ass-tastic."

Ass-tastic?

Was Jake referring to the weird conversation with his mother, the stuff about Kate and Caroline? Max had been swallowing questions about Caroline every time he saw the picture of her draped over Jake's shoulders, or on Friday nights when Jake seemed particularly anxious. He knew Jake went to see his daughter most Saturdays, but he hadn't realized the meetings were so strained. Or restrained. He'd imagined Jake playing with his little girl, not spying on her.

"You don't have a bunch of cousins?" Jake asked.

"Huh?" Processing the question, Max shook his head. "Mom was an only child. Her parents were already gone when I was born." Thank goodness. Probably not the most charitable thought, but Max reckoned it was a good thing his grandparents had passed before witnessing the decline of their only daughter. "Dad has family down in Virginia. We never saw them much." Max sucked on his lower lip as he recalled a road trip to see his cousins. He'd wanted to go to the nation's capital. They'd been so close to DC, he'd been able to see the distant point of the Monument. But, no, they'd pressed on until they ended up in some backwoods village way the heck up in the mountains. Mechanicsburg had hardly been a thriving metropolis, but his cousins lived in a town that had never left the last century.

"And the Hungry Man habit?" Jake asked.

"Dad is the old-fashioned kind of guy. I suspect he can cook. He's probably cooking now." Or heating up frozen dinners in a distant echo of his son, the idea of which made Max grimace. "But he always let Mom do the cooking and cleaning, until she got sick. Then it was up to me. Neighbors dropped food off sometimes. Casseroles." He shrugged. "Mostly we had sandwiches. Frozen stuff. I exploded some hot dogs in the microwave once." He aimed a careful look at Jake. "I think he liked that I was as useless in the kitchen as him. Made me seem less...." Gay.

Max reached for his coffee. Jake had made the coffee and it was good, of course.

"Was your mom sick for a long time?"

Max nodded. "Nearly seven years."

"I'm sorry, Max."

"Nothing anyone could have done."

Jake leaned forward and reached across the table. Max felt his own hand sliding to meet him, attracted by Jake's magnetism. He smiled as their fingers collided and tangled gently. Looking up into Jake's face, he noted a trace of weariness beneath his eyes and a shadow lurking within the steel-colored irises. Jake wanted to know about his family, and Max understood why. He shared the inclination—meeting Jake's family yesterday had served to whet his appetite further. He didn't want to know about Jake's cousins, though. He wanted to know about his daughter.

Squeezing Jake's fingers, he asked, "Why aren't you allowed to visit Caroline?"

Surprisingly, Jake's expression did not shutter. He didn't close down or draw away. In fact, he seemed to have been expecting the question. Maybe that had been the shadow in his eyes—it still lurked there, gray on gray. Then he pulled at his hand. Heart sinking toward his gut, Max let him go. He didn't apologize for his question. They were talking family, weren't they?

Jake set his coffee mug on the table and stretched his forearms across the wood. "Remember that night at Shay's, when I told you I'd done something stupid?"

Jake's big mistake. Max nodded.

"I put a guy in the hospital." Jake paused for a quiet but strained breath. "I was arrested, tried, and sent to prison for assault."

A ringing sound started up behind Max's ears. Assault? Sentenced? Jake had…. A cold prickle crept across his scalp. Reality became a weirdly detached thing, like a plate flying up off a yanked tablecloth. Max swallowed, and swallowed again. The bitter taste of coffee burned in his throat, and his breakfast curdled in his stomach. Had Jake really just said he'd beaten someone so badly they'd had to…? "I don't understand."

"I went to prison. For a year. I'm a criminal. An ex-con."

"You were in prison?"

Jake being in prison seemed to be the absolute least part of the issue, the abstract part, but Max latched on to it. Then he glanced down at Jake's hands, at those strong capable hands, dotted with scars and calluses, and shuddered. Those hands had caressed him last night and this morning. The finger of one had been inside him.

The buzz in his ears settled to a low-pitched whine, and the backs of his eyes burned. Putting his hands over his ears, Max glanced down at the plate in front of him. The crumbs of his breakfast seemed to stutter in place. He swallowed again in what felt like a new and disturbing habit and tried to rein in the panic speeding through his veins. God, if he threw up now, he'd embarrass himself more than he ever had before. He should go. He couldn't sit here and think, not with this noise in his head. Max pushed back from the table and stood on numb legs.

He was halfway to the door before he breathed again. The urge to glance over his shoulder nearly overwhelmed him. Looking back would be a mistake—he'd learned that lesson early on in his running career.

He looked back.

Jake hadn't moved. Hadn't turned around. Shoulders rounded and head dipped forward, he might have simply collapsed where he sat. His posture spoke of defeat and something familiar. Loneliness, isolation, the feeling of being trapped somewhere small. He didn't look strong or threatening, not right now. He looked broken. Max remembered then, the quiet yearning in Jake's eyes the night of their date, when Jake had asked him to stay overnight.

He couldn't leave Jake this way. Jake was a good man—he hadn't imagined that. Good, kind, and strong. A protector. Jake cared for his friends and he loved fiercely. Hadn't Max felt that care? Hadn't he even imagined he felt Jake's love? He'd woken up in his arms just over an hour ago and felt so safe. Needed. *Necessary.* And the very first time they kissed, hadn't it felt as if he'd come home?

I don't want to lose this. I don't want to give this up.

Max paced quietly back across the apartment and sat down. His fingers trembled as he reached across the table toward Jake's clenched fist, wrapped his hand around Jake's knuckles, and squeezed as hard as he could. "Tell me what happened. I want to hear all of it."

CHAPTER TWENTY-THREE

JAKE BLINKED at the young man sitting across from him, gripping his hand with all the apparent strength he could muster—at those sapphire eyes burning with sudden intensity. He might be seeing Max for the very first time. Not the shy Max who flinched if someone surprised him, moved too quickly. Not the passionate Max, the one who had writhed beneath him last night, crying out with need. The real Max, the man who dwelled within this spare frame. The man with the iron will—the man who had somehow forged himself on the strength of others.

Christ, he wanted to hold him. Pull Max close to his chest, bury his face in that soft brown hair and cry. Yep. He wanted to fucking cry. And thank Max for not leaving. Maybe kiss his fingers. His feet. But before he got to do any of that, he had to tell it all. He had to continue rolling out the risk and hope for reward.

Hope he wouldn't lose this. Lose Max.

Jake blew out a breath, drew in a shorter draught of air, and started at the beginning. "About four years ago, Kate started dating a guy named Dominick. I didn't like him from the first. Not because he was with Kate. I got over that a long time ago." Mostly. "But I still care about her. She's a good friend." Or was. "And she's the mother of my child." He looked into Max's eyes. "It's a weird bond, that."

Max nodded, the movement of his head a little jerky. That was all right. Max was allowed to be unsure. Jake felt just as edgy. He unclenched his fist and nearly gasped as Max's fingers slid across his palm. Gratitude warmed him a second later and he found the wherewithal to continue.

"We tolerated each other for Kate's sake and because I didn't want to lose out on time with my daughter. But then things got weird. Kate changed. She kept cancelling on me, which pissed me off."

He'd been luckier than a lot of part-time dads. Working for his uncle gave him a lot of flexibility. Brian let him go whenever he got a chance to see his daughter, but Jake wasn't stupid. He'd known, even then, making a proper go of his job with Brian was a big part of sorting out his life. Of being reliable and regular. He couldn't skive off whenever he wanted to. Juggling his schedule with Kate's changes had laid the second strand of tension across their relationship.

"Dominick was always a possessive ass, but when he started interfering with my time with Caroline, I got pissed."

Max's eyes widened.

Jake breathed in and out slowly before addressing Max's palpable fear. "There's more. I started showing up unannounced. Dom didn't like having me there and I'm pretty sure I made what was going on worse." He'd tortured himself with that little tidbit in prison. "He was nasty to Kate. A total ass. I couldn't understand how she put up with him. But when I saw the marks on Kate's arm, I kinda lost it."

"Marks?" Max whispered.

"Bruises. I asked her straight-out if he'd done it and they both acted like it was no big deal. He'd just grabbed her, they said." Another thing he didn't get. How Kate and Dom had collaborated in such shit. "So I gave him a warning, you know? Told him if he touched her like that again I'd…." Jake paused, swallowed and winced. "Beat the living crap out of him."

Max made an odd sound. "He didn't leave her alone, did he?" His expression hovered on a knife's edge. He needed to hear that Dom had started the fight, if only figuratively, and Jake appreciated the distinction. Max needed him to be on the white side of the gray.

Didn't he need the same thing?

"Nope. He hit her. She called me, crying. What the fuck she thought would happen is anyone's guess. Kate knows I have a temper. I'm not the touchy type, it takes a long time to stir me up, but when I go off, it's never pretty. I went over there…." Jake paused, just as he should have that night. If only he'd thought about it for longer. If only he hadn't gone off. "I went over there and I messed him up."

Max's fingers dug into his palm. He breathed in small, shallow gasps, and the sound sent Jake back to that night, to the way Kate had sounded on the phone. The way Dominick had sounded down there on the floor, nose broken, eyes swollen shut, ribs cracked. Dominick hadn't gone down without a fight, but he didn't have a fucking black belt. He didn't know where to hit or how to block. He'd just been a force of anger unrefined. A blunt instrument.

He'd never had a chance.

Then there had been the sound of Kate screaming, the sirens. Had Caroline witnessed any of it? Jake didn't know. He'd never had the courage to ask.

Chin dipping, Jake stared at the edge of the table until the smooth lines of the wood grain blurred. He felt a tear rolling down his cheek and did nothing to stop it. Swiping at his face would only invite sympathy and he deserved none. His throat closed, making breathing a chore, and his shoulders hunched forward. He slipped his hand out from underneath Max's and moved to grip his legs, putting pressure on the underside of his knees, digging his fingers into the little hollows so hard it hurt. There should be a reason for his tears, right? Something tangible.

Max's chair moved, the legs scraping along the floor. Jake let his head drop a little lower. He really didn't want to see Max leave. He didn't want to hear soft footsteps making their way back across the apartment. Irrationally, he thought to remind Max his shoes were in the bedroom, lined up neatly at the foot of the bed.

He jerked as Max gripped his shoulder. In the periphery of his vision, he saw Max hovering at his side. The hand at his shoulder tugged him around. Almost reluctantly he turned—he'd rather Max didn't say good-bye.

Max dropped to his knees and slid his arms around Jake, awkwardly, and hugged him.

"Why?" Jake croaked.

"I'm sorry," Max said.

Somewhere they'd gotten all confused. Jake should be the one apologizing. Unless…. "Okay." Jake tried to pull out of Max's embrace.

Max let him go and knelt back on his heels.

"Your shoes are in the bedroom," Jake said.

"I know where my shoes are."

"Don't you want to—"

"Go?" Max's throat moved as he swallowed. "No, Jake. I don't. I think leaving you alone right now would be about the most selfish and asshole thing I could ever do."

Max didn't swear, not really.

"I'm sorry I didn't tell you this before," Jake said.

"I get why. I mean…." Max's eyes darkened. "With me running out after that dinner and all."

"You're here now." Jake reached over to grip Max's hand, the one still lightly resting on his shoulder. "Thank you for staying."

"I can't believe you were in prison. Of all the reasons I figured you couldn't see your daughter, that would have been the very last one."

"I made a mistake. A really huge, fucked-up, and terrible mistake."

"Yeah, you did." Max nodded solemnly. "But I get why you did it. That's just you all over. Protecting the people you love."

He sighed and stood up, his expression thoughtful and cautious. Jake wondered if he would leave *now*, after offering his words of wisdom. Instead, Max wandered over to the sink and filled a glass with water. He stood at the counter to gulp it down and remained there afterward, empty glass clutched in his hand.

Jake stood slowly and crept into the kitchen area. He paused close to Max, but not too close. "What now?"

Max glanced over his shoulder at him and visibly considered the question. "I don't know," he finally said. He turned and reached toward Jake's face. Jake stiffened as Max's thumb swiped over his cheekbone, and sighed as he watched Max press that same thumb to his lips. Had he ever received such a curious and gentle caress? When Max circled him with his arms again, sliding them around his ribs, Jake had to sniff back more tears. He leaned into the sweet embrace, tucking his chin over Max's shoulder, his arms around Max's back.

"I'm not afraid." Max's voice was quiet, his cautious tone belying his words.

Jake hugged him a little harder. "I'd never hurt you, Max."

"I know." Max moved in closer. "I know."

After a quiet but solid hug that meant more than words, they moved the conversation to the couch.

"What I don't get is why you went to prison and Dom didn't," Max said.

"Kate didn't press charges against him."

"But she did against you?" Max looked appropriately horrified.

"No, that was Dom." Jake closed his eyes briefly. When he opened them, he looked down at his hands.

Max was looking at his hands, too. Jake could feel the attention. The skin at his fingertips tingled. Did he entertain the same thoughts Jake sometimes did? How these hands could be instruments of such violence? Jake tucked his hands under his thighs.

"It's not fair."

Jake glanced up at the plaintive tone. They sat close enough together that he could hear Max breathe, but not so close he could appreciate his warmth. Leather creaked as Jake adjusted his seat. As much as he wanted to bury himself in Max, literally and figuratively, he also needed the distance.

Max probably did as well. He'd yet to piece together the fact his most recent beating was related to Jake's major life malfunction.

Would that be when he left?

"Life isn't fair," Jake said. "C'mon, you of all people should know that." Max's dark brows twitched together. "How many times have you taken a beating you didn't invite?"

"That's different. I didn't—"

"Exactly. Did anyone stand up for you? Didn't your dad notice something was up? Your mom?"

Max's cheeks flushed. Jake knew the color would sweep down his neck and across his chest. Max tried not to give much away, but he blushed furiously. "My dad thought it might toughen me up."

Jake felt his jaw come unhinged. "He *what*?"

Max produced one of his patented shrugs. "He didn't like that I was, um...." He gestured abstractly. "I don't know if Mom knew what was going on. She had her own trouble."

A seven-year battle with cancer was more than trouble.

"What about your teachers?"

"There was this one teacher who wanted to know what was going on, but I couldn't tell him anything, could I? That would only have drawn more attention and probably got my butt kicked again."

Jake worked to tamp down the anger rising inside him, the heated flame that fizzed and popped toward explosive territory. "Doesn't sound like your silence bought you any favors."

"Can we talk about prison instead?"

Ouch. "You don't want to know about prison."

"You don't want to know about my career as a punching bag."

Oh, but he did. The flagrant abuse Max had suffered outraged him. "Tell me your father didn't let you get beat up because you're gay and I'll stop asking."

"He wanted me to learn the tough lessons," Max countered. "How to be strong, how to work hard. How to be a man."

All while expecting his son to tend and clean up after his sick wife. Jake held no delusion Mr. Wilson had been around to help with that. The way Max cleaned his apartment spoke of long habit, of an obsession drilled into him from a young age.

"So, um." Max licked his lips. "A year. Is that a long sentence for what you did?"

For what you did. Max couldn't know how those words stung, and Jake endeavored not to show him. The kid had been punished enough for simply being himself, and he obviously didn't want to talk about his father anymore. So… prison.

"No. I could've gotten fifteen years."

Max swallowed.

"I had a good lawyer and it was a first offense. I was lucky. Damned lucky. I was sentenced to three years and qualified for parole after just one."

"Good behavior?"

Jake nodded. "And a proper show of remorse."

"You're sorry you did it?"

"Hell, yes. Dominick is an ass. But I had no right." Jake considered Max's face. Max held his gaze steadily, eyes lit with a combination of curiosity and sorrow. "I meet my parole officer on Wednesday nights."

A dark brow quirked upward. "That's why you don't go to class."

"Not Wednesdays, for maybe the next year and a half."

"A year and a half."

"The rest of my sentence."

Max exhaled slowly. Jake looked away, less distracted by the vista of coffee table and entertainment console than simply requiring somewhere else to look.

"Listen, if this is all—"

"I'm fine, Jake. Well, not fine. This is…. No, you know what? I am fine. This isn't about me, anyway." Max looked down at his hands, and then his expression shifted, brow furrowing, his attention suddenly drawing inward.

Here it comes.

Jake watched helplessly as realization dawned. As Max figured out who the guys in the alley had been, and how they were related to Jake. With a gasp, Max leaned forward and gripped his knees.

Shit.

"Max, I know words can't make up for what happened, but you need to know I'm sorry. If I had even a clue, it wouldn't have happened. If I'd been there—"

"You knew who they were, didn't you?"

"Yes."

"Why me?" The question arrived on a curiously loud whisper. "Why did they get me and not you?"

It should have been obvious they had the wrong guy, right? There was a simple answer, though, and it made his stomach hurt. "They must have figured you were my friend or… boyfriend." Dominick hadn't been above taunting Jake about his sexuality. His friends had obviously put two and two together and gotten three, which was the magic fucking number or some shit.

Max stood. Fists clenched, shoulders tight, he rocked in place slightly. More, he vibrated. He was stuck, caught between two directions. Jake knew what they were—stay and go. Max had just discovered their entire relationship swung on the pendulum of Jake's past.

A sharp hiss cut the air, then another. Max squeezed his eyes shut. Breathed again. He turned so sharply his bare feet squeaked against the floorboards and stalked toward the door. He didn't pull it open and leave. He hit it. Raised his clenched fists and banged them against the closed door.

Jake sat, stunned, for two or three rounds—bang, bang, bang— before he found the wherewithal to stand. By the time he reached the door, Max was kicking it and swearing furiously under his breath. Jake actually hesitated to touch him. He'd seen Max angry before. Petulant, stubborn, and snappish. But this—he should recognize this. It was him, when he'd finally been tipped too far.

Oh God, what have I done?

"Max—"

Max whirled around, fists raised. Shock clenched his features, sewing his expression into a rictus of fury. He opened his mouth, but no sound came out. Then he slumped, all his stitches let loose at once. He grabbed Jake's shoulders and fell into him. Harsh breaths burned across Jake's neck as Max pulled him close, buried his face in Jake's shoulder and keened. "It's not fair."

No, it wasn't.

Max pulled back and looked up, the deep blue of his eyes shocking all over again. "You're my friend. A good friend, maybe the best I've ever had." He curled his fingers into Jake's shoulders and shook him. "I don't want to walk away from this."

A lump rose in Jake's throat. "I'm so sorry."

Max lifted a hand, fingers still curled. Jake didn't flinch, he waited. If this was what Max needed to do….

Max's fist hovered in the air for a long, drawn-out second before dropping out of sight as Max suddenly leaned in. Air brushed Jake's face, another furious breath. Max's lips touched his. Tentative, moving, but not kissing, as if he whispered secrets he wanted no one to hear. A choked sound passed between them. Then Max tucked his hand behind Jake's head and pulled him down into a kiss.

There was no doubt about the identity of the man kissing him. It was Max. He tasted like breakfast and coffee and toothpaste. He smelled like Max. The soap from Jake's shower, a faint whiff of bleach. Max. But the way he kissed. Hard, bruising… searching. He sought answers in Jake's mouth, from his tongue, from the flesh beneath his digging and squeezing fingers. If it weren't Max, the kiss would've been the equivalent of an emotional ransacking.

But it was Max—all of him. He was putting everything he was into this kiss. All of his anger and pain. His questions and the answers he hoped to find. Jake gave everything back. His hands shook as he collected Max against him, yanking him into an embrace as intense as the kiss. Molded himself to Max's slim form. Took on every tremble as his own, matched breath for breath, heartbeat for heartbeat.

When Max pulled away, Jake felt as though he'd lost a vital organ. His arms stretched as Max stepped back, out of his embrace. Then they were two separate beings, breathing alone, existing alone. Was Max as suddenly bereft as him?

Eyes wide, chest rising and falling with panted breath, Max shuffled back another step. A mottle of red cascaded across his face and down his neck.

Holding out a hand, Jake moved forward. "Max."

"I'm sorry," he whispered.

"Don't be."

"I don't understand why I…." He turned farther away and dipped his chin. "I don't know how to deal with this."

"I'm sorry." Those two words were starting to taste stale. "I should have told you everything. Not let it come between us."

"I'm so confused."

"I've had six years longer than you to figure out what's what," Jake said, "and I'm still confused by most of it."

Max returned a solemn nod. His breathing had calmed. He still looked upset, though.

"Listen, why don't we take a day or two?" Jake said.

"What do you mean?"

"A cooling-off period. Time to think things through."

"I...." Max plucked at his shirt. "Is that what you want?"

No. "I want you to be sure this is what you want, and I could use some time. Just to put myself back together." To rebuild his own patchy fence, and to stop entertaining fantasies of bending Max over the couch. That kiss....

Max looked so vulnerable standing there with his loose sweats and his big eyes.

"You missed your run yesterday," Jake gently reminded him.

He nodded carefully. "Yeah. Okay, yeah." With a decisive nod, Max turned to the door and cracked it open. "Just a day or two, right?"

"Go run. Breathe, think. I'll do the same. Then, if you want to talk, you know where to find me."

The quiet click of the door closing behind Max felt weirdly final, and not half-dramatic or painful enough.

The door opened again. Max stuck his head through. "Forgot my shoes."

Jake watched him cross the apartment to the bedroom and back again, his shoes dangling from one hand.

Max stopped in front of him. "This isn't good-bye." The intense spark returned to his bluer than blue eyes. "I don't want it to be good-bye."

Jake breathed out. "Not good-bye."

"Are you going to be okay?"

This kid. Asking if Jake was going to be okay. Jake put his hand on Max's shoulder and squeezed. "I'll be fine. Now go."

CHAPTER TWENTY-FOUR

MAX ALWAYS felt ridiculous bowing as he entered the dojo. Maybe he just wasn't comfortable pointing his ass out into the street. Straightening, he let the door close behind him and went to the bench lining the back of the room. Everyone was there, which was unusual for a Wednesday night. Apparently Jake wasn't the only one with a prior commitment. Max supposed none of his other classmates had regular meetings with a parole officer, though.

Nudging thoughts of Jake from his mind, Max shed his T-shirt and pulled on the top portion of his gi. In only a month and a half of lessons, he'd found the act of donning his uniform and belt served as a sort of meditation. His mind settled as he prepared to exercise, and he really needed to exercise tonight, because his thoughts had returned to Jake. Again.

Two days and no word outside of short answers to texts. *Work. Busy. Headache. Thinking to do.* Had agreeing to this cooling-off period been a mistake?

Max had needed the run on Monday. He still didn't understand the correlation between his anger and that kiss. He'd never felt anything so intensely in all his life—that need to connect and hold fast before he lost something.

Despite two days of thinking time, he also didn't understand the attack in the alley. Who beat up a random stranger in retaliation for... what? On the one hand, he figured it didn't matter. He had Jake now. On the other hand, maybe it should matter. On a third hand, which belonged to some mutant Thought-Max, sometimes a coincidence was just that. Awful, sickening, not quite random, but still a fluke. Bad luck. If anyone understood that, it was him.

The upshot of it all was that he missed Jake.

Elsa appeared in front of him and tugged at the ends of his white belt, tightening the already tight knot and jerking him out of reflection. "There. Wouldn't want you unraveling in the middle of class."

He was only in danger of doing that mentally.

She offered a handshake, as everyone did every week. The formal greetings weren't as weird as the bow at the door. In fact, they sort of made sense. A lot of their training circled the idea of respect—for their own bodies, their beliefs, and their goals. Naturally, the respect extended to those they trained with, and to the exercise itself.

After shaking everyone's hand, Max leaned into a wall, leaving everyone else to talk. Though he had just been in the middle of the group, exchanging handshakes and quiet greetings, he now stood apart—his default state of being, except when he was with Jake. Loneliness gripped him. Would Jake's regret be the thing that kept them apart?

"All right, let's line up," Sensei Fabrizio called, clapping her hands.

Max shuffled to his place at the back of the class. His head began to ache halfway through the jumping jacks, but he persisted in completing all fifty. He managed thirty push-ups and all fifty sit-ups. Afterward, lying on his side with one leg folded forward—they were stretching their backs or something—he wondered how Elsa kept up with the class. Or Arthur. Arthur had to be seventy. Or maybe he was just one of those folks who looked older, what with the gray hair and all.

He scrambled to his feet with the rest of the class and let out a constrained yell as he settled into a wide stance. A sharp pain pulsed around the side of his head, gripping his jaw. Ignoring it, he listened for instruction. By the time they moved into combinations, his blood hummed pleasantly and sweat clung to the back of his neck. His thoughts settled somewhere between interpreting the combination and anticipating the next one.

His head still ached. But he needed to be in class tonight.

After a short break, the diminutive Sensei called for them to pair up. Max looked for Arthur, but he'd already been claimed by Grant.

Barry sidled up with a familiar smirk. "Ready to lick the floor?"

Returning a version of the smirk, Max set his water bottle aside. He'd towel off the back of his neck, but couldn't find it in himself to care if Barry had to touch his sweat. He never showed the same courtesy and he always stank of onions when he got warm.

Directed to move through a series of grabs, from wrist to elbow to shoulder, Max and Barry faced off. Max wrapped his fingers around Barry's meaty wrist and prepared to be forced to the floor. Barry always went for the takedown, and he always snapped his moves, the shocked gasps of his partner obviously a joyful experience. Barry's palm just grazed Max's nose in a simulated strike, then Max's wrist was painfully locked. Max hissed as Barry stepped in, forcing him down.

When Barry didn't hear him tapping out, Max said, "Okay, that's enough."

Barry flexed his wrist again. "All nice and limp?"

Narrowing his eyes, Max huffed and stood up. "This side of broken." He rubbed his wrist and wondered again, briefly, why he had come to class. Oh, yeah, so he could learn to stand up to idiots like Barry.

He turned his shoulder in while Barry attempted to wrestle out of an elbow grab. Barry kicked him in the back of the knee. Yelping in surprise, Max dropped down, catching himself before he tipped forward. Barry's arm quickly circled his neck, forcing his chin up.

"Nice, Barry" came Sensei Fabrizio's voice through the rhythmic swish of blood blocking Max's ears. "But try not to kill Max. We like him, remember?"

Barry didn't. Max couldn't figure out why, but he hadn't put a lot of thought into it. He'd been running afoul of guys like Barry all his life. In fact, if he did put thought into the matter, he'd be more surprised by the fact the rest of the class did like him.

The pressure at his throat loosened and Max rubbed at his temple. His head was now a gong and that little stick with the ball was bouncing off his right temple in a relentless and steady beat. Every strike reverberated down his spine and jaw, sending chills to his fingers and toes. Swallowing, Max pushed to his feet and settled his hand on Barry's shoulder. He tapped out as loudly as he could before Barry got him halfway locked.

"Pussy," Barry whispered as they straightened.

The insults continued, verbal and mental, until they switched positions. Max tempered his rising anger by remembering who he was and why he was there. Barry's fingers locked around Max's right wrist, his grip firm and just short of painful, his lips slanted into his usual smirk.

That damned smirk.

Max's hold over his anger slipped—just an inch—but it was enough for his elbow strike to connect with Barry's jaw, snapping his head to the side. Barry's eyes widened. Max felt his shock. The fact he'd actually hit someone, not quite by accident, didn't stop him from completing the move, though. He captured Barry's hand, straightened his fingers beneath the joined clasp and angled up and over, slipping into the lock. Then he stepped in, forcing the surprised Barry to his knees.

Elation swept through Max. He felt high and shaky, as evidenced by his incomplete hold. Barry shook him off easily. But he'd done it. For the first time since attending class, he'd performed a combination without overthinking it, without weighing the cost of aggression, or worrying he might hurt someone.

Of course, he might have hurt Barry.

"Are you okay?"

Barry rubbed his jaw and grunted.

"Sorry, I...." Max trailed off, unsure how to apologize for not quite accidentally hitting someone.

In answer, Barry continued their practice by gripping Max's elbow, fingers curling painfully into Max's joint. Wincing, Max reached around to grab Barry's hand.

Barry's caught him across the ear with the other. "You forgot the strike."

Through the rest of the exercise, Barry used every opportunity to taunt him. Max gritted his teeth through it all, but a part of him rose to the challenge. Barry baited him, sure, but Max found he didn't mind being hooked. He wanted to hit the guy and, as the class progressed, he stopped even trying to examine his motivation.

Picking himself up off the floor for the umpteenth time, he found a smile. Hadn't Jake promised he wouldn't hit the floor until he got a colored belt? He quickly forgave Jake the small lie. He was learning, and enjoying the process. And... he wanted to share this with Jake. It was time to end this cooling-off period. With his blood singing and his head pounding, Max vowed to bang on Jake's door until he answered tonight.

Then he might hit him. Just once. Pay that damned regret bill.

Then he'd tell him they were moving forward.

With five minutes remaining in the class, Sensei Fabrizio called for them to line up and beckoned Max forward. "Feel like sitting on the wall for us tonight, Max?"

Tonight? Yes! If he succeeded, he'd gain a stripe, his first rank. More than the piece of yellow tape at the end of his belt, though, he'd have gained the respect of his sensei. The invitation meant she considered him worth training. Weirdly, he found he had to suppress a smile at the thought, respect notwithstanding. For the moment, the pain in his head and the myriad small aches spread across his body ceased to matter.

Max leaned into the wall, bending his legs until he achieved a rough ninety-degree angle, and breathed in. He did not look at the clock. The class would tell him when he could stand up. Seconds passed, every ten measured by a quiet inhale or exhale.

By the time he reckoned sixty, Elsa offered encouragement. "Nearly there. You're doing great."

He managed a smile, but remained concentrated on his task. One minute out of three hardly constituted *nearly there*. A mild burn crept across his thighs, working toward his hips. Max resisted the urge to rub at his muscles, knowing from long practice that it wouldn't help, that the action would only distract him. Better to fall into the sensation, embrace it, use it to push forward, just as he did when he ran. He breathed in and out. His headache pulsed along with each beat of his heart. Then, after an estimated minute and a half, Sensei Fabrizio called time.

Blinking in surprise, Max straightened up off the wall. His legs only wobbled slightly. The class cheered his bewildered expression.

"Not three minutes?" he asked.

Arthur laughed and clapped him on the shoulder. "Maybe you can do three minutes. For the rest of us, ninety seconds is downright heroic. Nice job." A large hand engulfed Max's in an enthusiastic shake.

Elsa grabbed his hand next, and he accepted congratulations from every student before attending the summons of Alyssa Fabrizio again. She gestured for him to face her, picked up one end of his belt, and wrapped it in bright yellow tape. Max grinned stupidly at the stripe. It seemed so casual, but he supposed sitting braced against a wall hardly constituted a harrowing test. That shiny band of yellow meant more to him than any award he'd received in school, however. He'd impressed someone he respected and she'd invited him to continue doing so.

Man, that felt good.

Class ended with another short meditation and another round of handshakes. Still smiling, Max moved toward the back of the room to retrieve his bag. He pondered wearing his gi home so he could show Jake the stripe at the end of his belt, but the heavy black cotton felt wet against his back. Rolling around the floor could be sweaty work. He undid the belt with shaky fingers and folded it into his gym bag. The top portion of his gi followed.

A whisper curled over his shoulder. "Did you practice by sitting on your boyfriend's cock?"

Max turned. He needn't have. He knew exactly who had offered the taunt. His elbow tingled as he turned around and he had to work to repress the urge to bring the sharply angled joint up and around with him, knock the smirk off Barry's face. Class had ended; he no longer had permission to strike someone, particularly in anger. But the urge surprised him. It felt foreign and sharp. Anger seethed beneath his skin, making him itch.

For another breath, he second-guessed himself. Hitting Barry would satisfy a need, yes. But Barry wasn't the guy who had taunted him throughout high school. He wasn't the prick who had cornered him at that party in college. He wasn't one of Dominick's friends, or the kind of man who might lurk in an alleyway, plotting violent satisfaction. He was a mattress salesman.

Gritting his teeth, Max sought a suitable reply. "Is that how you practiced?"

While Max wondered where on Earth he'd pulled that one from, Barry stuttered and spluttered. "I'm not a fucking faggot!" he said, his voice loud enough to draw the attention of everyone else.

Max felt the inevitable flush prickling his skin, across his cheeks, down his neck and over the top of his bare chest.

Alyssa elbowed her way through their small crowd of spectators and turned her dark brown gaze on Max, then Barry, giving each of them equal time. "What's going on?"

"Our special case here thinks I'm a fucking homo," Barry said.

Elsa clucked her tongue. "Takes one to know one, Barry."

What, a homo or special case?

"That kind of language is not welcome in this dojo," Alyssa said. "If any of you has an issue with the sexuality of another student, keep it to yourselves. If you can't, I do not want you here." She eyed all of them in turn, waiting for a nod before moving on. Then she turned to Max, one brow arched. "Do you have anything else to say?"

Max ran the possibilities through his mind. *Yes, I'm gay*, seemed like the incorrect response, on all levels. Thinking over the quieter purpose of the class—the bowing, the handshakes, the quiet words of respect—he extended a hand toward Barry. "Sorry."

Barry's eyes widened so the whites shone. Carefully, he took Max's hand, but he didn't return the apology.

Max turned away to don his T-shirt, the joy of his small success soured. Ignoring the quiet chatter around him, the exchange of farewells, he sat on the bench and pulled his socks and shoes closer. The bench creaked quietly beside him. He looked over to meet Alyssa's gaze, noting the brown of her eyes had warmed considerably over the last few minutes.

"Sensei, I'm—"

"I know you're sorry and I know you didn't start the fight. Barry has been gunning for you since the moment you stepped through the door. You did okay tonight. You might have thought out your reply a little better...." She paused to smile, the curve of her lips acquiring a distinctly conspiratorial lift. "But I'd have probably said the same."

Max tried not to smile.

"You're allowed to smile."

His smile felt stiff. Chuckling, Alyssa nudged his shoulder with hers. "You know what Barry's problem is?"

"He's homophobic?"

"Maybe. Maybe not. But he does have a thing for Jake."

A cold spike of jealousy pierced Max's chest.

"Regardless, I expect my students to remain professional in class."

"Ah...."

"Which you and Jake seem to manage."

"Right." Best to leave that one right there. Be... professional. "Do you know why Jake isn't in class on Wednesday nights?"

Alyssa studied Max's face for a moment. "Yes, and I'm going to assume you do as well."

"He just told me. On Monday."

"I see." Alyssa touched his arm. "I don't know what all Jake has shared with you, but he's a good man. He might have wriggled out of a conviction if he'd built a proper case against Dominick. He refused. I think a part of him was horrified by what he'd done, and rightly so. He should know better." She paused. "Jake is a pretty passionate guy. He doesn't always show it, he's got the cool and collected thing down. But underneath, he cares deeply about a few select people."

Alyssa didn't have to tell him that part. Max could see how much Jake loved his family and few close friends. It was obvious every time he spoke about them.

"He did his time," Alyssa continued. "Now he's trying to put his life back together." She nudged him again. "And he's got some good folks standing by to help him."

Max inhaled shakily.

"Are you okay with what he told you?" she asked.

Max found his chin dipping before he'd consciously chosen to nod. "It was a shock. I…. He surprised me. I'd never have guessed anything like that. Jake is so calm. He always seems so strong and capable and like he's got it all figured out."

"I think for the most part, he has."

"He just made a mistake?"

"We all have buttons. Dominick found the one of Jake's that has the lightest trigger." Alyssa stood and delivered a final smile. "Tell him I expect to see him in class on Friday."

While Alyssa tidied the dojo, Max pulled his phone out of his bag, selected Jake's number, and typed: *Got something to show you. Will be there in 15. If you don't stop brooding long enough to open the door, I'll ask Mrs. Wu to do it for me.*

CHAPTER TWENTY-FIVE

JAKE GLANCED down at the phone in his hand, the screen dimming toward dark. Demanding Max was hot, the idea of Max in command damned sexy. But he'd had to give him a pair of days, at the very least. Jake acknowledged he'd needed the time himself. More, though, he'd wanted to make sure Max had space—to breathe, to think, to digest the facts of his recent past. Max rejecting him for his sexuality would have hurt. The belief he had had twisted through Jake like a rusty blade. Max rejecting him because he'd screwed up his life was an altogether different enterprise. Max accepting him despite the same—it had to be his decision.

It seemed Max had made his choice. Now Jake could put this epic brood behind him.

Man, he'd missed Max. His kisses, his shy smiles, his surprise at ordinary things, even his quietness—the way he seemed to simply exist sometimes, without calling on others to help prop him up. He'd missed having Max in his bed, too. Sleeping, being available for all the small touches Jake couldn't help. He wanted to hold Max while he slept, cover every last inch of his pale skin with his hands and lips, his tongue, as he woke. Stroke him, stoke him, make him fly.

He wanted to love Max, and know Max loved him back, without reservation.

Jake looked down at the blank face of his phone. Max wouldn't knock on his door so late to break up with him, would he? No, and certainly not with Mrs. Wu in tow. Jake woke the phone display again to check the time. Nearly fifteen minutes had passed. He glanced expectantly toward the door. His legs tingled with the urge to unfold. He'd been sprawled across the couch since returning from his meeting an hour before. He checked the message again and a curl of uncertainty rolled in his gut. Fifteen minutes? Why would it take Max fifteen minutes to get upstairs?

Because Max wasn't downstairs, he'd gone to class.

Something more than an urge to move propelled Jake off the couch. He toed into one discarded boot, then the other, barely stopping to step down, let alone stoop to tug each over his heel. The anxiety in his gut curled tighter. The alley had been quiet for weeks. Nothing more than a puddle had lurked in the shadows. He hadn't received an answer from Dominick regarding his threat to involve the police if his buddies so much as drove along Beech Street again, but he hadn't really expected to. Dominick was a coward as well as an ass.

He half expected to find Max in the hall. The hallway stood dark and quiet. Even the odor of Chinese cabbage seemed subdued. Jake's descending footsteps were rude and loud. Max did not answer a knock at the basement apartment. Pressing his ear to the door, Jake listened for movement and heard nothing.

His panic felt unreasonable, as though he invited disaster by merely considering it.

Jake skipped back up the basement stairs and pushed through the door into the alley. He swallowed sharp fear as he scanned the pavement for trouble. He jumped the steps, boot soles clopping against the uneven concrete, and ran toward Beech Street.

If Max came around the corner, he'd call himself a fool. Pull the guy into a hug and kiss him senseless. Tell him he was happy to see him. Drag him back down the alley, take him upstairs and undress him. Make love to him. Hell, he'd happily admit his fright and encourage Max to laugh it off with him. Max wouldn't begrudge him one small weakness, would he? Not if he could forgive one major mistake.

Before Jake reached the end of the alleyway, he stopped short. His heart slammed in his chest and fear clawed the sides of his throat. A figure lay crumpled on the ground—dark pants, light colored T-shirt washed gray by the low light, gym bag pitched some two feet ahead.

"Max!" He didn't know it was Max, but he also, irrationally, knew it was Max.

Jake skidded forward and dropped to his knees beside the still form and all but froze in utter panic. Thought fled as his jaw worked and his fingers flexed, both actions entirely useless. For countless seconds he couldn't decide what to do. Anguish gripped him, held him fast. The echo of Max's name reverberated inside his skull, a buzz of sound timed to the frantic skip of his pulse. A honking horn in Cottman Avenue broke the spell. Jake slumped forward, hands fluttering over his lover's shoulders like dazed moths. He pushed dark hair aside, looking for Max's face, and found only the back of his head. His scalp felt warm.

"Pulse," Jake murmured. He should check for a pulse.

Jesus fucking Christ, why would he check for a pulse? Max wasn't dead! *Not dead.* Swallowing, Jake shuffled across the pavement on his knees, aiming to find Max's face. He needed to see Max's face. He brushed more hair aside and found an ear. A thin trail of blood leaked from the canal, leaving a diagonal stripe across Max's pale cheek. More blood spilled from his nose, down over his mouth. His eyes were closed and even in the shadows of the alley, Jake could make out the dark hollows beneath.

A narrow beam of light slashed across the back of Max's head, picking Jake's hands out from the dark strands of hair.

"Sir, I need you to stand up and keep your hands where I can see them."

Oh, God, he knew that tone. The stern voice of authority—the voice he dared not disobey. The panic he'd felt before? Nothing. Not a goddamned tick on a dog's ass compared to what he felt now. Rocking back on his heels, Jake raised his hands. Distractedly, he noted the way his fingers trembled against the tight white beam.

"Help," he croaked.

"Do you have any identification on you, sir?" A different voice. Lower pitched, softer, female.

"Y-yes. In my wallet." Jake cleared his throat. He forced himself to consider the cops as allies rather than a threat. "My friend is hurt. Maybe badly. Can you call someone? An ambulance?"

"We will surely do that," said the first policeman. "Can you tell us what you were doing here?"

The female officer stepped toward him, slowly, and knelt by Max's side. Her fingers disappeared into the shadow of Max's neck, probably checking for a pulse.

"I…." Jake's voice broke. "I was doing that," he said. "Checking for a pulse."

"He's alive," the female officer said, standing. Her tone far from gentle, but still reassuring.

The flashlight beam waved. "Show me your hands," the other policeman barked.

Understanding the command, the purpose of it, Jake displayed his hands, palms upturned, and then downturned so that the officers could check for blood or marks along his knuckles. Indignation had no place here. Still, his stomach churned with a mixture of fear and loathing. He hated that the mere sight of a police uniform could turn his thoughts upside down, but he had only himself to blame.

"Please call help for him," Jake said.

The male officer reached for his radio, called in the incident and requested an EMT. Then he jabbed the flashlight beam toward Jake. "Please show us your identification, sir, slowly, and run us through what happened here. Start with names."

Jake reached for his pocket, slowly as instructed. "My name is Jacob Kendricks. This is Max, er...." What was Max's first name again? "Gareth. Wilson. He calls himself Max. That's his middle name." Jake opened his wallet and waved it at the officer.

"Pull your license out for me please."

"He's my downstairs neighbor, my friend. He was supposed to meet me tonight. When he didn't show, I came looking for him."

He handed over his license to the female officer and listened as she read the details to her radio. Quietly, Jake debated dropping back to his knees. He wanted to be next to Max. He hated the idea of Max being alone on the ground. Had Dominick's friends jumped him again? He turned to look over his shoulder, scanning the alleyway for whatever he hadn't seen on the run to the end. Of course, whoever had attacked Max was more likely to run out into Beech Street than down a dark alley, right?

"Sir? Mr. Kendricks? You need to turn around."

"Whoever did this could be getting away. We need to check the alley and the street." Where had the cops been two months ago, when Dominick's friends had gotten away? The urge to go find them, now, slipped through Jake's legs, pulling him forward.

"I am advising you not to take another step," the male officer said.

One of the radios chattered and the female officer raised her hand to her shoulder. The details of Jake's record creaked into the night, surrounded by bursts of static. The policewoman looked from Max to Jake and back again. He couldn't see her face, but he felt the subtle shift in tension. Instantly, both officers became more alert. Fuck. Jake swallowed his panic, again and again, the taste of it sharp and bitter. They wouldn't take him back to prison under suspicion, would they?

I can't go back.

He took another step away from Max.

In the distance, a siren wailed. Jake's pulse rose accordingly, blood screaming behind his ears. An interminable minute later, filled with low conversation between the officers and their radio, the EMT vehicle coasted to a halt outside the alley. Colored light flashed from the brick walls, turning the scene into something more than a horrible memory. Jake felt his knees collapsing beneath him. He lurched toward the wall.

"Mr. Kendricks, you really need to stop moving." A flashlight beam cut across the still figure of Max before bouncing back up to Jake's face. "Are you sure this is a friend of yours?"

"Yes." Jake bit back the urge to divulge the full nature of his relationship with Max. Telling the cops he and Max were lovers or partners, that Max was his boyfriend, wouldn't invite sympathy or the help Max needed. "Please. We're wasting time here. Whoever did this is getting away."

"Who is your PO?"

"Officer Nathan Spet."

The male officer nodded as if the name was familiar and spoke into his radio again. Two blue-jumpsuited paramedics spilled out of the ambulance. The policewoman directed them to Max. Jake bit back the urge to yell at everyone. Why were they moving so slowly? Why were they all standing around while Max lay unmoving and bloody on the ground? Why wasn't anyone looking for Max's attackers? Dominick's friends could be halfway to Jersey by now!

"You need to calm down, Mr. Kendricks."

Jake gaped, then shut his mouth, realizing he'd vented his last questions out loud. Curling his fingers into his palms, he swallowed a growl and directed his attention to Max. The paramedics had snapped a brace around his neck and turned him over. Max's sharply angled face appeared more pale than ever, the clots at his nostrils obscenely dark.

"Is he okay?" Jake asked, his query more a plea.

"Any idea what happened here?" one of the paramedics asked.

"No. I just found him like that. He messaged me maybe half an hour ago? He attends a self-defense class on Castor Avenue on Wednesday nights. When he didn't show, I came down to look for him and found him here." Jake sucked in a breath. "There's blood coming from his ear, what does that mean?"

"Looks like he hit his head pretty hard."

"Bastards!"

The woman looked away, apparently used to being insulted by angry bystanders.

"Sorry," Jake muttered. He turned to the cops. "We need to find out who did this."

"Why are you so certain he was attacked?"

"Because it's happened before. C'mon, we need to do something."

"Mr. Kendricks, right now, I believe you are not responsible for Mr. Wilson's current condition. But if you cannot calm down, I'll be forced to reevaluate your presence in this alleyway."

Fuck, fuck, fuck.

Jake grasped for his precious anger management techniques and felt them slip through his mental fingers like so many useless grains of sand. His breath came hard and fast and his legs continued to shake. All of him shook, whether from fear or anger he couldn't tell. Remaining calm was just not going to happen. Neither was waiting until Dom and his friends got away. He started for the other end of the alleyway.

"Mr. Kendricks!"

Jake started running. The clamor behind him faded into aural haze, the cops' voices no more important than the obsessive need to find out who had done what to Max. He was done being good, with walking the line; the no drinking, no speeding, no crossing the goddamned street against the light. Counting his change, checking his pockets for sharp objects, not raising his voice, being everywhere on time. Observing his curfew, making every meeting with his parole officer. Pissing in a cup to prove he hadn't so much as looked at a poppy seed bagel, let alone indulged in anything illegal.

None of it had helped Max.

Something heavy hit him from behind and Jake flew forward an entire body length before skidding across the pavement. Before he could get his hands underneath him, his face was pressed into the gritty blacktop and one arm was yanked behind him. Yelling, Jake struggled against capture—even though he knew he was making it worse for himself.

What was rationality?

One of the cops sat on his legs while the other yanked his other hand back. Jake spit and struggled until a familiar sequence of words brushed past his ringing ears.

"...right to remain silent. Anything you say can and will be used against you...."

Jake stopped struggling.

CHAPTER TWENTY-SIX

MAX'S HEAD hurt, which was nothing new. Seemed his head hurt a lot. He was forever knocking it against something, breaking something, hitting something. Usually a fist, sometimes a wall. The relentless pounding inside his skull was like a heartbeat. Without it, he couldn't be sure he lived. But, lord, he was tired.

"Get your lazy ass out of bed."

The words echoed thinly, from the other end of a long tunnel. Max peered into the darkness, looking for the familiar outline of the man whose voice could pluck the tightest coil into a straight line. Lying in bed after dawn was a sin of the gravest variety. Wilsons rose with the sun. His father had never pulled him out of bed in the middle of the night before, though.

"Sssir." Max tried to get out of bed, but whatever afflicted his tongue also weighed down his arms and legs. "Can't get up."

"Are you defying me, boy?"

He still couldn't see anything and with every movement the pain in his head surged forward and back. He gagged.

"Stop that retching nonsense. A man carries his bruises with pride."

Bruises? At the thought, Max's body lit into flame, the memory of all his bruises spreading across his skin. His bones ached, all the ones that had been broken. His arm, a pair of ribs, his nose. Felt like someone had a boot on his face. Just stood there, grinding down. Was it his father? No, his father had never hurt him. Not really.

"If you stopped skulking around like a damned sissy, those other boys would stop beating on you."

True enough.

"Now get out of bed. I need your help in the shop."

"Sorry." The slur had returned. Why didn't his tongue work properly? "Sorry, sir."

"Damn right you're sorry. A sorry excuse for a man."

The insult hurt worse than all his aches combined. Max squeezed his eyes shut and worked to mask his pain. Real men felt pain, but they defeated it. Used the bite to move forward. A scream circled the inside of his head. Was it him?

"Are you whimpering, boy?"

"No, sir." If he did not get his lazy butt out of bed in the next breath, he'd have to make up the time doing the jobs no one else in the shop wanted to do: cleaning the pans and evacuators, scrubbing stains out of concrete bays that would never be clean, transferring oil from half-empty bottles and drums, stacking tires, weeding the cracks in the pavement.

His father saved those tasks for him, Max knew that. He also knew that his father looked for opportunities to punish him so those jobs got done. He wasn't stupid. Lazy, maybe. Small, weak, a coward and a sissy. But not stupid. What could he do, though? Defy the man? No. His mother needed him. She was sick and she needed his help. She couldn't look after herself, let alone her husband and son.

Gritting his teeth, Max fought to move his arms and legs. He would get up, regardless of how much it hurt. He would work, despite the pounding ache across his temples, the sharp pain drilling down between his eyes. What did it matter if he couldn't see? The stains on the concrete would never fade. He pushed and strained until black turned white, until the pain flared out from his head into a bright corona of light, swallowing him and his screams.

"SHH. IT'S okay. Don't try to move."

"Can't." The word left him on a sigh. He opened his eyes to regret. Bright light stabbed downward, pulling a broken yell from his sore throat. The heavy weight holding him down hadn't dissolved in the light. The nightmare still gripped him, pushing him down. If he didn't get up soon, he'd have to work all night to get through his list of chores.

Then who would look after his mother?

Maybe Jake could help. Where was Jake? Max made a sound that might have been Jake's name. Coordinating his lips required more work than keeping his eyes open. Why was he so tired?

"Shh," said the quiet voice that had spoken before. "Everything's going to be okay."

No, it wasn't. Everything felt wrong and Jake wasn't there. Oh, God. What if Jake had been nothing but a beautiful, golden dream?

"…going to give you something to help with the pain."

Wait, no. Max commanded his tongue to cooperate, but his mouth seemed fixated on a single word. "Jake."

MAX CURLED down, shame burning cheeks that already stung from the scrape of knuckles. He pulled his arms up over his head.

"Going to fight back?"

One of his arms was wrenched back, then across something. Max thought he heard a crack. White heat flowed along his forearm. He clutched it to his chest just before continued blows knocked him down. A boot caught him in the hip.

"Fucking pussy."

Sunlight poked through the bleachers overhead, bathing the scene in striped light. Max thought about rolling under the structure, but it would be a long roll to the front row and escape, and they'd only follow him.

Better to just wait it out.

HE SAT next to a bed in a quiet room. Max studied the gentle hill rising beneath the bedcovers, trying to figure out who occupied the bed. He had an idea it should be him. He was in the hospital, right? Something about his head. But that wasn't his arm resting alongside the covers, skin all yellow and papery.

He was dreaming again. Or still dreaming….

A quiet croak drew his attention upward to a face he barely recognized. Drawing in a sharp breath, Max swallowed horror and sorrow combined. His mother, her skin drawn tight over the bones of her face, regarded him with eyes the color of a puddle. Dirty and dull, from corner to corner, her irises barely distinguished from the whites.

Margaret Wilson had had blue eyes. Her long battle with cancer had leached the color away while rendering the whites a shade of parchment. The doctors said that was the liver failure or maybe her kidneys backing up. The same with her skin, which had thinned and darkened, the patches at her elbows and knuckles turning a deep purple. She had shadows under her eyes and in the hollows of her cheeks. Her ears sagged from the sides of her head, and what was left of her hair had been tucked beneath a floral kerchief that more resembled a wilted patch of wildflowers than anything remotely cheerful.

"Gary," she whispered.

His parents had never taken to calling him Max.

Max held her brittle hand, trying not to wince as the bones seemed to shift beneath her skin. "I'm here, Mom." His tongue still felt clumsy. His head still ached. His head always ached. Breathing out, he focused on the woman in front of him. "How are you?"

"I'm tired. I want to go home."

He knew the feeling, intimately.

"They won't let me go home," he said.

His mother looked at him oddly. "You should listen to your father."

Max frowned and a spike of pain shot through his skull. His father wasn't at the hospital. His father wasn't the one who said he had to stay there. In fact, he needed to go home before his father started bellowing. The chores would have stacked up by now, wouldn't they? Things would need doing. Things always needed doing.

His mother's fingers moved beneath his, twigs shifting under mulched leaves. Max loosened his grip. "I'm confused," he said.

"You hit your head pretty hard this time," his mother answered. Her arm shifted, as if she thought about reaching up to stroke his hair— except, she never did that. Jake stroked his hair, short nails scraping lightly over his scalp, and it felt so good. Soothing and regular, like a comb sorting his hair and his thoughts, putting everything in place.

"I'm sorry," he said.

"It's okay, Gary. I forgive you."

Throat tightening so his breath wheezed, Max struggled to contain his sorrow. He'd disappointed his mother. He'd failed her. Here she lay dying, and he couldn't bring her comfort, only distress. He couldn't tell her anything that would make her proud. He'd failed both his parents, over and over. He wasn't the son they wanted or deserved.

"I'm sorry," he said again, knowing the words were worse than useless. They were an insult, salt on the wound. Because he wasn't sorry, not really. Not for them. He was sorry for himself, wasn't he? Because he'd always been a selfish boy.

And he was confused and his head hurt.

And his mother was dying, the machine measuring the beat of her heart slowing inexorably to a quiet pulse. Soon he would hear nothing but the long, bland silence of death and he could do nothing to stop it. Nothing to change it. He could only watch and wait as her death settled across his shoulders, heavy and suffocating. Maybe that was why he couldn't move. His mother had died, leaving him paralyzed. Leaving him to the formless anger and hatred of his father, the man he could never and would never please, no matter how hard he worked, no matter how hard he tried.

I'm sorry.

CHAPTER TWENTY-SEVEN

ERIC HADN'T spoken since meeting him at the station, where Jake had been let off with a warning after a night of cooling his heels in a holding cell. God, he'd hoped never to see the world through a set of bars again. Thank every deity it had only been for a handful of hours. He was lucky. Damned lucky. They decided he hadn't resisted arrest, and Officer Spet had put in a good word. Apparently he was a model parolee.

This would be his one and only strike, however.

"Thanks for coming to pick me up," Jake said.

Eric maintained his silence, though Jake could see a response kicking around in his mind. The way his jaw flexed and his knuckles whitened as he gripped the steering wheel. His wisecracking best friend had been replaced by the man who got shit done. A man who had his life together and probably couldn't figure out why Jake was such a fuckup.

When Eric finally did speak, Jake wished he hadn't. "Do you know how many times I visited you in prison?" Eric asked.

"None. I told you all I didn't want visitors."

"We came anyway. Willa and I. We stood outside. Once we had a picnic on the lawn."

"Why would you do that?"

"Because you're like a brother to me, Jacob. Because you and Willa are family."

"Considering we've all been in bed together at one time or another, that makes us a pretty incestuous fucking family."

Breath whistled between Eric's teeth. "God, you are such an ass."

"I just spent the night in a holding cell."

"And whose fault is that?"

"Dominick's!" Except, it wasn't Dominick's fault. It was his, because he was fucking stupid. Running down the alley had accomplished nothing except to keep him away from Max at a time when Max really needed him. "Fuck. Shit. Damn. Fucking, fuck, fuck!"

"Are you done?"

"No." Jake glanced over at Eric. "Maybe."

"Jake—"

"I'm sorry, okay?"

"I'm not the one who needs to hear it."

"I mean for…." Pushing his hands through his short hair, Jake wished for the curls he'd have if he grew it out. Yeah, they made him look like a big girl, but gripping them and pulling on them always delivered a good, sharp pain. At fifteen, he'd imagined he might be tugging his thoughts into some sort of order. Apparently it hadn't worked.

He let go of his head and looked up. "Do you have any news on Max?" That should have been his first question. Would have been if Eric hadn't distracted him with this family bullshit.

"Not a lot. Willa has the full story. She can fill you in when we get to the hospital."

"Is he going to be okay?"

The set of Eric's shoulders relaxed. "As far as I know, yes." He turned to glance at Jake. "And that would be because you were there."

"But not quick enough. If I'd gone downstairs to wait for him, I might have been able to stop it."

Eric was shaking his head. "You couldn't have stopped it."

"Sure I could." Jake curled his fingers back into his palms. "I'd willingly go back into prison if it meant I could have saved Max another beating."

"No one beat him up. Not this time."

"What? He was lying on the ground with blood all over his face!"

"It was his head. Something popped in his head."

A curious numbness swept through Jake's limbs. He sat paralyzed for a moment. Unable to speak, unable to think. Then he gripped the door handle on his side. "Stop the car."

"What? We're nearly there."

"Stop the car, Eric. I'm not going to the hospital just yet."

"Why?"

Jake shook his head. "Best you don't know why."

Eric pulled over to the curb and put a restraining hand on Jake's arm. "Don't do this."

"You have no idea—"

"Oh my God, do you ever listen to a word I say? I know you, Jake. You're going to Dominick's place, aren't you?"

"He nearly killed my boyfriend!"

"So you're going to go mess him up again. Is that how it works?"

Yes! "No." *I don't know.* "He needs to know he went too far."

"He wasn't there. Not this time."

"It's because of his shit Max is in the hospital, though."

Eric mashed both of his hands against his forehead and groaned. "I really, really need a new best friend."

"I'm not asking you to come with me."

"Oh, I'm coming, and I am going to hold your fucking hand until you're done saying your piece, then I'm driving you back to the hospital."

"I don't want you there. And I don't want you holding my fucking hand."

"Someone has to stop you from making your next mistake."

Jake paused with his hand on the door handle. Fury burned through his veins and he could only figure one way of exorcising it. If he left the car, though, his friendship with Eric would suffer. But....

Man, his life was so full of suck right now, what was one more thing?

Everything?

Everything.

He'd known Eric for too long to let him go, and sometimes he thought Eric was the only person on the planet who truly understood him and loved him regardless.

Chest tight, sinuses burning, Jake pressed his forehead to the passenger side window. "I'm sorry," he whispered to the glass.

Eric rubbed the back of his shoulder, right over his tattoo. "I know."

DOMINICK'S SMALL brick house looked oddly domestic. The grass appeared freshly mowed and neat flower beds lined the short concrete path to the front door. Jake couldn't remember if the garden had been so tidy when Kate had lived there. His brain was too full of fog for that much abstract thought.

"He's probably not home," Eric said. "We should have called ahead."

Calling ahead would have killed his momentum—Jake's urgent need to take care of business, *now*, before he went to see Max. He strode up to the door and leaned on the bell. The ring inside the house sounded like a quiet appeal. Then footsteps, short and sharp, approached from inside. Jake stepped back.

A woman opened the door. Her honey-blonde hair, shorter than when he'd last seen her, fell loose to the tops of her shoulders. She wore a sundress, but he registered little more than the color—something between blue and green—before noting it hugged a figure rounder than he remembered. He looked up from her waist, attention skimming her cleavage with detached interest, and met her eyes.

"Kate." He hadn't seen her for nearly two years.

She greeted him as if it had been yesterday. "You shouldn't be here."

"What the hell are you doing here?" Jake asked. "Tell me you're not still living with Dom."

Kate made no answer.

Jake breathed out sharply and looked down at the scuffed toes of his boots. A night in a holding cell hadn't done his appearance any good. Mysterious stains darkened the knees of his worn jeans and his T-shirt stank of spent adrenaline and regret. Then there was the scrape across his cheek from where his face had hit the pavement. The scuffs on his elbows.

He'd shown up on Kate's doorstep looking like a bum.

Jake looked again at the woman he had once loved, the mother of his child. The woman he'd told himself he'd give everything up for. "Is Dom here?"

"No."

"Where is he?"

"You need to stop texting him. He hasn't contacted the police, but it's bordering on harassment."

"He put my boyfriend in the hospital. Did you know that? He sent his friends around for me and they got Max instead." Gaze dropping to the front of Kate's dress, Jake reevaluated the fit across her hips. His eyes widened. "Fuck." He looked up. "Tell me that's not his baby."

Kate lifted her chin.

"What the hell, Kate?" He reached for her arm, pulled it out from her side, turned it looking for bruises. "He's not a good guy."

"Jake…." Eric stepped between them and put a restraining hand on Jake's shoulder.

"And you are?" Kate retorted, tugging her arm out of his grip.

"I wanted to be!" Anger overrode the sorrow, lit inside him like a bonfire. "Jesus. Why him? Why not me? I wouldn't have hit you, ever."

"Once I might have believed that."

Rather than fuel his anger, the comment deflated him. Defeated him. "I would have taken care of you. I wanted to be Caroline's father, your husband. Why didn't you let me? Why wasn't I good enough?"

Eric stepped back off the porch. He didn't go far; he simply left the strained bubble so that it popped back around Jake and Kate.

Kate rubbed her arm. "Oh, Jake." Her eyes misted. "That's not… I didn't…."

"Didn't what? Didn't toss me aside and take up with an asshole who frightened you so much you called me back? What did you expect would happen? I wasn't good enough to be a father, but I was good enough to pound the man you wanted to take my place?"

Tears rolled down her cheeks. "I never wanted you out of my life. I just wanted you to be happy."

"Happy?"

"We were friends. Good friends, but not in love. We made a mistake. We've made so many mistakes. But letting you go wasn't one of them."

Letting him go?

"I didn't want to trap you," she said. "I saw the way you were with Eric, with guys after Eric. Maybe the right woman could have made you happy, but I didn't think I could have, and…." She sucked in a breath. "I didn't want to deal with having a husband who might leave me for another man."

Jake stepped back. Rocked back, his feet forced to follow. Well, fuck. There it was, the reason for the most painful rejection of his life. And, with that simple statement, so much finally made sense.

Kate didn't get it—few did. Why was loving a person simply for being a person such a hard concept to grasp? Or that for him, being with a woman had always been as fulfilling as being with a man? He'd loved Kate with all his heart. He'd have made her the most important person in his world.

That she hadn't known, or understood, meant either he'd failed, or she had. Fear had gotten the best of her, obviously, and he'd been just young and stupid enough to go along for the ride.

"Listen," Kate said, "I'm sorry your friend is going through this. Really, I am. But Dominick had nothing to do with it. You have to believe me."

"I saw Dom's friends there. They were waiting for us a week after Max got attacked. They were waiting for me."

"He didn't ask them to do that. In fact, he was very upset when he found out they'd been stalking you. He told them to stand down, Jake. Dom doesn't want this. Any of it." She laced her fingers over the dome of her stomach. "This baby has changed everything."

Jake looked at Kate's stomach again, at the swell across her hips. He was no judge, but if he had to guess, he'd say six months. With Kate's petite figure, it could be more. He turned toward Eric. "Did you know about this?"

Eric didn't have to say a word. The answer flickered across his face in large neon letters.

"I called Dominick," Kate said.

The world shimmied a little as Jake swung his attention back to Kate. "What?"

"When I saw you getting out of Eric's car. He'll be here soon. Look, you're already violating one restraining order. If you leave now—"

"Oh no. That's why I'm here. I came to see Dom. It's time we settled this, once and for all."

"If you hurt him, Jake, I'll have no choice but to call the police."

Jake clenched his fists. "I just want to talk."

CHAPTER TWENTY-EIGHT

THE ACHE in his head had receded. Recognizing the slow slide into consciousness, Max ignored the lack of pain, guessing even the mildest thought might summon the demon back. Sounds slowly intruded on numb-space, and Max spent several moments identifying them. He was in the hospital, he knew that. He preferred not to examine why. Classifying whispers of sound seemed a safer game. Mostly, he heard voices, all at a distance. Closer, he could hear the regular cadence of breath. His?

Easing his eyes open, Max prepared for the stab of pain. The universe did not disappoint him. Like the ache in his head, the stab was more a nudge. It didn't hurt... much. He rolled his head to the side, to where he thought the door was. He saw a window. Why had he thought the door was there?

Rolling his head to the other side took a lot more effort, but he was rewarded with a door, which opened to admit a flood of whitecoats.

"Good morning, Mr. Wilson," said one of them. Max had difficulty tracking so many faces. Three, four, five? There might as well have been ten people in the room with him.

One of them did the eyelid-peeling, flashlight-poking thing. Max tried to jerk his head away, but again, found the translation of thought to movement difficult. What was wrong with him?

He tried to lift an arm. Neither responded. Were they broken? A vague memory plucked at a corner of his brain. He'd struggled with this before—with an invisible weight against his arms, against his body. Mild panic burned in his chest, the sensation almost welcome. Something he could feel. He tried again, wriggling the fingers of his left hand first, then got his arm to move, but not gracefully. The limb flailed up off the bed and veered sideways, smacking one of the whitecoats.

She caught his arm and held it gently. "Well, this one moves!"

Max felt his eyes widen. Was he paralyzed?

Oh no, oh no, oh no....

"How are you doing?"

Max struggled to calm himself. Pain crept across the back of his skill. His headache returning. "Hurts," he croaked.

"Your head?"

Max tried to nod without nodding. Wow, so not a good idea.

"Not unexpected. You're about due something for the pain. Are you up to a few questions?"

They wanted to know his full name, the Gareth and Maxwell part, what year it was, and if he had anyone he'd like them to call.

"Is Jake here?"

"Who?"

"Jake." The name left him on a sigh. Making words happen was exhausting, and the light in here was too bright, and the quiet voices comparing notes and readouts behind the doctor made it hard for him to pick out what he was supposed to listen to. "Boyfriend," he managed.

"Do you have his number?"

"My phone." He opened his eyes again. Who kept pressing them shut?

"Why don't you rest now? We'll see if we can contact Jake, and talk more next time you wake up."

Rest sounded good. Keeping his eyes open was just too much work. Max let them slip closed. "When can I go home?"

A soft chuckle floated down from far, far away. "Not for a while. Don't worry. We'll take good care of you."

WILLA WAS there the next time he opened his eyes.

"What day is it?" Max asked.

"Thursday."

He'd barely missed a day of work. Good. He couldn't afford to lose his job at the market. "I need to get up." Max struggled with his traitorous limbs until it became clear he wasn't going anywhere. His left side responded just fine. His right was still taking voice mail messages. "Why can't I move properly?" And why did all his words sound like mush?

"Oh, Max, honey." Willa stroked his forehead. "It's going to be okay."

"I can't miss any more work." The more he spoke, the clearer his words got. Sort of.

"Not that you'd ever not have a good excuse for missing work, I think this time your employer is going to cut you some slack. Surgery is kind of a big deal."

"S-surgery?"

In careful, simple terms, Willa told him what had happened. He'd suffered a subdural bleed. If laughing didn't hurt, Max would've tried. He'd rather laugh about the fact he'd bled quietly, surreptitiously, inside his own skull until he'd passed out. He was so afraid of giving offense, he'd tried to die without a fuss. Now he had more attention than he liked, and a hole in his skull—under a flap of skin that had been shaved clean, peeled back and sewn shut.

"It's called a bore hole," Willa explained. "The blood from the hemorrhage needed to be evacuated."

Made his stomach turn just to think about it. Thankfully, the evidence of his surgery had been wrapped in a nice, neat bandage. Max really didn't want to see that scar. The good news was that the surgery had been a success. Mostly. His blood pressure had dropped too far at one point, causing a very minor stroke.

"Very, very minor," Willa made a point of saying. "Barely a blip."

"A blip."

"That's why you're slurring a little."

"Is that why I can't move my arm?" He glared at his right arm. Gritted his teeth and demanded the damn thing move. His hand jumped slightly. "I dreamed I couldn't move. I dreamed…." He'd dreamed about his father, a mishmash of nightmare and memory.

Willa collected his nearly numb fingers in hers. "You doing okay?"

"My father's not here, is he?"

"No, he's not. Do you want me to—"

"No!"

Concern furrowed Willa's brow. "Okay. Okay. Breathe, Max."

For several seconds, measured by the terrible pounding of his heart, Max feared he'd forgotten how to draw air. That his lungs were somehow as messed up as his arm.

Willa waited him out, and the feel of her fingers around his brought him slowly and steadily back. He breathed. His heartbeat slowed. The fear his father might find him lounging in a hospital bed receded.

But he couldn't stay here for long. He had to get back to work.

"When can I go home?"

Willa squeezed his hand. "Not for a while. Depending on the results of your physical assessment, you'll probably be moved to an SNF in the next couple of days."

"A what?"

"Skilled Nursing Facility. They'll have therapists there to help you get back on your feet."

How in heck was he going to afford all of this? "Willa—"

"Stop worrying and let us take care of you."

"But—"

"No buts."

He'd have cried if he could remember how, but his emotional response felt as heavy as his limbs. Or maybe it had simply been beaten out of him, along with the memory of the last time he had actually shed a tear. Had he been five? The pain lazily circling his skull intensified, acquired a rhythm. Exhaustion pulled at his thoughts.

"Where's Jake?" His question was slightly slurred.

"I'm sure he'll be here soon. He had to go get cleaned up."

He had to go? But he'd be back, right? Their cooling-off period was done. He'd sent a text, hadn't he? Max frowned at the haze that formed his memory of the past couple of days. Jake's confession, and his horror and anger. The kiss. Being confused. Missing Jake.

Would he be too much investment now? Did two dates really equal a relationship, a couple months of friendship aside? This bleeding inside his head thing made him complicated, and Jake sure didn't need complicated. He had enough to deal with.

"Why did this happen?"

"Oh, honey, I don't know." Willa stroked his forehead and though it was weird, in that she wasn't Jake, it also felt good. He'd come to think of Willa as a friend and was slowly coming to realize how grateful he was to have her there.

"It was the concussions, wasn't it?" he asked.

"Probably, and maybe not even the last one. You're going to have to take care of yourself from here on out. Not push yourself too hard and make sure you get enough rest."

Like that was going to happen.

Max sighed. "Head hurts."

Willa got up and walked around the bed. She pushed something into his left hand. "There you go. Press that button."

Max pressed the button. Before he could decide that it really couldn't be that easy, gray blots appeared at the edges of his vision. Billowing like storm clouds, they rolled toward the center and everything began to fade beneath them.

Heh. He needed a button like this. A life button.

CHAPTER TWENTY-NINE

KATE DIDN'T invite him inside. Eric went into the house with her, leaving Jake to pace the stoop. Jake supposed they expected him to either find some sense and leave, or wear himself down by the time Dom got there.

He did neither.

When Dom's car finally pulled into the drive, Jake leaped over one of the carefully tended flower beds and stalked across the lawn. He had his hands on Dom even before he got out of the car.

"What the fuck, man?" Dom jerked his arm out of Jake's grasp and pushed out of the car to stand next to him. "You can't be here. Kate did you a favor by calling me. But you can't be here. If you're not off my property in the next three seconds, I'm going to call the cops."

Jake could still smell last night's incarceration. Every time he moved, the odor of sweat and concrete rose up from his clothes. It was enough to make him step back and take a breath. "I just want to talk."

Dom folded his arms and leaned a hip against the car. "You got two seconds."

Jake opened his mouth and all the words he'd been saving up evaporated.

"One second."

"You made a serious mistake when you sent your friends after me."

"I didn't send no one after no one."

"I saw them, Dom. Weedy and Patrick. I talked to them outside Wu's."

Dom unfolded his arms and held both hands up. "I never asked them to look in on you. Yeah, things might not be settled between us—"

"Not by a long shot."

"I don't want any more trouble."

Jake stabbed a finger toward the house. "Then what do you call that?"

"My house."

"Don't play fucking games with me."

"What do you want?"

"I want to know what you're doing with Kate."

"I love her."

Not the response Jake had expected. He rocked back, shaken by the simplicity of both Dominick's answer and the ease with which he had delivered it. Both spoke of truth. And it cut deeply, because Kate was obviously drinking the same fucking Kool-Aid. She carried this man's baby. The same man who'd struck her across the face and left bruises along her arms. She'd rejected Jake because of his sexuality, only to embrace someone who obviously couldn't keep his hands to himself.

How fucked-up was that?

"I don't understand," he said as something unraveled inside him.

"It's not hard. You're a fuckup. Always have been. Always will be."

A quiet roar built inside Jake's head. He flung his head back and looked at the sky. The calm blue offered no answers. He could feel the rage returning, riding a wave of a simple statement. *It's not fair.* And it was Max's voice, over and over. *It's not fair.*

He'd worked hard to let go of Kate. He knew they weren't to be. He understood why it couldn't work between them, and if he were honest with himself, he'd known the facts for a long, long time. But this....

It just made no sense.

He wasn't aware he'd leaned forward, legs braced, fists raised, until Eric wrapped him up from behind. He lifted Jake from his feet. Jake kicked and yelled.

"Let me down, Eric!"

"We're going home."

"I'm not done!"

He drove an elbow back into Eric's side. With a grunt, Eric dropped him, but he didn't let go. Jake twisted until he'd loosened Eric's grip and surged forward, one destination in mind.

Dom backed up against the car and lifted an arm to cover his face. Fucking coward.

"Daddy!"

"Caroline!"

The shouts did what nothing else might have. They stopped him so abruptly, Jake nearly fell over. He turned to see his daughter running across the lawn, Kate hurrying after. Jake's legs failed him, dropping him to his knees. He hit the pavement hard, the shock rattling his bones. He let his chin drop down, and his eyes fall shut.

This was it, the final cut.

He didn't want to watch his daughter run into the arms of another man.

Caroline smacked into him, nearly knocking him the rest of the way down. Jake caught her automatically. His arms rising up to wrap around her without conscious thought. He pulled her into him, all gangly limbs and sunshine, and cupped the back of her golden head. He buried his face in her curls and inhaled the scent of her innocence.

"Don't hurt Dom." Her voice was small and urgent. "Please."

His heart broke into a hundred thousand pieces.

"Why are you crying, Daddy?"

The ache in his throat burned away his answer. Instead, he simply clung to his daughter. Pressed kisses to her head. Kisses that tasted of salt and sorrow.

"It'll be okay." She squirmed a little, loosening his hold, and reached up to pat his cheek. "You'll be okay."

Jake nodded in response. He was aware of Kate hovering over them, Dom at her side. Eric stood close by as well. None of them moved to separate him from his daughter. He pulled Caroline close again. "I missed you, Peanut."

"No one calls me Peanut anymore."

"What do you want me to call you?"

"Caroline, of course. Why haven't you come to visit me?"

It was just one kick after another.

Kate stooped down to pull Caroline away. "You know why Daddy isn't allowed to see you."

"But it's not fair."

I'm so with you, kiddo.

Jake sat back on his heels. He should probably stand. Being underneath his peers put him at a serious disadvantage.

Maybe he belonged down here.

Or maybe he'd finally come face to face with the person he really needed to see. The one he owed the biggest apology to.

"Caroline, sweet pea…."

"Hmm."

"I'm so sorry."

She regarded him with a solemn expression for way too many seconds before delivering her verdict with a nod. "Okay."

He should've said more, but words were not his friends today. He'd try next time. If Kate ever allowed him to see his daughter again. Eric helped him to his feet and another moment of awkward silence passed before Jake figured out what everyone else was waiting for.

He owed more than one apology.

Turning toward Dom, he opened his mouth.

Dom shook his head. "Forget about it."

"No. I need to say this. I want to see my daughter. I want to be a part of her and Kate's lives. That means we need to square shi—stuff between us."

"Then I'll go first."

Huh?

"I know an apology will never make up for what I did," Dom said. "For what went down between me and Kate, and you and me, but I want you to know a day hasn't passed that I don't regret it all."

Jake blinked.

"I ain't gonna say you did me right. You could've killed me. But...." Dom tilted his head. "You didn't. I believe you didn't for a reason."

"What's that?"

"It's not in you. You're just a really angry guy."

Jake's mouth worked in silence.

"So am I. But you knocked some sense into me. I got myself a shrink now. I hate him, mostly because he costs me money and a chunk of my pride. But I love Kate and I'm gonna love our kid as much as I love yours."

Jake desperately sought a point of balance. He'd wanted to kill Dom not five minutes ago. Now the guy looked so fucking normal and reasonable.

"You—"

"Not done," Dominick said.

"Two wrongs don't make a right, Dom," Jake ground out.

"No, but they sure do point a man in the right direction."

"You want me be believe this new leaf bullshit?"

"You want us to believe the State of Pennsylvania has rehabilitated you?"

Another grunt worked up through Jake's throat. "So what about your friends?"

"I never asked 'em to do that. I told them if they go near you again, I'd be the one calling the police. And their mothers."

"Why Max? Why not me?"

Dominick's brow pinched. "They thought he was your boyfriend. Same door, right?" A sigh gusted out of him, leaving Dominick looking pained and troubled. As if what he had to share disturbed him greatly. Jake found himself wondering why the guy would care so much, if he really had changed. Dominick continued quietly, "They wanted to hit you where it hurt."

God. Poor Max. He'd never stood a chance.

"I didn't even know him then," Jake whispered.

Dominick looked him in the eye. "We got a lot to answer for, you and me."

Jake held Dominick's dark gaze. Guilt surged through his veins, stinging his body, lashing him with the pain of his shame. No, he didn't like Dominick, but he held extreme dislike for what he'd done to the guy.

"I'm sorry," he said.

Dominick didn't make him sweat it. Instead, he stuck out his hand.

Jake studied the wrinkled palm and stubby fingers for a second and shook his head. "I can't. Not yet."

Dominick nodded and retracted his hand.

Kate stepped forward. "Jake." She licked her lips. "I love Dominick. He's not perfect, but he's trying. He's trying so hard."

Dominick looked at Kate, and his rapt expression told Jake everything he needed to know. For Dom, the sun shone from Kate. His days began and ended with her.

Goddamn it.

No anger answered his call, though. He had none left.

"When can I see Caroline?"

"You see her every week," Kate said.

"You... you knew?"

She offered a faint, sad smile. "How did you think the babysitter got your number?"

Jake darted a glance at Eric and Eric shrugged.

"I don't want to hold you to anything, Jake. But maybe one day you can shake Dom's hand and then we can, you know, try to move forward."

"I'd never hurt her, Kate."

"I know that."

Tears prickling the corners of his eyes, Jake nodded and dipped his chin. Should he shake Dom's hand now? Declare it over? He glanced sideways at Dominick and found a measured gaze waiting for him. Dom lifted his chin and Jake knew he understood.

Now wasn't the right time.

Jake turned back to Caroline and beckoned her forward. Kate let her go and Jake bent down to give his daughter another hug. "I've got some work to do. When I'm done, I'm going to come visit. I promise."

"Will you bring your boyfriend?"

God, she'd heard everything, hadn't she? A greasy feeling rolled around Jake's gut as he questioned whether he was worthy. For nine years he'd tried to be a father, and he'd messed it up more than he might ever have dreamed possible. Maybe it was time to quit.

God, no. Just the thought of quitting, of not knowing his daughter in some way, left him breathless. His chest ached with the imagined loss and his arms trembled. He'd just held her for the first time in more than two years. Nope. He wasn't giving up now. And maybe the fact she knew he had made mistakes was for the best. That's what knowing he had someone he cared about and wanting to meet that person meant, right?

"I'm sure he'd love to meet you." Jake bent to kiss her forehead. "I love you, Peanut."

She rolled her eyes, but smiled. "Love you, too."

If only the rest of his problems could be solved that simply.

Jake straightened on shaking legs and followed Eric back across the lawn.

"Thanks for… you know," he said. Lame and not an apology for the elbow to the ribs, but he'd used up all of his effective words.

Eric stopped next to the car. "Listen, about Kate—"

"Forget about it. I know why you didn't tell me she was pregnant. It's none of my business, right?"

"I figured you had enough to deal with."

Half an hour ago, Jake's temper might have flared at that. Instead, he simply nodded. "Can you drive me to the hospital?"

"Of course."

WILLA MET him in the ICU lounge. "Where have you been?"

"I had some business to take care of."

Her eyes narrowed. "Are you in trouble again?" She could smell jail on him, couldn't she? And maybe the vestiges of all the anger he'd burned since he'd stepped out into the early morning light.

Jake sighed. "No."

"What did your PO have to say?"

"I'll catch you up on my career as a criminal later. Can we talk about Max?"

Willa did her best impression of a puffer fish, bristling and softening before his eyes. The sight was so familiar, Jake almost chuckled. Exhaustion was making him punchy. Then she updated him on Max's situation and Jake's gut did another revolution through the spectrum of disbelief, horror, guilt, and sorrow. By the time she finished, he was swallowing bitter fluid and looking for somewhere to sit down.

Thankfully, Eric was still playing the part of best friend. He caught Jake before he fell and guided him to a plastic-looking couch. Jake sat and leaned forward, putting his head between his knees. The sharp scent of ammonia intensified for a moment, then faded, leaving him hollow. If he'd had any tears left, he'd probably cry.

This was his fault.

"He's going to be okay." Willa's voice started at a distance and came closer. She was sitting next to him.

"What about this weakness on his right side?"

"Temporary. He's already demonstrating a great response. Therapy should take care of the rest."

"Should?"

"He's going to be fine. This is Max we're talking about. He's not a quitter."

"Can I see him?"

"I wish you would. He asks for you every time he wakes up."

Jake shot to his feet. "Let's go."

Willa led him to a small room cluttered with complicated instruments. Thankfully, most of them were switched off and slipcovered. Max looked both as bad as Jake feared and not quite as bad as he'd imagined. A shocking white bandage wrapped his head and his eyelids were dark with bruise. His nose had another strip across it. He wasn't the same young man Jake had carried to his truck two months before, though. There was a new hardness to Max's jawline, an angle of strength. The freckles across his pale cheeks spoke of someone who didn't hide in dark spaces. His lips were dry, but pink with life. Jake could see him breathing. His chest rose and fell in a regular, calming rhythm.

Ignoring the chair in the corner of the room, Jake leaned his hip against the side of the bed. He had five minutes. Five minutes to watch Max sleep. He tucked his fingers under Max's limp left hand and squeezed. "I'm sorry I wasn't here last night. I fucked up. Again. Story of my life, right? But I'm here now, and I'm going to be here every day until I can take you home. I'm going to take care of you. Teach you how to take care of yourself. I promise."

Max breathed in answer. His attendant machines hummed quietly. The quietude snuck into Jake's soul and attempted to steal the cares of the day. He let them go. This was familiar territory, after all, and one of the aspects of Max's friendship he'd come to value.

The world kept knocking Max down, and he endured. Quietly, stoically.

There was a lesson there.

Willa tapped on the door and cracked it open. "Time's up. He'll be moved tomorrow and you can visit for longer."

Jake nodded and leaned forward to drop a kiss onto Max's forehead. He half hoped Max would open his eyes like a Disney princess. Smile at him. Give him the sense he'd ridden in on his noble steed.

Max breathed on with the regular cadence of sleep.

Jake was halfway through the door when a tickle at the back of his head had him turning back around. Max's eyes were open. Even at a distance, Jake could feel the blue. Was drawn by the color he adored so much. He stepped back toward the bed.

"Jake!" Willa hissed.

"Wait up."

Jake grabbed Max's hand again. "Max?"

Max gave him a tired and lopsided smile. "You're here."

Jake folded forward, tugging his hand free so he could wrap Max in a hug. He felt Max's left arm pat at his back.

"You're squashing me." Max's words were a little slurred, his voice dry as autumn leaves.

"Sorry." Jake pulled back. "How are you doing?"

"Tired. Want to go home."

His laughter felt perverse. Jake tried to keep quiet, but his chuckles were the product of another of Max's unique talents. He grabbed Max's hand and squeezed it again. "Of course you do."

"Don't let them call my father."

Jake glanced over at his shoulder at Willa. She shook her head. Jake turned back to Max. "No one is going to call him."

"He'll—"

"Shh. I'm going to take care of you, babe. Only thing you need to worry about is getting better."

CHAPTER THIRTY

MAX GRIPPED the parallel bars and concentrated on shifting his right leg forward. Despite the arctic air-conditioning, sweat rolled down his back. The bandage wrapped around his skull was probably wet, too. He wanted to wash his hair, what they hadn't shaved. Maybe buzz the rest to match his bald spot. He'd settle for a simple shower, but getting to the bathroom required more effort than walking a straight line. Bandages, IVs, monitors, getting out of bed without spilling into a pile of uncoordinated limbs on the ground—it all required *work*.

He glanced over at the solid figure standing to his left. Jake had his arms folded and his feet hip-width apart. Max recognized the pose as Jake's ready stance. He looked falsely calm until you got a glimpse of his eyes. There, the edge of steel burned. If Max faltered, Jake would be at his side quicker than the therapist standing to his right. Max met Jake's gaze and watched the effect he had on the larger man. Steel warmed and softened, lips curved and features animated.

Max lifted a brow in question.

"Not today, babe," Jake said.

Max scowled and turned away. He asked Jake to take him home every day. It had become something of a joke, but also a mantra. Max asked when he felt down, tired, defeated, or when he simply needed to hear Jake's voice.

His therapist, a calm woman by the name of Theresa, touched his elbow. "You're thinking too hard, Max. Just let go and see what happens."

He'd fall down, just as he had yesterday and the day before, and every day since Friday. Today was Wednesday, a week since his *incident*, and he wanted to walk without holding on to rails. He wanted to walk without thinking about walking. He wanted to go home and do his laundry. He wanted to run Pennypack Trail on Sunday. He missed Max-Space.

Throat tightening, Max turned away from Theresa and stared resolutely ahead. His head ached. In mildly fatalistic moments, he'd decided his head would ache until the day he died. In his more depressive moments, he wondered if that would be next week, or the day he left the hospital. He might fall down the steps and hit his head again, or burst another blood vessel.

He wouldn't just give up, though, much as the idea sometimes appealed. He had two legs and two arms. A whole body and a whole mind. Yeah, he felt sorry for himself right now. His life sucked. But no one had called his dad, thank goodness, and Jake was trying hard not to coddle him. Sometimes too hard.

You're thinking too hard.

Max looked over at Jake again, at the set of his shoulders, the quiet fire in his eyes, and blinked as a flash of memory caught him. Now and again he got bits and pieces of last Wednesday. Sometimes the images were a jumble of movement, sometimes a single frame. Someone's face or a bit of conversation.

"I sat on the wall," he said. "The night it happened. I sat on the wall. Got my yellow stripe."

Jake's face relaxed into a smile. "I know. Alyssa told me. She said you could have sat there for half an hour, no joke." His smile narrowed. "I'm sorry I wasn't there."

Max shrugged, his left shoulder moving up, his right thinking about it before twitching forward. "'S okay. I'm just glad I remembered it."

He turned back to the rail and took his step, hoping the buoyancy of remembering a single fact—a moment of pride—might carry him forward. It did. He managed another step and another, faltering only when he tried to transfer his weight to his right arm. Still, he didn't fall.

Jake stepped forward, arms half-uncrossed.

Max shook his head. "I'm good."

When Jake didn't immediately step back, Max narrowed his eyes at him. He didn't want to be Jake's new project. Another poor soul who needed picking up and holding up. Jake was good at it, no denying that, and every time he offered an encouraging word or touch, something inside Max fell over and died. He thought it might be the vestiges of his pride.

He turned to Theresa. "Can I go home now?"

Theresa laughed. "Soon, Max. Really soon."

"THEY WON'T let me go home."

Elaine's chuckle was strained. He'd laid some pretty heavy stuff on her. It had been hard to share the circumstances of his accident, surgery, and recovery, but he was learning it was harder to keep all his failures to himself.

"If you leave that hospital," she said, "I'm gonna fly out there and—"

"Kick my butt. Yeah, I know." It'd almost be worth it, just to see Elaine again.

"Right, so I forgive you for not calling last Sunday. Recovering from surgery is a good excuse. It means we've got more to catch up on, though."

Elaine rambled on for a while, sharing details of her life. Her voice had a comforting cadence to it—or perhaps the sheer normalcy of her doings was what soothed. Finally, she ended a story about her trip to the farmers' market with: "You're too quiet."

"Hmm?"

"Normally you ask what I'm going to make for dinner."

"Sorry. I'm tired."

"You sound kinda down, too."

"Today I walked fine. Tomorrow I might trip, fall, and hit my head again. I just wanna go home and rest. Being here is exhausting."

"How is everything with Jake?"

"He's good."

"That's not what I meant."

"It's what you asked."

Elaine laughed. "See, there. Now you sound like yourself."

He huffed softly. "It's…. I don't know if I could do this without him. And I don't know if that's—"

"Good."

"Huh?"

"It's good, Max. It means you have someone and there's no shame in needing someone."

A lump the size of a bowling ball swelled inside his throat. "We'd only been out a couple of times before I fell down." *Before my head exploded, turning me into a special case.*

"But he's your friend. Before anything else, Jake is your friend, and I already love him. He's looking out for my best bud, after all."

Max hadn't passed on the details of Jake's prison term or his suspicion that Jake thought himself responsible for putting Max in the hospital. He didn't intend to now. "So what are you going to cook this week?"

The phone produced a grumbling sound. "I'm going to let you get away with that this time. Special circumstances."

Just as Elaine sounded like she might be giving up trying to sell him on the benefits of kale smoothies ("they really don't taste like mulched up grass, trust me"), an attendant wandered into the ward with a bunch of colorful balloons.

"Max Wilson?"

Though he was alone for a change, Max raised his hand. "That's me." Heat already prickled his cheeks. Were the balloons for him? If so, from whom? If not, then why would he think they might be?

"Where do you want them?"

Max pointed dumbly toward his bed. He was sitting in the chair beside it, and would have to get back in there at some point, but he couldn't think where else to put the bobbing collection of smiley faces and "Get Well Soon" and "You Star."

"Max?" Elaine called from the forgotten phone.

Max lifted it to his ear. "Did you send me some balloons?"

"No. Though I wish I'd thought of it. Take a picture of the look on your face. You're doing your wary squirrel look, aren't you?"

"My what?"

"See if there's a card."

There was. Max pulled it out of the envelope and opened it up. It was from the dojo and everyone had signed it, even Barry. Had Alyssa held him down and forced his hand? Max squinted at the small print underneath Barry's scrawly name.

Need my nemesis back, fighting fit.

His nemesis. Max didn't know why that made him smile, but just like the blush prickles, he could feel his cheeks creasing. He had a sneaking suspicion Barry might be a comic book nerd, in which case, maybe they had something in common after all.

Elaine was demanding details from his forgotten phone. Max lifted it back up and read the card to her.

"RECKON THIS Jell-O would stick to the window?"

Max looked over at Jake, who had a small dessert cup in one hand, a plastic spoon in the other. He turned to look at the window, which was a square of glass separating his room from the corridor.

Ronald called out from the third bed. "Do it!"

Ron was probably in his thirties, but he acted younger. Max didn't know if it was due to a head injury—they all had gauze turbans in 4-C—or if Ron was just one of those guys who never grew up. Their other roommate, Cranston, was out wandering. He'd had a fairly major stroke and his travels required a walking-frame. Max shuddered every time he watched him push past.

He looked at the Jell-O cup and noted the chartreuse color. "Is that lime flavor?" he asked.

Jake assumed an expression of mock horror. "You think I'd throw lime-flavored Jell-O around?" He dipped the spoon into the cup and extracted a mouthful. Tasted it. "I think it's pineapple. Or maybe just 'yellow.'"

Max made a face. "Toss it."

Jake pulled out another mound that should've wiggled more and flipped the top of the spoon. The electric puke-colored gelatin flew toward the window. It landed with a light slap and clung for a second before dropping to the floor without pausing for a dramatic peel or slide.

"What about the ceiling?" Ron asked.

Jake dipped the spoon into the cup and pulled it back out again. The clump of Jell-O arced up, grazed the ceiling, and dropped back down to Max's bed. Jake leaned forward to scoop up the lump with the plastic spoon. "Might be tackier now," he said, preparing to flick it toward the window again.

Ron cheered. Max closed his eyes. He heard the Jell-O hit the window and Ron clap his hands. He leaned back into the nest of pillows and started to drift. He'd gotten good at tuning out the noise around him, pretending the babble of voices was something else, that the walls looming to either side weren't closing in, that his back didn't ache from all this lying around, his legs didn't twitch, his head didn't hurt. That his life hadn't fallen so far off badly constructed rails, he might never find a smooth track again. Man, he was tired. Tired of waiting for a miracle to happen. Tired of working so danged hard for mundane things.

"Hey."

At the warm touch on his hand, Max opened his eyes. Jake leaned in close. "You should finish your dinner."

"Not hungry," Max said.

"But it's fried chicken."

Max shrugged.

"You need to eat more. You need—"

"I need to go home, Jake." Except he probably couldn't afford to keep his hole-in-the-ground apartment.

Tomorrow would make two weeks since his head had exploded. A call to Melanie (not fun) had confirmed he'd have a job to come back to, but everyone seemed to think he wouldn't be ready to resume life as usual until July. Three more weeks without pay? Max didn't love his job—in fact, he was indifferent to it. But he had to support himself. He didn't have another home to go to, and after learning to do all these mundane, boring, and tiring things, he'd have a heck of a bill to pay. "I need to get back to work."

Did he have any clean clothes and change for the bus?

Jake's lips flattened into a firm line. "Even if you go home tomorrow, you're not going to be up for work for a long while."

Max ground his teeth together. "I haven't finished paying the last hospital bill. I could do half shifts, at least." His head spun as he thought about the walk to the bus stop. Top of the alley and turn right onto Beech Street. Walk half a block to the corner of the avenue. He could make that, easy. He'd lapped the PT suite five times that afternoon.

Being on his feet all day at the market, though....

Some nemesis he made. For the past few days, the bright bob of his get-well balloons inspired a rash of anger every time he looked at them. It was that expectation again. Alyssa thought he could do it. Now Barry did as well.

Jake always thought he could, he just wanted him to take it slowly.

"There it goes!" shouted Ron, pointing at the window.

Seconds later, Max heard the soft plop of another spoonful of Jell-O hitting the floor. He didn't look over, instead he held Jake's gaze. Jake looked tired. The gray of his eyes had dulled to gunmetal and his lightly tanned skin had paled. He had shadows beneath his sockets. Small pouches, another shade of pale. His hair seemed a little longer than usual. Bushier. His lips thinner. For a moment, Jake's face was that of a stranger, of a person Max didn't know. Then he became the man Max had been intimate with. Max remembered what Jake looked like when he climaxed, the sounds he made, and a shiver skipped down his spine. Another blink, and Jake became the upstairs neighbor, the friend Max tried to cling to while maintaining the necessary distance. Jake's mouth changed shape and Max remembered the feel of those lips on his.

"If you've got other stuff to do, you know...." Max chewed on the dry skin of his lower lip. "You don't have to be here." Jake's sad expression deepened. "It's not your fault, you know. You don't have to keep—"

Jake cut him off with a kiss.

Max froze. He knew his relationship with Jake was obvious to anyone who saw them together. Kissing in public, though, he didn't think....

The memory of Jake's lips returned. The firmness and softness and the way Jake often sighed into a kiss, as if he'd been holding on, waiting. Max had to answer. He always did. Jake's lips, Jake's kisses. He opened his mouth in invitation and Jake's tongue swept inside. They played, briefly, and then Jake pulled back and bumped their noses together, stirring another memory. Jake might've been big and broad and every man's (or woman's) dream of masculinity, but he was the sweetest, most tender person Max knew.

"I'm here because there's no place I'd rather be," he murmured.

"But—"

Another quick kiss. "Trust it, Max. What we have. I do."

CHAPTER THIRTY-ONE

JAKE PULLED his tool belt from around his waist, grimacing as it peeled away from his shirt. He could already picture the imprint of the stitched leather across his hip where the belt had slipped. He'd been in too much of a hurry that morning to fasten it properly, and Brian had kept him hammering all day, literally and figuratively. In retrospect, staying busy could only be a good thing. Kept his mind occupied.

Max was getting stronger every day. He struggled with his limitations, though. Got depressed easily. It'd pass, right? Once he got properly back on his feet? Max shy and a little awkward was cute, especially because Jake understood and appreciated the strength and fortitude he held within that spare frame. Down in the dumps Max was… worrying.

Jake tossed his belt into the paint bucket he'd adopted to carry his shit to and from his truck and asked his boss, "We 'bout done for today?"

One of the other laborers called out and Brian raised a hand. "Hold on. Let me see what Cam wants and then I want to talk to you about this quote I'm putting in."

Jake felt his brows rise. "Uh, yeah. Sure."

Was that code for talking about how he wouldn't fit into the next quote because he'd been taking too much time off?

Shit. He loved this job.

Brian stepped back around the side of the house. As he approached, Jake measured his expression. Like Jake's father, Brian Kendricks didn't give much away. He was a staid and solid man. Both were qualities Jake counted on. When Brian said something, he meant it. His words came with a guarantee, making him a reliable builder and a respectable guy.

Brian pulled his cell phone out and scrawled his finger around the screen a bit before angling it toward Jake. "Remember that house we looked at a month ago? They wanted a second story."

Frowning, Jake looked down at the phone. He saw the picture of the house and instantly recalled the place. "Hey, yeah. They got back to you?"

"Yep. They want to go ahead." Brian looked up at him. "It's a big job, Jake."

"Yeah, it is."

"To pull it in at the price I quoted, we're all going to need to put in a lot of hours."

Ah, right. "Listen, Bri—"

Brian held up a hand. He then darted a look over his shoulder. When he turned back, his face had acquired a few creases. "Some of the other guys are making noise, Jake. You know how it is. You're family, my nephew, and they know where you were last year." Jake opened his mouth, but Brian raised his hand again. "I didn't hire you back on because I felt sorry for you. You're one of my best workers. Have been since you started with me. I know this isn't particularly glamorous work, but I feel like you found a niche with me. That construction suits you. I know you get that same satisfaction out of a finished project as I do." Brian drew in a quiet breath. "I like this being a family business, but my girls don't want to do more than help out in the summer. This isn't what they want to do after college and I respect that."

What was Brian building toward—or skirting around?

"So, I guess what I'm saying is I feel like this is your thing. I just want to check that out with you, though, because your head has been elsewhere the past couple of weeks. Now I know Max is in trouble and you need to be there." Brian's expression shifted and, for a second, he looked exactly like his brother Tony. Then he smiled and the effect softened. "I get that you and he are, ah…."

"Together."

Brian scratched an imaginary itch on the side of his face. "Right." He fiddled with his phone and looked up. "Until we finish this place, if you need to duck out early sometimes, I'm good with it. I mean, if it was Peggy in the hospital, or one of my girls. I get it."

Jake swallowed. Even though he hadn't been missing it, another puzzle piece of his life had just been slotted into place. "Thanks, Bri. So, this job?"

Brian tapped the darkened screen of his phone. "Right. I need you in on this with me. All the way. This is going to be a big one. Long hours, but big money. It's a game changer. The business I could get from this could have us adding a man or two and that could mean you moving up the food chain."

Jake's eyes widened. Here he'd thought Brian might be trying to find a way to let him go and his uncle had been thinking in the opposite direction. "Seriously?"

"Yeah. That sound like something that would suit you?"

"Yes!" Jake paused for the sober second the invitation warranted, then grinned. "Yeah." He nodded over Brian's shoulder toward the small crew of guys tidying up the work site. "Is that going to be a problem?"

Brian shrugged. "You've got seniority over everyone except Vince, even with your year off, and he's only in it for the wage. He doesn't care about the projects the way you and I do."

Jake's throat tightened. "I don't know what to say."

"Say you'll put as much effort into this as you do everything else and we're set."

"You got it. Thanks."

"Anytime, son. Anytime."

MAX SEEMED bound and determined to punch a hole in Jake's big yellow balloon of happiness. He walked the treadmill belt to nowhere as though it would take him somewhere… anywhere. Away from the nursing facility, no doubt. Every now and then he'd scowl at the display and poke a button. The rhythmic slap of his shoes against the rubber would increase in pace and he'd scowl harder.

"The job doesn't start until September," Jake said, meaning *I'm not abandoning you.*

A small part of him was crushed by Max's reaction to his news. He'd hoped his boyfriend of all people would be happy for him. Yeah, Max was having a hard time right now, and he hated physical therapy—which was fucking weird. If anyone would get off on regularly scheduled exercise, it should've been Max. But Jake had been working hard, too. Trying to right his wrongs and put his life in order. His potential promotion felt like a huge step up, right when he really needed it.

When Max didn't answer him, Jake moved back to his customary place by the wall. Maybe it was best to just let him run it out. He'd heard Max talk about the mental space he reached when he ran. Maybe that was what he sought. His runner's high. A measure of peace.

Would he be more reasonable when he got there?

Max stabbed the treadmill console again.

Jake glanced over at Theresa, one eyebrow raised. Shaking her head slightly, she made a "be patient" gesture with her hands. Max had seriously lucked out with the hospital's choice of physical therapist. Theresa knew when to push, and when to hold back. More, she seemed to understand Max's moods. His petulance, frustration, and brooding silences.

She'd probably seen it all before, at least a hundred times.

Sweat stood out against the short length of Max's newly shorn hair by the time he slowed the treadmill belt. Color flushed his cheeks and his chest rose and fell in a steady rhythm as he settled into a fast walk. He looked good. Both legs moved evenly and his right arm had a good swing. Except for the haircut and slight pallor, he looked much the same as he had before his accident—but still different in some way Jake hadn't finished defining.

Max leaned forward to slow the belt again, then straightened, and the difference became clear. It was his posture. Not the straightness of his back, or the square set of his shoulders. Max had always had that. It was the looseness of his limbs. An almost carefree swing to his arms, his stride. It matched that new angle to his jaw, the way he held his head. Somewhere over the past two months, Max had found confidence. He wasn't fully comfortable with it yet, but he didn't wear it like a shirt chosen at whim—one he could discard if it seemed too loud, too bright. It came from within.

Max came to a halt and looked up with a shy smile that only enhanced his new posture. He'd never be cocky—and shouldn't be. "That was a mile," he said.

Ah, fuck it. Celebrating his promotion could wait. Max needed cheers now. Jake let out a small whoop and Theresa clapped her hands.

"Can I go home now?" Max asked with a wider grin.

"How about tomorrow?" Theresa said.

Max's grin dropped away, replaced by disbelief. "Really?"

"Really. You're ready."

Jake was so busy being proud, he nearly missed the stumble as Max stepped off the treadmill. Theresa caught his left arm and just managed to keep him upright until Jake got there. Jake grabbed his right arm and held on until Max found his feet.

He complained, of course. "I'm fine, you can let go."

"Take it easy, Max," Theresa said.

He started pulling at his arms. *Here we go.* "I just tripped. I'm fine."

The weight against Jake's side suggested Max was far from fine. Jake helped guide him to the plastic seats lining the wall near the door. Max sat heavily and pulled his arms in. Jake sat next to him. He knew better than to ask Max whether he was okay.

"This is nothing to worry about," Theresa said. "Your right leg might quit on you now and again. Especially when you're tired. It'll come back. You could probably stand up and walk another mile right now. I don't want you to. You push yourself hard enough as it is. But I promise you that you can."

Max had his fists clenched. Jaw, too. He nodded as Theresa spoke, but gave no indication he agreed or understood or even took comfort from her words.

Theresa went over to her bag and returned with a small sheaf of papers. She sat on Max's other side. "I've printed out all your exercises for you to take home. I know I don't have to encourage you to keep up with your PT. You're probably the most determined client I've ever had." She glanced around Max's shoulders at Jake, then returned her attention to her client. "Just remember that getting enough rest is as important a part of your recovery as running a mile, okay?"

She handed Max the papers and stood. "I'll try to stop by in the morning, to say good-bye, but if I miss you, it's been a pleasure, Max."

Max looked up then. He still wore his belligerent expression, the one that Jake personally thought made him look about as cute as an angry chipmunk. Theresa must have thought the same. Her smile softened, broadened. Became more personal.

After taking a deep breath, Max pushed to his feet, moving slowly and carefully, and extended his hand. "Thank you."

Grinning, Theresa knocked his hand aside and hugged him. "Oh, never mind that. Just be good, hmm?"

She gave his cheek a last maternal pat and left the PT suite.

Jake stood up behind him. "You know, you could totally work that boyish charm thing you've got going."

Max turned, frowning.

Jake held up a hand and ticked off fingers. "Willa, my mom, Alyssa, now Theresa. I bet you've got half the nurses in this facility sneaking you cookies after hours, too."

Instead of sharing the joke, Max scowled. Then he flopped back into his seat, sending Theresa's papers flying, and dropped forward, his head in his hands. His newfound confidence seemed to flutter toward the floor with his exercise printouts.

Jake sat back down and touched his shoulder. "What's up?"

Max shook his head. For a moment, Jake thought he might be crying, which would've been weird. Max wasn't the crying type. Besides, Jake wept enough for the two of them.

Maybe he was just tired?

Jake rubbed his shoulder for a while and fell into a meditative sort of state. Worry bubbled below the surface, and he was still a little pissed that Max hadn't immediately cheered his good news. But as always, Max's quietude soothed him, even when he could feel Max doing his own worrying.

When Max finally looked up, the answer to every question was written clearly across his face. Brows low, lower lip pinched between his teeth, eyes dark. Max was afraid. Of what?

"Talk to me, babe," Jake said. "Tell me what's going through your head."

"What if I never get better than this?" The question was sharp-edged. Furious, but also cut with fear.

"What do you mean? You're doing great."

"It was a mile. And I nearly fell off the treadmill after it. My leg is still numb."

"It's been a little over two weeks since I found you in that alleyway. A mile on the treadmill is fucking fantastic."

If anything, the line of Max's jaw got harder. "I don't want to have to go home."

It was Jake's turn to frown. "I don't understand."

"Back to Mechanicsburg."

"Why would you—" Jake flashed back to Max's early insistence that no one call his father. The urgency and fear underlining every request. He also remembered Max's few stories about the man who raised him. Family was forever, but Jake could easily understand Max never wanting to return to his. "Has your father been in touch with you?"

"No!"

"Then why would you think you had to go back there?"

Max's dark brows pinched together. "Before I woke up, I kept having these dreams, like nightmares, sort of. Stuff that happened when I was a kid. I couldn't move. I didn't know why. In the dreams, my dad was so angry, so disappointed, and I couldn't move! I tried so hard that it hurt. He didn't care. He never did. He made me clean the garage with a broken arm." Max gripped his upper arm as if in memory. "He used to say it was my fault that Bryce and his friends kept cornering me." He looked up. "It wasn't really my fault, was it?"

"God no. None of it."

"Why did this happen? I was so close to making it. To being able to say I was doing okay on my own."

"You did that over a year ago when you moved to Philly. Might not have felt like it, but the minute you left your father's house—"

"He kicked me out. He caught me sort of flirting with a customer at the garage and gave me an hour to pack my stuff."

Fucker. Gareth Wilson Sr. had a lot to answer for. But Jake had him figured. To have kicked Max down so constantly before kicking him out spoke of one primal emotion. Fear. Jake didn't think Max was ready to hear that, though. "That might have been the kindest thing he ever did."

Max's mouth dropped open.

"Because you came down here and rocked it, babe."

"I came down here and got my ass kicked."

"And stood up, dusted off your hands, and got on with it."

Max swallowed audibly. Then, jaw hardening again, he nodded.

"Listen," Jake continued. "I know you're worried about your job and money and all sorts of stuff. I wish I could tell you that you don't have to. But we live in the real world. Shit happens. Shit also gets fixed. Your boss is a good guy. Not everyone would keep a job for you. Hold on to that. Your boss obviously respects you. And you've got friends looking out for you. Willa has been watering your plants, and Eric and Rob still expect you to work with them in the gardens this summer. Cherish that.

"And you've got an amazing boyfriend. Someone who loves you so damned much, he thinks he can make it all better every time he kisses you." Okay, talking about himself in third person was weird. "I wish I could make it all work with a kiss. I really do. But you know wha—"

Max was now looking at him with something akin to horror on his face.

"What's wrong?" Jake asked.

"You…. You…." Tears misted his beautiful blue eyes. "Did you, do you…?"

Max hadn't required speech therapy for more than a couple of days. It was his leg and arm that gave him the most trouble. This sudden difficulty with words was worrying.

"Do I need to call someone?"

Max squeezed his eyes shut and shook his head. When he opened his eyes again, he looked a little more composed. "Did you mean you love me like someone loves a cat or…."

Jake's grin spread so wide, so quickly, he wouldn't have been surprised if he'd split the sides of his mouth. "I mean I love you for you, Max," he said. "I know saying it here isn't all that romantic. I could have planned it better. But you know what? I'm glad it slipped out. Because now is when I needed to say it. When I needed you to know that I love you."

Max's mouth moved. He was forming words and discarding them. Finally, he said, "I hate that I still feel like a project. That I'm so down on myself all the time. I wish I was a happier person."

"Happiness is so subjective. And so damned fleeting. It's moments, Max. You know what I value? Contentment. That's what I feel when I'm with you. Like all's right with the world. Mine, yours. That's deeper than happiness. You make me happy, too. By God. I love the highs and I'm okay with the lows. The steady line, though? That's what it's all about."

Holy fuck, how profound was that? Jake sat back and thought about what he'd just said and nodded to himself. There was another puzzle piece, right there.

Max looked as though he was searching for words again.

"You don't have to say it back, you know," Jake assured him.

Max's brow pinched.

"Take your time, babe. I'm not going anywhere and you can only walk a mile. Also, you know you're really cute when you scowl, don't you?"

Clenched teeth, flashing eyes. Perfect.

Jake grabbed Max's hand and rubbed his thumb over the knuckles. "I just want you to understand…. No. I want to hear you say that you know I'm not with you because you're a project or because I feel guilty.

We're friends, Max. Of course I want to help you. Of course I feel bad about you getting caught up in my shit. But what we have is more than that. Tell me you know that."

Max considered him for a long time, his blue gaze intense and unwavering. Then he gave a short, decisive nod. "I know it." His lips twitched toward a smile, faltered, then relaxed. It was the shy smile, of course. Jake's second favorite.

He leaned in to kiss it. "Good."

"Jake?"

"Hmm?"

"That's really awesome about your job. The new project. The promotion. I...." Max massaged his chest. "I'm sorry I got all spooky about it. I was scared, you know? That maybe you wouldn't have time for me, or that—" Jake tried to kiss him, but Max pushed him off with a quick grin. "You can't kiss me every time you don't like something I say."

"Watch me."

There was the sly smile. Jake's absolute favorite.

"I'm happy for you," Max said.

"Good. Can I kiss you now?"

CHAPTER THIRTY-TWO

"MORNING, BEAUTIFUL."

Max slit his eyes open to the gray light of predawn. "'S not morning yet," he mumbled. If any day came with a sleep-in, it was this one. They weren't due at the Kendrickses' annual Fourth of July celebration until noon.

Jake's hands captured his, one by one, and slid them up toward the headboard. Max allowed himself to be drawn up and laid out, eager, despite his lassitude, to feel Jake's lips coast across his bare skin. Jake began with the side of his neck, the spot just below his ear that seemed connected to every nerve in his body. Sighing, Max arched upward. Skin kissed skin, every brush sending a thrill to his groin.

Jake hummed against his ear. Then he kissed his way down Max's neck to his shoulder, poked his tongue into the groove between musculature there, tickling and delighting, and moved on to Max's arm, skimming his tongue under before tracing a line to his elbow. Max had never had his arm licked before. No one had ever loved his arm.

Over the past two weeks, Jake had loved nearly every inch of him. He cooked for him, cared for him, picked him up when he fell down—which happened less and less often, thank goodness—and rubbed his head to send him to sleep. They bickered about Max wanting to do more than he should, and about Jake wanting him to do less than he could. It was the stupidly mundane things Max enjoyed the most, though. Doing Jake's laundry for him, or learning to make drinkable coffee. Each small task made him feel like an essential part of Jake's life.

Then there were times like this, when Jake spent countless hours licking, tasting, kissing, and nuzzling. With every kiss, Max felt himself being opened, as if he'd been buried for nearly twenty-two years, waiting for Jake to find him.

Max bumped his hips up again. Jake rocked into him, the knee between Max's legs sliding back as he did so. The hot brand of Jake's erection brushed his thigh. Max arched, his cock almost folding against

Jake's hard abdomen. The pleasure of touch and the slight friction far outstripped the discomfort of the angle—so much so, he did it again, and again, sliding his length across Jake's stomach.

Jake continued to tease with his lips, pressing kisses to his wrist, nipping the inside of his forearm, sucking each finger in turn. As Jake's warm mouth enclosed each digit, Max thought about coming. His nuts tightened and his dick jerked. He pushed into Jake's skin, moaning. Jake's need was just as obvious in the hot slide against his hip.

If his wrists weren't pinned, Max might've reached down and taken Jake in hand, tried to encompass them both, initiate another grinding rut. Or maybe Jake would eventually work his way down to enclose him in the moist heat of his mouth. Max licked his lips. He'd done just that last night, kissed his way down Jake's beautifully sculpted torso to suck his cock. He loved the feel of Jake's silky, hot flesh against his tongue, the combination of hardness and softness, the male scent, the simple fact that with his mouth, he could make Jake come.

"Jake," he whispered, using his lover's name as encouragement and plea.

"Mmm?" Jake's lips were fastened to his neck. He lifted his head and swiped his tongue across Max's mouth. Max forgot voicing his need and fell into communicating it with his lips instead. Jake's tongue thrust past his, urgent and rhythmic, every stroke intensifying the ache in his groin.

When Jake pulled away for breath, he smiled. "I love waking you up."

Smiling in return was easier than articulating the fact he both did and didn't love being woken so early just so Jake could molest him. Orgasm was its own sort of reward, wasn't it?

Jake let go of one of his hands to trace his arm. The one that hadn't been loved yet. Max shuddered beneath the new sensation. Jake passed a thumb over his nipple, just flicking it, and a fresh jolt of pleasure shot to Max's groin. Warm fingers followed, pausing as Jake traced the angled line from his hip across the top of his thigh, then down, beneath his harder-than-hard cock to nudge his sac. Max hissed with pleasure.

"I knew you'd be like this," Jake said.

Max found a pair of words. "Like what?"

"Not quiet, not meek. Hot as hell."

Jake nudged his balls again, and stroked a finger backward, teasing the soft skin of his perineum. Max moaned and thrust himself at Jake's hand. He loved being touched there. The tease frustrated him, but only in the best way possible. And every time Jake ventured behind his balls, Max got a little closer to asking him for more.

Max bent one of his knees, opening his legs wider, and pushed his heel into the wreckage of the bedcovers—every movement designed to guide Jake's finger to where he so desperately wanted it.

Jake's finger moved farther backward. "This what you want?"

"Yes," Max hissed, caught between trembling and pushing forward.

Jake stroked his tight entrance and Max bucked, catching them both by surprise. Jake had fingered him before. They both knew he enjoyed it. This morning his want felt sharp-edged, though. Needier.

Jake eased his hand away and paused for breath, the sound of his inhale and exhale quiet, thoughtful.

"What?" Max worked hard to keep that one word steady and clear.

"Have you bottomed before?" Jake asked with a sweetly earnest expression.

Max exhaled softly. "Yes."

"Did you like it?"

Yes and no. And the *yes* part was the hardest to come to terms with, especially when he'd spent so much time denying who he was and what he wanted. He thought about the best way to express that, along with the fervent belief he would enjoy it with Jake, aware with every passing second that Jake was watching him. Thinking alongside him.

Finally, Max said, "I really want to do it with you."

"Are you sure?" Jake's hand disappeared under his nuts again. "Because I want to get inside you in the worst possible way."

Max rocked into Jake's fingers. "Yes, please."

Jake stroked him once in a quick and maddening tease, then clambered off the bed to gather the necessary supplies. Max lifted his other knee, ready to roll over. Jake caught his hip and pressed him back down. "Can we do it this way? I want to see you, watch you come."

"Okay." Max spread his legs and tried not to blush. Tried not to think about blushing. This was no different to what they'd done before, right?

Jake moved back over him and dropped small kisses across Max's chest, lips plucking at his skin while he stroked a lubed finger between his asscheeks. Max clenched. While everything else tightened, his blush worked free, claiming his cheeks, neck, and upper chest in a hot blaze.

Crawling off the bed to hide beneath was not an option—and he shouldn't have wanted to. He was with Jake. He wanted to do this with Jake, give himself to Jake. Having a man like Jake want him should be the pinnacle of sexual fantasies.

So... why was he suddenly so tense?

Because this was Jake, and he wanted to be exactly what Jake saw, wanted to see. He wanted to be *hot as hell*, but wasn't sure how.

"You doing okay?"

"Um...."

"We don't have to," Jake said.

"I want to. It's just been a while."

Jake smiled at that and moved up to kiss him. "For me, too. An embarrassingly long while."

"I want to, Jake."

"I believe you."

Max felt his brows pull down.

"Want to try the other way 'round instead?" Jake asked.

"Other way?"

"I'll bottom."

Max's brows popped back up. "You'd do that with me?"

"Hell, yes." Jake kissed him to punctuate the sentiment and drew back. "Just 'cause I'm big doesn't mean I can't lie back and take as good as I give."

Laughter bubbled up inside Max's chest, relaxing lines of tension. "As good as you give?"

Jake rocked against him. "Babe. We've agreed you're hot." No they hadn't. "But it's kind of a given that I'm on fire."

Max laughed again, his dick twitching against Jake's abs. He could feel Jake's hot length against the back of his thigh. "You are," he agreed.

Jake's mouth drew into a more serious line for a moment. "I don't know how it works for everyone else, but for me being bi means being open to experience. To loving someone for being a unique person. And that means being able to make love with you in all the ways we can think of."

Max reached up to stroke the side of his face, his fingertips catching on Jake's bristly cheek. "I want you inside me." His blush hadn't faded, but for now, he didn't care. He was with Jake. He was ready.

He revised that opinion once Jake eased inside him. After preparation that had nearly sent him through the roof, the press of Jake's hardness, the burn and the absolute fullness of having another man inside, had Max drawing on every ounce of control he possessed not to come.

Quaking over him, Jake appeared to be fighting the same battle. "Jesus, Max."

"I know."

"You couldn't possibly. I can't move. Man, I cannot move. If I move, I'm gonna come."

"Don't move," Max said urgently. He didn't want it to be over yet. Not yet.

Nothing but panted breaths breached the quiet of early morning until Jake spoke again. "I have to move."

Having given warning, Jake moved and Max cried out, the pleasure of it overwhelming the discomfort of a stretch he had not felt in a long, long time. And he'd been caught in a lie—he hadn't done this before, not this exact thing. He'd bottomed, but not face to face. Having Jake over him as well as inside him, having Jake's face pressed into his shoulder, his hands planted to either side of his ribs, was different... and just about the most incredible and wonderful experience, ever. Max felt truly connected to his lover, and he knew they were doing more than getting off. They were making love and that thought should have scared the heck out of him. But he felt too damned good.

Arching up, Max pushed into Jake's next stroke. Jake reached down to capture one of his legs, angling Max's knee over his shoulder. Max curled toward him, then fell back, away, abandoning his body to Jake's attention. Jake framed the side of his face with one hand and their lips met in a butterfly graze. Their hips swayed together and apart, every slide of Jake's thick cock touching off a thousand points of pleasure inside him. The friction and the fullness combined into one drawn-out sensation that all but overwhelmed.

"More," Max moaned.

"God, yes."

Jake leaned back, bracing himself with his strong arms, and began thrusting with more urgency and power. The new angle caught that one point of lightning inside and Max yelled, drew in a breath and whined. He reached for his dick and tugged, his touch rough and unsteady, but he was too gone for subtlety.

"Jake, I'm so close," he warned before another cry overtook him. His hand jerked up and down, and his hips followed, moving into Jake's.

"Good," Jake panted. "'Cause I'm about to blow."

He did, on the next thrust. Max had about a second to mourn the fact it was nearly over—much too soon—before his desire to join Jake in that heady high took over. He needed to come. His existence narrowed to a pinpoint of friction and rhythm, his hand on his cock, and the overwhelming desire to push through the passage of his fingers, over and over, until he lost himself. He felt Jake climax inside him, condom swelling appreciably. Jake kept thrusting. Max kept stroking. Then he was there. He shouted nonsense and squeezed his dick. Hot semen splattered across his skin, shooting as high as his shoulder, and his body rang like a tuning fork, singing and whining. He looked up and met Jake's wide-eyed stare. Jake grimaced, for which Max quickly forgave him. It was hard to come and smile at the same time. But he understood why Jake had wanted to see his face; if he looked half as blown apart as Jake did, then it would be quite a sight.

It seemed as if they rocked together forever, shaking and senseless, but it wasn't until they stilled that Max fully realized Jake had come as hard as he had. As completely. *I'm on fire*, he thought, eyes slipping closed.

"Open your eyes, Max." Jake's breath tickled his lips.

Max opened his eyes and met Jake's gray gaze. Again, they stared at one another for an unmeasured moment, and Max felt his thoughts and feelings rearrange, the movement subtle, but profound. Emotion rolled through him, another quiet orgasm, and he couldn't separate the joy from everything else. He just felt, and *felt*. Jake's eyes reflected the same, and when he inhaled, breath seemed to catch in his throat. Max's shoulders hitched.

Jake leaned down to kiss him, softly, sweetly. Their tongues got involved and small aftershocks slid beneath Max's skin. Then came that awful moment when they had to separate. They kissed through it, parting with a sigh.

Jake bumped his nose to Max's. "I think we need a shower."

"Mmm," Max agreed in an abstract sense, but he wasn't ready to move yet. He didn't want to jumble the kaleidoscope of thought and feeling rolling behind his eyes. The color of pleasure, the shape of contentment.

The picture of happiness. He did have to blink, though, and when he did the image changed and reformed, becoming brighter and warmer.

He wasn't afraid.

He'd invited a lover inside him and… it'd been good. Amazing, in fact. Not furtive, not scary, but wonderful. Completing.

He didn't have to be afraid of Jake. Of what he felt for him. Jake loved him, treated him as though he were precious, or simply worth holding on to. Yet for all his care, Jake never made him feel delicate, or less than a man. Even in this. Even while inside him, Jake treated him as an equal. A partner.

What could he give back?

Max touched Jake's stubbly cheek again. Danced his fingertips over bristly blond hair. "I should go downstairs and get my razor. And my toothbrush."

Jake's brows quirked together. "You're naked, and covered in spunk."

But ready for so much more than this.

"After a shower, then," Max said.

Jake leaned back, caught his hand, and hauled him upright. "After *our* shower. And I'll help. You've got a lot of bathroom stuff."

"I have hardly any bathroom stuff."

"I might have to carry something else upstairs, then."

"Okay."

Jake tilted his head. "Seriously? I've been asking you move your stuff up here for weeks now and all it took was—"

Max pressed his free, sticky hand to Jake's lips. Jake licked his fingers and continued talking. "You're doing it wrong. If you want me to stop talking, you have to kiss me."

"I'm not moving in today." But as soon as he could say the three words jumping beneath his skin, he would. Not just to make Jake happy, but because he wanted to be with this man. Wake up to him every morning and feel this loved.

Behind the fan of Max's fingers, Jake offered a sober nod. "Okay."

"We're just packing one box."

"It's more of Max in my space than I had this morning." Jake poked his tongue through Max's fingers.

Max chuckled. "You make every day a happy day, did you know that?"

It wasn't exactly what Jake wanted to hear, but he accepted it with good grace. Because he was Jake, and that was his thing. He returned the grin. His wider, because Jake gave his all to everything he did. His answer, though, was very, very simple. "You make it easy, babe."

CHAPTER THIRTY-THREE

TAKING ONE hand off the wheel, Jake smacked the fingers sneaking toward the radio. "You think because we moved a box upstairs you've earned the right to fiddle with Tanya's knobs?"

Max reached for the radio again. "I said we could do another box tomorrow."

Jake grinned at his almost, not quite, but totally getting there live-in lover. "With your two plates and two glasses. You live large, babe."

That shy smile caught Max's mouth. "If I had more stuff, we'd have less time to, you know."

"You're a fiend."

"You're a bad influence."

"I'll own it. So long as it means I get to keep you in my bed."

Max looked as though he was considering a petulant response, then the music changed from top forty hits to some twangy country shit.

"Oh, no you don't." Jake punched the first preset button and swatted Max away from the radio again. "Tanya and I don't do country. It's all my wife left me for my dog."

"My wife…. Wait, what?"

Jake laughed, then broke off to sing along with Justin Timberlake.

Snickering, Max reached for the radio again. Jake affected a long-suffering sigh and let him change the station. Max got to enjoy the taste of victory for about thirty seconds, his grin set to shit-eating, before Jake said, "You know you have to sing now, right?"

Max's grin fell away and his beautiful eyes narrowed. "No."

"Oh yeah, them's the rules."

Jake watched as Max sucked on his top lip, chewed his lower lip, and maybe even thought about singing. He pushed the first preset. "Okay, you win this round."

"One day you'll sing for me."

"I'm about as likely to sing as I am to go to the moon."

"Dream big, beautiful."

Forty minutes and two one-man sing-alongs later, Jake pulled up outside his parents' place and hopped out of the truck. He stretched his legs and reached over the back to unstrap the cooler he and Max had packed. He'd taught Max how to make deviled eggs and they'd put together two dozen. It had been a simple exercise, but Max's obvious enjoyment over creating something that didn't come out of a freezer or microwave was one of those small delights that would make living together such a joy.

Max probably didn't get that part of it yet. Maybe he did on some subconscious level? But when it all clicked, when one of those small moments captured him properly, Jake figured that was when Max would tell him he loved him.

Max had barely stepped out of the truck before Willa had her arms around him.

"You're here!" she said, unnecessarily. She then put color in his cheeks by kissing both. Letting him go, she raised a hand in a wave to Jake. "Hey!"

"Where's my hug?"

Willa slung an arm around his shoulder and pulled him into a sideways sorta hug. "What's in the cooler?"

"Deviled eggs."

"Ooh, awesome."

"Max made them."

"Oh, yeah?" She turned to Max, who hadn't recovered from his hug and kisses yet. "Next you'll be making pies. Don't even pretend they're better than Mom's, though. She'd be all sad and stop baking."

"I don't think I could ever bake something as good as that." Max was adorable in his sincerity.

"You can do anything you want to do, Max."

He snorted softly. "You sound just like Jake."

"Of course I do. We Kendrickses are optimists. Hasn't he told you that?"

Jake pressed a kiss to his sister's cheek. "I've tried." He nodded toward Max. "His cloud is getting smaller, haven't you noticed?"

Willa pretended to inspect the space over Max's head. She pursed her lips. "Hmm. You know, I think you're right!"

Snorting, Max turned around and made his way toward the front door.

Jake called out, "Only guests use the front door, babe. Family goes through the side gate."

There was so much family packed into the yard for the Kendrickses' annual July Fourth bash, they might have been better off sneaking through the house. By the time every aunt, uncle, and cousin had greeted Max, he looked like a wilted rag. A bewildered and wilted rag.

"How do they all know who I am?"

Jake scratched his head. "Let's see. You've been out here four times now, right?" Sunday visits to Doylestown had resumed the week after Max had blown his hospital coop. "And my family loves to gossip. I've got three sisters, man. But the guys are all just as bad. Seriously, my dad can out-gossip those folks on *The View*."

"The what?"

"Sometimes it's like you lived in a cave until I found you."

Max produced one of his cute forehead wrinkles. Then, apparently noticing how it affected Jake, twisted his lips. "You've ruined me. I can't even scowl properly anymore."

"I know." Jake mussed his too short, unmussable hair and Max barely flinched. Every day he got a little more comfortable with being touched. It was a wonderful thing.

"Jake, thank God you're here." Abigail dropped Antony into Max's unsuspecting arms. "Hold this, will you?"

Max and T mirrored one another's stunned expressions until T reached up to touch Max's nose.

"Watch out, he likes to stick his fingers in small places."

Max cut him a look combining horror and amusement. "I'm not going to follow that thought to the end."

"Best you don't."

Abigail pulled on Jake's arm. "You have to talk Bernat out of extending his deck."

"Bernat and Dawn don't have a deck." They had a foot-wide balcony affair outside their bedroom window.

"My point exactly."

"Be right back, Max."

Max lifted T. "Ah...."

"You'll be fine. Just bounce him around a bit."

As he followed Abigail, Jake glanced over his shoulder at Max. He and T were still looking at each other, all bemused. Holding a toddler meant he couldn't flail and he'd yet to look for someone to offload his burden to. More, he seemed focused on figuring out a new puzzle.

"He looks good with a baby in his arms." Abigail had never seemed to take much of an interest in his affairs. That was Willa's job. The sparkle in her eye was pretty obvious, though.

"Is there a deck issue?"

"Oh, yeah. But Brian is handling it. I just wanted to see what Max would do if I handed him an unexploded bomb."

"You're evil."

Abigail chuckled. "Maybe. But tell me you're not enjoying watching him."

Max was talking to T, his expression animated in a guarded way. T had his head cocked, all his attention on Max. Jake wondered what they were talking about. While he wondered, his chest tightened and his throat got all dry. There was so much he already wanted to share with Max, and this hadn't been on the list. Was he moving too fast? Falling too hard? Max laughed suddenly, and T's face wrinkled in the toddler version of extreme mirth. Then Willa appeared at his side and relieved him of his young bundle. She tickled T until he squealed. Both she and Max laughed and the three of them melted into the crowd of family.

"You are so gone," Abigail said.

Jake turned to regard his sister and, as sometimes happened, he couldn't think of anything to say.

Grinning, Abigail reached up to squeeze one of his cheeks. "Aww," she crooned. "My little brother is in love. Looks good on you."

"Thanks," he croaked.

Abigail sauntered back into the crowd, her mission apparently complete, and Jake stood in his quiet pocket for a while, happy to just observe the seething mass of family spread across the patio and yard. The only thing that would make the day more perfect, the only *person*, was Caroline.

He was working on that. Working on forgiveness, working on being the father he always imagined himself to be. Because watching her play wasn't good enough. Jake wanted to be a part of his daughter's life and that meant Dominick being a part of his life. Jesus H. Christ it was a tall order. But with Max by his side, Jake felt he could accomplish anything.

That was love; what love was.

A hand closed around his shoulder, distracting Jake from the warm swell in the center of his chest.

"Where's Cute Stuff?"

He turned to find Eric and Rob standing side by side, both of them dressed rather soberly—except for the color scheme: blue jeans, red shirts, and white belts.

"Where on this Earth did you find white belts?"

"That old department store at Neshaminy Mall. You know the one. Where they sell the off-the-rack sort of stuff."

Jake couldn't remember the name, but he did remember the store. "You drove around town looking for these, didn't you?" He glanced at Rob and noted the studiously polite expression. "And you made Rob wear one. Jesus. You guys must be in love or something."

"Mmm-hmm, and you'd know all about that, wouldn't you?"

"I thought this was Independence Day, not 'tease Jake because he has a boyfriend' day."

"Where is the boyfriend?"

"Mingling."

Rob took the opportunity to step forward and extend a hand. "Thanks for the invitation."

Jake shook his hand. "Eric's family, that means you are, too."

Eric would never settle for a handshake. He pulled Jake into a hug. While Eric had him there, he whispered, "Everything good?"

Jake leaned into his friend and hugged him back with more feeling than he might've for a while. "Yeah."

Over Eric's shoulder, Jake saw another small cluster of people push through the back gate. A woman and a leggy nine-year-old girl. A man hanging just behind them. A fluttering started up in his chest before moving to his throat. He let go of Eric and sidestepped him as though he weren't there. He heard Eric turn behind him, then heard nothing but the weirdly muted sounds of the party as he scuffed across the grass toward his daughter.

Kate met him first and they spent three seconds figuring out how to say hello—both extending a hand before deciding on an awkward half-hug arrangement.

"I didn't think you'd come," Jake said. He'd texted her an invitation a week ago—along with some other thoughts he hoped might convince her he was ready to try things her way. Or a new way.

"I made the mistake of mentioning it to Caroline." Kate's reply was a little stiff. She was nervous.

Jake bent to greet his daughter. "Hey, kiddo."

"Did you see me waving at you at the playground yesterday? I waved. I wanted to come over, but the babysitter said I can't. So I told mom we had to come today." Caroline wrapped herself around his waist.

Jake circled her shoulders with his arms and held her close. He looked up at Kate. "Thank you."

She nodded and smiled.

Annabel and Tony Kendricks joined the small side party. Annabel scooped her granddaughter up into a hug while Tony offered a more sober greeting. "Kate, Caroline." He attempted to burn holes in Dominick with his not-laser vision. "Just dropping them off?"

Ducking his head, Dom sidled back toward the gate.

"He's staying," Jake said, probably surprising himself more than anyone else.

Dom glanced up, one brow lifted in query. The expression was so close to the one inviting a punch, Jake almost made a fist. Then he breathed and let go. Turned to his dad. "He knows if he ever so much as disturbs a hair on Kate's head—"

"Jake," Kate hissed.

Jake started again. "As long as he's good to Kate and Caroline, he's welcome."

Dom chose then to find his balls. "And what about you, Jake? You going to be good to our girls?"

Our girls. It sounded… damn it. It sounded right. After giving Dom's question—and point—the moment it deserved, Jake offered a nod, stepped up, and offered his hand.

Dom accepted the shake immediately.

It didn't seal any kind of deal. But it did give their audience the go-ahead to start drawing oxygen again. It wasn't the final puzzle piece, either—and that was okay. Having his daughter back in his life completed an important part of the picture. It meant Kate hadn't given up on him, neither had his family. Nor Eric. Nor, for all his inability to recognize his own strength, had Max.

Jake turned to put his hand on Caroline's shoulder and looked to Kate. "Can I take her to meet someone?"

Kate smiled. "Sure."

CHAPTER THIRTY-FOUR

MAX WAS chatting with Brian, Jake's boss, when they both saw Jake approach, his hand on the shoulder of a young girl.

"Caroline!" Brian stepped off the edge of the patio to greet Jake's daughter.

"Uncle Brian!" She wrapped her arms around her uncle.

"You remember me."

"Of course!"

Wow. She sounded like Jake. Looked like him! A more delicate and much younger version, but she had his hair—longer, curlier—big gray eyes and legs that went all the way up, even on her smaller frame. There was no mistaking her genetics. And no mistaking the mix of pride and joy in Jake's face as he stood next to her, still holding her shoulder as though she were the world's greatest prize.

A flicker of jealousy held Max still a moment. It was a weird feeling. He'd experienced envy before. Heck, he'd envied everyone who wasn't him at some time or another. This was different. This girl had a portion of Jake's heart he'd never get.

"Max, I want you to meet my daughter. Peanut, this is Max."

Nothing for it, he had to be polite. Max stepped off the patio and dithered for a couple of seconds before holding out his hand. "Hi."

Caroline shook his hand solemnly. "Hello."

Well, this was nice and awkward.

Then she said, "I told him no one calls me Peanut anymore, but he's not a very good listener. Does he listen to you?"

Yep. Jake in miniature.

Max chuckled. "No, he doesn't. Ever."

Caroline grinned. "He's also a terrible singer."

"Hey!"

Ducking his chin, Max grinned. "Actually, I think he's a pretty good singer. He just has terrible taste in music."

"I'm standing right here." Jake was also terrible at pretending to be annoyed, especially when he wore an ear-to-ear smile.

A knot of cousins arrived to whisk Caroline off to play. Max followed her progress for a while, noting how nearly everyone stopped what they were doing to hug her as she passed. Then he saw a woman who could only be Caroline's mother talking to Willa. She was beautiful—and very pregnant.

"Is that Kate?" he asked, hoping his renewed jealousy didn't affect his tone.

Jake put an arm around his shoulders. "Yep."

"She's…." Would it be weird to comment on the fact she was pretty?

Jake kissed his ear. "Not you."

Annabel Kendricks threaded her way through gathered knots of family to claim her pie helper, and Max let himself be dragged off in yet a new direction. Kendrickses were good at that. At picking people up and putting them somewhere else. They fully believed it was for the best, too.

Sometimes it even was.

Several hours later, Max trailed in the wake of another group of Kendrickses.

Slowly.

He had to pause halfway up the small slope. His right leg was trembling. He'd felt the telltale tingle before they even hit the incline and bit his lips together and trudged on, determined to make it to the top without help. Now he faced one of those impossible choices that seemed to crop up every other day: ask for help, or experience a catastrophic limb failure.

Jake turned around and strode back to his side, his gait easy and relaxed. "You okay?"

Opening and closing his fingers in half-conscious mimicry of one of his exercises, Max considered lying. Instead, he slung his arm around Jake's waist. "Need more practice on hills, I guess."

"And it's late, *and* you didn't take much of a nap."

Because it was embarrassing to have to take some quiet time in the middle of a party. He'd spent most of his nap on the phone with Elaine anyway, delivering his weekly update.

Jake scooted in close, slipping his arm around Max's shoulders. "Nearly there. The view is worth the effort." He nuzzled Max's cheek. "I'll give you a piggyback ride on the way down."

Only Jake could make infirmity seem like fun.

"You better help me get to the top, then."

Jake smiled brilliantly. "See, asking for help isn't so hard."

Yeah it was, but it was getting easier.

At the top of the hill, Eric spread out the blankets he carried and Willa dropped the cooler, bottles rattling quietly inside. In the warm circle of Jake's arm, Max took a moment to admire the view. Doylestown stretched below them, scattered clusters of houses threaded by winding roads. Jake's other arm intersected the vista as he pointed toward the center of town.

"Central Park is a couple of miles away, but the show is about as good from here. Plus, we don't have to find a parking spot."

Jake moved behind him a little and Max leaned back into his comforting bulk. If he concentrated, he could still feel a small ache inside, the sweet reminder of how this long day had started. He smiled.

"C'mon, let's sit."

Max collapsed into an untidy sprawl on the indicated blanket. Jake sat behind him and pulled him into the inviting nook between his legs so Max sat enfolded by his lover, his back warm, his sides all protected. Briefly, he wondered if he should be embarrassed about being so close to Jake in front of others. Then he decided he was being ridiculous and snuggled in, murmuring his gratitude. Willa sat with a pair of cousins, and Eric and Rob formed their own huddle, both parties close enough to talk, not so close Max felt crowded. Much as he enjoyed Jake's family, a little space was nice.

It was amazing how far under his skin the Kendrickses had managed to get. He'd let Willa fuss over him, held a baby for Abigail, passed out drinks for Dawn, played with Caroline, helped Tony flip burgers and, while they served pie, consulted with Annabel on the menu for Labor Day—as if he'd still be around then, as if it was expected. He'd requested a peach cobbler and she rewarded him with a beatific smile and an invitation to come out a day early to help bake.

Sniveling in front of Jake's mother would have been embarrassing. Thinking about it now, his eyes still wanted to tear up.

No one had yelled at him all day. No one had nudged him aside or held him accountable for something he couldn't do or hadn't done. People had wanted to talk to him, they'd sought him out. They hadn't all simply asked after his health, either. They wanted to know what he was interested in. He'd talked to a cousin for half an hour about Formula One racing.

No one had looked at him sideways or whispered slurs in passing. People smiled indulgently when Jake kissed him on the cheek or hugged him from behind. No one called him a freak or sissy.

Max knew not every family was as warm and wonderful as Jake's, and the Kendrickses weren't perfect. But to him, they were everything he'd imagined might exist. They were a wonderful dream he never wanted to wake from. And the man behind him? The one humming softly in his ear? There were no adequate words. Well, except for those particular three.

Jake kissed his ear. "Feeling good?"

Max nodded. "Mmm." He nestled back into Jake's chest. "I might be in love with your family."

Jake's arms wrapped him a little more tightly. "Oh yeah?" Lips nipped at his ear again. "What about one Kendricks in particular?"

Swallowing a sudden lump, Max nodded, the motion jerky. *Just say it.* He'd wanted to that morning and the urge had tickled his heart all day.

A sudden explosion overhead pulled a startled yelp from his throat. Over his shoulder, Jake chuckled and issued a soft "Whoop." Fireworks continued to soar into the sky over the middle of the town, the sound carrying just before and just after each one. Every now and then, music would weave into the small lulls and voices would carry up from the houses below. Max shifted just so he could see Jake's face, watch his lover watch the fireworks. As he'd imagined, Jake was enraptured. Of course he would like fireworks—the bold light and color, the explosion of sound.

Max waited for another of the pauses in sound to lean in and whisper in Jake's ear. "I love you."

A firework popped and whistled overhead at almost the same moment, light flashing across the sky. Max didn't have to wonder if Jake had heard him, though. He was smiling broadly, and he'd torn his gaze away from the sky to look at Max.

"You're missing the fireworks," Max said, nudging him.

"You sure know how to pick a moment, don't you?"

Max tilted his head. Another blast of light and color interrupted them.

"Say it again," Jake said. Shaking his head, Max turned his grin toward the sky. Jake pulled him into another hug and shook him gently. "Say it!"

Fighting laughter, Max shook his head again. Jake dug fingers under his arms and poked him in the ribs. Squirming, Max fought off the tickles, missing some of Jake's offensive moves to darkness, startled by others as light flashed overhead. The distant boom of the fireworks barely covered his laughter.

"You're not blocking, Max. C'mon, show me your moves."

Max tackled Jake to the ground only to find Jake had him caught from beneath. He might've been on top, but Jake's grip was stronger.

"Say it," Jake said.

Max looked down at that handsome face and felt the words crawl up out of his chest, tickle his throat and trip off his tongue. "I love you."

Of course, no fireworks covered the declaration. Everyone heard it. Everyone cheered.

"Woohoo!" Willa yelled.

"We need a kiss!" put in Eric.

Cheeks burning, Max murmured, "Happy now?"

Jake smiled up at him. "Now I'm beyond happy."

He looked it. More than ever before, Jake simply glowed. Throat all closed up again, Max slid down into Jake's arms, then off to the side. Jake rolled with him so that they were cuddled together. There, Max lay buzzing, as though he and Jake had just made love. High above them the explosions continued, filling in for the aftershocks of a climax. It didn't matter that they were clothed and surrounded by friends and family, that his confession had been more public than Max had planned.

Nothing really mattered but this moment. He might be clumsy and tired, but his heart was light and his thoughts free. Best part, though? He still felt like *Max*. Like himself. He'd found the courage to tell Jake how he felt, the strength to say it twice. He'd claimed something he wanted, made it his. That was what men did, right? That was standing up to be counted.

Finally, he was on his way to who he wanted to be.

KELLY JENSEN was born in Australia and raised everywhere else. Currently, she lives in Pennsylvania with her husband, daughter, and herd of four cats. After disproving the theory that water only spins counterclockwise around drains north of the equator, she turned her attention to more productive pursuits such as reading, writing, writing about reading, and writing stories of her own. She also enjoys volunteering at her local library, playing video games, and holds a brown belt in Kiryoku, a martial art combining Shotokan, Aikido, and Tang Soo Do. Her family is not intimidated by her.

Twitter: @kmkjensen
Website: kellyjensenwrites.com
Facebook www.facebook.com/kellyjensenwrites

BEST IN SHOW

KELLY JENSEN

Solitary mystery writer Julian Wilkes doesn't want a pet, but his sister persuades him to visit Lingwood Animal Rescue, where he is immediately taken with a large ginger tabby cat. Before he can settle into the joys of cat ownership, however, he discovers something very unusual about his new companion.

Macavity Birch is cursed. By day he is a large tabby cat. At night he can be himself—a human male with ginger hair and oddly yellow eyes. He didn't mean to end up in the animal rescue, but he never meant any harm when playing the prank that resulted in his curse, either. Happily, Julian adopts him. But while exploring his host's home, he discovers the diary of a long-dead relative.

Unfortunately, not all of Mac's ancestors are dead and buried. His great-great-great-grandmother is very much alive, and she's a powerful witch who doesn't take kindly to the sharing of family secrets. When Mac reveals himself to Julian in order to save him from bigger trouble, he achieves just the opposite, plunging Julian deeper into a magical mystery with him.

www.dreamspinnerpress.com

Counting
FENCE POSTS

KELLY JENSEN

There are over two hundred thousand fence posts between Syracuse and Boston. Henry Auttenberg likes numbers—it's his job—but he isn't going to count them all, even if the view outside the rental car is less confounding than the driver, his attractive but oh so obnoxious colleague, Marcus Winnamore. It's Christmas Eve, and Henry would much rather be home with his family. When the blizzard that grounded their flight forces them off the road, however, he's stuck with Marc until the storm passes—or a plow digs them out.

As the temperature outside plummets, the atmosphere inside the car slowly heats up. Henry learns the true reason for Marc's chilly distance—he's not exactly straight… maybe… and he's been fantasizing about Henry's mouth, among other things. Confession laid out, Marc is all for sharing body heat… and more. Henry isn't interested in being an experiment, but as the night and cold deepen, he could be convinced to balance certain risk against uncertain reward.

www.dreamspinnerpress.com

out
in the
blue

KELLY JENSEN

At forty-five, Jared Tailler suddenly feels old. When his employer grounds him, he starts thinking in terms of measuring his coffin. Well, not quite, but he's creakier and hairier than he was ten years ago, and his closest relationship is the one he has with his frequent-flyer card.

It's time to get out there.

On the first day of a five-day hiking trip, he meets Finley Macrae, a younger, seemingly brighter man. As they inch together in halting steps, Jared learns he's not the only one lost out in the blue—Fin's good cheer hides a turbulence deeper than Jared's midlife crisis. Maybe together they can find the trail to happiness.

www.dreamspinnepress.com

WHEN WAS
THE LAST
TIME

KELLY JENSEN

Paul Summerfield is stunned by the gentle reminder it has been over a year since he and his partner, Evan Akkerman, have made love. He vows to take Evan out for Valentine's Day. Dinner and sex. Lots of sex. There's only one catch—he's supposed to be in San Francisco that week cataloging the art collection of an important new client. No problem, he'll just change his schedule and cut his trip short by a day.

In San Francisco, Paul struggles with regrets and the fear his love is slipping away from him. Every call to Evan seems only to prove the distance between them is increasing. All this, and a key piece of his client's catalog is caught up in customs. To keep their Valentine's date, Paul will have to choose between the career he's built over fifteen years and the man he's loved for just as long.

www.dreamspinnerpress.com